PLENTY AND SATIETY,
PLEASURE AND EASE,
LIBERTY AND POWER.

# VAMPIRATES

## TIDE OF TERROR

by Justin Somper

LITTLE, BROWN AND COMPANY

New York ✖ Boston

Also by Justin Somper

*Vampirates: Demons of the Ocean*

Little, Brown and Company

Hachette Book Group USA
1271 Avenue of the Americas, New York, NY 10020
Visit our Web site at www.lb-kids.com

First U.S. Edition: June 2007
First published in Great Britain by Simon & Schuster UK

ISBN-13: 978-0-316-01374-1
ISBN-10: 0-316-01374-9

10 9 8 7 6 5 4 3 2 1

Q-FF

Printed in the United States of America

Book design by Alison Impey

The text was set in ITC Charter, and the display type is Exlibris.

*For my mum, Thelma Somper,*
*who is always in search of a good read.*
*I hope this makes the grade!*
*With love and thanks for all your support.*

# NIGHT SURFER

Sunset. A deserted cove. The waves reach out hungrily for the sand, which changes hue from white to honey gold to fiery amber as the sun grows weary and dips down into the inky waters. The hungry waves soon swallow the ball of light.

Now it is a world of shadow upon shadow. No human eyes could discern the border between land and water or between water and sky. No human eyes could make out the insistent rush and tumble of the ocean. For this isn't the lackluster darkness of towns and cities. This is *real* darkness — deep and strong and velvet black.

Where is the moon? It's as if she chose not to come out tonight, reluctant to witness the happenings of the coming hours. Where are the stars? They, too, seem to have elected to keep a quiet distance. On a night like this, you could be forgiven for thinking that the world was about to end. And, for one of you, that might be true.

For the dark waves protect a secret. A man — at least, the *semblance* of a man — riding a surfboard. It's no free ride. The black waves are as tall as they are fierce, testing the surfer to the very limits of his strength and endurance. He never loses his footing, in spite of the swell, in spite of the lack of light to guide his way. His muscle-bound body twists and turns, locked to that board. It's a battle for re-spect that he fights with the waves. And he's holding his own out there.

At last, the waves seem to grow tired of their sport and reward the surfer's determination by easing him into the shallows. Still, he moves at high speed, the knife-edged surfboard skimming the thin sheet of water.

He jumps from the board, his feet touching the sandy floor. The waters make a final teasing grab for the board but the surfer reaches into the foam and lifts it out of their clutches. Board under his arm, he strides across the dry sand.

He does not pause for an instant, in spite of the weight of the board. Nor does the night air chill him. And, strangely, though he has come from the depths of the water, his skin and hair are already dry. His clothes too are dry as bone. He isn't wearing a wet suit, just regular clothes — trousers and a shirt, the sleeves ripped off at the shoulder to allow his arms maximum motion. His feet are bare.

He comes to the foot of a cliff and props the board against the rock, leaving it behind as he begins his ascent. At first there's a path for him to follow but, as the rock climbs higher, so must he reach out with his hands to haul himself up, using his feet, too, with equal dexterity. Now he seems less like a man, more like a wild animal. In truth, he's a little of each. And a little more besides.

He reaches the top of the cliff and pauses for an instant, looking back with satisfaction down the sheer rock he has climbed, looking out across the sand to the rough sea by which he arrived here. No human eyes could make out the border between land and water. But his eyes drink it all in. *His* eyes are at ease with darkness.

He wastes no more time on self-congratulation but turns forward instead. There's a high fence but, after all the other hurdles he's jumped, this one is easy. His feet land on soft grass. He looks ahead, far ahead, to the house in the distance — its windows lit up, even at this late hour. It's almost on fire with so much light. It brings a lightning crack of pain to his eyes but he bites it down and keeps on walking.

His long strides make short work of these grounds, as sizeable as they are. He passes a field where horses are running. For a moment, he pauses to watch them. They do not see him but sense him, freezing still for a moment. They are frightened by the stranger, as well they might be. But tonight, they need have no fear. He moves on.

There's a vast swimming pool and, ever the showman, he can't resist diving into it and swimming a powerful crawl from one end to the other. He hauls himself back out, and again his clothes are bone-dry.

Up ahead is a tangle of trees, a fruit orchard. As he walks through it, brushing against the branches, ripe fruit falls to the ground. Carelessly, he crushes peaches and pomegranates under his thick feet.

Beyond the orchard is another stretch of lawn, this one even softer than the last. He smears the fruit off his soles as he continues on. He's almost at the house now. All that stands between it and him is a garden of roses — a profusion of twining stems; sharp thorns; and thick, velvet blooms. And, in the center of the flowers, is a woman. He knew she was here. Now he stands still to view the curious sight.

She's a middle-aged woman, round in the figure from a life of too much ease. Dressed in a pink silk kimono, she has a basket looped over one arm and, clasped in her plump fingers, a pair of pruning shears. On her head is a band with a small flashlight at the front. She looks utterly ridiculous but is smiling happily to herself as she reaches out to the roses and snips at their stems, before sniffing at the blooms and laying them tenderly in the basket.

For a time she is oblivious. Then his foot, half unintentionally, crushes a fallen branch.

"What was that? Who's there?"

She spins around, the light on her head darting about like a firefly.

Still she does not see him. After a moment's pause, she returns to her sweet labors, humming to herself. She sounds like a demented bumblebee. He decides to have some fun and breaks another twig underfoot. It works. She jumps into the air — well, as high as her plump body will propel her.

He steps out of the shadows, directly across the pool of light.

Now she sees him. She looks up to take in the vast measure of him. Still, to give her credit, she's not as scared as he might have expected. Instead, she bristles with anger.

"Who are you?" she asks. "What are you doing here?"

He stares at her.

"Who are you?" she repeats.

"Who are *you*?" he asks.

"I'm Loretta Busby, of course. And this is my rose garden. And you have no business being here."

He smiles at her, reaching into her basket and grabbing one of the roses. He lifts it to his nose. It smells sickly, overpoweringly sweet. He crushes the bloom in one hand and tosses it away.

"How dare you, you monster!" she cries. "Do you know who I am? Do you know who my husband is?"

"Busby," he says. Does she think he's stupid? He isn't stupid.

"That's right," she says. "Lachlan Busby — Director of the Crescent Moon Bay Cooperative Bank, President of the North East Region Board of Trade, Elder of the Crescent Moon Bay Progressive Church, and the most powerful man for miles around." She fixes him with a glare, literally, as her flashlight catches him in the eyes. "You've walked into the wrong rose garden tonight, you half-wit."

He's insulted now. Insulted and irritated. The light is boring into his eyes and the smell of the roses is thick and syrupy. He looks down at the woman, who continues yapping at him like an annoying little puppy. Finally, he can take no more.

He reaches out his muscular arms and lifts her up, until her face is level with his. Shocked, her legs paddle through the air, as if she still thinks she might run away from him. She stares at him indignantly but now, for the first time, she sees his eyes properly. Or rather, the holes where the eyes should be. For now, they are merely pools of fire — deep pools of spitting flame. There are no more words for her voice has gone. Her legs cease their useless motion. Her flashlight slips lower and she sees his teeth. Twin gold teeth, like daggers, bearing down toward her.

Just then, the clouds shift above them and a shaft of moonlight beams down into the rose garden. Light showers Loretta Busby as she hangs suspended in the air. Light bathes the man — the thing — who holds her there.

And, somehow, the light changes him. The fire is drawn out from his eyes. Now they are just empty pools of unfathomable darkness. She watches, not daring to breathe, as he closes his eyelids. He frowns and she can see he is in excruciating pain.

His hands grow limp and he drops her. She tumbles down onto the grass, bouncing lightly before coming to a rest. For a moment, she lies there, thinking this is the end. But suddenly her nostrils fill with the sweet scent of the blooms she has nurtured. It's her favorite rose — *Summer's Promise*. She knows, deep inside, she is going to be okay.

The creature turns away, oblivious of her now. He strides across the manicured lawn, breaking into a run as he reaches the pool, sprints back through the field of horses, until once more he stands at the edge of the dark rock.

Here, the moon is high. Her golden light showers down over his vast body. There's a searing pain in his head, like an electric current from the top of his head to the back of his eyes. He does not care. No longer will he cower under the light. As he opens his eyes, the clouds close across the moon. The world is pitch-dark once more.

*That's it,* he laughs. *That's it. Run and hide! You'd all bet-ter hide!*

He is bigger than this. Bigger than all his enemies. They do not know it yet, but he is going to show them. He smiles, feeling reborn. Then, he jumps from the edge of the cliff, somersaulting down through the soft night air.

The adrenaline rush is enormous. This is what it means to be free, he thinks. How he endured so long aboard that ship is a mystery to him. How he ever put up with that captain — with his rules and regulations . . . No more of that for me, he thinks, as his feet thud back onto the sand. No more rules for Sidorio. From now on, I make my own way through this world. No limits.

# THE THREE BUCCANEERS

Cutlass Cate strode across the deck of *The Diablo*, surveying her elite pirate attack force. The attack would commence within the hour and already her chosen pirates filled every space on the deck, preparing themselves mentally and physically for the challenge ahead. Cate walked slowly down the center of the deck, monitoring them all as they trained, making mental notes to pass on to individuals and teams. It was still strange, but exciting, to think of herself as deputy captain. Much had changed aboard *The Diablo* in the past few months. Cheng Li had left the ship — on a teaching assignment of all things! — and opened up the post of deputy, which Cate had needed little urging to fill. Captain Molucco Wrathe was back in his old high spirits now that Cheng Li had gone. She had always been something of a thorn in his side. He seemed far happier having Cate as his number two. They might not always agree on strategy but they maintained a friendly respect and, in matters of attack-planning, he generally let her have the final say. But, of all the changes that had occurred these past few months, to Cate the most important had been the arrival on board of the Tempest twins.

Their advent had been in the most tragic circumstances. Connor had turned up first, a week or so ahead of his twin sister, Grace. In the days following their father's death, they had fled from their hometown — Crescent Moon Bay — in the family's old wooden yacht. But misfortune had piled upon misfortune and the boat had been caught in the fiercest of storms. The twins had almost drowned, but fate had brought them to safety, though it had kept them separate for a time.

Cate knew what a testing time that separation had proved for Connor but, to the boy's credit, he had thrown himself into life aboard *The Diablo* with every fiber of his being. She could see him now, at the very end of the deck, practicing his swordplay with his two best buddies — Bartholomew "Bart" Pearce and Jez Stukeley. She hastened her pace toward them. Bart and Jez had each been members of the crew for several years and were two of the most popular pirates on board. Both were in their early twenties now but had signed up to the articles while in their teens. Even as a teenager, Bart had been one of the strongest men aboard. But under her guidance, he had acquired expert swordsmanship to complement his muscles. Jez was smaller and leaner but, truth be told, the more accomplished swordsman. While Bart used the broadsword and often led the attack force, Jez — like Cate — was a precision fighter who, with his rapier skills, could determine the success of the day.

And then there was Connor Tempest — still just fourteen years old. He had only been aboard a little over three months and had no previous pirate training. Cate had introduced him to the rapier and was delighted with both his natural ability and his commitment to training. Now, as Cate observed the three young pirates executing their maneuvers, there was very little to separate them in terms of talent. Cate was especially delighted that Jez had taken Connor under his wing. Hopefully, the full genius of his rapier-handling would rub off on his young apprentice.

"And how are the Three Buccaneers, this fine day?" Cate asked, with a smile. She had come up with the nickname and it had stuck. The three pirates were inseparable. Each one looked out for his comrades — in and out of attack.

The three of them looked up from their swords, smiling as they saluted the deputy captain.

"We're doing good, thank you, ma'am," said Bart, with a grin. He and Cate had an ongoing flirtation, which she secretly enjoyed but could not encourage when she was on attack duty.

"At ease, lads," she said, drawing closer. Though she was giving them permission to relax, the command also served to demonstrate her authority over them.

Bart took the hint. "So," he asked, "tell us more about this ship we're pursuing."

"It's a containership," Cate said. "We've been following it all morning. Captain Wrathe received a tip-off early yesterday from one of our most reliable sources. Apparently, the ship's loaded with cargo — and under-defended. Better yet, it's in our own sea-lane."

"Should be an easy victory then," said Jez Stukeley.

"Never assume that," Cate said. "The odds are in our favor, but we mustn't be complacent."

"No, sir!" exclaimed Jez.

"No, *sir*?" echoed Bart. He and Connor grinned at their mate's slipup.

Jez shrugged, flushing red. "I'm sorry, *ma'am*. I don't know what . . ."

"That's *quite* all right," said Cate, amused but keen not to let it show. She turned her eyes toward Connor. "And how's young Mister Tempest feeling today?"

Connor looked her in the eye. "Poised and ready for attack!"

"Excellent!" said Cate. "And how's Grace?"

Connor shrugged. "Fine, I guess. I haven't seen her

since breakfast. She was on early swords-maintenance duty, I think."

"She's making good progress with her own sword skills," Cate said. She noted that Connor immediately tensed up, as he always did when the subject of Grace and swords came up. Surely he couldn't be worried that she would prove a rival to him? As good as Grace was — and she certainly showed some natural flair for attack — she just didn't apply herself as consistently to swordplay as Connor. It was a shame, Cate thought. Why should the boys have all the glory for themselves? She must have another word with Grace and get her to take things a bit more seriously. Maybe a little one-on-one training with another of the women pirates — perhaps Johnna? — was the way forward.

"You're not going to put her into attack for the moment, are you?" Connor asked.

"No," said Cate, shaking her head. "No, she's not quite ready." She saw Connor's shoulders immediately relax. Now she thought she understood. He was simply a brother, being overprotective. He didn't like to think of Grace putting herself into danger. But there was no free ride on a pirate ship and, besides, Grace had proved that she was able to deal with significant danger. After all, she had been "rescued" by a ship of vampires — or rather *Vampirates* — and lived to tell the tale. In spite of her crewmates' urging, Grace had said very little about what she had endured aboard that ship. She had only confided in Connor and, though he had steadfastly kept his sister's secrets, he had hinted that she had faced some truly horrific situations on board. It was understandable that he wanted to protect her from further trauma.

"You mustn't worry about her," Cate said to Connor. "She's as tough as the leather on my sword hilt."

Connor smiled, but only faintly. "She's my sister, Cate. She's all I have left in the world."

"Na-hah, buddy," said Bart, reaching out a hand to Bart's shoulder. "What about us?"

"Yeah," added Jez, digging Connor in the ribs. "What about the Three Buccaneers?"

"All for one and one for all!" added Bart.

"Very original," said Cate, with a sigh.

But their clowning had done the trick. Connor was smiling again.

"All right, lads," Cate said, "I'm off to make the final preparations for attack."

"Yes, *sir*!" Bart said, saluting her.

Cate tried to frown but she couldn't stop the laughter breaking through. "Enough of your cheek, *Mister* Pearce. Any more lip and you'll be on toilet duty tonight, while the rest of us are off to Ma Kettle's." She turned and walked away, before another wave of laughter broke through her serious demeanor.

"Ohh, I love it when she gets all uppity," said Bart to his mates.

Connor rolled his eyes at Jez.

"Come on, Connor," Jez said, "let's leave Mister Pearce here to his lovesick fantasies while we get on with some serious rapier maneuvers."

"You're on," agreed Connor.

—⁓—

After spending the morning cleaning swords, Grace Tempest was in need of a good wash herself. She scrubbed away at her hands and arms but, though she managed to get rid of most of the grime, she couldn't extinguish the smell of oil and metal. Oh well, she'd just have to let it wear off, she decided. Bidding farewell to her fellows, she headed back down to her cabin for a well-earned break. As she walked down the corridor, she could hear the pirates on the top deck getting ready for the attack. Connor would be among them. She felt an instinctive wave of nerves for him. After three months, it was still strange to think of her twin brother as a pirate prodigy.

Sometimes, she wondered at the way things had turned out. After their father's death, there had been nothing left for them in Crescent Moon Bay — nothing save a life of drudgery at the orphanage or being adopted by the lunatic bank manager, Lachlan Busby, and his demented wife, Loretta. And so they had taken to the ocean in their old boat, *Louisiana Lady*, not exactly sure where they were heading, but certain that wherever they ended up would be better than what they left behind.

Neither one of them could have ever imagined what lay ahead though, thought Grace, pushing open the door to her small cabin. Her brother had been rescued by this pirate ship. And as for her, well, she had been brought to the Vampirates — creatures she had only heard of in the strange shanty her dad had sung to both twins.

*I'll tell you a tale of Vampirates,*
*A tale as old as true.*
*Yea, I'll sing you a song of an ancient ship,*
*And its mighty fearsome crew.*
*Yea, I'll sing you a song of an ancient ship,*
*That sails the oceans blue . . .*
*That haunts the oceans blue.*

As many times as they had heard the shanty, they had never thought that the ship might actually exist. But it did! And she had found herself on board, coming face to face — or rather, face to mask — with its enigmatic captain.

*They say that the captain, he wears a veil*
*So as to curtail your fright*
*At his death-pale skin*
*And his lifeless eyes*
*And his teeth as sharp as night.*
*Oh, they say that the captain, he wears a veil*
*And his eyes never see the light.*

The captain did *not* wear a veil, but rather a mask. This was just one of the ways in which the reality of the Vampirate ship contrasted with the words of the shanty. The ship *was* as mysterious as she might have anticipated. But it certainly *wasn't* the place of unalloyed horror that everyone expected. At least, it hadn't been for her.

"Wasn't it a *terrible* place?" one or other of the pirates would ask her each and every day. "What was the *worst* thing that you endured?" was another popular question. And "What were they like, those *demons*?"

Faced with these questions, Grace had decided the best strategy was to say, "I'd rather not talk about it, if you don't mind." That generally did the trick. Poor Grace, they thought. Of course, she doesn't want to conjure up memories of that awful place.

This was far easier than trying to persuade them that

she had actually been treated well on board that ship. The masked captain had seemed a benevolent creature, with Grace's best interests at heart. And though the Vampirates did — of course — drink blood, they did so in a measured fashion at the weekly Feast. And the blood was supplied by donors, who were treated well in exchange for their gift. She had told Connor about this, but even he had struggled to understand how she could be so accepting of it all. The mere thought of blood-taking — or "the sharing" as the Vampirates called it — filled him with horror. Grace smiled. As tough as Connor might appear to his pirate comrades, the very thought of blood made him nauseous. It was a good thing, she reflected, that it was *she* who had found herself on the Vampirate ship and *he* on the pirate vessel — and not the other way around!

As strange as it sounded, Grace had made good friends on the Vampirate ship. Why, the very clothes she was wearing had been given to her by Darcy Flotsam — the ship's figurehead by day and, in her own words, "figure of fun by night."

Sitting down on her narrow bed, Grace drew back the thin curtain over her porthole. Outside, the ocean was dazzling blue. It made her think — as she so often did — of Lorcan Furey. He was the "young" Vampirate who had rescued her from drowning. He had guarded her on the ship and, when the pirates came to find her, he had protected her one last time. She had left the ship in much more of a rush than she would have liked. She hadn't even had the chance to say a proper good-bye to Lorcan. She had lost track of him after Connor arrived. Her brother's arrival had been such a surprise!

Of course, Lorcan must have headed inside the ship as daylight fell. But, when Grace went to his cabin to bid him farewell, he wasn't there. She had made Connor wait while she searched the rest of the ship for him, but she hadn't found him. Even the Vampirate captain was unable to tell her where Lorcan might be. Finally, she could stall Connor no more. Grace said her good-byes to the Vampirate captain and then returned to her cabin one last time. She took a small case of possessions — including the notebooks from her cabin and some of Darcy's cast-off clothes — and headed back up to the deck to depart.

When she had unpacked the case in her cabin on *The Diablo* later, she had discovered a small wooden casket that she didn't remember packing. There was a small cloth bundle inside. As she unwrapped it, a small note-card fell out. Written in a familiar scrawl were the words:

*Dear Grace,*

*Something to remember me by.*
*Travel safe!*

*Your true friend,*
*Lorcan Furey*

Grace's heart was beating fast as she lifted the card. Just the sight of Lorcan's scrawled signature was enough to move her. But, folded within the cloth, lay an even greater shock. For there was Lorcan's Claddagh ring. She remembered the first time she had seen it, as he'd brushed a stray hair from her wet face, after rescuing her from drowning.

Now she looked down at the ring — at the strange icon of the hands clasping a skull, a small crown set upon the skull's head. She took the ring in her fingers. This was too great a gift, she thought. It was almost a part of Lorcan. But perhaps that was the point, she thought with a thrill. He *wanted* her to have a part of him. She'd have to return it to him one day, she decided. In the meantime, it would be her talisman — a reminder of the time she had spent on the Vampirate ship and an omen that one day, in the future, she *would* return.

For now, she unfastened the chain Connor had given her, and slipped the ring onto it, so that it nestled beside Connor's locket. They were her two most precious possessions.

Grace reached up her fingers to touch the ring now. Sometimes, when she touched it, she closed her eyes and had such a clear vision of the Vampirate ship, it was as if she were able to see it for real. If only this were true!

How were they all — the captain and Darcy and Lorcan? — she wondered. Where were they now? Once again, she wished she had had longer to say her good-byes. It had been impossible to argue with Connor when he had said she must come to live with him on *The Diablo*. She would never have been able to convince him that they should stay on the Vampirate ship. That would be *madness*, wouldn't it? Choosing to live amongst a crew of vampires? She remembered something her father had once told her. *"Sometimes madness is wisdom, Gracie."* She had the feeling her dad would have understood.

Grace let her hand fall from Lorcan's ring. She would have chosen to stay with them if she had had a real choice. Only one of the crew had threatened her. As always, she shuddered as the image of Lieutenant Sidorio came into her mind — his eyes flaming pits of fire, his gold incisors as sharp as daggers.

Sidorio — who had killed his donor and held Grace hostage in her cabin until the captain rescued her.

Sidorio — who had told her that he had been killed by Julius Caesar himself before he crossed.

Sidorio — who had been banished from the ship, and sent into exile.

He had been the only truly dangerous one aboard that ship, thought Grace, as she stared out into the translucent ocean. But Sidorio was gone. The danger had passed. Surely it would be safe to return now, if she could only find a way.

2

# AN EASY VICTORY

"Sound the cannon!" cried Cate. The attack was on.

Now *The Diablo* was alongside the target ship. Cannon fire signalled the raid had begun and the sound of grinding metal signalled that the grids the pirates called the "Three Wishes" had swung down from above to make bridges onto the containership. Connor had not yet cured his fear of heights and his heart did a familiar somersault as he heard the wishes descend, anticipating his imminent run across the wishes, high above the water. Mercifully, it all happened quickly, and today, there was further compensation in the relative gentleness of the ocean.

"Fours — go!"

The instant the wishes were near horizontal, the teams of four raced heavy-footed across them. These were the teams of muscle — mostly grown men, including Bart — who began the attack by swirling their broadswords and inducing fear and apparent chaos on the other deck.

"First eights — in!"

Cate's cry signalled the movement of three teams of eight rapier and épée bearers across the metal grids. This was the first flank of precision fighters. Though the broadsworders appeared more fearsome, it was the first eights who posed the deeper threat. As Cate had once told Connor, using her épée was like "fighting with a needle." If that needle pierced a human target in the right spot, it would puncture a vital organ and trigger a slow, painful death from the inside out. Jez was the last of the first eights, ahead of Connor.

"See you on the other side!" he cried to Connor as he jumped onto the wish.

The 4–8–8 formation in which the pirates of *The Diablo* launched their attack on the containership was one of Cate's favorite and most successful maneuvers. It was her preferred mode of attack on a medium-sized craft, such as the current target, and involved sixty pirates, divided into three teams, which then further subdivided into 4–8–8. Each pirate in the second team of eight was paired with one in the first — the second acting as a backup to the more experienced and accomplished fighter. Today, Connor would act as Jez's backup. They'd been working as a pair during every attack for the past eight weeks and Connor was learning a lot from his good friend and mentor.

"Second eights!"

The head of Connor's team made the cry and now the teams of second eights flew across the wishes to join the battle. Connor was the last of his team. Again he thought back to his first attack, when Cheng Li had nudged him forward. Now, Cheng Li was gone and there was just his own will to push him on. Taking a deep breath, Connor leaped onto the wish and ran into the fray. Now it was all about instinct and timing and precision. Now Connor Tempest inhabited not just the clothes of a pirate but a pirate's skin and soul. As he let out a cry and drew his rapier from its sheath, he felt the blood pumping through his veins. He felt truly alive.

As Connor raced through the melee aboard the containership, he saw that Jez was running rings around two of the opposing ship's crew. They were dressed head to toe in black and brandishing curved swords with sharp outer edges, which Connor recognized as scimitars. To be brandishing such weapons, he realized that the cargo of the containership must be precious indeed. The stakes of today's battle would be high.

"Welcome aboard!" Jez greeted Connor, with a laid-back smile. "Come and meet my new friends!"

At the sight of Connor — charging forward, rapier in

hand — the two crew members promptly surrendered, dropping their scimitars to the deck.

"An excellent decision, my friends," Jez said, beaming. "Connor, keep them under guard here. I'll be back in a flash."

"No problem," Connor said, standing in the ready position with his rapier covering both men. This was not the end of the battle. He'd been caught out before and he knew that one slip mid-combat could result in a very different result at the end of the fight.

He did, however, allow himself a quick glance across the deck. The attack seemed to be going in their favor. Although the defending crew were well-armed, they seemed to be insufficiently skilled at fighting techniques, and the pirates of *The Diablo* had them on the defensive with Jez's maneuver repeated all over the deck. The containership's crew was brought to the center of the deck, their scimitars dropping like pine needles onto the boards. Connor felt flushed with pride. *The Diablo*, under the instruction of its new deputy captain, Cate, was truly an elite fighting machine.

Connor looked into the eyes of his captives. "Always watch your opponent's eyes," Bart had once told him. "The sword can lie, but the eyes don't." During past attacks, he'd grown used to reading the fear in his prisoners' eyes. This was the part of the operation he found the hardest to deal with. Bart and Jez had told him that this would change in time.

"There's nothing wrong in it," Jez had told him. "It's good to remember that your prisoner is just another guy — just like me or you — another guy with mates and family and dreams of glory. It *only* becomes a problem if you let your guard slip for an instant and allow him back into the fight." Connor was already an experienced enough pirate to know that that wasn't going to happen here.

Careful not to let his captives out of his sight, he again cast his eyes swiftly around the deck. It looked like the battle was coming to a close. He could see Cate and Captain Wrathe circling the core of prisoners, all clustered around the mast at the ship's center. Farther in the distance, Connor saw Bart and his team of broadsworders, guarding the periphery. Everything was under control. Now, just one important maneuver remained — the surrender of the defending captain. But where *was* the captain? Who was he — or she? All the pirates were dressed identically, with no distinguishing marks of rank. Why, Connor himself might be holding the captain captive.

Connor watched his prisoners' faces as he heard Molucco Wrathe call out.

"Captain, come and show yourself. Your ship has been boarded and I, Molucco Wrathe, of *The Diablo,* lay claim to your cargo."

There was no response. Captain Wrathe's words hung in the air like the residue of cannon fire.

Jez rejoined Connor. Connor turned to him, expecting his comrade to be smiling, but Jez's face was serious.

"I don't like this," he whispered. "I don't like this at all. It's been too easy."

"Easy is good, isn't it?" said Connor.

Jez shook his head. "There's easy, and there's too easy. Something's wrong."

Connor trembled at his words.

Captain Wrathe called out again. "Come and show yourself, Captain. We'll do no more harm if we can agree to terms swiftly — and fill our hold with your treasures!"

This time, there was an answer. It came with the sound of a bell. The ship's bell. As the strange tolling rang out three, then four, then five times, the pirates of *The Diablo* looked from one to the other, wondering what was going on. Connor could just make out Cate's face in the distance. He could see that she was as perturbed as the rest of them.

Now, he was *really* worried. He looked back at his prisoners' faces. One of them was smiling at him. Then he began to laugh. His fellow followed suit. Connor turned to Jez, confused, as the wave of laughter spread from one prisoner to the next, until a crescendo of laughter took over the deck.

Suddenly, Connor became aware that his crewmates

no longer formed the outer periphery of the deck. They were now surrounded by a circle of pirates, dressed head to toe in black like their prisoners, brandishing the same deadly scimitars. How had the captives done it? The deck was now full of them. The pirates of *The Diablo* werc completely outnumbered.

"They tricked us," Jez said. "Look over there!"

Connor followed his gaze to where a line of black-clad figures were rising from two holes on the deck. Trapdoors!

"And look behind you!"

Connor twisted his head. More crew members were climbing out from two farther trapdoors at the starboard end of the ship. The defending crew had lulled the pirates of *The Diablo* into a false sense of victory by only fielding a skeleton crew for the initial fight. It was a bold move — for how did they know that the pirates would not go in for the kill? But the risky stratagem had paid off and now four times as many black-clad crew stood ranged about the deck, scimitars outstretched.

"What do we do?" Connor asked Jez.

Jez shrugged, looking beaten. "Know any good prayers, mate?"

Connor had never seen Jez so dejected. He looked from Jez's ashen face to the smiling prisoners before him — or, at least, the men he'd thought were his prisoners. Suddenly, Connor felt very, very sick.

"Lay down your weapons, attacking scum!"

The captain's voice at last called out across the deck. Still, Connor held tight to his raised rapier. No pirate of *The Diablo* could lay down his or her weapon without instruction from a commanding officer. It was one of the articles Connor had signed up to when he joined Molucco Wrathe's command.

But now, to his surprise, Connor heard Cate cry, "Lay down your weapons, fellows."

He could scarcely believe his ears. In the three months of his tenure on the ship they had been in some scrapes, but nothing compared to this. All around him, weapons thudded to the floor. He turned questioningly to Jez, who nodded sadly. Together, they lay down their rapiers. As they did so, in a clearly well-rehearsed movement, the former prisoners swept up their scimitars. Now the crew of *The Diablo* were held under swords from both sides. They had no chance of escape. But where was the enemy captain?

"Let the shamed captain announce himself!" It was the same voice that had commanded them to lay down their weapons. A voice that spoke of violence and no mercy. Connor and the others glanced about the deck. But it was not clear who was speaking. "Let the shamed captain announce himself!" repeated the voice.

"I have already made my presence clear," called Molucco

Wrathe in response, "which is more than can be said for *you*, sir."

Connor looked over to Captain Wrathe. Even now, in the face of disaster, Molucco had lost none of his grandeur. He was, and would ever be, a larger-than-life character.

Suddenly, there was a noise high up above. Connor glanced up to the crow's nest. A man stood there — clad in the same costume as his crew, head to toe in black. The other pirates began looking upward, too.

Then, to Connor's amazement, the captain jumped from the crow's nest. He dived down onto the deck, flying past the sails and rigging, trailing a black cord behind him. As he neared the deck — and certain death — the cord held him tight, like a bungee. He bounced for a moment, then hung upside down — and perfectly still — like a sleeping bat. Finally, the captain unsheathed his scimitar and sliced through the cord. As the cord broke free, he executed a perfect somersault in midair, landing neatly on the deck a few feet from where Molucco stood.

The mysterious captain strode toward Molucco. His scimitar flashed in the sunlight like cut diamond. He ran it across Captain Wrathe's neck. Still, Molucco did not flinch.

Now the captain lifted his other hand and removed the dark coverings of his head. The black cloth unfurled like ribbons, which flew away in the breeze.

Only now, did Captain Wrathe pale and seem to shrink in stature. Only now, did he seem at a loss for words, gulping for air. Until, at last, he managed to open his mouth and speak.

"*You!* But it can't be . . . can it?"

Connor turned to Jez, wondering if *he* knew what was going on. But, for once in his life, Jez Stukeley was utterly silent.

3

# THE DEVIL AND THE ALBATROSS

The captains stood face to face. Well, as close as was possible, given that the captain of the containership was a good head taller than Molucco Wrathe. His face was tanned, angular and smooth as soapstone, save for a deep scar, which dissected his cheek like a purple river.

"Narcisos Drakoulis," Captain Wrathe exclaimed in wonder. "I thought to have seen the last of you."

"I'm sure you did, Wrathe." Captain Drakoulis smiled, without a trace of warmth. "Many winters have come and gone since Ithaka."

Connor looked from one captain to the other, wondering what dark history lay between them.

"Your crew mutinied. They took your ship. You were marooned. How did you do it? All this . . ." Captain

Wrathe's voice trailed off as he surveyed the deck, taking stock of Drakoulis' hoards of fighters, their scimitars flashing like fire in the sunlight.

Drakoulis smiled again through tight lips. "Always have a Plan B, Wrathe. It's the first rule of captaincy, is it not?" He raised his scimitar in the air, prompting his crew to repeat the gesture, so their weapons surrounded the pirates of *The Diablo* like a lethal fence.

"Keep still your weapons," Drakoulis ordered, "for now."

Connor shuddered, wanting to check Jez's reaction but unable to tear his eyes away from Captain Drakoulis. There was such danger in the captain's cold eyes and in his emotionless voice. Connor realized that today's attack had been doomed. He cursed himself for being so gung ho. Now, he might never see Grace again. After everything it had taken to find her, now it might all come to an end on this very deck — at the hands of one of Drakoulis' crew.

"There's been a mistake, Drakoulis," Molucco Wrathe said. "You know I'd never order an attack on another pirate captain's ship."

Drakoulis shook his head. "I know nothing of the sort."

Molucco forged ahead, unperturbed by the icy tone of his enemy. "We thought this was a containership. We were misinformed . . ."

"Yes," Drakoulis said, smiling again. "You were misinformed." He paused, as if carefully weighing his words. "It's curious how these . . . confusions, occur."

Connor looked over at Jez now, and found him frowning. "We were tricked," Jez hissed. "This was a set-up."

"It's time that you paid for your errant ways," Drakoulis continued, "There's a Pirate Code, Wrathe, which you seem to have conveniently forgotten — or else think you are somehow above. You have some fanciful notion, perhaps, of the Wrathe name — you and your brothers. You dive in and out of other captains' sea-lanes — laying siege here, taking plunder there. Oh it's all sport to you and your . . . playmates, is it not?"

Connor had heard other pirates rail about Captain Wrathe before. He thought back to his first visit to Ma Kettle's Tavern, when a dozen other captains had unleashed their anger on Captain Wrathe. That had been frightening, but this was an altogether more dangerous situation. The other pirates had only wanted to vent their fury. Captain Drakoulis had planned and executed a cold-blooded mission to ensnare Captain Wrathe and his crew. Connor sensed that Drakoulis was seeking revenge for some ancient hurt. What had Molucco done to him? Connor looked with new eyes at the captain to whom he had pledged his allegiance.

"What do you want, Drakoulis?" Captain Wrathe's question pulled Connor roughly back into the present — dire — situation.

"I already told you, Wrathe. The time has come to pay for your actions."

"Let's talk terms then, man, and we'll both be on our way." Captain Wrathe sounded as cocksure as ever.

Drakoulis resumed in his cold voice, "There is a price to be paid for your misdemeanors."

"Name your price," answered Molucco. "And remind me, is it gold or silver that tickles your fancy?"

Drakoulis looked at Molucco in disgust, shaking his head slowly. As he did so, Connor noticed that in contrast to Captain Wrathe — who was dripping in silver and sapphires — Captain Drakoulis wore no jewelry. His uniform was the same as the rest of his company — simple, black and unadorned. When he spoke again, his voice was full of disdain.

"How typical of you to think that I would wish for the same ephemeral rewards as you, Wrathe. The price of your transgressions will not be paid in metal, Captain. It will be paid in the only currency that matters — blood."

At their captain's words, the crew raised their scimitars once more. It was a perfectly smooth, coordinated movement. How well Drakoulis had rehearsed them. Connor could not begin to think what fresh horror would now be unleashed. But he knew that Drakoulis' pirates would be perfectly prepared, while he and his crewmates would be left floundering. He felt a flash of anger at Captain Wrathe for putting him and the others into this position. But the anger soon dissipated. Molucco Wrathe had welcomed him aboard his ship like a father. He had given Connor sanctuary in his darkest hour — given him back hope. Molucco might be an unruly rogue, but he was not an evil man. In stark contrast, it appeared, to Captain Narcisos Drakoulis.

"A duel," Drakoulis announced. "The matter will be settled by a duel — to the death."

Molucco flinched. It was no secret that his best fighting years were behind him. He was still a force to be reckoned with, but he had long since delegated the key combat to the younger members of his crew. Connor looked from Molucco Wrathe to Narcisos Drakoulis. In the stark white sunlight, the contrast was all too obvious. Captain Wrathe appeared overweight and overindulged while, beneath his tight black vestments, Narcisos Drakoulis was lean and hard and primed for the fight. It was no contest. If it came to swords, Connor and his mates would be returning to *The Diablo* without their captain.

But Drakoulis smiled at Molucco once more. "Of course, I'm not suggesting that you and *I* engage in direct combat. Why, it would hardly be worth oiling this scimitar for such sport. No, Wrathe, you shall put forward your best swordsman and so shall I." Drakoulis' dark eyes narrowed. "Best decide quickly who it shall be."

Molucco frowned. He sought out Cate in the crowd. Connor held his breath. Was Captain Wrathe going to choose her for the duel? She must rank as one of the best fighters on the ship, certainly the most knowledgeable.

But to risk losing her would be a terrible gamble. And, as her friend as well as her protégé, Connor felt a wave of dread at the thought.

"All right," Drakoulis announced, "while you dither about, allow me to introduce you to your combatant. Gidaki Sarakakino, step forward!"

There was a united cheer from the ranks of Drakoulis' crew as one of their number began a slow march to the center of the deck. Connor felt a flood of fear as he heard the heavy footsteps approaching. The man brushed past him and the weight of his tensed muscle sent a searing pain into Connor's shoulder. He turned and saw a dark bruise already forming on his flesh. Looking up again, he watched Drakoulis smile and extend his hand to his chosen swordsman. Sarakakino shook it and then turned to salute his crewmates. Connor felt his heart sink. Few of the pirates of *The Diablo* could take on an opponent such as this.

Molucco was locked deep in conversation with Cate.

Captain Drakoulis shook his head. "It comes as little surprise that you struggle so to make a decision for yourself."

For the first time, Molucco gave way to anger. "My ship is a democracy," he snarled, "and I will have the opinion of my deputy on this matter."

Drakoulis shot Molucco a contemptuous look but did not, for the moment, say anything more.

It was agony watching Captain Wrathe and Cate

discussing the dire situation. Connor knew how much it would pain them both to have to elect a pirate to fight alone like this. Life on *The Diablo* was based on teamwork and there was real friendship among the crew members, cutting through the hierarchy without weakening it. There was no sense on *The Diablo* that even one pirate was expendable.

At last, Captain Wrathe turned from Cate and addressed Narcisos Drakoulis.

"Our decision is made."

Connor, together with the rest of his crew, awaited the verdict.

"We will not submit to a member of our crew engaging in a duel."

For a moment, Drakoulis said nothing. Then he turned to Sarakakino. Both men started to laugh. Drakoulis composed himself and turned back to Molucco.

"You act as if you have a choice," Drakoulis said. "This isn't a game, Captain. I have told you — it is time to pay the price."

Molucco stepped up to Captain Drakoulis, infused with a new energy. "You spoke of rules before, Captain. And yet you issue your dictate like some kind of demigod."

"Demigod?" sneered Drakoulis, "Why, isn't every ship its own universe and every pirate captain god of all he surveys?"

Connor felt the blood in his veins turn to ice. There was

madness in Drakoulis. Allied to his violence, who could tell the extent of the danger he posed?

"I'll report you to the Pirate Federation," Molucco said.

Drakoulis shook his head. "I don't think so, Wrathe. You are on *The Albatross* now, *my* ship."

*The Albatross*, thought Connor, grimly. It was a curious name for a ship. The long-winged seabird was a portent of doom to sailors. And so it had proved to the crew of *The Diablo*. Clearly, the devil was no match for the albatross today.

"You're out of your sea-lane," Drakoulis announced coldly.

"This isn't your lane, either."

"It matters not," said Drakoulis dismissively. "The Pirate Federation is cutting you loose, Wrathe. They've grown weary of your transgressions. Lord knows that they've tried their best to correct you. Even sending one of their spies into your crew —"

"A spy?"

Molucco stopped in his tracks, aghast.

"Yes — a spy!" Drakoulis imitated Molucco's wide-eyed confusion. "Chang Ko Li's daughter. You thought she was in training to be a captain, but all the time she was spying on you and reporting back to the Feds."

This was news not only to Captain Wrathe. Connor watched the troubling accusation ricochet around his crewmates. It hit him hard too. He had experienced at close hand Cheng Li's frustrations with Captain Wrathe, but he had never thought she was a *spy*. As his mind frantically rewound their conversations, he realized that it all fit. If only she were here to explain herself . . . but he hadn't seen her in almost three months.

Captain Wrathe shook his head. "This is more of your madness, Drakoulis," he said. "Mistress Li was completing her academy training. And the Federation chose *The Diablo* for her apprenticeship."

"So where is she now?" Drakoulis asked, with a sneer.

"She's back at the academy, on a teaching assignment."

"Oh, that's right, isn't it? She resigned from your command due to *an exceptional offer* from the Federation. Or was it, perhaps, because she had failed in her mission to bring you into line?"

"No!" shouted Molucco.

"Why not ask her yourself, next time you bump into her at Ma Kettle's? I think you'll find Mistress Li to be *full* of interesting stories. That is, of course, if she still deigns to speak with you."

Molucco looked thunderstruck. Connor felt equally bewildered. He knew only a little of the Pirate Federation. Was it true that the Federation was spying on Molucco Wrathe and his pirates? Was Narcisos Drakoulis acting independently or had he been contracted as an assassin? Had

Cheng Li really tried — and failed — to contain Molucco's roguish ways? It seemed as if all Molucco's chickens had come home to roost this time.

"We've talked enough," Drakoulis spat. "It's time to settle the matter. Which of your crew will fight the duel with Sarakakino here?"

As he spoke, his chosen combatant let slip his shirt, revealing a taut, muscle-bound chest and arms, channeled with thick veins. As Sarakakino's shirt fell to the deck, he turned around and clenched his biceps. Across the tanned skin of his back was a vast tattoo of a bird, its long wings stretching out over his shoulder blades. Another albatross, Connor realized. If ever there was a portent of doom, this bird tattoo was it.

"I told you before," Molucco said, "I'll put no pirate of mine to the sword."

"And *I* told *you*," Drakoulis said, exploding with rage, "to put one man forward or I'll unleash hell on the entirety of your crew!"

All about the deck, the curved scimitars were raised.

The two captains stood, face to face, in deadlock.

Then, to Connor's surprise — and horror — he heard a familiar voice cry out.

"I'll fight him, Captain Wrathe. Let me fight him!"

# THE VISITOR

Grace lay on the bed in her cabin. Above her, the deck of *The Diablo* was quiet. That meant they'd gone — all of the pirates involved in the attack. Now, those that were left behind could only wait. This was the time she hated. She could just about cope with the idea of Connor going into battle — there was precious little she could do to prevent it — so long as she didn't have time to dwell on it too much. While he was away, she liked to keep busy. Whenever possible, she used this time to do her duties, but today she'd been on the early roster and now she had a couple of hours to herself. She could always go and offer to help with more of the work, but time off aboard *The Diablo* was a luxury not to be wasted. Besides, she had slept badly the night before, and that — combined with her early start — had left her dog-tired.

She glanced about her small cabin. It was decidedly more spartan than the grand cabin she had occupied aboard the Vampirate ship. There, she had slept like a storybook princess in a vast bed, piled high with cushions and hung low with tapestries. Now, she bedded down on a simple single bunk with one pillow, which itself had seen better days. But Grace wasn't complaining. She rather liked her new abode. It was comfortable enough, and it was certainly nice having daylight filter in, even if it was through a somewhat grimy porthole. Besides, better to have a cabin to yourself than to sleep — like Connor – in a dormitory where the other pirates' snores and wheezes, coughs and farts played like a strange symphony through the night.

Besides the bed, there was little other furniture in the room — a small wooden chair that she chiefly used to hang her clothes at night, a small cupboard, and some shelves. But it was more than enough room for someone who had as few possessions as Grace. Uncurling herself slowly, she slipped down from the bed, and knelt on the floor. She reached her hand under the bunk, moving aside a box of old rope and a blanket, which were simply decoys to prevent prying eyes from finding the small case that she kept there.

Now, she took it in her hands and climbed back up onto

the bunk. It was Darcy Flotsam who had given the case to her. "Because every young lady needs a place for her secret things," she had said. It was typical of Darcy — the kind gesture, the rationale, and the case itself. It was, strictly speaking, a "vanity case," deep red leather on the outside and shocking pink silk padding on the interior. It was intended for storing combs and brushes, makeup compacts, lipsticks, and the like. Grace had none of these and no desire for them. But with its hidden compartments and, most usefully, its small lock and key, the case was the ideal place to keep her secret things.

She turned the small key and lifted the lid, smiling as she surveyed the contents. There were the notebooks and pens she had brought with her — at the Vampirate captain's urging. She reached in and extracted the small leather notebook in which she had started to write the "crossing stories" of the Vampirate crew — the accounts of what their lives were when they were mortals and how they had gone from that world to this. So far, few of the pages had been used. It only had Darcy Flotsam's story — written in Grace's best handwriting — and Sidorio's much darker tale, hastily scrawled under somewhat different circumstances.

Her eyes ran over these last words. His tale was as thrilling to her as it was horrific. Lieutenant Sidorio had revealed that, many centuries before, he had kidnapped Julius Caesar and later been killed in revenge. In spite of the raw fear Sidorio instilled in Grace, she was glad to know his story and to have captured it in this book. She had plucked a dark secret that few others in this world knew, and to Grace that was as heady a thrill as if she had pressed the rarest of orchids between the pages of her notebook.

As she came to the last page of writing, she sighed. She would dearly love to add to the journal. Aboard the Vampirate ship, she had hatched a plan to chronicle the crossing stories of each and every member of the crew. That thought still sent a shiver of excitement through her, though she knew she had little hope of making it happen.

Grace's eyes were growing as tired as the rest of her body. She closed the journal and placed it beside her on the bed. She lay back on the sheets and she closed her eyes. She brought her hand up to her neck, tracing the chain hanging around it. As her index finger followed its path down below her shirt, it found the heart-shaped locket Connor had given to her. Her fingers pushed it to one side and made contact with Lorcan's Claddagh ring. As she touched it, there was a moment of electricity — real or imagined — as she remembered Lorcan's gift to her when she left the ship.

Now, it was the ring, above all, which gave her hope. It reminded her of Lorcan's words, his soft brogue, the way he looked at her as if there were depths of feeling he could not yet give voice to. The ring was the best kept of

Grace's secrets, hanging there where no one could see it, hidden under the locket. Sometimes, just sometimes, as the band of metal pressed against her clavicle, she felt a strange sensation — as if Lorcan were speaking to her, reassuring her that everything was going to be okay and that they would be together again. Sure enough, it was his voice that spoke softly to her now, pulling her away from the pirate ship into the sparkling blue waters of her dreams.

—◦—

"Grace! Grace, wake up!"

"What?"

She was floating in such a delicious dream. She felt so rested and comfortable.

"Grace!" The voice came again. Louder. She recognized it but could not place it. And the dream was too comfortable to leave. She resisted.

"Grace Tempest! Please wake up!"

As the voice poured directly into her ears, Grace opened her eyes. She knew that voice — that strange, squeaking cockney accent.

"Darcy!" she exclaimed, twisting her head on the pillow. "Darcy Flotsam."

Sure enough, Darcy was sitting beside the bed. Her brow was furrowed. "Well, I must say, you sleep awful heavy for a young lady." Her frown quickly gave way to a smile.

Grace smiled back, drawing herself up to a sitting position and swinging her feet round toward Darcy. "Darcy! I can't believe it's you! How did you get here?"

"It's a long story," Darcy said. "Listen, I'm not sure how long I can stay. But I had to see you."

Grace was beaming. She couldn't have wished for a nicer awakening. There she had been, lost in a dream about the Vampirate ship and now one of her friends had appeared — not only on the ship but in her very cabin! Elated, she stood up, opening her arms to hug Darcy. Darcy rose to meet her and stepped forward.

But as Grace flung her arms about Darcy's waist, Darcy must have moved suddenly, or else the ship did, because Grace's arms flailed through thin air. She opened her arms again and reached for Darcy. This time, they were face to face. Darcy was looking at her strangely. Grace watched . . . as her arms moved straight through Darcy. It was if she were made of air. Grace lifted her hand to her friend's face, reaching out a finger toward her button nose. It poked straight through Darcy's nose into nothingness. Grace recoiled, looking at Darcy curiously.

"What's going on?" she asked.

Darcy looked serious, folding her arms across her chest. "You see, I'm here, but I'm *not* here, Grace."

"I don't understand," said Grace. "Can *you* see *me*?"

"Yes, yes of course I can see you," she said, stepping forward. "And I can see you've made an awful mess of that pretty blouse I lent you."

Grace glanced down, guiltily. It was true — the blouse was stained with oil from her earlier sword-cleaning duties.

"I'm sorry," Grace said. "I had to get up really early to work and it was the first thing I threw on. I didn't think."

"Hush!" said Darcy, raising a finger toward Grace's lips but not touching them. "We have more important things to talk about than stains and spills."

"Yes," Grace said. "Of course." She still didn't quite understand how Darcy came to be here but she could see from her friend's anxious expression that she had come for a reason. "Let's sit down," she said.

Grace sat on the bed and Darcy sat down next to her. Only she didn't exactly sit, Grace noticed, but hovered just above the mattress. It was very curious.

"How is everyone?" Grace asked. "How's the captain? And Lorcan?"

Darcy's head dropped for a moment. When she raised it again, there were buds of tears in her eyes. "That's just it," she said, "that's why I had to come. Since you left, everything's horrible, just horrible."

Grace's heart sank. "What do you mean? Whatever's happened?"

For a moment, Darcy was unable to speak as the tears

fell from her eyes, mixing with her eyeliner and falling like dark petals across her fine complexion. "Just a mo," she managed to sniff, fishing in her pocket, "I think I've got a tissue in here somewhere." But her hand came away empty.

Grace reached in her own pocket and instinctively offered Darcy her own handkerchief. They both looked at each other for a moment. Then Grace let the handkerchief go. They both watched as the small square of cloth floated straight through Darcy's phantom hand and down to the floor of the cabin. Somehow, it made them smile. Darcy sniffed and brought the back of her hand up to her face, wiping away her tears and then wiping her hand clean on her dress. It was an uncharacteristic gesture for someone who cared so much about her appearance. Darcy shrugged. "Like I say, Grace, stains and spills."

Grace nodded, smiling reassuringly at her companion. "Darcy, you must tell me what's wrong. Perhaps I can help. You were all so good to me — well, *almost* all of you. I'll do anything I can to help. You don't know how many times I've dreamed about coming back to the ship. Why, just before you woke me up —"

A dark look crossed Darcy's face. "You can't come back!"

Grace was confused. "Why not?"

"It's not a safe place anymore. You mustn't even think of coming back."

"Not safe?" Grace said. "But I was there when the captain

banished Sidorio. And *he* was the only rebel Vampirate, wasn't he?"

Darcy shook her head. "Not the *only*," she said, "the *first*."

"The first?"

Darcy nodded. "Sidorio *was* the only rebel, but since he was banished — since you left — there are others who challenge the captain's authority every day and every night. They won't settle for just taking blood at the Feast. They want more blood, more Feasts . . ." She broke off, tears in her eyes again.

"And what does the captain say?" Grace asked.

"He tells them 'no.' He says that these are the ways of the ship. Always have been. Always will be."

"Well then," Grace said. "The captain will keep control. He always does."

Darcy shook her head. "It ain't never been like this before. For as long as I've sailed on that ship, there's always been . . . there's always been respect for the captain. But, after he sent Sidorio away, something changed. No one was ever sent away before."

Grace remembered thinking at the time that it might be dangerous to send Sidorio away. But the captain had been so intent upon it. But Grace had been more concerned with what dark mischief Sidorio might cause in the world outside, than with what would happen on the ship after he'd gone.

"I wish I could help you," Grace said. "I wish I could come back and talk to the captain."

Darcy shook her head. "No, Grace. No, you must stay here — with Connor — where you're safe."

Grace smiled. "It's a pirate ship, Darcy. It's hardly safe. Even now, Connor's off on an attack."

"You two sure have a knack for landing yourselves in trouble," Darcy said.

"Out of the frying pan and into the fire," agreed Grace, ruefully.

They smiled at each other. Grace reached out her hand as if to take Darcy's.

"We can't touch," Darcy reminded her.

"I know," said Grace, keeping her hand extended. "I know we can't, but let's just pretend we can."

Darcy nodded, stretching out her own hand until her phantom palm lay almost against Grace's flesh-and-blood one. It was near enough.

"So," said Grace. "Tell me about Lorcan."

But as Darcy opened her mouth to answer, she started to fade.

"Wait!" Grace cried. "What's happened to Lorcan?"

Darcy shook her head, tears filling her eyes again. Then she melted away into the air and Grace was alone once more.

# 5

# DUEL

"I'll fight him, Captain," Jez Stukeley called once more.

Connor turned to his friend in shock, but Jez was already pushing forward through the crowd. Up ahead, Connor turned toward Bart. He was clearly as shocked as Connor was. This couldn't be happening to the Three Buccaneers!

Some of Drakoulis' henchmen barred Jez's way, but Captain Drakoulis himself berated them. "Let him through. Let him show himself."

The ranks of black-clad warriors duly opened up and Jez Stukeley walked bravely through them, coming to a stop in front of the two pirate captains and the mountain of muscle that was Gidaki Sarakakino. Sarakakino looked down at Jez and smirked. You didn't need to be a mind-reader to guess what he was thinking.

"Mister Stukeley," Molucco Wrathe said, placing his hand on the young pirate's shoulder, "you're a brave and honorable man, but I can't let you put yourself into such danger."

Jez shook his head. "It's my duty, Captain Wrathe. When I signed the articles, I agreed to defend *The Diablo*, my captain, and my crew mates. There's no way off this ship unless one of us agrees to this duel."

"He's right," Narcisos Drakoulis cut in. "All I require is one of your pirates to enter a duel with Sarakakino. Fail to submit to that and neither you nor the rest of your crew will ever see *The Diablo* again."

Connor trembled at Drakoulis' threat, made all the more tangible by the sight of the scimitars poised across the deck. He weighed this up against his friendship with Jez. There had to be another way. Wasn't it Captain Wrathe's responsibility to head off the danger? It couldn't fall to Jez. It just *couldn't*.

Molucco shook his head. "I never cared for you, Drakoulis, but you used to have morals — of a fashion. I don't know where you've been rotting all this time, but your years in the wilderness have made a putrid villain of you. Your actions today cannot have been endorsed by the Pirate Federation. You act out of your own twisted desires and some warped notion of revenge for a small and ancient grievance."

In spite of this verbal assault, Drakoulis said nothing for a time. His face was a mask, betraying no emotion. At last, he spoke. "If your lecture is over, Wrathe, let us get down to business. The duel will commence on the fifth strike of the ship's bell." He turned to his company. "Clear the center deck now."

At his word, Drakoulis' pirates surged back to open up a fighting area on the center deck, about the size of a boxing ring. And, just as in the preamble to a boxing match, Drakoulis now drew to one side to conspire with Gidaki Sarakakino, who was binding dark ribbons of cloth around his hands.

*"No!"* Connor wanted to cry. This was madness. Why had Jez put himself forward to the slaughter? And why hadn't anyone stopped him?

Jez walked over to join Molucco and Cate on the other side. Connor took advantage of the movement of the crowd to slip through and nearer to the front. He found Bart and darted in beside him.

"Hey, buddy." Bart flashed Connor a weak smile, but could not maintain his pretense of lightheartedness for more than a moment. He turned away and looked over at Jez, his eyes heavy with concern.

"Has he got a chance?" Connor whispered to his mate.

"He'll give it a bloody good go," Bart said, "but look at that Sarakakino guy. He makes *me* look puny."

Connor wondered if Bart was tempted to take Jez's place in the duel. But, he reminded himself, although Bart had more bulk, Jez was the more skilled swordsman. He was strong enough and, what he lacked in bulk, he more than made up for in technique and agility. Connor thought of Molucco Wrathe's watchwords of "good training and good fortune." In the next few minutes, Jez Stukeley would need to draw upon every last drop of each.

The bell of *The Albatross* tolled once and all eyes turned to the two men. For Connor, the next few moments seemed to stretch out, as if in slow motion.

A second toll. Sarakakino dipped his hands into a bucket of chalk dust, presumably to enable a better purchase on his sword. As he leaned forward, the spread of muscles on his back and shoulders became even clearer — the tattoo of the albatross stretched out as if about to fly away.

A third toll. One of Drakoulis' men offered the bucket of chalk to Jez. Turning from Molucco and Cate, Jez stepped forward and rubbed the chalk over his hands, shaking off the excess. Then he wrapped his left fist tight around the hilt of his épée and looked to the sky, perhaps sending up a quick prayer through the pink ribbons of cloud.

A fourth toll. Sarakakino was motionless, his back to his opponent — gathering himself, perhaps, with a prayer of his own. Jez waited, his body balanced and poised to fly in either direction.

The fifth and final toll.

Now, all hell broke loose.

Sarakakino turned and faced his opponent, his scimitar slicing through the air in a warning of what it would do if it met Jez's flesh. Undeterred, Jez moved from side to side, holding his own sword in a ready position. Even Connor knew that Sarakakino's swordplay was all mental war. Cate trained her pirates to blind themselves to such bravado. How well Connor remembered her and Bart telling him to watch the eyes of your adversary — even more so than the tip of his sword.

And now Sarakakino's sword drew still. He stared into Jez's eyes, as if questioning him. *Do you really want to do this? Do you really think you can fight me?* In answer, Jez stared back coolly but, as he did so, he thrust with the épée. It cut across Sarakakino's muscled forearm and slashed the skin. First blood had gone to Stukeley and *The Diablo*. Connor watched the crimson drops of Sarakakino's blood spill onto the deck boards.

"Bloody hell," whispered Bart, "I wasn't expecting *that*!"

Connor grinned.

Sarakakino was clearly surprised and Jez wasted no time capitalizing on that, moving lithely around the bigger man and darting in for a second attack. But now Sarakakino was primed and, like a monster stirring from sleep, he gave a roar and thrust out his scimitar to meet Jez's épée. Steel clashed upon steel and Connor could see Jez struggle to maintain his grip as the full force of his adversary transferred through the sword like an electric shock.

Now the two opponents' swords were held together like magnets. Whoever broke away first, and dared to attack, risked exposing himself for an instant — a fleeting instant, but potentially a decisive one.

Their eyes were locked as tightly as their swords. Combat was, as Connor had learned, as much a battle of will as of strength. Jez was doing really well. The wound he had cut into Sarakakino's arm was only shallow, but it had sent a warning to the cocky fighter and doubtless made him reassess his opponent.

And now, once more, it was Jez who took the gamble. He lifted his épée, throwing back Sarakakino and his sword for a moment. Jez leaped up and forward, lunging toward Sarakakino's chest. But his opponent recovered fast and swung his scimitar out to block the attack. Never mind, thought Connor. Again, it had been Jez who had made the attack. Again, Drakoulis' hulk was on the defensive. His friend had a real chance of victory here.

Connor glanced over at Narcisos Drakoulis, hoping to see some sign of fear in his eyes, but the captain's face gave nothing away. In contrast, Connor saw that Molucco was smiling softly, willing Jez on to keep up the momentum of attack. Beside him, Cate was also watching the fight intently. Connor knew that she'd be thinking through every move Jez made. To her, it was all about tactics — like a game of chess. She might be on the sidelines, but in her mind she was there with Jez, maneuvering the blade. He wondered how she thought Jez was doing.

A sharp clash of metal drew Connor's eyes back to the

duellists once more. Their swords were high, giving Sarakakino an advantage in height. Sarakakino held the posture, knowing that the longer he did so, the more of Jez's fire would be drawn away. Jez would have to do something amazing — and fast — to regain the advantage now. But could he take the risk of disengaging his épée?

In the end, it was Sarakakino who broke off first, as if bored by the stalemate. He drew down his sword and leaped beyond Jez's clutches. It was a sign that, though bigger in frame, he too was nimble. The two men were getting the measure of one another and discovering with every gambit that they were in fact quite evenly matched. And, with that knowledge, the fight proceeded with more fluency. Instead of posturing, Sarakakino let his scimitar do more of the work. Jez too realized that he could not rely on being more fleet of foot than his more muscled opponent.

Connor watched as the swords spun through the air, colliding and then flying away again. It was as brilliant a display of fighting techniques as he had ever seen. His own adrenaline was pumping now, and a good part of him itched to reach for his own sword and try out some of the dazzling moves he was witnessing. Of all the sports he had learned, there was something unsurpassable about sword fighting. But there was more to this than mere sport, Connor reminded himself.

Jez parried Sarakakino across the full stretch of deck

left open to them. They came to a stop just in front of Captain Drakoulis, Jez holding the advantage. Then Sarakakino broke free and parried Jez's sword back across the boards to where Molucco and Cate were standing. The transfixed crowd was utterly silent. The only sounds were those of the duellists. The effort of their breath. The thud of their boots. The infinite echo of steel on steel.

Jez and Sarakakino were like two wild beasts, and yet there was as much poise and synchronicity in their movements as if they were dancing. Although they were adversaries, they were partners in this strange dance. It was a beautiful thing to watch, full of skill and grace. Connor marked every move, mesmerized. One day, he would fight such a fight as this.

A new noise.

A cry.

Jez Stukeley is bleeding — profusely from his chest. He tumbles, slow motion, back toward the deckboards. The boards seem to buckle to meet his body, which crashes down, arms and legs flying out. It has happened so quickly that only now does Connor see Sarakakino's blade withdraw, stained with Jez's blood. The dance is ending. The elusive beauty is gone. It is revealed as a dance to the death. Connor and the others stare at Jez Stukeley, whose body jerks like a fish on a hook — the life running out of him in a dark, pulsing river, all over the deck.

6

# DEATH OF A BUCCANEER

Connor could not believe his eyes. The fight had changed so quickly. Only a few minutes earlier, he had been lost in admiration of Jez's swordplay. Now, his friend was lying on the deck, fatally wounded. It was the most horrible of sights. Shock and stunted adrenaline rose up inside him and for a moment he thought he was going to vomit. He felt the bile rise in his throat, but somehow he managed to keep it down.

Connor turned to Bart, in time to see him rush forward. Two of Drakoulis' men raised their swords to halt Bart's steps, but Drakoulis signaled to them to drop their weapons and let him through.

Bart approached their dying friend, dropping down to his knees and reaching out a hand to clasp Jez's. His friend's were already white — life was draining out of him at a terrifying speed. Then Connor realized — Jez's hands were still smeared in chalk dust. It was a momentary relief.

"You fought well, buddy," Connor heard Bart say, as he attempted to staunch the flow of blood from his friend's chest with his neckerchief. "You're a real hero."

Connor turned his eyes to Gidaki Sarakakino. He wanted to hate the killer, but found he couldn't. The fight might just as well have gone the other way, and it could have been Sarakakino laid out on the floor in a pool of his own blood. Even now, the victor was not gloating. He had only done his captain's bidding, like any pirate. Now, sedately, he unwrapped his wrist bindings and wiped his sword clean. He seemed to have withdrawn mentally, finding his own way, perhaps, to justify his actions and their consequence.

So it was to Narcisos Drakoulis whom Connor now glanced, awash with hatred. Jez's blood was on *his* hands, though they might appear perfectly clean and smooth in the pale pink light of the setting sun.

"Your price has been paid, Wrathe," Drakoulis said, his voice devoid of emotion. "You and your crew are free to go."

Molucco Wrathe was incandescent with rage and not afraid to show it. "That lad gave his life in vain, Drakoulis."

"No," Drakoulis snapped, "he gave his life to remind you that piracy is not merely sport."

"Don't lecture me about being a pirate," Molucco roared. "No one here knows more about what it means to be a pirate than I do."

Drakoulis remained calm, in spite of Molucco's outburst. His voice, as he continued, was passionless — robotic. "Your actions, your transgressions, have consequences, Wrathe. Let this be a timely reminder for you. Stick to your own sea-lanes. Respect the domain of other captains. Pay heed to the rules of the Federation. Next time, it could be *your* fetid blood on the deck. Now, round up your crew and leave *The Albatross*."

"Captain!" Connor heard Bart cry.

Molucco and Drakoulis turned at once.

"Captain *Wrathe*," Bart clarified, "Jez isn't dead yet. His pulse is weak, but I think there's a chance he can be saved if we could just get him back to *The Diablo* and see to his wounds properly."

Molucco broke into a smile but Drakoulis stepped in front of him, his body blocking out the setting sun so that it seemed to form a halo of light around his dark frame.

"Leave now, without the vanquished."

Molucco was incredulous. "You taught me a fine lesson today, Drakoulis. And your henchman has nearly butchered this boy. Are you really so twisted that you'd see him die on your deck rather than have us carry him back to his ship and let him take his chances?"

"He fought a duel and lost. He should be grateful that death is coming to wash clean his failure."

Molucco was momentarily speechless. Connor was stunned. Just when you thought you'd descended to the base depth of Drakoulis' darkness, you fell deeper and deeper into the well.

Bart took up their friend's cause. "Please, Captain Drakoulis. You've made your point. I don't reckon he's long for this life anyhow. At least let us take him and give him a proper . . . farewell."

Drakoulis didn't flinch. He looked straight at Molucco. "Please remind your subordinates not to address me directly." The two captains glared at each other. Drakoulis sneered, "Take the fallen man if you wish, Wrathe. Just get off *The Albatross*. I'm weary of you and your miscreant crew." He turned and walked away, dispensing orders among his own company. The black-clad crew began herding the pirates of *The Diablo* into lines to disembark.

Connor stepped forward to join Bart and Captain Wrathe at Jez's side. Molucco put a hand on Bart's shoulder and leaned closer to look down at Jez. Captain Wrathe had removed his hat, and Scrimshaw (the pet snake who lived in Molucco's hair) was inching forward to see what was happening. The snake stretched out over Jez. Stukeley's face was as pale as his chalk-stained hands and, in spite of Bart's efforts, he was losing too much blood for his pain to last much longer.

"You did a fine job for us today, Mister Stukeley," Molucco said. "A fine job, d'ye hear? We'll fire the cannon in your honor. And each of your comrades will drink a cup of rum for you at Ma Kettle's. Just like the old days, eh?" There were tears in Captain Wrathe's eyes as he forced out the words. "And whenever we have a chance, we'll speak of Jez Stukeley as the very stuff that pirates are made of. You hear me?"

"Yes, Captain," Jez managed to rasp. Then he looked up at Bart and Connor and a faint smile flickered across his violet lips.

"Time for this buccaneer to say good-bye."

He closed his eyes. His head rolled slowly to the side.

Scrimshaw recoiled at the sight, burrowing back into the safety of his master's dreadlocks.

"He's gone," Molucco said softly, placing a hand on Bart's shoulder.

Connor turned away in disbelief. His crewmates were already leaving the deck, flowing back across the three wishes to *The Diablo*. There was no sign of Drakoulis. But Gidaki Sarakakino stepped forward, his boots heavy on the deck.

"He fought well," he said, surprisingly softly. "He carries no shame."

The words had not come easily to him, thought Connor.

Perhaps even this brief speech might be construed as disrespectful to his own captain. He nodded briefly, then withdrew.

"Let me help you to carry him," Connor said to Bart.

"Thanks, buddy," Bart said, biting back his tears. "Come on, Stukeley, shift a leg. Time to get you back home again, mate."

———

Grace heard the noise above deck. The pirates were back. She couldn't wait to see Connor. She had to tell him all about Darcy's phantom visit to her cabin. She flung open the door and raced along the corridor up toward the top deck.

As she stepped out into the open air, she sensed immediately that something was wrong. The deck was crowded with both the returning pirates and the crew they had left behind. But Grace could tell from the quiet aboard the deck that the attack had not been a success. Her heart dropped, like an anchor plummeting to the ocean floor. Where was Connor? She had to see Connor.

She began pushing through the pirate hoard, trying to stem her rising panic. Where was he? At last she caught sight of some of the pirates who had led the attack. They looked all right. They bore a few cuts and bruises but she had got used to seeing these during her time on *The Diablo*. Cuts and bruises were all part of the pirate's trade.

"Where's Connor?" she asked.

The pirates seemed dazed.

"Where's Connor?" she repeated. "Is he all right?"

At last, one of the pirates stepped aside and she saw Connor standing behind him.

"Connor!"

His shirt was stained with blood. But no one was tending to him. Someone should tend to him . . .

"Grace!"

He smiled wanly and opened his arms to her. She ran into them, not caring about the mess his blood might make. They hugged. He held her tightly. She could feel the strength of his arms and his beating heart. She knew instinctively that he was okay.

"I'm fine," he whispered into her ear. *"I'm fine."*

After a few moments, he released her from the hug, but kept her in a looser hold. She looked down at his bloodied shirt. "I thought you were . . ." She couldn't bring herself to say the words. The thought itself was too upsetting. She had tried to be so cool, so matter-of-fact, about him going off into battle. But she wasn't cool with it. She never wanted to see him go off into attack again.

"I'm fine, Grace," Connor said. "But we lost a man today."

Grace nodded. It wasn't Connor. That was all that mattered.

Then Connor stepped back and she saw, behind him, Bart — kneeling on the deck, also covered in blood. She instantly regretted her previous thought. But Bart looked up at her sadly, then dropped his face once more. She looked down onto the deck and saw the motionless, butchered body of Jez Stukeley. His eyes were closed. Now, she understood.

She stepped closer. "Jez," she said. Her eyes moved from Connor to Bart and back to their fallen comrade. She knew how much the three of them meant to each other. "Oh no," she said, "I'm *so* sorry, so very sorry."

Bart nodded sadly at her. He was still holding Jez's hand. Connor took her in his arms once more.

"Don't ever leave me," he said. "You won't, will you? You'll never leave me."

"No," she said. But an image of Darcy flashed through her head. Then Lorcan. Then the Vampirate ship.

Connor pulled her in closer. She felt him shaking.

"No," Grace said, shutting out all the images. "No, Connor, I promise I'll never leave. And you have to make me a promise, too."

He nodded.

"I don't want you to fight again. No more attacks. No more fighting."

He said nothing but drew her closer, planting a soft kiss on the very top of her head.

⟶•⟵

That night — the night following Jez Stukeley's death, the night before his funeral — Connor stayed with Grace in her cabin. After everything that had happened, they needed to be together.

It was a tight fit on Grace's narrow bunk but it didn't matter. It was like being kids again. Sometimes, when one or other of them had had a bad dream, they would share a bed at the lighthouse. With their father upstairs, tending to the lamp, they had learned to draw comfort from one another.

As the bedside candle burned low, Connor told Grace all about the attack and how the pirates of *The Diablo* had been tricked by the evil Narcisos Drakoulis. Grace listened with mounting horror. How could Captain Wrathe and his deputy Cate have been so easily tricked? Were there other crews out there planning similar attacks? Where would this end? Grace couldn't help but feel that Molucco himself bore at least some responsibility for Jez's death — he had received more than one warning about venturing into other captains' sea-lanes. But she didn't voice her thoughts. There would be a time to share her concerns. Tonight what Connor needed was comfort, not confrontation.

"He was so brave," Connor said.

"Jez?"

"Yes."

"Connor," she said, reaching out her hand and twisting his face toward hers. "If it *ever* happens again, *don't* be the brave one."

## 7

# THE CLADDAGH RING

Morning came all too soon. Grace opened her eyes. She had slept only fitfully, her mind churning with thoughts. Connor was standing over her, bleary-eyed.

"I'd better go," he said. "I want to make sure everything's set for the funeral."

Grace nodded. "I'll see you there," she said, "I won't be long." She stood up from the bunk and hugged him once more.

As the door closed behind him, she sat back down. Her lack of sleep and all the anxieties running through her head had made her feel rather sick.

Grace steadied herself sufficiently to look out through the porthole. There was little to see out there, beyond the slap of water and gray sky and sea, for the most part indistinguishable from one another. It was appropriately grim weather for Jez's funeral.

Suddenly Grace felt a searing pain in her eyes. It was so sharp, it threw her away from the window and down onto the bunk. She lay there, catching her breath, her hand instinctively covering her eyes. What had happened? She opened her eyes again but, as she did so, felt another stab of pain. She closed them once more, trying not to panic. She didn't understand *what* was going on.

Instinctively, she moved her hand up to Lorcan's Claddagh ring. As her thumb and finger closed around it, she felt instantly calmer. Was it her imagination, or was the ring slightly warm to the touch? She gripped it and, as she did so, the heat of the metal increased.

As it did, she began hearing noises in her head. She heard the sound of footsteps and distant voices. Somehow, without opening her eyes, she knew that the noises were not from *The Diablo*. She was having a "vision" — if you could call it that when she could see nothing, save a dull, foggy darkness.

The ring grew still warmer in her hand. She had the sense that she was moving. Her footsteps were far louder than any she had ever made before. It was as if she were wearing heavy boots, thumping irregularly onto deck boards. She felt her hand reach out and push against something. A door. Her hand extended. The door must be opening. She could hear the creak of an old hinge. And then a voice.

"Lorcan."

The name electrified her.

She listened, waiting to recognize the voice.

"Lorcan," it said again. It was a girl's voice, but she could not place it. "What are you doing here? It's morning. Time to rest." There was caution in the girl's voice, fear, even.

The ring was almost too hot to touch now. But Grace was desperate not to let go, sensing that if she did, the vision would be lost to her.

"I'm sorry." She immediately recognized Lorcan's soft brogue. It was magical to hear it again, whatever the circumstances.

"Have you lost your way?" It was the girl again. Fear had given way to pity. Grace could hear it in the changing tone. *Lost your way*? What did she mean?

If only Grace could see the ship as well as hear it. She pressed her thumb and finger to the ring even more tightly. It was burning her now. Still she saw nothing beyond the fog but, as the metal seared into her skin, Grace heard the sounds of the Vampirate ship even more clearly.

"I'm sorry." Lorcan again.

"No," the girl answered. "It's okay, Lorcan. It's okay. Give me your hand. I'll take you back to your cabin."

"I can find my own way back," he said, his voice uncharacteristically proud and angry.

"Wait!"

But the girl's voice was fainter now. Grace had the sense of movement again. Uneven movement. Hands reaching out. And then a tumble. She felt sick as the sensation of falling took over her body. The ring was too hot to hold now. She gasped and released her hand. Her eyes pulled open.

She lay on the bunk in her small cabin on the pirate ship, breath racing through her. Her thumb and finger felt raw and painful where the Claddagh ring had burned into her. And yet, when she lifted her hand, there was no mark. Nothing at all. She couldn't understand it.

She knew she had made a journey to the Vampirate ship. Not a journey like Darcy had made to *The Diablo*. This was more of a vision — like the first time Grace had met the Vampirate captain and her head had been filled with a sudden image of flesh tearing and crimson blood on dark skin. This new vision was more sustained than that though, more *linear*. It was as if she had been inside Lorcan's head. She had been able to hear his conversation. She had felt the movements of his arms and feet. She had, she realized now, felt something of his pain. It was something to do with his eyes. As if . . . please, no . . . as if he couldn't see properly.

Now Grace felt ice-cold panic spreading through all the veins in her body as memories flooded back to her, like the returning tide. The morning that Connor had boarded the Vampirate ship, Lorcan had stayed out on deck to protect her. He stayed out even *after* Darcy struck the Dawning Bell — when all Vampirates were called back inside, out of the light. Light was dangerous to them — extremely dangerous. Only the Vampirate captain himself could venture out into the light. But Lorcan had stayed there, because of *her*. Was it possible that, in doing so, he had wounded his eyes? Blinded himself even?

What had Lorcan's note to her said? *Something to remember me by. Travel safe.* Travel safe! Could Lorcan be sending her a message through the ring? She *had* to get back to the Vampirate ship. But how?

Just then the cannon sounded. Grace jumped. Cannon fire was the signal to come up to the main deck. Jez's funeral was about to begin. She was late!

# 8

# BURIAL AT SEA

The first thing that Grace noticed as she stepped out onto deck was how quiet it was. This was all the more unusual, given that the full crew of *The Diablo* now stood across it. She shut the door carefully and joined the crowd. The pirates opened up their ranks for her. Gratefully, she moved forward until she had a clear view of proceedings.

At the stern of the ship stood Captain Wrathe and Cate. They were at the right of Jez's coffin, which was draped in the skull and crossbones flag. To the left of the coffin stood Jez's pallbearers, including Bart and Connor. Grace watched them from the crowd, wondering how Connor was holding up. The last funeral they had attended was their father's. How long ago that seemed already. Then they had stood together, at the front of the congregation, leaning upon one another for support. She scanned Connor's face, but he looked distant. Jez's loss was written all over his features.

The cannon sounded once more and now Captain Wrathe, dressed in funereal black velvet — trimmed with silver — turned to address his crew.

"Pirates of *The Diablo*, this is a dark morning indeed. But the darkness in the skies above and the waters below are only mirrors to the darkness in our hearts. For today we say good-bye to one of our finest men, Jez Stukeley.

"Jez came to us as a young lad — eight years ago — and from the start he kept us amused with his sharp wit and his love of a good tale." Molucco smiled. There were a fair few nods and muted chuckles among the ranks of pirates.

"He was one of the most companionable of crewmembers," Molucco continued. "He was never too busy to help out another fellow in need, whether it be with a shipboard chore or in the field of battle. . . ."

Grace winced at the term. *Field of battle.* He made it sound so noble. It wasn't.

"And it was here that Jez Stukeley marked himself out, time and time again, as one of our most capable, courageous, and effective men." Molucco glanced at Cate, who was nodding solemnly. "Yesterday, I'm afraid that my actions placed all of us in mortal danger. . . ."

Grace's ears pricked up. She hadn't been expecting

such frankness from the captain, but perhaps she had underestimated him.

"I regret this, deeply. Let me assure each of you that I have been searching my soul and that I shall continue to search it when the events of this day are complete. But whatever the circumstance, brave, honorable Mister Stukeley came to our aid. He threw himself into the fire so that we might be saved. He fought a fine fight, full of flair and determination. He might well have prospered." Again Cate nodded. "But fate has taken Mister Stukeley from us . . ."

Grace wondered at that. Where did you draw the line in the sand between fate and your own actions? Was it simply Jez's destiny to die on that other deck, or was it Molucco's actions which had led him there?

"We find ourselves at a terrible loss, knowing that no more shall we be entertained by his wisecracks, and no more shall we be able to depend upon one of our most able." Molucco raised a large handkerchief to his eyes and wiped away the tears that were welling there. "Bravest, dearest comrades, I know you all have your own memories of Mister Stukeley. And now, I'd ask you to spend a minute or two remembering him as you would wish to."

Silence fell once more about the deck. The only sounds were the churning waters beneath and the flapping of the sails in the wind. Grace looked up to the crow's nest, thinking back to the very first time she had met Jez.

It was the day after she had joined the ship. As excited

as she had been to be reunited with Connor, she had felt disorientated by leaving the Vampirate ship — and her friends there — so precipitously. She had gone up to the deck of *The Diablo*, just as she had sometimes made for the deck of the Vampirate ship. She had stood at the deck rail alone — until Jez had joined her, bringing two hot mugs of tea with him. They had sat chatting — or rather, he had talked to her, nonstop. She couldn't remember exactly what he'd said but he had been kind and warm and funny. Just as he always was. She remembered how at that moment she had felt she could make a home for herself on *The Diablo*.

Remembering this brought tears to her eyes. She fished in the pocket of her coat and found a lacy handkerchief. Wiping her eyes, she glanced over at Connor. He smiled back at her faintly. He was trying to be strong, she knew. But she saw there were tears in his eyes too. Devoid, as always, of a handkerchief, Connor simply lifted his hand and brushed the tears away.

"Well, then," Molucco said softly, bringing the spell of silence to a close. "We come to the next part of our proceedings. Jez's longtime comrade — and great friend — Bartholomew Pearce, will now say for us the Pirate's Prayer. Bartholomew . . ."

Molucco turned. Bart stepped slowly forward, clutching a piece of paper in his hand. He lifted his eyes to the assembled and began to speak.

*Mother Ocean, Father Sky,*
*Send this pirate to his rest.*
*He was one among the best —*
*Set his spirit free to fly.*

*Brother Sun and Sister Moon,*
*Bathe him in your balmy light.*
*Now no longer need he fight —*
*The one you called back far too soon.*

*Lightning, thunder, wind, and rain,*
*Let his cutlass blunt and rust,*
*As his body turns to dust —*
*Free from every mortal pain.*

*Spring tide, neap tide, morning, night,*
*All you things that frame our days,*
*Carve him out a resting place —*
*Wherever will his cares be light.*

*Creek and harbor, gulf and reef*
*Waters shallow, waters deep,*
*Grant him now eternal sleep —*
*And anchor us who reel with grief.*

Bart hadn't had to look once at the piece of paper in his hands. Grace guessed that it was an old poem, but the way Bart spoke it, each word seemed fresh and potent.

There had even been a temporary lull in the wind, as if the elements themselves were paying heed to the pirate's pleas for his lost comrade.

Now, Bart turned and signalled to Connor and the four other pirates beside them. The six men, all wearing black armbands, arranged themselves around Jez's coffin. On a quiet count, they lifted it as one and walked slowly and somberly to the prow of the ship. The skull and cross-bones flapped in the breeze.

They held the coffin aloft for a moment and then let it drop down into the waters below. It met them with a terrible thud. Grace's heart wrenched at the sound. But the noise was soon overwhelmed by a volley of cannon fire, during which Bart, Connor and their fellows resumed their positions.

At the close of the cannon fire, Molucco Wrathe turned to his crew.

"This has been a sad day, my friends, but there are two halves to mourning a death — first, the sadness and then, the celebration of a fine life. Tonight, we shall direct ourselves to Ma Kettle's Tavern to drink a toast or two to Mister Stukeley."

There were sounds of approval across the deck — and although they were more muted than usual, the noise was a sign that things would soon return to normal about *The Diablo*. It seemed terribly sudden to Grace, but perhaps this was just the way things had to be aboard a pirate ship.

"And now," said the captain, "go about your business. Let no man say that *The Diablo* isn't the finest pirate ship on all the seas."

Connor stood with Bart on one side and Grace on the other. He needed them now, more than ever. He had always known that the life of a pirate could be brief. His first night aboard ship, Bart had told him, "I'll be lucky to see my thirtieth birthday." Connor had registered the words, but only now did he really understand how true they were. The Three Buccaneers were supposed to have been invincible. Jez was only twenty-three — far too young to die. But, thought Connor, when you sign up to be a pirate, you accept that you are never too young to die. He was only fourteen, but he could just as easily lose his own life during the next battle. He couldn't risk leaving Grace all alone in the world. He'd have to smarten up and stop daydreaming. And he'd have to watch Captain Wrathe a little more carefully, too. He couldn't shake the feeling that, in spite of the captain's fine eulogy, Jez Stukeley had died a needless death.

9

# THE GIFT

Sunset. After a day of rough, squally weather, the surf is good tonight. The lone surfer is out again, pitching himself against the waves. Every night, he grows stronger — every night, more proficient. And every night, in spite of himself, more lonely. Yes, he can admit this now. He is not made to be alone. It is life — and death — that have contrived to separate him from others. But he is not one to be dictated to by the fates. Just now, he might be dependent on the ebb and flow of the tide, but soon he will start to direct the flow of events. This time of waiting will be over.

The moon is on the rise, shooting golden darts across the dark water. He is careful to avoid the light, steering the board toward the dark places in between. Now he is fighting both the pull of the tide and the moon's flaming arrows but, muscle-bound as he is, he is holding his own against them both. His footing is firm as he shifts the board from left to right, feeling the energy of the waves beneath him, propelling him toward another empty cove.

As he cruises into the shallow water, there are rocks to negotiate. He jumps down from the board, the water scarcely higher than his ankles now. He pulls the board from the water, before it comes to grief on the waiting rocks, and walks the last remaining feet onto dry land. As always, the moment he emerges from the water, his clothes and flesh are bone dry.

The cove is as rocky above the water as it is beneath. He rests the surfboard lightly against a jagged boulder and climbs up to a ledge. There, comfortably cloaked in the darkness, he can safely survey the scene.

A ship enters his vision in the distance. The sight of it makes him wistful, thinking of ships he has left behind. But there will be other ships in his future. And, this time, *he* will be the captain. No more will he do another's bidding. This is his destiny — of that he is certain.

The ship sails across his line of vision, torches flaming about it. They light up the skull and crossbones flag. A pirate ship — hardly uncommon in these waters. Yet the ship looks familiar to him. He closes his eyes, shutting out the light to think more clearly. In the darkness, he sees the girl. The strange girl who escaped from him. Grace. That was her name. Why is he seeing her — an insignificant girl to whom he once told his story? He crushes the mental picture of her — as if it were an insect that dared to land on his palm, and opens his eyes.

The ship has sailed past, but now something much closer takes his attention. Something which bumps against the rocks in the shallow water below. Something which is pummelled by the white horses, bobbing in and out of the shards of moonlight. He leans forward. His vision cuts through the dark shadows and he sees the wooden box brought to him on the tide. He decides to take a closer look at the gift the ocean has delivered to him.

Leaping down from his ledge, he strides back into the water, his feet deftly avoiding the jagged rocks beneath. The box is within his reach now, buffeted between twin rocks, like a football kicked back and forth between them. His large hands find the edges of it. It is bigger than it seemed from above, and as long as a man. To others, it would be impossibly unwieldy, but to him it is manageable. He frees it from the dueling rocks and lifts the coffin — for that is what it is — out of the water, carrying it effortlessly to the sanctuary of the small stretch of beach.

He sets it on the sand and, unsure of his next move, looks for somewhere to sit and think. Then he realizes that the coffin itself will make the perfect seat so he eases himself down on it and looks out to sea once more. Beneath his weight, the tender wood begins to crack and splinter. Quickly, he jumps up, surveying the damage he has done.

The coffin is not in a good way. Wherever it has come from, its journey through the water has not been smooth. More than one rock has lashed out at it, judging by the marks around its sides. In one corner, there is a hole and he brings an eye to this now, looking down into the darkness within.

It's hard to see much. Some seawater has got inside — not yet enough to weigh it down but enough to confuse his vision. He leans away again, contemplating breaking off a bit more wood. *Snap.* The timber breaks like a bar of chocolate in his fingers and now he has a clear view inside. His eyes come face to face with a boot. It is a sailor's boot, still laced tight. It is not, after you stare at it for five minutes, the most interesting of sights.

If only the other end of the coffin had been broken, he thinks, looking up. But the other end is still intact. After another minute in the water, the wood would almost certainly have cracked there too. Because really, if you just reached out your finger and pressed with any kind of strength, you could crack this wood, without even really trying and . . .

*Snap.* The feeble wood has broken in his thick hands and a nail buckles. He leans forward. Now he is looking down on part of a face — on an eye that is shut tight, long wet eyelashes resting on the linen-white pillow of a cheek.

Of course, he wants to see more and since the wood is broken anyway, there's no harm in prying it loose so he can see the whole of the face. Now he can see that it is a young man, his features fully at rest. The mouth is lifted in a small, frozen smile as if he is dreaming. What might he be dreaming? If only he could speak again, you might ask him this question — and a fair few others besides.

Thoughts are rushing in now, as fast and as furious as the tide. His hands reach out and make short work of the rest of the lid, until broken shards of wood are piled on the sand like discarded orange peel. Now the coffin is open to the elements. And there lies the young mariner, cooled by the night air again, as once he was in life.

This is not just a gift. It is a sign. A sign that the tide is turning in his favor — that his plan is the right, true one. He smiles to himself, his gold teeth revealed once more.

There are things the surfer knows — things, at least, that he has been told, if he can only remember them. Things he wishes now he had paid more heed to. Gestures and incantations that — if he can only focus and squeeze them back to the forefront of his memory — might just yield a result. He looks down at the man before him. From his garb alone, you can tell he was a pirate, even were his hands not folded about a cutlass and even if the skull and bones flag was not tied around his wrist.

If only he could remember the right procedures. He scratches his shaven head. He must try to remember. He owes it to this pirate now. Now that he has invaded his rest, he owes it to him to try. He closes his eyes, shutting out all distractions as he scours the dark passageways of his memory for the right words.

He is transported back to a shadowy, smoke-filled den, where incense once pervaded his senses. Now, he is back in that darkness. Once more, cedar and sandalwood lull his mind. He sees again that other face through the gloom, teaching him the ritual. The words are coming back to him. He is not speaking them, only hearing them, letting the other one tell him now as he told him before.

He feels a growing pressure about his hand. He cannot yet open his eyes, for the ritual is not complete. But the flesh of his hand is being compressed on all sides. As if . . . no . . . as if . . . *yes* — as if another hand is clinging onto his.

At last he opens his eyes. And, yes, his hand is stretched down to the coffin and, sure enough, a hand has risen out of the darkness and taken his own, much fleshier, hand. And now they pulse together as if they share one heartbeat.

He looks down at the figure in the coffin, searching for other signs of life. He thinks he sees something stirring somewhere beneath the mask of the sleeping face, but he cannot be sure it is not simply his own imaginings. He thinks he senses life — or whatever you might call *this* — beginning to flood the muscles of the dead pirate's limbs.

He imagines life — or its alternative — taking hold of the dormant organs caged in his chest. And still he smells cedar and sandalwood and senses the ritual is not yet quite complete.

At last, he hears a sigh. At first it is as soft as the waves lapping the rocks in the distance. And then it comes again, louder. Mouth open in curiosity, he looks down as the wet eyelashes flicker and part. White eyeballs appear like glistening pearls from a dark oyster.

Then the pale violet lips open, too. They splutter to expel a small pocket of air and seawater. And a voice follows, surprisingly clear and strong.

"Is it time to get up already? I was having such a nice old dream!"

# 10

# LIEUTENANT STUKELEY

"You all right, mate? You look like you've seen a ghost!"

Sidorio looks down into the coffin at the pirate, dead just moments before, now stirring and stretching and beaming at him as if he is a long-lost friend.

"I'm all wet," the man says now. There is a thin layer of water in the coffin and it has soaked his clothes. He smells of the sea.

"Here," Sidorio says, reaching out a hand once more. The pirate grips it and Sidorio pulls him up onto his feet.

The pirate stands for a moment, then his legs wobble and he staggers. Sidorio has to move fast to prevent him from crashing back down and doing himself an injury on the sharp edges of the broken coffin.

"Thanks, mate," the pirate says, still holding tight. "I'm feeling a little funny. Like I've had a bit too much rum!"

Sidorio holds him until he seems to be bearing his own weight.

"Oh, that's much better. Yes. There we go!"

But as Sidorio takes his hand away, once more the mariner's legs buckle and he falls down in a heap onto the sand.

"Maybe I'll just sit here for a moment and get my bearings."

"Good idea."

Sidorio stands back and looks down at the pirate, still stunned by his own achievement. He has brought him back from the darker shores. He, Sidorio, has performed the ritual. It is a sign that his powers are growing. The tide is already beginning to turn.

"You're a big fella, ain't you?" the pirate says, looking up at him.

Sidorio shrugs.

"What's your name?"

"My name is Sidorio, but you must call me Captain."

"Right you are, Captain. I'm Stukeley, Jez Stukeley. You can call me Jez."

"Henceforth, you will be known as Stukeley," Sidorio says. "I will be your captain and you will be my lieutenant."

"Lieutenant? That's a nice promotion!" He seems pleased.

Sidorio hesitates. The pirate seems quite unfazed by what has happened to him. He remembered the ritual but he doesn't remember this part. What are you supposed to say to the returned? How fragile are they? Now that Stukeley is growing used to breathing again, he hardly seems fragile at all. He is sitting straighter, and his wet clothes have dried out. Now, he starts unbuttoning his shirt.

"I just want to see it," he says. "I never got the chance before."

What is he talking about? Sidorio watches as Stukeley unfastens the first few buttons of his shirt and reveals the flesh of his chest, which is pale as marble except for a deep indigo gash.

"So that's it," Stukeley says, nodding. "That's the fatal wound. Have to confess, I'm a bit disappointed. I expected something more dramatic."

Sidorio crouches down to his level.

"So you know . . . you know you were killed?"

Stukeley stares at him, his eyes twinkling in the moonlight. "Me — killed? No, I . . . What *are* you going on about, mate?"

Sidorio is lost in confusion until Stukeley breaks out laughing.

"Of course I know I was killed, mate. I don't just hang out in coffins for a lark! I'm not some vampire, you know."

"Well . . . ," Sidorio begins.

"No!" Stukeley exclaims. "You're having me on! Me —

a vampire? That's impossible. Are you serious? Have I got fangs and everything?"

"Not yet, but you will. If everything turns out right."

"Wicked! I don't s'pose you've got a mirror, have you?"

"Go take a look at yourself in the water, if you wish."

Stukeley pauses for a moment, then draws himself up to his feet and staggers forward to the edge of the ocean. Sidorio watches him as he bows forward, trying to get a clear reflection in the agitated waters. The pirate turns, shell-shocked.

"I can't see my reflection."

Sidorio nods his head, smiling. "That's right. You *are* changed. You see?"

"Yes, Captain." The voice is different now — full of respect and awe.

Sidorio wonders at his actions. It is all happening so fast. Barely an hour ago, he was thinking how things might change, how he might have company. Now, he has a lieutenant, but already his excitement at his own power has given way to a stirring sense of the burden of responsibility. Stukeley turns from the water and runs toward him, smiling.

"I can't believe I'm back. Thank you," he says, smiling. "Thank you for bringing me back."

"What was it like there?"

"You've been there yourself, haven't you? You must know."

"It's different for everyone."

Stukeley shrugs. "Honestly, I can't remember much. Just losing the duel — which was quite unfair if you ask me — and lying on the deck, feeling like I was being pulled away from my mates, their voices getting softer and softer. But after that, I don't know. It's all a blank." He turns and looks at the remnants of his coffin. He smiles again. "They must have given me a proper burial at sea. Not everyone gets one of those, mate. I'm pleased to bits about that. Oh, and I remember the captain saying they'd have a bash for me at Ma Kettle's . . ."

"Which captain?" asks Sidorio. "Which ship?"

"Captain Wrathe's ship," Stukeley answers. "*The Diablo*."

"*The Diablo*, eh? The Devil." Sidorio smiles once more. "*My* kind of ship."

A curious look crosses Stukeley's face. "How long was I gone?"

Sidorio shakes his head. "I don't know. But I don't think your coffin would have lasted much longer."

"What day is it now?"

"I don't have any interest in the passing days."

"You say some strange things, mate. I'm just trying to establish how long I've been gone."

"My guess," says Sidorio, "is that you weren't . . . gone . . . for very long. But why does this matter?"

"Do you know a place by the name of Ma Kettle's Tavern?"

Sidorio thinks for a moment. "Yes, I've been there before."

"Well, I think there's every possibility that my wake is happening there this very night."

Sidorio smiles. "And you'd like to go?"

Stukeley beams back. "Seems kind of rude to miss it, don't ya think?"

Sidorio pauses. "If we do go, no one must see you. Nothing must threaten my plans. *Our* plans."

"What exactly *are* our plans?"

"All in good time, Lieutenant. All in good time."

"Whatever you say, big guy."

"Whatever you say, *Captain.*"

Stukeley nods. "Whatever you say, Captain."

"This is the beginning," Sidorio says. "This is the turning of the tide. I have been waiting for so long. Before I am finished, the ocean will turn red with blood. Now, at last, the tide of terror begins!"

## 11

# REUNION AT MA KETTLE'S

Grace stood beside Connor as *The Diablo* made its way toward a rocky outcrop.

"There it is!" Connor said.

A neon light came into view, flashing erratically through the darkness.

"Ma Kettle's Tavern," Grace read.

"I hope you're ready for this, Grace," said Cate, who stood on her other side.

"Is anyone *ever* quite ready for Ma's?" asked Bart, with a smile.

After the sorrows of Jez's funeral, the pirates already seemed in better spirits. Grace still found it difficult to put aside her sadness, but perhaps Captain Wrathe was right when he said there were two halves to mourning a death — the painful good-bye and the celebration of a life. It was just unbearably sad that the life in question had been snuffed out so soon.

As the ship docked, the excited crew surged to the front of the deck to disembark, and Grace had to focus all her attention on keeping together with Connor and the others. For a time, she had her head down, battling to find room for her feet among the thronging crowd. Connor reached out his hand and pulled her through the crew to join him at the front. When she next glanced up, Ma Kettle's Tavern stood directly before her — its huge waterwheel illuminated by the moon. Above it, a skull and crossbones flag was flying at half-mast.

"Out of respect for Jez," Bart said proudly. Grace nodded, squeezing his arm comfortingly.

They climbed the stairs to the first platform of decking. "Watch your step, Grace," Connor told her.

She looked down and saw the treacherous gaps in the wooden floor, giving way to the ocean below. The dark water was placid now and she could see her face reflected in it, as if there were another Grace trapped beneath the surface of the water, waiting to be rescued. The mirage was strong enough that she might even have dipped her hand into the water to check, but the others were surging on ahead and she didn't want to be left behind.

The crew made their way forward, deeper into the tavern toward a roped-off section, where their tables were waiting for them. "Look," Connor said, pointing at the wooden placard saying *The Diablo* which marked their territory. "Only the VIP captains have these." He beamed at Grace. She smiled back faintly. This world seemed to make such easy sense to him. He was so accepting of its rules.

The pirates arranged themselves around the tables, and the volume of chatter increased as they began bantering among themselves and with other crews at the neighboring tables.

A distinguished-looking man, with a neat white beard and moustache, appeared at Captain Wrathe's side. "I was sorry to hear about what happened, Molucco," he said.

"Why, thank you, Gresham."

"That Drakoulis is a nasty piece of work. I thought we'd seen the last of him."

"As did I," Molucco said with a shake of his head. "As did I."

"Let me stand your crew a round of rum," Captain Gresham said. He turned and called out, "Can I get some service here? I say, can I get some . . ."

"What's all this din?"

A woman appeared between the two captains. She was dressed in a vast gown of dark cloth, patterned with white skulls and bones. Connor nudged Grace. "That's . . ." But Grace needed no introduction. She knew at once that it was Ma Kettle. Today, Ma was wearing a black lace veil, which she now lifted, to offer first one cheek then another to Captain Wrathe.

"I'm *so* sorry, Lucky," she said. "These are dark times."

"Dark times indeed, Kitty," said Molucco, clasping Ma Kettle tightly in his arms.

Ma Kettle now turned to the rest of the crew. "Tonight, the drinks are on the house, boys and girls. A sign of my love and respect to Jez and the rest of you." There was thunderous applause and Ma Kettle blew a kiss to the approving crowd. Before she had finished speaking, her serving girls had lined up shots of rum along the length of each table. Grace glanced down at the glass which had been placed before her. She had never had rum before. But she didn't look down for long. Ma Kettle was too intriguing to remove your eyes from for any period of time.

"Bartholomew," she was saying now, clasping Bart to her rather ample bosom, "this must be a particular blow to you. You were like brothers, I know."

Bart nodded. "For all of us, Ma. But for me and Connor especially."

Ma nodded sadly, turning her gaze on Connor. "Hello again, Mister Tempest. Well, what a difference a few months makes! Look at you, Pirate! And I hear such things about you. A superstar in the making, they say!"

Connor flushed the color of an overripe tomato. Grace wondered if Ma Kettle would embrace him too —

knowing that Connor would die with embarrassment if she did — but instead Ma simply reached out a hand and rested it on Connor's shoulder.

"I've no doubt you're feeling a stew of emotions," she said. "It's terrible when we lose a close comrade — a friend. Bloody terrible, so it is."

Connor nodded. But Ma hadn't finished with him just yet.

"Now Ma's going to give you some free advice — which you're at liberty to take or leave, my sweet. Number one — death. It never gets easier. Whether you're fourteen years young like you or . . . well, as old as the coral reefs like me . . . losing someone close to you will always be the most bitter blow. Number two . . . don't bottle up your emotions. You have to let them out. That's one of the reasons we lay on a party, see." She swept her hand across the panorama of the tavern. "When a good pirate like Jez is lost, we must celebrate his life. We must drink and be merry and tell tales of the times we had together. Some people think it's *distasteful.* They'd have us keep silent and stoic and walk around in black from head to foot all day and night. But we have to celebrate life itself, d'you see? Life! It's the most wonderful treasure, my sweet. And Jez Stukeley may only have had three and twenty years of it, but he made his mark. He left people behind who love him, who will remember him. In the end, that's the best any of us can hope for. Don't you agree, Lucky?"

Molucco stepped up behind her and took her hand, kissing it tenderly. "You always were most eloquent, Kitty. I couldn't have spoken truer words myself."

Ma smiled at Connor. "I wish you a long life, Connor Tempest," she said. "But, more important than that, I wish you a life of love and laughter, friendship and adventure and not a minute of boredom." She kissed her hand and rubbed it on his cheek. "An old pirate tradition," she said, smiling.

Then she turned her gaze on Grace. "And who's this young beauty?" Now, it was Grace's turn to blush.

"This is Mister Tempest's twin sister, Grace," Molucco said.

"Yes," Ma Kettle said, coming closer, "I see the resemblance now. What a pretty young lady you are." She reached out her hand and ran a finger down Grace's cheekbone. "Such beautiful skin. Smooth as silk. To think I had skin like this once. And now look at me, a wizened old sea monster!"

At once, all attention turned back to Ma Kettle as Molucco, Bart, and the others plied her with compliments. Grace watched, fascinated by this extraordinary woman.

"Yes, yes, boys, stop fussing over an old shipwreck like me. Now, enough gassing. Why don't you make yourselves comfortable? The girls and I have put together a little entertainment for you, to cheer you up from your sorrows."

She turned and called — or rather, screeched — over her shoulder. "Sugar Pie, are you ready?"

"Aye, aye, Ma!" came the call of a much sweeter voice.

"Come on then. Sit down, everyone. That's right. Lucky, you come next to me." Ma Kettle fussed about with her vast skirts as the lights of the tavern were suddenly dimmed and blackness fell all about them.

Then there was the sound of an accordion, and suddenly a pool of light broke on a stage, revealing the prow of a ship, and its beautiful figurehead. This must be Sugar Pie. She was wearing a pirate captain's hat and looking out at the audience through a telescope. Grace could not help but think of Darcy Flotsam, especially when the figurehead tucked the telescope away and winked at the audience.

Now two further pools of light appeared on either side, revealing two more ships' figureheads. Each blew a kiss out to the audience and each was rewarded with whoops of approval. Now, the accordion was joined by other instruments, as the three figureheads disengaged themselves from the ships' prows and slipped down along blue and white ribbons to land on the decking below. The shapes of waves had been set among the wooden planks. It was quite an elaborate set. They might have been at a proper theater, not a rough tavern, thought Grace.

The crowd burst into applause. The central figurehead,

still wearing a captain's hat, put a finger to her lips. All at once there was silence.

"That's Sugar Pie," Connor whispered to Grace, a dreamy look on his face.

"Oh really," said Grace, smiling at her brother. "And who might she be?"

"Just . . . ," Connor began, but was at a loss for words.

"An old friend," said Bart.

Grace smiled, nodding and heartily enjoying Connor's embarrassment.

And now, Sugar Pie set her hands on her hips and began to sing:

> *I've grown a little bored of ocean-faring.*
> *To me the ocean's just not what it seems.*
> *I was promised loot and plunder,*
> *but I guess I made a blunder*
> *And now I'm calling into question my ocean-faring dreams.*
> *I was told the sea was quite the place for action . . .*

At this, she winked.

> *High adventure was sure to come my way.*
> *Well I've been sailing day and night,*
> *looking out for Captain Right —*
> *But all I've seen is ruddy reef and bay.*
> *I've done everything my officer commanded,*

*Kept my cutlass oiled and ready for attack.*
*But a girl can't wait forever — I'm at the end of my tether!*
*So I'm furling up my sails and changing tack.*

There was a whoop from the crowd.

*I used to dream of capturing a captain*
*Who'd join me up and take me 'board his junk.*
*He'd sail the seven seas,*
*taking plunder where he pleased*
*And share out all his riches — my ocean-faring hunk!*

*I used to dream of marrying a captain*
*And being his trusted deputy on board.*
*The crew'd respect my rank,*
*else I'd make 'em walk the plank!*
*But I'd be fair — if somewhat firm — with my*
*thronging pirate horde.*

At this Ma Kettle cried, "You go, girl!"

*But all my dreams of love have come to nothing —*
*It seems no pirate captain wants a wife.*
*So it's time to jump this ship,*
*and give piracy the slip —*
*Yes, I've had it with the nautical life!*

*I had ocean-faring dreams*
*But nothing's what it seems.*
*Yes, I've had it with the nautical life!*
*Oh, I've well and truly had it with the nautical life!*

At this, Sugar Pie removed the captain's hat from her head, shook down her long blond hair, and beamed at the audience.

Grace smiled despite herself. She and Sugar Pie had something in common, she thought wryly. If only it was so easy to give piracy the slip!

—◠◠—

A short distance away, a small boat docks at the jetty.

There are three people inside — the ferryman and two passengers.

"This is the place," the ferryman announces.

"Excellent," says the heftier of the two passengers. "Stukeley, out you get while I settle our tariff."

Stukeley needs no further urging. "Ma Kettle's Tavern," he says in wonder, as his feet land on the jetty. "I never thought I'd see you again!"

"Don't go too far ahead!" the other passenger calls after him. "We must be careful."

"No, Captain. I'll wait for you just here."

"Good, Lieutenant," says the other, turning his attention

to the ferryman. "This gold buys your silence," he says, "but, I wonder, can you be trusted?"

The ferryman nods eagerly, his hand reaching out for the payment. But the other's fist suddenly closes about the gold. "I'm afraid my trust issues have gotten the better of me again," he says with a sigh.

The ferryman looks at him in surprise. Something is very wrong here. The surprise soon turns to indignation, then raw terror.

Stukeley has been lost in thought as he watches the glorious waterwheel turning in the distance and hears the familiar slosh of the waters. But now there is a bigger splash close by. He turns and sees Captain Sidorio striding toward him.

"What was that noise?" Stukeley asks.

Sidorio shrugs. "What noise?"

"Isn't that the boat we came in? Where is the ferryman?"

Sidorio turns. "Ah, yes. The ferryman seems to have disappeared. That *is* strange," he says, wiping his mouth and picking at something between his teeth. Turning back, he slaps a firm hand down on Stukeley's shoulder. "Come on, Lieutenant. We don't want to linger here a moment longer or we'll miss your party."

Stukeley has an uncomfortable feeling. But he knows that Sidorio doesn't like to be questioned. And, after all, it is Sidorio who brought him back. Sidorio is his captain. And it is only right that he should do the captain's bidding — whatever it might be. This is a second chance. And Stukeley intends to be the very model of a good and trustworthy lieutenant.

～

The pirates roared their approval for Sugar Pie, but she raised a finger to her lips to silence them. She held her hat aloft, poised to throw it.

"Whoever catches this, wins himself a kiss from Sugar Pie!"

She sent the hat in a high arc through the air, above the whooping pirates, their arms and hands flailing about like reeds to catch it. It eluded the majority, sailing on toward the tables where the pirates of *The Diablo* sat. All eyes turned as the hat finally made its descent. It was plummeting toward Connor and Bart, whose hands both reached out for it. Grace leaned back to give the two of them more room. Bart had the advantage in height and he grabbed the hat before Connor could do so.

"Better luck next time, buddy," chuckled Bart, placing the captain's hat on his head and playfully pushing Connor aside as he strode off to claim his prize.

"So near yet so far," said Grace, digging Connor playfully in the ribs. She was enjoying herself now. She felt a flush of guilt, thinking of Jez. But then she remembered

Ma Kettle's words. They were here tonight to celebrate Jez's life. And there was no doubt in her mind that this was what Jez would have wanted. Why, if he had been here, he'd have been fighting Bart and Connor for Sugar Pie's attentions!

The show over, the lights went up and Grace saw that a fresh batch of drinks now lined the table. One mouthful of rum had been more than enough for her, but the other pirates lifted their glasses gleefully and threw the fiery liquid down their throats.

"I'm going out to get some air," she said to Connor.

"Okay," he said, giving her hand a squeeze. "If you need me, just holler."

She nodded, moving away from the table. When she glanced back, she saw that one of Sugar Pie's backing dancers had come over to the table and Connor, along with the others, seemed utterly transfixed by her. Shaking her head in amusement, Grace turned and walked away.

She traced her path back to the entrance of the tavern, careful to avoid the gaps between the decking. Once more, she glanced down into the water below. There she was again, staring back at herself. Like she was drowning all over again. Like before Lorcan had rescued her.

*Lorcan.* Instinctively, she moved her fingers to the chain around her neck, finding his Claddagh ring. The metal was cool to the touch at first. But, as her thumb and finger lingered there, it began to grow warmer. Was she about to have another vision? She felt a thrill of excitement but also fear. More than anything, she wanted to know the truth about how he was and what had happened to him. And yet she feared what she might discover.

As the ring continued to heat up, she sat down on the decking and closed her eyes, waiting for the wave of nausea she had experienced the last time. But, although the ring grew warmer and warmer, there was no accompanying pain or feeling of sickness. Added to which, she heard nothing and there was no dull fog in her head. What kind of a vision *was* this? Was she doing something wrong? Puzzled, Grace opened her eyes.

As she did so, she gasped. Down in the water, down beneath the decking, she saw Lorcan. He was stumbling along the corridor of the Vampirate ship, his hands reaching out to steady himself. Grace gasped. It was as if she was experiencing the same scene as before but this time as an external observer. It was painful to watch Lorcan struggling so. She wanted nothing so much as to hold out her hand and help him. Instinctively, she found herself reaching a hand down to the water's surface. She still held tightly onto the ring, which grew hotter all the time. It was an awkward maneuver to say the least, but she was overcome by the strongest of urges to touch the water.

But the instant Grace's fingers brushed the dark surface,

the vision of Lorcan disappeared. The waters became a mirror again, reflecting her own disturbed face and the lights of the tavern back up at her. She frowned.

Then the waters grew dark once more. She leaned closer, waiting for the vision of Lorcan to return. But instead, she saw another face. She shuddered. It was Sidorio. He was looking directly at her — just as he had on the Vampirate deck that fateful night. And now, just as then, his eyes suddenly became empty, then full of fire. He opened his mouth in a horrible smile, the dagger-like incisors seeming to rise up, out of the water.

"No!" Grace cried.

The Claddagh ring was burning her fingers now. She wanted to release it, but somehow she was unable to. Suddenly, her hand jolted forward. The ring had come free of the chain. She was still gripping it between her thumb and forefinger but there was no telling how much longer she could hold it. Any moment now, the heat would force her to release it into the water. *No!* However painful it was, she couldn't lose it. The ring was her last connection with the Vampirate ship, with Lorcan. If she let it go, she might never be able to return, never be able to help her friend. It was this thought which, in spite of the pain, enabled her to remain holding the ring, even as the excruciating heat seared through her nerves.

In the waters below, Sidorio watched her. He was

laughing at her. What did it mean? Was this another vision? Was he close? Was he coming back for her?

Suddenly, she felt a hand on her neck. It pulled her firmly backward. As it did so, she felt the temperature of the ring cool at last. She slumped back onto the decking, gasping with relief and weakness — and pure fear.

12

## CONFESSIONAL

"Well, well, well. What have we here?"

Grace opened her eyes and looked up into a familiar face.

"Cheng Li!" she exclaimed.

"Hello, Grace." Cheng Li nodded, crouching down beside her. "How nice to run into you — albeit in somewhat curious circumstances. If you're intent on practicing acrobatics, I can think of better places for you to do so."

Grace looked up at her. Cheng Li seemed softer than Grace remembered her. But they'd only met briefly on *The Diablo* and her memory had perhaps been tarnished by Molucco Wrathe's harsh words about his ex-deputy captain.

"I wasn't practicing acrobatics," said Grace.

"I didn't really think you were," said Cheng Li. "But

whatever you were doing, you look rather pale. I think I'd better get you something to drink."

"Do they serve non-alcoholic drinks here?" Grace asked. "I had a mouthful of rum and I'm feeling a bit queasy."

"Hmm, you might find that's what happens when you suspend yourself upside down over stagnant water! What exactly *were* you doing down there?"

Grace smiled. "It's a long story."

"My very favorite kind." Cheng Li smiled at Grace and extended a firm but graceful arm towards her. "Come along, dear. We'll share a pot of Sea Lily Tea. That, as they say, should put some color back in your cheeks."

Cheng Li led Grace back inside the tavern. Up ahead, in the VIP section, the pirates of *The Diablo* were getting rowdier by the minute. Grace saw Connor in the thick of it, but he was evidently too preoccupied to notice her. Cheng Li reached for Grace's hand and led her to a dark stairway to one side of the tavern. They climbed up the narrow stairwell, emerging in an upstairs gallery. It was lined with booths. Each booth was separated from its neighbor by wooden panels, which were intricately carved with images of ships and waves.

The booth they entered reminded Grace of a church confessional. It overlooked the downstairs bar but there was a red velvet curtain you could draw across to shut out prying eyes and drown out some of the hubbub below.

This Cheng Li did, with a sharp tug. "There," she said. "Now, we can be private."

It was dark inside the booth and Cheng Li's face was illuminated by a single candle, flickering from a glass lantern in the center of the table. The meager light softened Cheng Li's features, reminding Grace that in spite of her aura and rank, her companion was actually only a few years older than herself.

Cheng Li was quite different from how Grace remembered her. Her glossy black hair had grown in the months since they had last met and she had styled it a little less severely. Then Grace noticed that Cheng Li wasn't carrying the twin katanas on her back. Now that she was a tutor at the Pirate Academy, had she relinquished her weapons?

"What does it take to get some service around here?" Cheng Li said, extending her hand out of the booth and snapping her fingers. Grace spotted the katanas laid out on the bench. Not relinquished, then, just resting.

One of Ma Kettle's servers arrived at the booth. It was, Grace was surprised to see, a boy. He bowed low. "How may I be of assistance?"

"Bring us a pot of Sea Lily Tea," Cheng Li said.

"Right away, Mistress Li!" He scurried off.

Cheng Li smiled at Grace. "It really is a nice surprise running into you," she said, "I've thought of you often."

Grace flushed at her words. "It's good to see you too," she said, a little embarrassed.

The serving boy swiftly returned, bearing a tray crowded with jugs, glasses, and different-sized caskets. Could all this be just for the two of them? Clearly there was quite a ritual to this tea drinking.

Grace could feel Cheng Li's eyes upon her as she watched the serving boy. He placed two prettily painted tea glasses on the table. Next, he set a tall glass teapot in the center. It was empty, Grace noticed. Bowing, the boy opened a small onyx casket. It was full of flower buds. Taking a pair of silver tongs, he carefully dropped two of the buds into the glass teapot. He closed the casket and took up an elegant silver pot, pouring hot water in a high arc over the buds until the tall glass pot was almost full.

"Now be patient!" he smiled, removing the casket and the tray. "Oh, I almost forgot, here's some honey." He set down a small black jar, a tiny spoon jutting out from its lid.

Cheng Li dropped a coin onto the tray. "Close the curtain after you," she said.

He smiled and bowed once more, then disappeared, drawing the curtain around the booth. The two young women were completely enclosed.

"Now watch," Cheng Li said, indicating the glass teapot.

Grace followed her gaze. The clear water had turned a pale shade of pink — a shot of more intense color spiraling through the clear liquid as if a used paintbrush had been dipped inside. Grace saw that the two tiny buds at the base of the pot were spinning about like the smallest of sea creatures. Then, very slowly, the buds began to open out. Petals gradually fanned out from each bud, like arms gently stretching after a long night's sleep. As the petals extended farther, the two flowers touched. All the time, the water was turning a deeper and deeper pink — like the sky at sunset.

Now the buds were fully open and began to rise to the top of the pot — until the flowers were floating together on the surface of a jewel-pink ocean.

"Wow," Grace said, intrigued by this small piece of theater.

"Now it's ready to drink," Cheng Li said, reaching for the pot and pouring the hot tea into Grace's glass. Steam spiraled up and hit Grace's nostrils. The tea had the most unusual and intoxicating perfume.

"Some people like to add a spoonful of honey," Cheng Li said, nodding at the small black jar on the table, "but I prefer mine without."

Grace decided to follow Cheng Li's lead and lifted her glass to her lips.

"Wait," Cheng Li said. Grace paused, wondering how much more there might be to this ritual.

"A toast," Cheng Li said, raising her own glass to meet Grace's. "To new friends!"

"New friends!" Grace echoed.

They gently chinked the delicate glasses. Then Grace took a sip of the Sea Lily Tea.

"Well?" Cheng Li said, her smoky eyes flashing at Grace. "What's the verdict?"

"I think it's the most delicious drink I've ever tasted," Grace said.

Cheng Li nodded and smiled. "I thought you'd like it," she said. "Sea Lilies are a rare delicacy, full of good things. They're hard to come by — but Matilda Kettle has connections."

"Matilda?" Grace was surprised. "I thought she was 'Ma' as in 'Mother.'"

Cheng Li shook her head. "No, dear, her name is Matilda."

"But Molucco called her Kitty before."

"People call her many names, but her real name is Matilda."

Grace sensed that Cheng Li knew many, many secrets. She took another sip of tea, feeling its sweet warmth flood through her body. It felt as if all the tension she had been carrying around had drained away. Was it possible that just a couple of sips of the delicately perfumed tea could have such a strong and immediate effect?

"Now," Cheng Li said. "Tell me everything."

Where should she begin? There was so much she could tell. So many thoughts and experiences that she was suddenly burning to get off her chest. So many questions too.

But could she trust Cheng Li? She was aware of her companion's reputation — the former deputy captain was talked about aboard *The Diablo* with a mixture of fear and disdain. Connor, though, had spoken highly of her — describing her as harsh but fair — and his opinion mattered far more to Grace than that of Captain Wrathe or his all-too-easily influenced subordinates. But one thing that Connor had told Grace gave her real cause for concern. He had told her of Captain Drakoulis' insinuation that Cheng Li had been spying on Molucco — that this was the reason for her arrival on *The Diablo*, and for her sudden departure.

"What would you like to know?" Grace said at last, deciding to let her companion start off. She would proceed with caution and then make her own decision as to Cheng Li's trustworthiness.

Cheng Li shrugged. "Well, for a start, how do you like life aboard *The Diablo*?"

It was a simple question but Grace took a moment to compose her answer. Cheng Li waited, taking another draught of tea.

"I like it well enough," Grace said.

Cheng Li observed Grace with her bright almond eyes. Clearly she was waiting to hear more. Grace decided to take a chance.

"I don't know that I want to stay there forever."

"Really?" said Cheng Li, one eyebrow raised quizzically.

"Forgive me if I'm wrong, but hasn't Connor signed up to the articles now?"

Grace nodded. "Yes," she said quietly.

Cheng Li took a sip of tea. "That's a little bit of a problem."

Grace hardly needed reminding of that. The articles were a constant thorn in her side.

"The articles are generally considered to be binding for life," said Cheng Li. She gazed at Grace. "But there are always ways around little problems."

Grace's heart lifted. Was Cheng Li about to throw her a lifeline?

"Tell me, how is Connor faring on the ship?"

"Pretty good," Grace said.

Cheng Li smiled. "Only pretty good? The word on the nautical newswire is that he's a pirate prodigy!"

"He's doing really well," Grace said. "He's shaken up by Jez's death. We all are. But Jez and Connor . . . and Bart . . . were especially close."

"Yes." Cheng Li sipped her tea ruminatively. "Of course — the Three Buccaneers and all that."

Grace nodded. "Connor will bounce back. He's happy enough living the pirate life."

"But it doesn't sound as if *you* are."

"I like it well enough."

"You've already used that expression, Grace. Why are you being so cagey? Don't you trust me?"

Wow! Leave it to Cheng Li to get straight to the point.

"You *don't* trust me," she continued. "I can tell. It's okay, Grace. I'm used to being the 'bad cop' on *The Diablo*."

Grace was impressed by her companion's frankness. And it felt so good to be able to talk to someone about all her worries. Despite her doubts as to Cheng Li's trustworthiness, she already felt something of a bond with the older girl. She felt too that Cheng Li might be able to help her.

"It's just that . . . ," Grace began. She might as well spit it out. "It's just that Captain Drakoulis made an accusation about you."

"I see. What exactly did Narcisos Drakoulis say? And to whom?"

"He told Captain Wrathe — well, all the pirates really — that you were undercover on *The Diablo* . . . sent by the Pirate Federation, to spy on Captain Wrathe. That Captain Wrathe thought you were on a regular deputy captaincy apprenticeship and all the time you were operating as an agent of the Federation."

Cheng Li nodded, refilling Grace's glass. "Pray continue, dear."

"You were supposed to bring Captain Wrathe into line but your mission failed. And that's why you were suddenly called away again — to the Pirate Academy."

Cheng Li gazed intently at Grace. Grace felt nervous. Had she said too much?

"It's all true," Cheng Li said.

Grace couldn't believe her ears.

"I'm telling you this because I think you'll understand. I *do* work for the Pirate Federation. They recruited me some years ago at the Pirate Academy and I've been working for them ever since."

"What exactly *is* the Federation?"

"I'm coming to that," Cheng Li said. "The Federation exists to further the cause of piracy throughout the world — to consolidate the power we have on the oceans and to develop a global network of pirate fleets, working in peaceful cooperation."

It sounded admirable stuff, thought Grace.

"Molucco Wrathe is a lingering migraine as far as the Federation's concerned," continued Cheng Li. "He's yesterday's man but he just won't go quietly into the night. In spite of our urging, he simply won't come into line. Indeed, he operates willfully in isolation. He fails to respect other captains' sea-lanes. He is motivated solely by the lure of a quick buck and a colorful adventure to swell his ego still further." She paused. "This may sound extreme to you, Grace, but I'm afraid that Wrathe's disregard for the Federation was the trigger which resulted in Jez Stukeley's death."

Grace nodded. She had come to the same conclusion herself, though without — until now — the advantage of the bigger picture.

"Narcisos Drakoulis is another loose cannon," Cheng Li

continued. "If I was given to more dramatic language, I'd say he was 'psychotic.' He's certainly no poster boy of the Pirate Federation himself. But he had legitimate cause for argument with Molucco Wrathe. Wrathe has angered many other pirate captains through his wanton behavior. There were two differences here. First, Drakoulis and Wrathe have ancient history — a dispute over some treasure in Greece, which led to Wrathe sinking Drakoulis' ship. Second, Drakoulis decided to do something about Wrathe's recent wrongdoings. Don't misunderstand me. I'm certainly not endorsing what Drakoulis did. Nor is the Federation. But Captain Wrathe invited that attack. If it hadn't come from Drakoulis, it would — sooner or later — have come from one of a hundred other pirate captains he has wronged. And make no mistake, if he doesn't mend his ways, it *will* happen again." Cheng Li gazed deeply at Grace once more.

"And next time it happens, Connor could get hurt."

Grace knew that Cheng Li was speaking the truth. "I know," she said. "Believe me, I know. But what can I do? Connor is dead set on a career as a pirate."

Cheng Li shook her head. "The problem isn't Connor wanting to be a pirate," she said. "The problem is his choice of his captain."

Cheng Li had been so straight with Grace, and so trusting in giving all this information. More importantly, it was clear that she could help. Time was of the essence.

Grace decided she had to trust her back. She took a deep breath.

"Is there *any* way we can get Connor out of Captain Wrathe's articles? Is there a way we can both get off *The Diablo*?"

"Of course," said Cheng Li, matter-of-factly. "I was about to come to that."

## DECISIONS

"Pirate Academy?" Connor repeated. "You want us to jump ship and go to *Pirate Academy*?"

"It isn't a question of jumping ship," Grace said. "It would all be aboveboard. And it would just be for a week. Captain Wrathe would sign us off . . ."

Connor stared incredulously at his sister over the now-empty pot of Sea Lily Tea. Cheng Li had disappeared to the bar and Grace had fetched Connor to join her in the booth.

"But Pirate *Academy*, Gracie? You know me and schools . . . it's just not a good combination."

Grace smiled. "I know, Connor. But we're not talking about Crescent Moon Bay High. We're talking Pirate Academy. Forget dull old tests and required reading lists. We're talking classes in combat and navigation and EMS . . ."

"What's EMS?"

Grace smiled. "Extreme Maritime Survival!" she announced proudly.

Connor laughed. "Wow! Cheng Li did a good selling job on you." He paused. "And that's another thing. Just suppose I *did* think this was a good idea — and I'm not saying that I do — but just *suppose* I did . . . how on earth would we get Captain Wrathe to agree, knowing that Cheng Li invited us and that she'd be looking after us there?"

Grace nodded. "I've thought of that," she said. "We can't pretend that Cheng Li isn't involved. Captain Wrathe is no fool. But we'll play down her involvement. We'll just say that we'd like a chance to see what the Academy is all about — and to bring back some new skills to *The Diablo*. Maybe even a new recruit or two?"

"I don't know if he'd go for that." Connor shook his head.

"You know him better than I do," Grace admitted, "but we're only asking for a week away . . . initially."

"Initially? What do you mean 'initially'?"

Grace took a deep breath. "Connor, I've been wanting to talk to you." She could see a wave of caution cross over his face, but she gritted her teeth and persisted. "It's about your articles."

"What about them?"

"I just wish . . . Well, I just wish that you hadn't signed up to Molucco quite so quickly."

"He saved my life, Gracie."

"And now he's endangering it."

"What do you mean?"

She hadn't meant to lay it so bluntly on the line. But now it was out there, so she might as well be frank.

"Cheng Li told me that it's only a matter of time before one of the other captains turns on Molucco . . ."

"Drakoulis is a fruitloop, Grace, a nutjob, a psycho. We were unlucky . . ."

"Jez was a little more than *unlucky*," she said. She saw Connor's face fall. "I'm sorry Connor, but I'm concerned about you. I'm concerned about *us*. I think we're in grave danger if we stay on *The Diablo*."

Connor grinned at her. "Hey, kiddo. We thrive on danger, you and I."

She couldn't return his smile. "Please, Connor. You have to take me seriously. I have nothing against Molucco Wrathe personally. I'm grateful to him — he gave you a home and now he's offered me one, too. But Cheng Li says it's only a matter of time before one of the other pirate ships attacks *The Diablo*. With you in the attack line, I'm worried — really worried — that you'll be killed."

Connor reached out a hand toward hers. "I understand how you feel," he said. "And, for what it's worth, I've had the same thoughts since Jez was killed. Molucco isn't a bad man but the way he behaves does invite trouble. I'd never say this to anyone else, but I think Jez died needlessly."

Grace gripped Connor's hand tightly. She hadn't expected to hear him say such things. After their separation — and all that had happened to them subsequently — it was sometimes too easy to forget the deep bond they shared. It was good to know it was still there.

"So, will you ask Molucco, then?" she chanced.

"For one week's leave to visit Pirate Academy?"

Grace nodded.

"I'll ask him. But I'm not at all optimistic that he'll agree."

"Thanks, Connor. Apart from anything, it'll be great to be away, just for a bit. We can have a proper talk about the future. About where we want to go, what we want to do."

"Gracie, I'll ask Captain Wrathe to give us a week's leave but when that's over, I have to go back to *The Diablo*."

"And I have to go back with you." She couldn't stop the words from spilling out.

Connor frowned. "What does that mean?"

"You've signed up to the articles," she said. "I haven't."

"Not yet," he said. "But you will, won't you? Isn't the only thing that matters that we're together?"

Grace let go of his hand. "We *won't* be together if you get killed in an attack, Connor. And you know me well enough to understand that I won't just wait around for that to happen."

"What will you do, then? Where will you go?" He looked her in the eye.

She couldn't tell him but she wasn't quick enough to disguise her thoughts.

"Oh no, Grace. *No!* You're not thinking of going back to the Vampirate ship?"

She sighed. "There are people there who need me."

"Not people," he said, shaking his head. "Vampires. Monsters. Demons."

"You're entitled to your views," she said quietly.

Connor was angry now. "You lecture me about keeping safe and all the time you're planning on hitching another ride on a ship where they sleep all day and drink blood all night."

"You don't know what you're talking about," she said. Now she was getting angry, too. He knew next to nothing about the Vampirate ship. If only he understood the pain Lorcan was in — how much he needed her.

"Grace, I can't believe you. I can't believe we're even having this conversation."

"Look," she said, with steel in her voice, "I don't want to fight you, Connor. You're the most important person in my world, you know that. And you're right — we should stay together. But there are things we haven't talked about — things we haven't had *time* to talk about with everything else that's gone on around us. If you could just persuade Molucco to let us off the ship for a week, we'd have that chance."

Connor shook his head in resignation. Somehow, she always managed to argue things around to her way of thinking. "All right," he said. "All right, I'll go and ask him. But don't expect miracles."

He drew back the curtain which separated the booth from the balcony. Leaning over, he could see Molucco, sitting with Ma Kettle and feeding bar snacks to Scrimshaw.

"Captain Wrathe!" Connor called. "Captain Wrathe! Could I have a word with you?"

"Of course, my boy. Come on down!"

---

In the next booth along, Sidorio and Stukeley hear Connor's cry.

Stukeley sits bolt upright. "That's Connor," he says, "and Molucco." Instinctively, he reaches for the curtain that closes them off from the bar below.

Sidorio reaches out and catches his wrist.

"I told you. No."

"Okay, Okay. Ow, you're hurting me."

"Sorry," mumbles Sidorio, releasing his grip but pushing Stukeley's hand back toward the table. "Just leave that curtain alone."

"Well this is no fun," Stukeley says. "No fun at all."

"No?" Sidorio surveys his lieutenant once more.

"Well, I can't drink anything," he says, tapping his tankard. It is still three-quarters full of beer — and the remaining quarter has been spluttered out and spilled on the table. "Can't seem to keep it down," he goes on.

"Things are changing inside you," Sidorio says. "Be patient."

Stukeley frowns and lifts the tankard once more.

"No!" Sidorio exclaims, infuriated.

Defiantly, Stukeley takes a sip of ale. Sidorio shakes his head with frustration as Stukeley begins to choke once again. He leans over and thumps his companion on the back.

"Ow! Stop attacking me!"

"STOP trying to drink. You *can't* take it."

"But why?"

Sidorio sighs wearily. "Be patient."

"*Be patient! Be patient! Don't look at anyone. Don't speak to anyone. Leave the ale alone.* Captain, you're sounding an awful lot like my mother."

Sidorio shakes his head. Maybe it is time to cut this crackpot loose? But no. It is the early days. It is so long since he went through the metamorphosis himself that he can't predict what will happen next. If he can just wait this out, treat it as an experiment, things will surely be easier with the next one he brings back. And the next one. And then the one after that. Sidorio's army. Sidorio's crew. These are comforting words. Just what he needs to cheer himself up.

"Forget the beer. We're leaving."

Decisively, Sidorio draws himself to his feet.

"Why? Where are we going? What more thrills do you have in store for me?"

Sidorio laughs. "Thrills? I'll give you thrills! I know what you need."

He charges out of the booth. Stukeley grabs his coat and follows his new master.

"What are you talking about? Where are we going? What *do* I need?" Stukeley says, following on his tails.

Sidorio has reached the stairwell. He freezes for a moment and turns back to face his tiresome lieutenant.

"Blood, Stukeley. What you need is blood."

---

"Well," Connor said, rejoining Grace, "It's all decided."

"He said yes?"

"Yes," boomed Molucco Wrathe, appearing at Connor's side. "The captain said yes."

Grace flushed with embarrassment. "I'm sorry, Captain

Wrathe. I didn't see you there. But thank you . . . for letting us go. That's great news."

Captain Wrathe waved her thanks away. "It's been a difficult few days aboard the ship," he said. "I'm sure a break will do you both some good."

Grace couldn't believe that he was being so easygoing about it.

"Well, I must say," said Cheng Li, returning from the bar, "that's refreshingly forward thinking of you."

"Mistress Li," Captain Wrathe said. "What an unexpected *dis*pleasure."

"Ha! Ha! Ha! Ha!" laughed Cheng Li, sarcastically. "It's good to know that the recent turn of events has not robbed you of your rapier-like wit."

Molucco fixed her with a look. "The man who cannot laugh, Mistress Li, is a very poor man indeed," he said.

He was joined by Cate on one side and Ma Kettle on the other. More pirates began turning toward them or getting up and walking over. Everyone was aware that this was the first meeting between the captain and his former deputy since Drakoulis had leveled his accusation that Cheng Li was a spy.

Unintimidated, Cheng Li ignored the crowd and addressed Captain Wrathe and Cate directly. "I was so very sorry to hear about Jez Stukeley," she said. "He was a fine pirate." She fixed her smoky eyes on Cate. "Congratulations, by the way, on making deputy captain. I hope the additional responsibilities are not proving too oner-ous for you."

The two women looked at one another — the former deputy captain and her successor. Grace had noticed that Cate was growing into her new role, showing more confidence and authority daily. But now, face to face with her predecessor, she looked a little unsure of herself.

Molucco placed his arm around Cate's shoulder. "Cate is a very fine deputy," he said. "At last I have someone at my side I can trust."

Cheng Li smiled. "You could always trust me, Captain."

"Yes," Molucco laughed. "I could always trust you to have an objection to my plans, to place obstacles in my way, to question my motives and my authority. On matters such as these, you were one hundred and ten percent reliable."

"Oh, Captain," said Cheng Li, smiling, "once more your good humor has the better of me. But now, I'll take my leave of you. There are preparations to be made for Grace and Connor's arrival at Pirate Academy. That is . . . so long as you're sure I can be trusted with them."

What *was* Cheng Li saying? Grace was alarmed. Talk about raising a red rag to a bull! But Molucco remained unusually composed.

"I don't trust you any farther than I can smell you," he said. "But I trust Connor and Grace implicitly. They are keen to visit the Academy and I see no reason to decline their request."

"We have very different ideas about piracy there," said Cheng Li. "Aren't you worried we might corrupt their young minds?"

Once more Grace felt a sharp stab of panic, but Molucco only laughed.

"Base metals like you, Mistress Li, are more easily corrupted than pure gold like the twins." He lifted his arm from Cate's shoulder and stretched out his hands, one settling upon Grace's shoulder, one upon Connor's. "Go and have your fun, my friends. You're young. It's no more than you deserve. There are some good people at the Academy. Keep your minds open to what they teach you." He squeezed both their shoulders. "And then come back to *The Diablo* and we'll get on with the real business of being a pirate."

Captain Wrathe took Ma Kettle's hand and began walking away. Then he stopped and turned back.

"They're members of my crew, Mistress Li, but they're not my slaves. I encourage individual thinkers and freedom of expression on my ship. Can you, your precious headmaster, Kuo, and the others say the same?" He glared at her, then took Ma's arm once more.

"Well," said Cheng Li, "we will see, won't we? Oh, Captain Wrathe, I almost forgot. Captain Quivers asked to be remembered to you."

"Lisabeth Quivers," he said, his face lighting up at once. "Now *there's* a name I haven't heard in a full moon or two!"

He turned to the twins. "Lisabeth Quivers! There was no finer captain in her day."

Ma Kettle cackled. "No finer captain and no greater *heartbreaker*. With those eyes and that flame-red hair. Oh, Lucky, she certainly kept you and your brothers in line! Wasn't *she* a one-off?! What larks we had back in those days!"

"Yes," Molucco said, his voice tinged with sadness. "Yes, those *were* grand old days." He turned to Cheng Li. "Please send Captain Quivers my very best wishes."

"Best wishes!" exclaimed Ma Kettle. "Pah! Send her our love! And tell her to sail by for a drink one night." She looped her arm through Molucco's and walked him away to a small private room.

The pirates began to disperse, realizing that the fireworks display was over. Cate grabbed Connor and set off in search of Bart. Grace turned to face Cheng Li.

"Why did you taunt him like that?" she asked.

"Watch and learn," said Cheng Li with a wink. "He said you could come, didn't he? Now whoever would have thought that could happen?" She smiled at Grace. "I'll come and pick you and Connor up at nine o'clock sharp tomorrow morning. Pack a small bag each and be ready on deck."

In spite of the severity of Cheng Li's tone, Grace couldn't help but smile. "We're really doing this, aren't we?"

Cheng Li nodded. "Yes, Grace. By this time tomorrow, you and Connor will be free of *The Diablo* and settling down to your first night at Pirate Academy."

14

# PIRATE ACADEMY

The academy's harbor was enclosed by a seawall, the entrance marked by a tall stone arch rising out of the water. As Cheng Li's small boat sailed closer, the twins saw that the arch bore an inscription. Grace read it out.

> PLENTY AND SATIETY,
> PLEASURE AND EASE,
> LIBERTY AND POWER.

"That's the Academy's maxim," Cheng Li said, with a great sense of pride. "The words come from a famed captain of the old times."

"What does 'satiety' mean?" Connor asked.

Cheng Li smiled. "Taking everything you want, and then everything else besides." Connor's eyes lit up but Grace couldn't help frowning, thinking of Molucco Wrathe's unquenchable thirst for treasure. "Of course, these days, piracy is a much more complex and subtle business." Grace kept her eyes on her, awaiting further explanation. "You'll see what I mean after a few days at the Academy." Cheng Li turned away and busied herself with the sails.

As Cheng Li steered the boat through the arch and into the harbor, Grace and Connor gasped at the first sight of their surroundings. The Academy was a colorful oasis — a sprawling mass of old buildings, painted in bright yellows, pinks, and oranges and set among lush gardens, leading down toward the dockside. As they approached the dock, a flotilla of small sailing boats passed them, full of young kids — with one exception.

"Captain Avery!" Cheng Li called out. The old man jerked to attention and looked up, then smiled and lifted his cap to wave at her. "He's taking the juniors out for their sailing lesson," she explained to the twins. Now the young students noticed Cheng Li and began waving. As they did so, some of the boats began to veer out of line.

"Focus!" Captain Avery cried at his students with exasperation. "Now, let's pay a little *less* attention to Mistress Li and a little *more* to our own navigation, shall we? Come on Mister McLay, look alive! And you, Miss Conescu —

pull in the sheets now, that's it. Oh yes, Miss Webber, nice recovery. Much improved! Very much improved!"

Grace and Connor watched as the pirate apprentices attempted — with varying degrees of success — to bring their boats back into line. Meanwhile, Cheng Li eased their own craft into its slip. She was poised to jump out to tie it to its moorings, but a man appeared at the dockside, held out his hands, and said, "Here, allow me."

"Thank you, Commodore Kuo," Cheng Li said, throwing out the line toward him. The man caught the coil of rope in one hand and deftly wound it around the mooring pin. He stretched out his hand to help Cheng Li out of the boat.

Commodore Kuo was smartly dressed in calico britches tucked into tall, black leather boots, which seemed to shimmer in the sunlight. He wore a crisp white shirt — open to reveal the beginnings of a strong, tanned chest — and a red silk waistcoat. Hanging around his neck was a chain with four charms on it. He wore his silver-gray hair to his shoulders, like Molucco, but — in contrast to Captain Wrathe — his hair was smooth, well-groomed, and noticeably free of reptiles. His handsome face was tanned and his dark-brown eyes sparkled as brightly as the sun on the water.

Standing beside him on the dockside, Cheng Li addressed the twins. "Grace, Connor, it's my very great pleasure to introduce you to Commodore John Kuo, Headmaster of the Pirate Academy."

Connor jumped from the boat to the dockside.

"Welcome, Mister Tempest," said Commodore Kuo, shaking him firmly by the hand. "Connor, I've heard so much about you already — from Mistress Li and others. It's an absolute delight to have you here."

Now, Commodore Kuo reached out his hand to help Grace cross over onto the shore.

"Miss Tempest, welcome to Pirate Academy."

As the headmaster leaned forward, Grace saw more closely the chain hanging around his neck. Suspended on a thin gold thread were four charms — a sword, a compass, an anchor, and a pearl. The headmaster caught her looking.

"I see you've noticed my chain," he said, running a finger along it. "Each of the charms has an important meaning. They symbolize the three core talents required to be a successful pirate. The sword represents the ability to fight and is modeled on my very own Toledo Blade. The compass represents skills in navigation. The anchor recognizes that we must ground ourselves in pirate history. And the pearl . . . well the pearl is perhaps the most important — it marks the capacity to take the most dark and unprepossessing of situations and break through it to find the treasure within."

Grace felt she knew something of what the headmaster was saying. "Well," said the headmaster, placing a hand lightly on each twin's shoulder and brushing them forward, "what are we waiting here for? Let's go inside!"

The four of them set off along a twisting footpath, through the grounds of the Academy. The gardens smelled wonderful. After breathing little more than sea air for weeks, the scent of the tall jacaranda tree near the dock was heady enough to knock you out. Its branches hung low, under the weight of its bundles of blue flowers. Running around the tree was a circular seat, on which two boys were sitting, both engrossed in the same book.

As they passed, the boys glanced up and straightened their posture.

"Sebastian, Ivan," said Commodore Kuo. "Catching up on some reading?"

"Yes, sir!" said the first boy, holding up the book's cover.

"Ah, *The Book of Five Cutlasses*," said Commodore Kuo, "A piratical classic!"

"Mistress Li recommended it to me," the boy said, excitedly.

"Indeed I did," Cheng Li said. "Sebastian has made such excellent progress in Combat Workshop, I thought he'd find Captain Makahazi's biography an engaging subject."

"Ambitious — and violent — reading for a ten-year-old," exclaimed the headmaster, "but it seems to have engrossed Sebastian, and it appears young Ivan is equally gripped."

"Yes, *sir*," said the other boy.

"Very good," Commodore Kuo said, smiling. "Well, we shan't disturb you any more, young *pirates*."

The boys beamed at the word and returned to their

study beneath the blue bower. Could there be a more ideal place to sit, wondered Grace — shaded by the branches, immersed in its scent, looking out to the glistening harbor.

"Come on, slowpoke," Cheng Li called, already a good way ahead, standing in front of a dazzling fountain made of colored glass and seashells.

Grace hurried to catch up with her. "It's all so beautiful," she said with a sigh.

"So, you're glad you came?"

"Oh yes," Grace said, her eyes wide with wonder and delight.

"You're a very long way from *The Diablo* now," Cheng Li said, taking Grace's arm. They walked side by side past the fountain, splashes of cool water bouncing up and onto Grace's face. It felt delicious on her tanned skin, warmed by the morning sun. For the first time in ages, Grace found herself properly beginning to relax.

Connor and Commodore Kuo had made swifter progress and now stood, deep in discussion, at the entrance to a tall, domed terra-cotta–colored building. Grace could see that Connor and the headmaster were already getting along famously. She felt a strong sense of optimism. This was a new beginning. With Cheng Li's help, she felt sure that she had rescued Connor from certain death as one of the pirates under Captain Wrathe's leadership.

Cheng Li and Grace joined Connor and Commodore Kuo at the building's entrance — a pair of vast, elaborately carved wooden doors. "These doors were plundered by one of our founding captains," Cheng Li told the twins, "after an especially successful raid off the coast of Rajasthan." She touched a hand to the intricate carvings. "Whenever I see these doors, I feel as if I am coming home."

"The Academy *is* a home for all our students — old and new," Commodore Kuo said, pushing open the doors. "And, wherever you travel in this world, our doors will always open to welcome you back from your adventures."

As he finished speaking, he stepped back and Grace and Connor found themselves on the threshold of a vast circular room, bathed in cool blue light.

"This is the Rotunda," said Commodore Kuo, "but our students' affectionate nickname for it is 'the Octopus' — on account of all its tentacles." He smiled, indicating the various corridors spinning off from the center.

Grace's attention was drawn up above her head. The domed ceiling of the Rotunda was studded with circular glass panels, in every shade of blue — from pale turquoise to bright lapis to deep indigo. Sunlight streamed down through the glass filters, drenching the Octopus and those inside it in watery blues. The effect was stunning, as if you were wandering upon the ocean floor itself.

Following Grace's gaze, Connor also looked upward. But his eyes were drawn by something different.

Hanging down on steel wires from the very top of the Rotunda were glass cases, forming a giant mobile. The cases came to a stop just a couple of feet above their heads and, as Connor examined them, he saw that each case contained a sword. It was strange — and not a little disconcerting — looking up at all these blades, swimming in the blue ocean of light like a school of beautiful but utterly deadly fish.

"Wow," said Connor. "What's the deal with all these swords?"

"Impressive, aren't they?" Commodore Kuo said. "We're very fortunate at the Academy to have swords belonging to some of the most celebrated pirate captains of our time. Most of the swords are bequeathed to us when the captain retires but, in some instances, it is the sword which retires first! That one up there, for instance, was once used by your friend Captain Molucco Wrathe. Do you see?"

The Commodore pointed up at three swords which hung together in a group.

"Which one?" Connor asked.

"Ah well, it's true they're almost identical. You see, those three swords once belonged to the three Wrathe brothers — Molucco, Barbarro, and Porfirio. But that one, in the middle, was once Molucco's rapier. If you look carefully, you'll see the telltale sapphire in its hilt."

Connor was a little surprised that Molucco had bequeathed a sword to the Academy, given the rather dismissive way he spoke about the place. But he knew the captain well enough to know that he was a changeable man. Besides, Bart had told him when they'd first met that Molucco and his brothers were pirate royalty — so of course they would want the swords of the Wrathes in the Academy.

"What about *this* sword?" Connor asked, his eyes suddenly drawn to a simpler long sword, the hilt of which was leather-bound and glittered slightly.

"Did you prime our guests, Mistress Li?" Commodore Kuo asked with a smile.

Cheng Li returned his smile, shaking her head.

"What do you mean?" asked Connor.

"That's *my* old sword," Commodore Kuo said. "My Toledo Blade. It was my ally in many a conflict. It's a quite unusual weapon." He stood at Connor's side, their eyes fixed on the sword hovering above them.

"It's forged in the most exceptional way," explained Commodore Kuo. "Iberian blacksmiths are masters of their art — and they surpassed themselves with this sword. The steel blade has an iron core inside, making it extraordinarily hard. That's why Hannibal himself chose a Toledo Blade, along with great kings and leaders throughout history." Commodore Kuo glanced across at Cheng Li. "Even Japanese samurai traveled to Toledo to have their katana and wakizashi forged there. And so did I."

Commodore Kuo's hand rested on Connor's shoulder. "The weapon's creation is a complex process. The smiths must forge hard and soft steel simultaneously and at exceedingly high temperatures. Then the sword is cooled with water, or oil, to weld the seam. The master blacksmith who forged this sword blew upon the blade 20,000 times to achieve the perfect consistency. Just imagine! He only makes three blades each year. And you see the hilt? It's bound in stingray skin — exceptionally tough and waterproof. My boots are made of the same material."

Grace glanced down at his boots, realizing that they were not — as she had first thought — crafted from leather. She was reminded of her similar mistake over the Vampirate captain's cape and the mysterious ship's sails. Though Commodore Kuo's boots shimmered in the light, she didn't expect that they flickered with veins like the Vampirate captain's cape or the ship's sails. Nevertheless, the Academy felt similar to the Vampirate ship in at least one other respect — it appeared to have many exciting secrets to unlock.

Connor couldn't take his eyes off the Toledo Blade. It sounded amazing. A thought crossed his mind. "Commodore Kuo, would I be able to try it out?"

"I'm afraid not," the headmaster said with finality, though his voice was still soft and smooth. "The swords are only taken out of their cases once every year, on Swords Day. It's when we celebrate the founding of the Academy and the accomplishments of our students. Those who have shone most brightly through the year are rewarded with the honor of exhibition fights with these swords." He turned to Connor. "But alas, this is an opportunity only open to *students* of our Academy, *not* guests."

Connor felt a sense of disappointment and frustration. Right now, he'd give anything to hold that sword in his hands, even if it meant signing up to a year at the Academy.

"The Academy has many different treasures to appeal to every taste," Commodore Kuo continued, his voice echoing around the Rotunda. "Over the next few days, you must feel free to explore whatever seizes your interest and passion. Ask for whatever you need and, wherever possible," he glanced up at the Toledo Blade, "it shall be yours. Mistress Li will be your guide and the door to my study is always open to you. But now, I fear, I must step away to finalize revisions to our Navigation curriculum. Mistress Li, I'll leave you to show Grace and Connor to their quarters?"

"Yes, Headmaster."

Commodore Kuo began walking away along one of the corridors. Then, apparently seized by a fresh thought, he spun around — his eyes flaming with passion. "Once I was captain of a thousand-strong crew. Now, I am captain of the brightest future stars of the pirate world. Should you feel, after a few days here, that you might want to join us, well, I'm sure that we could find a way to accommodate that. Don't you think so, Mistress Li?"

"Yes — yes, of course, Headmaster."

Commodore Kuo turned and this time disappeared along one of the twisting tentacles of the Octopus, his stingray-skin boots thudding on the checkered tiles.

Connor stared up above his head at the swords of a hundred or more pirate captains. Each sword had seen so much action and adventure. If only they could tell their stories!

As Connor's eyes excitedly took in the details of the different swords, the cases began to move. The whole giant mobile turned slowly like a lethal carousel, the swords rising and falling like fairground horses, gathering pace. His eyes hungrily drank in the identifying marks of different captains — a precious jewel on the hilt here, a mysterious carving on the blade there. But soon the swords were spinning too fast to make out their individual details. This was out of control. The swords spun faster and faster until the glass cases they were in shattered and shards of glass rained over him. Still he stood there, in the heart of the meteor shower, too enthralled to feel any pain. And now, as he stared up, he saw and heard the heart of a battle. He saw the flash of sunlight on flickering blades of steel; billowing white sails; the timber of decking and masts. He heard swords clashing against each other; rigging being torn; cannon firing and the cries of pirates running in and out of the fray. He listened more closely to the cries.

"Captain," he heard. "Captain Tempest."

No. It couldn't be.

"Come. Captain Tempest."

There again, as clear as day.

"Come. Captain Tempest. He is wounded. He needs . . ."

Connor tried to make sense of what he saw but his vision had blurred. The cries were growing faint. Then he saw the swords above him once more, turning back to their original position and coming to a standstill — each one still enclosed in glass. He tore his eyes away, glancing down to the floor of the Rotunda. It was perfectly clear. No shards had fallen around him.

"Come along, Captain Tempest."

Connor looked up to see Cheng Li fixing him with a smile. He blinked. Had she said "*Captain*"?

"You're going to make yourself giddy, staring up at those swords," she continued, "and heaven knows what harm you're doing to your neck. Let's go and get some lunch."

Connor saw that she was speaking, but the words made little sense to him. He was confused by the vision he had seen through the swords above him. Had he simply imagined it, or was this a glimpse into his future? Was he going to be a pirate captain himself?

"*Lunch*, Connor," Cheng Li said, with only a mild sense of exasperation. "Even pirate prodigies need to eat once in a while. And the Academy chef prepares quite the most delicious dumplings you'll ever taste."

15

# NO ORDINARY SCHOOL

"Well," said Cheng Li, raising her cup of jasmine tea. "Welcome again to Pirate Academy." Connor and Grace lifted their tea bowls and clinked them against Cheng Li's.

They were eating lunch on the Academy terrace, surrounded by the other students and staff, in the balmy heat of the midday sun. As Grace chatted animatedly to Cheng Li, Connor surveyed his surroundings. This was like no other school he had ever seen. Though, to be fair, the only other school he *had* seen was Crescent Moon Bay High — and you would have to go a long way to find a nastier, more down-at-heel, more narrow-minded institution.

"How many students are there here?" he heard Grace ask Cheng Li.

"One hundred and fifty," Cheng Li said, "ranging from

seven-year-olds to seventeen-year-olds. There are just fifteen students in each of the ten year groups. With the Academy's high teacher/student ratio, every pirate apprentice is given the very best opportunity to thrive. In this — as in many other ways — Pirate Academy is no ordinary school."

"Where do the students come from?" Grace asked.

"Good question," said Cheng Li. "Our students come from the very best pirate families. And, believe me, it's no easy feat securing a place at Pirate Academy. We have rigorous entrance exams and interviews. You can't buy your way in here by simply donating a new training boat or a case of cutlasses. Every student has to walk through the door on his or her own merits."

"It sounds like you have to be rich, though," Connor said.

Cheng Li shrugged. "By definition, most successful pirate families are wealthy. You wouldn't be much of a pirate if you couldn't manage to educate your kids, would you? Of course, in rare cases — yours, for instance — scholarships are available."

Connor shrugged. "Well, we're only visiting, anyhow."

Cheng Li nodded. "Yes, that's right. For a moment, I forgot!" But there was something in Cheng Li's voice that signaled to Grace that she had not forgotten. Not even for a second.

"And do pirates really prefer their kids to come here,

rather than training them on board their ships?" asked Grace.

"Think about it," Cheng Li said. "Think about how hectic life is aboard a ship like *The Diablo*. There's no real time for a working pirate to educate his or her children. Of course, all ships must groom their young pirates in swordplay, but there's simply no opportunity for the broader education we provide here — in History and Navigation, Strategy and Captaincy skills. Our offer to pirates is this — give us your children for ten years and we'll return them to you — not only ready to become full-fledged members of the crew, but ready to take on the role of captain."

"That makes sense," said Grace. "Don't you think, Connor?"

Connor did not reply. He was lost in thought. He was thinking about the vision he had had in the Rotunda — the vision of becoming a captain.

"Don't you think, Connor?" Grace repeated.

"What? Oh, erm . . . yes, absolutely." He wasn't entirely sure what Grace had asked him, but she seemed well pleased with his answer.

"Now," said Cheng Li, "I've brought each of you an Academy timetable." She passed a folded card to each of the twins. "This is the schedule of classes you would be taking if you were Year 8 students here — along with the other fourteen-year-olds. I've marked the subjects I think you will find the most interesting, but it's entirely up to you. You're my guests. You're here to get a flavor of the place, so feel free to attend as many classes as you wish."

Grace unfolded her timetable, but Connor had already tuned out Cheng Li's voice and was excitedly scanning the class schedule. There were no boring subjects here! From Pirate History on a Monday morning to Friday afternoon's Combat Workshop, each day seemed to be jam-packed with interesting stuff. Okay, so maybe he *could* take or leave a double dose of Marine Biology on Tuesday mornings, but triple Practical Piracy and Ocean-faring sounded great and he couldn't wait to attend the class in Extreme Maritime Survival. Connor beamed at Grace — he had to hand it to her for suggesting coming here in the first place. She smiled back.

The only off-putting thing about the timetable was the length of each day. Every morning kicked off at 7:00 a.m. with something called "Strength, Stamina, and Motivation" and the Academy day didn't end until 8:00 p.m. — although the final hour after dinner was set aside for private study or clubs and other social events. There were also classes on Saturday mornings and even one — a Meditation class, taught by Cheng Li — late on Sunday afternoon. Still, Connor mused, if the students here were preparing for life aboard a pirate ship like *The Diablo*, it made sense for them to get used to very long days. He'd never been a "morning person" back in Crescent Moon

Bay, but since signing up to the articles of Molucco Wrathe's ship and taking his share of the duty rosters, he'd developed more than a passing acquaintance with sunrise.

Connor took a last mouthful of dim sum — savoring the delicious flavors of ginger and lemongrass — then set his chopsticks back on their china rest. Cheng Li was right. The food here was delicious — and the portions were generous, too. He lifted the cup of jasmine tea to his lips and felt a heady sense of well-being. For a moment, his thoughts flashed back to *The Diablo* but already it was exerting less of a pull on his emotions. He'd be back before long and, in the meantime, there was plenty to distract him here — from the delicious and plentiful food to the extremely cool classes.

"Don't you think, Connor . . . ? Connor!"

He glanced up to find both his sister and Cheng Li staring at him. He had been so engrossed in thoughts, he'd completely zoned out.

Cheng Li smiled. "I was just saying that there's no need to attend any classes this afternoon. Instead, I'll show you around and we'll get you settled in your rooms. Tonight, you will join all the teachers for a special dinner. They are all former captains — every one a pirating legend — and they're all very eager to meet you both."

Connor beamed. "I could get used to the VIP treatment," he said, stretching out his arms in a contented yawn.

Grace and Cheng Li shook their heads at him. Secretly Grace was delighted that Connor was so enthusiastic about the Academy. And she was grateful for all the preparations Cheng Li had made in such a short amount of time. Dinner with the pirate captains was an especially nice touch. Grace knew the inner workings of her brother's mind, and the more he felt a sense of belonging to the Pirate Academy, the better chance she had of persuading him to extend his stay and never return to *The Diablo*. She felt a little guilty when she thought of their friends aboard the ship — especially Cate and Bart — but she was only looking out for her brother's safety. She wasn't prepared to see him suffer the same fate as Jez Stukeley. Everyone would understand — eventually.

—~—

The twins each deposited their bags in their rooms and then followed Cheng Li back outside for a full tour around the grounds of the Academy.

"So, how do you like your quarters?" Cheng Li asked. "I trust they're to your satisfaction?"

"Oh yes," Grace said. She had never expected to be given such a large, well-appointed room. It even had its own balcony, looking out toward the harbor. Connor's was just as generous, though it was on the other side of the building, overlooking the "inner circle" — a secluded courtyard of manicured grass, where a class of kids were practicing their martial arts skills.

As expansive as the grounds of the Academy had appeared from the terrace, when the twins and Cheng Li wandered through them, they seemed to open out still farther. Trees and bushes which had appeared from above to mark the Academy's boundaries, in fact disguised new parts of the Academy — each one painted in the same soft, sunny palette as the main cluster.

Cheng Li pointed out all the different buildings to them — from the student dormitories and staff lodgings to the combat workshop, from the archive store to the lecture theaters and classrooms. The Academy was a world all its own and it was a lot to take in, especially in the soporific heat of the early afternoon. Grace found that some of the details of Cheng Li's excited monologue passed her by, but she was struck by her deep sense of pride in the Academy. Connor noticed it, too. This was a very different Cheng Li to the one he'd known aboard *The Diablo*. She seemed calmer here — like she belonged.

"Wow!" Connor exclaimed. He had run a little ahead but now turned and waited for Grace and Cheng Li. "What is *that*?"

As the girls caught up to him, Grace saw that he was pointing to a large amphitheater, set back a little from the harbor, but an amphitheater with a *difference*. In place of a stage, was a sparkling pool of water. And, in the center of this was a ship — a galleon not dissimilar to *The Diablo* or, indeed, to the Vampirate ship.

"That," said Cheng Li, her eyes sparkling as brightly as the water, "is the lagoon of doom!" She laughed. "Well, that's what the students call it, at least. We use the ship there for attack practice and for combat demonstrations. It's one of my very favorite places in the Academy!"

Connor looked toward the deck. It was empty now, like a ghost ship. But it was all too easy to imagine pirates running across its boards. He thought once more of his vision in the Rotunda. The deck he had seen looked a lot like this one. Maybe there, on that deck — in the "lagoon of doom" — he would learn how to become a captain.

"Time for a little refreshment," announced Cheng Li, pausing by the thick foliage of a pomegranate tree. She reached out and twisted two fruits from its branches, dropping them into the twins' hands. The fruit was still warm from the sun as Grace's fingers enclosed it.

Cheng Li twisted off another pomegranate for herself. She lifted one of her katanas, tossed the fruit in the air, sliced it, then caught the two halves in her hand. With a smile, she performed the same deft operation for Grace then Connor. The exposed seeds twinkled in the sunlight like jewels. The three of them took a seat on the grass to savor the snack. Grace felt the fruit burst on her tongue, surprisingly cool and thirst-quenching in the heat. She turned her eyes to the boats in the harbor below. Captain Avery was getting ready to set off sailing with another class of students. The prospect, Grace noted, didn't appear to be filling him with the greatest of pleasure.

"No, no, no, Mister Webb!" she heard him cry out to one of his young charges.

Closer to them, a stream of the Academy's older students were walking purposefully along the harbor path to a pale-gold-colored building.

"That's the main lecture theater," Cheng Li explained. "And this is the Year 10 class — our final year students — heading off to a lecture by Captain Larsen, if I am not mistaken."

"Good afternoon, Mistress Li," one of the students called politely. Others turned and nodded respectfully in her direction.

"Mister Blunt," Cheng Li called out. "Mister Blunt, come over here a moment."

A tall, good-looking boy with flushed cheeks and pale straw-like hair turned toward them, his eyebrows raised in query. He had been walking along, deep in conversation with some friends, but now he disengaged himself and cut across the path to greet Cheng Li.

"Have you been stealing pomegranates again?" he asked Cheng Li, with a smile. "Naughty, naughty! But I promise I won't squeal to the gardeners."

"I want to introduce you to Connor and Grace Tempest," Cheng Li said, ignoring his cheek. "You remember I told you about our guests?"

"Oh yes, of course!" the boy said, extending a hand to Connor. "Hello, Connor, I'm Jacoby Blunt." He smiled. "Mistress Li tells me you're a *brilliant* swordsman."

"Jacoby is perhaps *the* finest fighter at the Academy," Cheng Li said. "I think the two of you would be very well matched in combat."

Connor looked into Jacoby Blunt's gray-blue eyes. They seemed cold and glass-like for a moment. Connor felt his heart sink — Cheng Li had set them up as rivals from the outset. He knew from experience how this would play out. It was like CMB High all over again! But then, to his surprise, Jacoby Blunt broke into a wide smile. "It *would* be great to have some decent opposition for a change," he said.

Cheng Li gave a satisfied laugh. "Well, Jacoby, I'm sure you and Connor will get a chance to put that to the test. Connor will be here all week and, as I mentioned to you earlier, I'd like you to look after him and his sister, Grace."

Cheng Li indicated Grace and now Jacoby leaned forward and shook her hand. "It certainly won't be a hardship looking after *you*, Grace," he said. Grace blushed at his words and his handsome smile.

"Well, off you go to your lecture," Cheng Li told Jacoby. "But remember that you're invited to dinner tonight with Grace and Connor and the captains. Commodore Kuo thought you might like to collect the twins and bring them to his study at seven-thirty sharp."

"No problemo," said Jacoby with a laid-back smile. "Enjoy your afternoon, Tempest twins . . . and I'll come and fetch you a little ahead of nineteen-thirty hours! Dress to impress!"

Grinning, he jogged off to catch up with his classmates.

"Come on, then," said Cheng Li, drawing herself upright. "Break's over! Let's continue with the tour. You *have* to see the freshwater pool!"

"Definitely!" Connor jumped up and began following Cheng Li. They were already some way down the path when they realized that Grace was not with them.

"Grace?" called Connor.

"Grace!" Cheng Li shouted. "Where are you?"

They stopped and turned back for her. She was standing still on the grassy hillside, looking out at the harbor. She was barely moving a muscle. The only thing to indicate she was a person and not a statue were the strands of her long hair, lifting and falling in the harbor breeze.

"Grace!" Connor called, increasingly impatient. His sister didn't even turn.

Suddenly, Grace's body went limp and she slumped down onto the grass.

"Grace!" Connor and Cheng Li cried, simultaneously. They raced back across the grass to see what on earth was wrong.

16

# JOURNEY

"I'm all right. I'm all right," Grace said, opening her eyes to find Connor and Cheng Li staring at her intently.

"What happened?" Connor asked. "One minute you were standing there, looking out at the harbor. The next, you were taking a tumble."

"I don't know," Grace said, shaking her head slowly. The fall had taken her by surprise. It had been preceded by a rush of sensations — some familiar, others new. But she wasn't ready to share this with the others.

"Let me feel your head," Cheng Li said, "we should get you to the infirmary."

"Really, I'm fine," Grace insisted, as Cheng Li's fingers gently probed the back of her head. "I think I just need to sit still for a bit."

"There don't *seem* to be any lumps or bumps," Cheng Li said, "nevertheless, I'd feel happier if Nurse Carmichael took a look at you."

"Don't worry about me," Grace said. "I'll just catch my breath. You guys go on with the Academy tour. I know Connor's dying to see the freshwater pool!"

"It doesn't matter," Connor said quickly. "I can see it later." But he didn't do a good job of hiding the disappointment in his voice.

"No, no. You go along now. I'll be fine." Just ahead of them, she saw the jacaranda tree with its circular seat. An idea came to her. "If you will just help me over there, I could sit in the shade for a little bit."

"Yeah, no problem," Connor said. He reached out to lift her. "Cheng Li, can you give me a hand?"

The two of them helped Grace to her feet. With her arms around both their shoulders, they walked her over to the jacaranda tree.

"How embarrassing!" said Grace.

"Don't worry about it." Cheng Li shook her head. "It's a hot day. Could have happened to any one of us."

They settled her on the seat. Grace felt instantly better, sitting amid the soft blue bower, out of the glare of the sun.

"Here," said Cheng Li, reaching into her pack and producing a bottle of water. "Take some sips of this."

"Thanks," said Grace, gratefully taking the bottle. The others watched her carefully as she took a sip. The cool water felt good. "I'm fine now," she said. "I'll just sit here for a bit. You go on."

Cheng Li placed her palm on Grace's brow. "You still seem a little hot to me. I'll go on with Connor but we'll be back to check on you within the hour."

Grace nodded, unnerved by the intensity of Cheng Li's stare. Really, all she needed was some peace and quiet.

After Cheng Li had gone, Grace slid back, deeper under the branches of the jacaranda tree, her arms brushing its trumpet-shaped flowers and releasing more of its sweet perfume. She felt cocooned there, looking out toward the harbor, where Captain Avery had at last successfully guided his charges out of their slips and off toward the harbor wall. Grace's eyes fell to the glistening waters. She felt as if she were sinking. It was the same sensation she had experienced just before falling. This time, she didn't fight it but instead let herself give in to the feeling.

She closed her eyes and felt her body grow limp once more. This time, she was able to cushion her fall by lying down on the seat before regular consciousness left her. It soon felt as if she were afloat on a more pliant surface than the wooden bench — possibly the ocean itself.

Her eyes remained closed and yet she could see that she was traveling through the air at a furious rate of knots — out across the dock and the harbor, out to the harbor wall and through the Academy arch, out beyond into the open ocean.

The speed of her motion was as exhilarating as it was giddying. The craggy coastline rushed past in a blur, the weather changing from sun to cloud and rain and then, just as quickly, back again. She continued to breathe deeply, letting this strange tide carry her wherever it wanted. She was unsure whether she should be fearful or excited about this journey.

She came to a point where she lost all sense of speed and she found herself swathed in a soft white mist, through which nothing was visible. The giddying sensation gave way to a deep calm. She felt safe. She sensed she was being looked after, held and guided by unseen hands. She waited.

Gradually the mist lifted and she was exactly where she had hoped to be — back on the deck of the Vampirate ship. She was standing up and yet she could not feel the deck-boards beneath her feet, nor the rocking motion of the ship. It made her understand that she was not really there, not wholly there — not in any normal sense. Grace thought of Darcy's visit to her cabin on *The Diablo*. Somehow, she had managed to make her own spirit journey! How had she done it? How was she going to get back? She brushed the questions aside for a moment, just thrilled to be here.

It was daylight and the deck was deserted, as she would have expected at this time of day. She stood for a moment beneath the ship's dark, winglike sails. A breeze was blowing and they billowed above her. Grace reached out a hand toward the strange leathery material. Her hand could not touch it — just as Darcy's hands could not touch anything during her visit to *The Diablo*. Grace's fingers moved through the sail, as if it were a hologram. Even so, as they passed through it, a spark of light shot up through the veins of the material. Grace watched the light rise and spark like a firework. It filled her with wonder and delight. It was so good to be back.

She walked over the familiar red deckboards to the very front of the ship. Beneath her, Darcy — in her daylight incarnation as the ship's beautiful wooden figurehead — stretched out over the waves, watching the horizon with her wide painted eyes. Grace leaned forward against the deck-rail, but here there was an invisible buffer, preventing her from touching the rail itself. The breeze was strong and strands of her hair flew back into her eyes. She brushed them away, looking down at the perfect painted hair of the ship's figurehead.

"Hello, Darcy," she called, unsure if her friend would be able to hear her above the roar of the breeze and the noisy flapping of the ship's sails.

"Grace!" She heard Darcy's cockney accent and her heart leaped. "Grace, you came back. You shouldn't have! I told you not to . . . but I'm glad you did!"

"Me, too," Grace said, her voice suddenly choked with emotion. "How are you? How is everybody?"

There was a pause. Then perhaps a sob — or it might have been the slosh of the waters below.

"Things are worse and worse, Grace."

"Why? What's happened, Darcy?"

"It's not . . . it's not for the likes of me to say, Grace. Besides, I can hardly hear you at the moment. My head is filled with the sounds of waves during the day. My ears and mouth are only wood until it grows dark. It's not easy to talk until after nightfall. What's more, the captain was ever so angry when he found out I'd been to visit you."

"Angry? Why was he angry?" Grace asked.

"He says we must leave you be. That this ship is for creatures like us, not girls like you. Says we must let you be free to get on with your life."

"But how can I?" asked Grace. "How am I supposed to just carry on when I know that you are suffering . . . that Lorcan is suffering?"

"That's what I told him, Grace," said Darcy, "but he got angrier and angrier, until he threw me out of his cabin and told me I was . . . troublesome. That I was nothing but a troublesome piece of . . . ," she sobbed, "piece of driftwood!"

Grace was shocked. She would never have expected the captain to have spoken such cruel words. She wondered, with a shiver, what he would say when he found out *she* had come back to the ship. Perhaps he already knew. Little passed on the ship that he was unaware of. How much time did she have left here?

"Darcy, I'm going to look in on Lorcan."

"All right, Grace. But be careful!"

"Careful of what?"

"Just careful, Grace."

Grace felt a deep sense of foreboding. But what was the point in coming here, if not to see Lorcan? "I'll see you later, Darcy," she said, turning back across the deck.

The door to the captain's cabin was closed, she noticed. She walked past it and instead opened the door that led into the main corridor. The lights were on — though dimly — and she eased her way down toward Lorcan's cabin. As she turned the corner, she saw a couple of unfamiliar faces — a tall, well-built black man with short silvery hair, and a slighter, rather jaundiced man, his head covered by a cowl. She quickly identified them as vampires not donors. They were locked in conversation with each other and didn't appear to notice her even as she brushed past them to proceed along the narrow passageway. How strange!

She paused outside Lorcan's cabin, suddenly nervous to enter. Summoning her strength, she raised her hand to knock. She failed to make contact with the wood but, nevertheless, the door opened. She stepped forward into utter darkness.

"Hello?" she said, her eyes struggling to adjust to the gloom.

There was a pause and then a familiar voice spoke. "Hello, stranger."

"Lorcan!" she said, feeling a strong surge of emotion but trying to fight it. "It's so good to hear your voice."

"Yours, too," he said. "Yours, too. How the devil have you been?"

"I'm fine," she said. "I just miss you — all of you — so much."

"We miss you too, Grace."

His voice trailed off.

Her eyes were adjusting to the darkness, but still she could only just make out the outline of his head and body. His bed was a four-poster, with hangings, making it hard to see inside. She walked around it but, whichever angle she glanced through, his face seemed to be turned away from her, as if he didn't want her to see him. Tentatively, she sat down on the edge of the bed. Much like when Darcy had sat on the bed in Grace's own cabin, she found herself hovering — albeit quite comfortably — a inch or so above its surface.

"Darcy told me that things have been difficult since I left."

"Sometimes, Darcy might think more and speak less." His words were suddenly stripped of the sunny tone he had adopted before.

"No, Lorcan. If something's wrong I want to know about it. I want to help."

"You're so kind, Grace." His voice was weary now. "But

I'm afraid this time you cannot help. Even the captain's powers are being tested as never before."

"What do you mean? Is this to do with the rebel Vampirates?"

"What do *you* know about them?"

"Darcy told me," she said, "that Sidorio wasn't the *only* Vampirate to rebel against the captain. That he was only the *first*. But now others challenge his authority. They want more blood. They want more Feasts."

"Grace, you mustn't interfere in such things. You mustn't even think of them."

If only he would turn toward her, or at least light up a candle. "But I want to help," she said. "You were so good to me. All of you . . . but especially you and the captain."

"It's best you leave us to find our own way," Lorcan said, his voice heavy with defeat. "You were only ever a visitor here. You know only a little of our world."

"Yes, but I want to know more."

"It's too dangerous. You came closer than any mortal ever has. I don't even know how you managed to come back . . . like this."

Grace took a deep breath. Had she *willed* herself back here? "I think I journeyed back here because I care." Her voice cracked with emotion.

Lorcan sighed. "Then you must stop caring, Grace. You must let us go."

"How? How am I supposed to do that? Should I just extinguish any feelings I might have and forget all about you?"

"Yes." His voice grew weaker each time he spoke. Her urge to see his face was impossibly strong.

"Lorcan, do you have a taper? It's so dark in here. If you could just light one of the candles —"

"No, Grace," he said, with sudden ferocity. "No candles. There's the difference between us. I need the darkness, not the light."

"Lorcan, please don't talk this way. I thought you'd be pleased to see me."

His only answer was another sigh. It was almost as though words were too much of an effort for him now.

"Lorcan, aren't you even a little pleased to see me?"

Still, there was no answer.

Suddenly, the room was filled with smoke. No, it was too cold to be smoke. It was the mist again. And, as much as she fought through it, it only grew thicker and thicker. Filled with frustration, Grace waved her arms about, trying to cut through the screen that separated her from her dear friend.

But it was no good. She had only been a visitor and, however she had got there, her stay was not in her control. The mist took hold of her, filling her eyes and ears and nostrils. And then she was traveling again, this time backward. Flying off the deck of the ship, light as a seagull feather — pulled back over the ocean, so the rocks and reefs and lagoons all rushed by in a blur that made her head spin. Until finally, there was darkness and stillness once more, and a heady scent, which, though familiar, she couldn't immediately place.

Grace opened her eyes and found herself staring into the blue. It took her back to her first arrival on the Vampirate ship, when she had looked up for the first time into the intense blue of Lorcan Furey's eyes. But this blue was different. As her gaze steadied, she watched the color separate into the trumpet-like shapes of flowers. Now, she remembered. She was lying on the seat beneath the jacaranda tree. She propped herself up, letting out a breath, wondering at her strange journey. Had she really been on the ship or only imagined it? It had all seemed so very real.

"Grace."

The voice was soft but close. She twisted her head.

Cheng Li was sitting beside her, holding a small bag which hovered over Grace's forehead.

"I brought you this ice-pack," she said. "Nurse Carmichael thought it might be soothing to you. She recommended that I take you back to your room so you can get some rest. Do you think you might be able to walk there, with my assistance?"

Grace drew herself up. She actually didn't feel too bad, just a little shell-shocked and confused, her head swimming with unanswered questions.

"I'll be fine to walk," she announced.

"Good," Cheng Li said, taking her hand. "Come along then." They stood face to face for a moment. "And, on the way, you can tell me exactly what's going on."

"What do you mean?" Grace asked, looking at Cheng Li in shock.

"You're *not* suffering from sunstroke, Grace," Cheng Li said. "There's something far more complicated going on with you. You'll feel better if you let it out. Secrets have a way of eating away at us from the inside."

Grace shuddered at the thought, imagining all the secrets of her time on the Vampirate ship — secrets she had only shared with Connor — eating hungrily away at her insides. The gnawing sensation felt all too true. And then there were the fresher secrets that even Connor didn't know — that she could communicate with the Vampirate ship and journey to it, in her mind at least.

Cheng Li smiled softly and looped her arm through Grace's. "Don't look so anxious, dear. I'm not going to *force* it out of you. It's fine if you don't *want* to tell me — if you still don't think you can *trust* me." Cheng Li's smoky eyes bore directly into Grace's. "I think you should know, Grace, I am an excellent listener — if I do say so myself. If and when you *do* decide to talk, you could do a lot worse than talking to *me*."

*Could* she trust Cheng Li? It would be such a relief to share her secrets. And the older girl had shown her nothing but kindness, so far.

"Thanks," Grace said, as they began walking. "I'll bear that in mind."

They walked on up the hill in silence. Grace still felt exhausted but exhilarated by her first journey back to the Vampirate ship. She was excited too by the possibility of unburdening her secrets upon Cheng Li. She badly needed someone to talk to — if only as a sounding board for her own questions. But her thoughts kept circling back, like a school of sharks, to one very big question. Could Cheng Li be trusted?

When they came to Grace's door, Cheng Li said her good-byes. "Get some rest, Grace. You've clearly been through some kind of ordeal today, but you'll want to be on your best form for the captains tonight." She patted Grace on the shoulder, then turned to walk away.

"Wait!" said Grace. The word came out more forcefully than she had intended. Cheng Li turned, one eyebrow raised in surprise. Grace took a deep breath. "Why don't you come inside?" she asked. "There *are* some things I'd like to talk to you about."

Cheng Li nodded, looking very serious all of a sudden. "I regard your trust as a great gift," she told Grace. "And, of course, it goes without saying — but I shall say it nevertheless — whatever you tell me will be in the strictest confidence. Just between us two."

## THE GOOD LISTENER

Once Grace started speaking, she found it incredibly easy to talk to Cheng Li about the Vampirates. Frankly, it was a huge relief to talk to *anyone* other than Connor, who was so overprotective and so ready to condemn the Vampirates — every last one of them — without even trying to understand their ways.

Unlike Connor, Cheng Li did not interrupt Grace with her own judgments. Instead, she listened closely, only interrupting very occasionally to ask for clarification of one thing or another. For the most part, Grace talked and Cheng Li listened, nodding supportively and encouraging Grace to share more and more of her experiences.

Looking at the clock by her bed, Grace realized she had been talking solidly for over an hour and a half. There was still so much to say. Initially, she had intended to censor the more extreme things that had happened to her during that time, but she decided that if she was going to confide in Cheng Li, and seek her help, then she had to tell her the full story. Either you trusted someone the full one hundred percent or you didn't trust them at all.

And so Grace found herself recounting everything, from her first arrival on the ship to her realization that Lorcan, dear Lorcan, was not a seventeen-year-old boy but a seven-hundred-and-nine-year-old vampire! She told Cheng Li about breaking out of her cabin and going to confront the Vampirate captain himself — and finding out that he was far from the monster that she had expected. And then she told Cheng Li the full story of the Feast and the donors and her horrific encounter with Sidorio.

"*He* sounds fascinating!" Cheng Li said. "Terrifying, but fascinating all the same. I wonder where he is now?"

"I dread to think," Grace said. "I hoped that when the captain banished him, he would just disappear into the wilderness. But I have a feeling that hasn't happened. And now there are other rebellions aboard the ship. I just wish I could help."

"But Grace, what could you *do*?"

It was a question worth asking. Grace thought hard. "I don't know," she said. "I don't know. But I just have a feeling, deep inside, that I *could* help them. I really want to.

You see, I think in many ways I'm responsible for what is happening."

"How?"

"Well, Sidorio was exiled because he attacked me. If I hadn't been aboard the ship, he might still be there."

Cheng Li shook her head. "No, Grace," she said. "You're being unfair to yourself. Sidorio wasn't only banished for holding you hostage and threatening you. He killed his donor, remember? That was his open challenge to the captain's authority. From what you've told me, the captain would have exiled him for that, whether you had been on board or not."

Grace felt a sense of release at Cheng Li's words, but then the heaviness returned. "That may be true, but what about Lorcan?"

She told Cheng Li about how Lorcan had protected her when Connor and the pirates came back for her, how he had stayed out after the Dawning Bell had sounded. And now she told of her two mysterious visions involving Lorcan, and the way he had acted during her spirit journey to the ship.

"Well, I know this isn't what you want to hear, but I agree with you," Cheng Li said. "It sounds like Lorcan did injure his sight when he stayed out in the light."

"If he did, then it's my fault," Grace said.

"You're being so hard on yourself. He knew the dangers, Grace. He must have. He made a choice . . ."

"To protect *me*!"

"It was still *his* choice."

They sat in silence for a time, thinking over each other's words. Then Cheng Li spoke again. "How did his eyes seem to you when you journeyed to the ship?"

Grace shook her head. "It was hard to see. His cabin was dark and he kept his head away from me, hidden by the bedding." She smiled, ruefully. "It was as if *I* had the sight problem."

"Grace," said Cheng Li, at length, "I think your journey to the ship took you by surprise — as well it might have. You did well to get there. But, for your own reassurance, next time you journey there, you must ask more questions. Find out the truth about Lorcan's sight. Find out if you can help. Perhaps they know how. Perhaps that's why they are calling you back like this."

Grace looked at Cheng Li curiously. "You really think *they* are calling me back?"

"Yes, of course," said Cheng Li. "Don't you? First, Darcy makes a spirit journey to you. And then you have these two visions of Lorcan . . ."

"But they came through the ring," Grace reminded her. "I touched the Claddagh ring and it heated up and that's when I had the visions. In fact, the ring grew warm before Darcy came, too. I felt really sick. And when I opened my eyes, there she was."

Cheng Li thought for a moment. "So, the first contact

you made after you'd left the ship was through Lorcan's Claddagh ring. When you touched the ring, it appears you somehow triggered a response from your friends aboard the ship."

Grace nodded.

"I'm sure they planned this," Cheng Li said. "I'm sure that's why Lorcan gave you the ring in the first place."

"He left me a note," Grace said. "He said it was something to remember him by. He said . . . he said to 'travel safe.'"

"Well, there you are, Grace," said Cheng Li, triumphantly. "He virtually told you what to expect. It was his way — the Vampirates' way — to help you travel back to the ship." She paused, allowing a fresh thought to arrive and flower in her mind. "When you went on your own journey to the ship — a spirit journey, we might say, or astral journey — did you touch the ring to initiate this? Did it heat up like before?"

Grace shook her head. "I don't think it had anything to do with the ring that time."

"Fascinating," said Cheng Li. "Okay. Then it seems to me that your connection is getting stronger. It's as if they used the ring just to get your attention — to prepare you, as it were. And now . . ."

"Now what?" Grace was anxious to hear Cheng Li's thoughts.

"Now it seems like they are ready to call you back more strongly."

"So now, I just have to wait for them to call me again?"

Cheng Li thought for a moment. "Let's try an experiment, shall we? Try touching the ring now."

Grace raised her thumb and forefinger to the ring. "It's cool," she said.

"Keep on holding it," said Cheng Li. "Tell me the moment its temperature changes."

Grace kept hold of the Claddagh ring, just as she had so many times before. Cheng Li sat there, watching. Finally, after several minutes had elapsed, she asked Grace, "Anything?"

Grace shook her head.

"All right then," said Cheng Li. "I think the ring is yesterday's news. Now you have to wait until they call you. But be prepared. It could happen at any moment."

"But how can I get back to the ship *properly*?" asked Grace.

"Don't ask me," Cheng Li said, with a smile. "Ask *them*! The next time you find yourself on that ship, that's the first question you must ask them."

Grace nodded. That made sense.

"It's getting late," Cheng Li said. "This has been fascinating, Grace, but I do think you should get some rest ahead of dinner. We will talk more of this. I shall keep thinking about it. Whenever you want to talk to me again, just say the word."

"Thank you," Grace said. "Thank you for listening."

"No, Grace," said Cheng Li. "Thank *you* for trusting me. It means a lot." She smiled as she headed toward the door, then turned. "I would advocate saying very little to the other captains about this. They'll doubtless want to know about your background. When they ask, I'd say nothing about the Vampirates. Not everyone is as open-minded as I am."

Grace nodded. Cheng Li stood by the door, observing her with a curious look.

"What is it?" Grace asked. "What are you thinking?"

"I'm thinking that the most fascinating part of all this," said Cheng Li, "is the connection you felt — that you still feel — to them. Other people would be grateful that they had escaped from that ship with their life. But you — you would willingly return."

"Of course!" Grace said. "Wouldn't you?"

Cheng Li considered the question. "Honest answer? I don't know. I'm a survivor, Grace. Like you, I'm curious about the world and its mysteries. But to willingly throw myself into danger . . . I really don't know if I *would* do that." She paused. "I remember one time, I asked your brother about you. And the way he spoke of you, he made you sound like the most extraordinary person."

Grace flushed with surprise and pleasure.

"And now that I know you for myself, Grace Tempest," Cheng Li continued, "now, I see that it is true."

With those words, Cheng Li finally slipped out, smiling,

into the corridor. Grace was exhausted — from her journey; from talking so much and from the relief of unburdening her secrets. As the door clicked shut, she lay back on the bed, her head seeking out the soft pillows, and immediately fell asleep.

18

## THE CAPTAINS' TABLE

At seven-thirty sharp, Jacoby Blunt knocked on Commodore Kuo's door.

"Come in," called the headmaster.

Jacoby pushed open the door, allowing Grace and Connor to step inside the headmaster's study before following them in.

"Good evening, everyone," Commodore Kuo said, looking up from his desk, where he still seemed to be hard at work. He was dressed as he had been earlier that day, but with the addition of a small pair of spectacles.

"I'll be with you in just one moment," he said, glancing back down to read over a document. Apparently satisfied, he inscribed his signature with a flourish of turquoise ink and slipped the document into his out-tray. Then he replaced the lid on his pen, removed his glasses and set them both down on the desk.

"A headmaster's work is never done," he said, standing to push back his chair and step away from his immaculately tidy desk. "Quick, let's make an escape before something else crops up requiring my input."

Slipping a dinner jacket over his waistcoat, he flashed a smile at Grace and Connor. "I trust you've enjoyed your first afternoon at the Academy?"

"Oh yes!" said Connor. "We had a great look all over. I had a long walk around the harbor and we saw the 'lagoon of doom' with its practice ship. And then I went for a swim in the pool. It was awesome."

"Excellent," said Commodore Kuo. "How about you, Grace?"

Grace flushed, remembering Cheng Li's advice to keep her counsel. "Oh yes, it's all wonderful," she said, hoping she could get away with being so vague. It appeared that, on this occasion, she could.

"Terrific," Commodore Kuo said, leading them over to the French windows at the back of his study. "I thought we'd all eat on the terrace as it's such a fine night." He opened up the doors and they immediately heard the buzz of chatter. Their audience was already waiting for them, it seemed.

"No going back now," Jacoby whispered, from behind the twins.

Commodore Kuo stepped out onto the terrace. Grace, Connor and Jacoby followed. A long table had been set out there, lined with candles and groaning with food — from mountains of king prawns to platters of dressed crab and lobster and, sitting simmering on hot plates, bowls of unimaginably sweet-smelling curries, rice, and noodle dishes.

The other teachers were already crowded around the table, drinking wine and nibbling on canapés. There were, Connor noticed, just four empty seats at the table — two at the head and two at the foot. Just enough for the headmaster, Jacoby, himself and Grace.

"Now, Jacoby," Commodore Kuo said, "why don't you take this seat here, while I introduce Connor and Grace to everybody?"

Jacoby did as instructed, slipping into the seat. At the same time, Commodore Kuo clapped his hands together. "Everybody, if I might have your attention?"

Ten men and women turned. Most were silent, looking toward the twins with interest. One of the women was still finishing off a conversation.

". . . certainly *not* in my day. It's a complete nonsense if you ask me."

Commodore Kuo beamed at her. "Captain Quivers, I'm as keen as mustard to know what you're talking about."

"I'm sure you *are*."

"Well, perhaps we may return to that presently, but

first, allow me to introduce you all to Grace and Connor Tempest."

There were various nods and smiles from along both sides of the table. And then Commodore Kuo put his hands together and started clapping. The applause was taken up by the seated teachers, though not quite uniformly. Grace noticed that Captain Quivers was the last to join in and didn't do so for long. She rather wished the others had proved so unenthusiastic. This was getting really embarrassing! She noticed that Connor seemed to be far less embarrassed. In fact, he was clearly enjoying the attention.

"Now," continued Commodore Kuo, "as you know, the Tempest twins are our guests at the Academy this week. Mistress Li extended an invitation on our behalf, and Connor and Grace agreed to take a break from their valuable duties aboard *The Diablo* to come and see what we're all about. And I'm sure that we're all very grateful to Molucco Wrathe for agreeing to allow these young pirates shore leave."

"Here's to Molucco!" cried Captain Quivers wildly, raising her wineglass and sloshing a little of the liquid on the otherwise pristine tablecloth. "Oops."

"Yes," Commodore Kuo said, smoothly. "Here's to Molucco." He raised his own glass, gave a chuckle, then moved briskly on.

"Well, I think it's high time that we tucked into this tempting feast," he said. "But just before we do, of course I would like to make some personal introductions."

He placed a hand on each of the twin's shoulders and began introducing each of the captains ranked along the table.

"Grace, Connor . . . this is Captain René Grammont, formerly of *The Troubadour* . . ."

"*Bonsoir, Monsieur et Mademoiselle Tempest.*" Captain Grammont nodded formally in the twins' direction.

"Next to René: Captain Francisco Moscardo, formerly of *The Santa Anna* and *The Inferno* . . ."

"*Buenos noches,* Tempest twins."

"Then," continued Commodore Kuo, "we have Captain Lisabeth Quivers, formerly of *The Passionflower.*"

"Hello, Grace. Hello, Connor. A great pleas —"

"And at her side, Captain Pavel Platonov of *The Muscovite.*"

"*Dos vadanya,*" said Captain Platonov, rising and giving an exaggerated bow. Grace noticed Captain Quivers give a little laugh at this.

"I hope you're keeping up," laughed Commodore Kuo. "Next we have Captain Apostolos Solomos of *The Seferis.*"

"*Kalispera,* Connor and Grace." Captain Solomos gave them a broad smile.

"And then there's Mistress Li, to whom you need no introduction." Cheng Li nodded formally to them. It was as if she and Grace had never had their recent heart-to-heart. Grace was pleased — Cheng Li was playing her part so that no one would suspect. "Now, Mistress Li has yet to captain a ship, of course, but we know that her future will be as illustrious as any of us seated here today. Indeed, I might go so far as to say she may well eclipse a reputation or two."

"Hear, hear!" cried the woman seated next to Cheng Li. "May I present Captain Kirstin Larsen of *The Krönborg Slot*."

Captain Larsen had the whitest blond hair Grace had ever seen, intensified by a deep suntan and eyes as blue as a mountain spring. Captain Larsen raised a glass to the twins, then drained it in one draught.

"Next, we have Captain Floris van Amstel of *The Koh-i-Noor*."

"Good evening."

"And Captain Shivaji Singh of *The Nataraj*."

Captain Singh bowed. Grace was tempted to mirror the gesture, but felt too inhibited so just nodded in response. She glanced at Connor. He was smiling from ear to ear. She could see how much he was enjoying meeting these captains who, according to Cheng Li, were among the most accomplished pirates in the world. Better yet, they appeared to be only too eager to meet Connor and Grace!

"And last of all, Captain Wilfred Avery of *The Barbary Corsair*."

Of course. They had glimpsed Captain Avery several times from afar since they had arrived at the Academy, but now here he was across the table from them, his tanned face covered with white wisps of mustache and beard.

"We'll be testing you both on all our names before dessert," he beamed at the twins. Grace found herself instantly liking Captain Avery. She smiled back.

"Now, you sit here, Grace," Commodore Kuo said, pulling out a chair for her between Cheng Li and Captain Solomos. Then the headmaster strode to the other end of the table and indicated for Connor to sit on the chair between himself and Captain Grammont. Jacoby was already sitting opposite and had begun tucking into the food.

"Connor, shall I help you to some of this green curry?" Captain Avery said. "It's really rather good."

"Yes, please," Connor said.

"What about a crevette?" Captain Grammont said, following suit.

A crevette? What was he talking about?

The captain extended a wooden spear bearing a plump king prawn toward Connor. "A crevette," he repeated.

"Oh, great, yes — thanks."

Gradually, Grace's plate filled up, too, and she joined the captains in their hearty feast. She wondered if they ate like this every night. She'd ask Jacoby later. She imagined that the other students, who had eaten an hour or so earlier, had received somewhat simpler fare.

"So tell us about yourself, Connor," Captain Grammont

said. "We know little about you except what an impressive start you have made aboard *The Diablo*."

"Yes, tell us," added Grammont's neighbor — Captain Moscardo. "Did you always want to be a pirate?"

"What he really means is," Captain Avery interjected, "did you read all about our exploits and dream of being one of us?"

Connor shook his head. "No, absolutely not."

Captain Moscardo looked disappointed, but Commodore Kuo laughed at Connor's answer. "Go on, Connor, tell them where you come from."

"Well, we were born in Crescent Moon Bay . . ."

There was a chorus of sympathetic sighs.

"You know it?"

"Connor, it's our business to know every bay, reef, and creek on the map," Captain Avery said softly.

"Oh, of course. Well, my dad was the lighthouse keeper there. But he died and we didn't have anyone left, so Grace and I —"

"What about your mother?" interjected Captain Quivers, directing the question at Grace.

"We never knew our mother," Grace said sadly. "She died . . . giving birth to us."

"How terrible . . . for all of you."

"So," said Captain Moscardo, "you two had nothing left in that godforsaken bay."

"No," Grace said. "So we took our dad's yacht and sailed away."

"But where were you going?" Captain Grammont asked.

"We didn't know then," said Connor. "We just knew we had to get away. We thought we'd sail down the coast and see where we ended up."

Captain Avery's eyes twinkled at him. "The first sign that you *do* have pirate's blood in your veins."

"And where *did* you end up?" Captain Moscardo persisted.

"We were caught in a storm," Connor said. "Our yacht was decimated by it and we both thought we were going to drown."

"Oh!" exclaimed Captain Quivers. "You poor, poor children."

"But," Connor continued, "I was rescued by Mistress Li and taken aboard *The Diablo*."

"And you, Grace?" inquired Captain Larsen, turning her crystal-blue eyes upon Grace.

Grace could sense, without looking, that Cheng Li was watching her carefully. The other captains now also stared in her direction. She took a breath, then spoke.

"I was rescued by another ship."

"Which one?" pressed Captain Larsen. "We know pretty much all the pirate ships in these waters."

"It wasn't a pirate ship," Grace said.

"Then what? A private vessel?"

"Something like that," Grace said, praying that Cheng Li would step in and rescue her. But help came from another side entirely.

"Details, details," Captain Avery said, with a smile. "The important thing is you both *were* rescued. And you found yourselves upon *The Diablo*. And what, pray tell, were your first impressions of Captain Wrathe?"

Connor knew he had to tread carefully, unsure of how the others felt about Molucco. Molucco wasn't a big fan of the Academy so perhaps the teachers here were similarly disparaging about him? On the other hand, Molucco's old sword *had* taken pride of place in the Rotunda.

"Captain Wrathe has been very good to me . . . to us," Connor said.

"He always had a keen eye for young talent," Captain Quivers said.

"And, Connor," Moscardo pressed forward again, "you weren't at all scared to learn swordplay?"

Grace felt the attention turn back to her brother. Part of her was a little resentful but mostly she was relieved. The less questions they asked her the better, she suspected. She took the opportunity to exchange a brief smile with Cheng Li.

Cheng Li winked at her supportively, then offered her the platter of salt-and-pepper squid.

"No." Connor shook his head. "I wanted to learn. It was my reward."

"Your reward?"

"For helping Captain Wrathe in an attack."

"You remember, Captains," Commodore Kuo interjected. "Wrathe pillaged Governor Acharo's house, up at Port Hazzard — and Acharo's two boys staged a revenge attack on *The Diablo*."

"Oh, yes." Captain Grammont nodded. "I remember."

"And Connor defended Captain Wrathe," added Commodore Kuo. "Saved his life, by all accounts."

"More's the pity," muttered Captain Singh. Connor made a mental note that here at least was one captain definitively opposed to Molucco.

Commodore Kuo caught Connor's expression and was quick to respond. "You'll hear some divided opinions here about Captain Wrathe, but I'm sure you're no stranger to those already."

This Connor had to admit was true.

"Frankly," Commodore Kuo continued with a smile, "Captain Wrathe has always divided opinion. As any character that large might. You're aware, perhaps, of the Pirate Federation and the rule of the sea-lanes?"

"Yes." Connor nodded. "Of course."

Grace listened intently, and carefully watched Connor's changing expressions. She wanted to see if his sympathies stayed resolutely with Captain Wrathe or if he might be wavering.

"Well, the Academy works closely with the Federation," continued Commodore Kuo. "Indeed, many of us here are involved in the hierarchy of the Federation. And we share and teach beliefs, such as the unequivocal respect for our captains' sea-lanes."

"We also," added Captain Grammont, "strive to build and develop productive relationships with the land powers, such as Governor Acharo. Acharo was always lenient to us. It was a major . . . well, let us say a major nuisance, Captain Wrathe attacking him like that. In the months since that attack, Acharo has changed his attitude and his policy toward us quite considerably. And that doesn't just cause problems along the coastline of his territory, he has powerful allies in the north, too. So this random action by your captain has caused ripples far across these waters."

Connor understood what they were saying, but he would not betray Captain Wrathe to them, not after everything Molucco had done for him. However, the other captains were warming to their theme.

"The more Captain Wrathe acts like a loose cannon," said Captain Singh, "the more danger he puts himself and other pirate crews in. Why, look at what happened just days ago with Captain Drakoulis."

Connor dropped his head sadly. "I was there," he said.

Grace could see that he was thinking about Jez. Of course he was.

"How terrible," Captain Avery said sadly.

"I was there," Connor repeated, "and I saw my comrade — my good friend . . . killed."

"A milestone in any young pirate's life." Captain Avery nodded, sadly.

"These are changing times," Commodore Kuo observed, as he pushed back an empty plate. "The world is progressing rapidly and piracy is changing and growing with every turn of the tide."

"Wrathe's sun is setting," announced Captain Singh. "The future lies not in individual attacks but in coordination, alliances, and proper strategy."

Connor listened to Singh's words. It was a tension he'd been aware of since he'd first arrived on *The Diablo*, when Bart had clued him into the different philosophies of Captain Wrathe and Mistress Li. Now, he saw just how much the mood of the time was with Cheng Li and the captains gathered here — and, more importantly, *against* Molucco. It made him fear for Captain Wrathe and his crew — and it made him question his own future. But he had signed up to the articles of *The Diablo*. There was no escape from that. He had pledged his duty, his very life, to Molucco. A decision, which — as Grace had told him — was now beginning, perhaps, to look a bit hasty.

Commodore Kuo suddenly clapped his hands together.

"Enough of this talk, everyone. I fear we've placed Connor in a difficult position with our . . . *observations* about Captain Wrathe."

Connor shrugged. "It's nothing I haven't heard before — at Ma Kettle's."

Captain Larsen gave a hollow laugh. "There's some difference between the tittle-tattle you pick up at a tavern and the opinions you receive here in this august company."

*Okay*, thought Connor, *she's another one not to tangle with. I'm learning.*

"Now now, Kirstin," said the headmaster. "Let's not vent our grievances on young Connor here. We want him to enjoy his stay at Pirate Academy, don't we?"

"Yes," chorused Captain Quivers and Captain Avery. Others around the table nodded.

"And," added Commodore Kuo, "when your stay comes to an end, Connor, we'll see how you feel about where your future lies."

Grace bit her lip. She hadn't expected the headmaster to make such an open offer to Connor. How would he respond? She watched, but her brother only smiled, saying nothing.

"And now a toast," said the headmaster. "To Connor and Grace. Please fill your glasses, everyone."

A decanter of inky-black liquid was quickly passed around the table. Shot glasses were filled.

"Has everyone got the cuttlefish grappa?" Commodore

Kuo checked. "Excellent. Well, please raise your glasses to Grace and Connor Tempest, who triumphed over the darkest of circumstances to make their way into the pirate world. Grace and Connor, we thank you for joining us here at the Academy this week. Here's to a most enjoyable and enlightening stay and, in the words of a far greater pirate captain than I — Plenty and Satiety, Pleasure and Ease, Liberty and Power to you both."

The other captains joined in the toast. Connor and Grace recognized the words as the Academy motto. They watched as the captains downed their glasses of grappa. It looked and smelled disgusting. Grace was happy not to have a glass herself.

After the toast, the spotlight fell away from Connor and Grace and the captains began chatting about the business of the Academy day, much like any other group of teachers — albeit these ones had cutlasses at their waists.

At last, Commodore Kuo glanced at his watch. "It's getting late," he said. "You kids had better get some sleep."

"Especially if you're planning on joining me for SSM tomorrow morning," said Captain Platonov with a smile.

"SSM?" asked Grace.

"Strength, Stamina, and Motivation," explained the Russian captain.

"It's the first class of the Academy day," added Cheng Li. "All the captains take it in turns to lead it so it varies from forms of yoga to inspirational discourses to —"

"A brisk ten K run!" interjected Captain Platonov. "We set off from the terrace at seven o'clock sharp."

"Sounds cool!" Connor said. Jacoby grinned.

Grace smiled too, but decided she might start *her* Academy day in a more leisurely way. "I'm going to bed," she announced, standing up. "Thank you for dinner. It was lovely to meet you all."

"You too, my dear," said Captain Quivers. The other captains nodded.

Connor drew himself to his feet. "On behalf of my sister and I, I want to thank you all for inviting us to Pirate Academy."

Grace smiled. She wasn't used to hearing him take to the stage in such a formal fashion.

"You're very welcome, Connor," said Commodore Kuo. "And please, do not let yourself be swayed by our petty squabbles with Captain Wrathe. We understand how good he has been to you and your sister. And we admire your loyalty to him."

Connor managed to smile, but his expression masked the increasingly complex thoughts swimming in his head. He was looking forward to getting to his room, where he could think about everything he had heard tonight. He was starting to feel a real sense of anxiety about the articles which bound him to Captain Wrathe. Suddenly, Grace's fears made absolute sense to him. He glanced along the table. Gathered here were the most influential pirates of their day and they all seemed to think that Molucco Wrathe's sun was setting. They also seemed to think that he, Connor, was something very special. Connor remembered the vision he had had of becoming a captain. He was determined to make that happen. In the future, perhaps, he'd have to select his allies and mentors far more carefully.

"Come on," Grace said, appearing at his side. "Let's walk back to our rooms."

"What? Oh yes. Yes, sure. Jacoby, are you coming, too?"

"Actually," said Commodore Kuo, "I need a brief word with you, Mister Blunt."

Jacoby nodded his assent to the headmaster. Grace and Connor said good night to their new friend. Then they set off across the terrace toward their accommodation block. The twins said not a word to each other as they walked along in the moonlight, each locked in their own secret world of thoughts.

19

## POWDER CREEK

The moon is high and full and illuminates the small ferry-boat, beating its way steadily along the creek.

"I see land, Captain," Stukeley says. "Is this the place?"

"Yes," answers Sidorio. "Why? Are you hungry now?"

"Yes, Captain. I'm hungry indeed."

A sly laugh. "Good."

Sidorio rows the boat right up to the shallows, then jumps out into the water, pulling the boat, with Stukeley inside it, up onto the meager pebble beach. Now Stukeley jumps out, too.

"What is this place, Captain?"

"Powder Creek," Sidorio answers.

"I swear, Captain — you know every last place along this coast." Stukeley is impressed.

At that moment, Sidorio steps forward. Behind him is a wooden sign, flapping in the breeze.

# WELCOME TO POWDER CREEK
### "Leave nothing but footprints, take nothing but memories."

"Come on," Sidorio says brusquely. "Let's not lose any time." He begins trudging across the beach. He seems to know where he is going. Stukeley follows, struggling to keep up with the captain's lengthy strides. Something has caught the captain's interest and Stukeley has learned that when that's the case, you just have to keep up the best you can and await further instructions.

So far — all things considered — events haven't gone too badly. Although there has been rather a lot of talk of a glorious future, an army of men, and a fleet of ships when, right now, there just appears to be a stolen ferryboat, two surfboards and the two of them. Still, you have to start somewhere, Stukeley supposes. At least the captain has dreams. *Big* dreams.

Sidorio is standing still. Is he waiting for Stukeley to catch up? How decent of him, thinks Stukeley. He doesn't usually exhibit such courtesies. He runs toward the captain — and feels water between his toes, thinking that his old boots have seen better days.

As he draws level with Sidorio he sees that the captain is talking to someone — in fact, to two people. Two young women. At Stukeley's arrival, one of them looks over and laughs.

"Oh aye? Who's this then — little and large?"

"This is my lieutenant," Sidorio says. "His name is Stukeley."

"How do," says Stukeley, giving a little bow.

"Well, you're a curious pair and no mistake," the girl responds, nudging her friend, who begins to giggle.

"All right?" Stukeley says with a grin. "What are you two lovely lasses doing out here at this hour?"

"Ain't it obvious?" answers the first girl in a bored tone. "We're waiting for our ship to come in."

Sidorio smiles and points over his shoulder, back toward the ocean. "Maybe your ship *has* come in."

Stukeley sees something in that smile. The girl misses it. Of course she does. But Stukeley has seen it before. It is a sign. The game is on.

"I can't see any ship," the girl says, utterly oblivious to what is about to happen. "Just some third-rate rowing boat."

"*Third-rate?*" Sidorio says, always quick to rise to anger. It will be down to Stukeley to provide the charm. It is always down to Stukeley to provide the charm.

"It's big enough to take two beautiful young ladies out on a moonlit voyage," Stukeley says. "Well, it is once we take the surfboards out."

"You surf?" asks the first girl, her interest suddenly heightened.

"We surf," Stukeley confirms rather proudly, only lately having acquired the skill.

"Let's see you in action then." She likes him. He can tell. Ladies tend to like him.

"No," Sidorio says, shaking his head. "No surfing."

"What the captain means," Stukeley interjects, "is that we'd much prefer to take you for a voyage first. While the water is so calm."

"It *is* calm, isn't it?" says the girl, stepping toward Stukeley.

"It's a small boat," Stukeley says, "but it's big enough if you squeeze in tight."

"We'll all keep nice and warm that way, won't we?" says the girl, taking Stukeley's arm. He trembles. In times past, he'd have been feeling a hundred other desires at this point — but now there is only one.

"Come on, Lily," the girl says, looking back over her shoulder. "I'll take David and you can have Goliath to yourself and we shall all have a spin around the creek."

Her friend, Lily, giggles and steps toward Sidorio. He smiles at her, his mouth opening to reveal his twin gold teeth. Lily gasps, suddenly sensing the danger that her friend has been blind to. Stunned by fear into silence, Lily allows Sidorio to propel her toward the boat.

Stukeley gets there first, removing the surfboards and throwing them onto the shingle. The other girl watches him, oblivious to Lily's alarm.

"I'm Pearl," she says, "and this is my cousin, Lily. Where did you two fellas come from, anyhow?"

"From Hell," Sidorio says, lifting the terrified Lily into the boat.

"Your mate's a joker, isn't he?" Pearl says to Stukeley as he lifts her into the boat and pushes it free from the shingle into the water.

"Oh, yes," Stukeley replies. "The captain's a big ol' joker."

⊱—⊰

The sound of two limp bodies falling overboard doesn't register much, out in a dark, deserted creek in the very depth of night. Now you see them, now you don't, as the molasses-like waters suck them down to their resting place. Down where we'd best let them lie. It doesn't pay to dwell on such things.

Back on the surface, the ferryboat floats in the moonlight.

"That went well," Stukeley says, licking his lips to draw the last drop of blood into his mouth.

"You're learning fast," Sidorio says.

"We're a pretty good combination, I reckon."

"Perhaps."

"And how could I ever be lonely around such a sparkling wit and conversationalist?"

Stukeley's irony is lost on Sidorio. It is probably better that way, thinks the lieutenant. Sidorio is calm now. Soon he will sleep.

There they lie, on either side of the ferryboat, rocking gently on the oily waters of Powder Creek. Another night, another little adventure. Stukeley brings up his arm, resting his head on his hand. He gazes up at the moon, watching as the globe of light is smothered by smoky clouds. Now there is no light to pierce the darkness of the night. Trying to block out the sound of Sidorio's snores, he closes his eyes and falls into a happy little dream.

# BELONGING

Connor zipped up his black and gold Academy tracksuit and glanced at the clock on his bedside table: 6:50 a.m. He'd already been up twenty minutes. He would never have leaped out of bed at 6:30 for a day at CMB High. But here at the Academy, even after his late night, he woke up raring to go. Just like on *The Diablo*. Maybe, he thought with a slight pang of guilt, even more so. Was it really only two days since he'd left the ship? Already, it seemed a world away. Now he felt even more disloyal. *But*, he reminded himself, Captain Wrathe had given his blessing to the stay at the Academy.

Perhaps it would have been better if he had never come. Then all he'd have known of the pirate world was *The Diablo*. But Connor's ideas about piracy were changing fast. Now, he saw what Cheng Li had told him time and time again. There *was* a bigger world of piracy out there. And now it was opening up to welcome him in. *If* he had the guts to go for it.

A knock at the door pulled him out of his thoughts. He opened it to find Jacoby, dressed in the same tracksuit. It bore the Academy insignia — the dagger, compass, anchor, and pearl, just like the charms which Commodore Kuo wore on the chain around his neck.

"Top of the morning!" Jacoby said. "I hope you're ready for some punishment."

"Always," Connor said, with a smile.

"Shall we pick up Grace?" Jacoby asked as they headed along the corridor.

Connor shook his head. "My sister isn't a big fan of early morning exercise."

Jacoby nodded. "Well, in that case, she certainly won't enjoy what Platonov has in store for us."

As he followed Jacoby outside, Connor saw that Platonov and a gaggle of other students were gathered on the terrace, all dressed alike in their tracksuits — performing their warm-up stretches. A pretty girl smiled and waved at them both.

"Hi, Jasmine," Jacoby said, smiling goofily. "Meet Connor Tempest. Connor, this is Jasmine Peacock." He added, in a whisper, "The foxiest girl at Pirate Academy."

Jasmine smiled at Connor. He was dazzled by her green

eyes and silky black hair. He struggled for something to say to mask his awkwardness. "Perfect weather for a run, eh?" It was lame, but it was words.

She smiled, then she bent her body in two and smiled up at him again through her outstretched legs. He flushed. She could see he couldn't take his eyes off her, but she didn't seem to mind. Connor's embarrassment was saved by Captain Platonov blowing his whistle and clapping his hands. Then the captain set off at a brisk run across the Academy lawns and the students fell into line behind him. Jacoby was right behind Connor, close enough to whisper in his ear.

"She wants you, Tempest! The Peacock has staked her claim."

Connor shook his head and increased his speed. They began their run around the Academy gardens. As anticipated, Platonov set a challenging pace. Connor felt his legs waking up and his heart pumping. There could be few better ways to start the day than with a run.

As they descended the hill toward the harbor, he looked back to the balcony outside Grace's room. The curtains across the French doors were closed. He smiled to himself. Grace must still be fast asleep. Lazy bones!

---

Fifty minutes later, Platonov's runners were nearing the home stretch. The captain had drawn them together so they were running in a closely organized pack, three in each row. Connor had Jacoby on his left and Jasmine on his right, their steps in perfect unison. The end of their run was in sight. Connor could feel himself hitting "the wall," but knew he could push on through. It was just a matter of willpower.

"Now, let's chant," Captain Platonov said.

It was just the distraction Connor needed. He heard the captain and his fellow students begin to chant as they ran:

"Pirate captains rule the sea," began Platonov.

*"Pirate captains rule the sea,"* chanted back the students.

"A ship for you and one for me!"

*"A ship for you and one for me!"*

"My sword is ready to attack."

*"My sword is ready to attack."*

"No one's gonna hold me back."

*"No one's gonna hold me back."*

Connor beamed from ear to ear as he too began to join in the chant.

"We hoist the skull and bones up high."

*"We hoist the skull and bones up high."*

"To let you know the end is nigh!"

*"To let you know the end is nigh!"*

"Don't tangle with this deadly crew."

*"Don't tangle with this deadly crew."*

"'Cause we'll make mincemeat outta you!"

*"'Cause we'll make mincemeat outta you!"*

Connor looked first to Jacoby, then to Jasmine. It was great running as part of the pack.

"We're in command of the High Seas."

*"We're in command of the High Seas."*

"We're taking power by degrees."

*"We're taking power by degrees."*

"Goin' out to cause commotion."

*"Goin' out to cause commotion."*

"This is our time and this is our ocean!"

*"This is our time and this is our ocean!"*

Now the others were quiet but Captain Platonov called out:

"Who's the baddest?"

Without hesitation, the students called back:

*"We're the baddest!"*

Captain Platonov continued: "Who's the meanest?"

Connor joined the others in shouting back:

*"We're the meanest!"*

Platonov shouted once more: "Who rules the ocean?"

Connor, Jacoby, Jasmine, and their classmates all roared back:

*"We rule the ocean!"*

At that moment, Connor felt powerful, unstoppable. They *were* the future of piracy. In years to come, if all went to plan, they'd each have a fleet of ships and thousands of pirates at their command. The ocean *would* be theirs — and much of the land, too. It was a heady thought.

Platonov turned. They had made it back to the terrace. He gave a brief clap. "Okay, class. That was a good run. Now, make sure you cool down properly. Then showers, then breakfast. And *don't* be late for the first class of the day!"

# 21

# THE WOUND

Grace opened her eyes and was thrown into deep confusion. She had slept heavily, but for how long? What time was it? And where was she?

The room in which she found herself was large and unfamiliar. An expanse of black-and-white marble tiles swept off toward a pair of open French doors, with sheer curtains billowing in a faint breeze onto a balcony beyond. Where was she? Was it possible that she hadn't even properly awoken and was trapped in one of those strange dreams which opened up like a Russian doll — tricking you into thinking you'd woken up when in fact you were still just as tightly enclosed in sleep?

She raised herself up on a large mound of pillows to gain a better view of her surroundings. As she did so, her head felt heavy. However long she *had* been sleeping, it hadn't refreshed her. She felt decidedly groggy. There was a small carafe of water at the side of the bed and she poured out a glass. The water was deliciously cool on her tongue. She drained the contents of the glass in a few gulps and refilled it. As she drank again, she glanced about the room.

It was light and airy. There was a tall ivory-colored armoire, with mirrors on the front reflecting a matching chest of drawers. Across the room was a dressing table made entirely of mirrored glass, off which the light bounced back into the center of the room. A tall cabinet was filled with books, but it was glass fronted and this too was bathed in light, making the panes opaque and preventing Grace from reading the titles on their spines. On the walls were navigational charts and paintings of fine old ships. Above the chest of drawers hung a particularly imposing woodcut of a ship.

Grace pushed back the bedclothes to take a closer look. Her head was still heavy but she was sufficiently *compos mentis* to realize that she was in the room she'd been assigned at the Pirate Academy.

She stood staring at the ship, a distant memory stirring inside her. At the foot of the picture were the words *The Pequod*. Of course! Grace recognised it as the "whaler" from *Moby Dick*. It had been one of her dad's favorite books and he had read it to the twins several times. He had a wonderful old edition of it, with woodcuts just like this one. Perhaps there was a copy of it in the cabinet of books. She walked across the floor, the marble tiles cool under her feet. The glass doors of the cabinet were closed and a small key was resting in the lock. She twisted it and the lock released. Even so, the wood had warped a little and she had to pry the door open.

The shelves were crowded with books, some familiar — including *Moby Dick* in what looked to be the very same edition as her father's — but others less so. Her eyes were drawn to an old volume called *Lives of the Most Notorious Pirates*. The book was covered in navy-blue cloth with the gold outlines of a skull and crossbones and a ship at sea decorating the spine. She reached into the case and took out the book, finding that it was encased in a three-sided box. It must be quite old and precious, she thought. Gently, she eased it out of the box and carefully opened up the yellowed pages.

Then there was a sudden noise, like footsteps. Grace turned, jumping to find another girl across the room. The girl looked equally surprised to find Grace there. For a moment, they stood still and silent, taking the measure of each other. Slowly, Grace realized that she was simply looking at her own reflection in the mirrored door of the armoire. She felt exceedingly silly. She must still be half asleep. She stepped nearer to the mirror, examining her reflection. She looked a mess — her eyes bloodshot and her hair sticking out in a hundred directions. Still holding the book, she raised her other hand and tried to push the strands of her hair into some kind of order.

This, she realized, was going to be a job for two hands, so she set the book carefully on the floor and returned to the mirror. She continued to tweak her hair until it met her satisfaction. It wouldn't have been good enough for Darcy, she thought with a smile. "A young lady really oughtta give her hair a hundred stokes of the brush at night," she had once told Grace. Grace had taken her advice but had grown bored, lost count, and then felt incredibly sleepy. Just like she did now.

Even after a few minutes' standing, she felt as tired as before. It was rather like being back on the Vampirate ship during those first days. Indeed, if she hadn't been able to see, beyond the sheer curtains, the balcony and the view of the harbor beyond, she might have imagined herself to be back on the ship. Her eyes thirstily drank in the turquoise water of the harbor, glinting temptingly in the sun. She realized, from the direction of the sun, that it was morning.

Feeling woozy again, she decided she was going to have to sit or lie down once more. Well, perhaps she'd at least be able to read rather than simply fall back into sleep. She reached down for the book and, having retrieved it, stumbled back toward the bed. As she threw her body down on the counterpane and closed her eyes, she felt as if she were in motion. The bed itself seemed to be moving.

As Grace lay there, her limbs still and heavy as boulders, the movement of the bed increased. It was both a familiar sensation and a new one. She realized, with excitement, that she was being taken back to the Vampirate ship again. But this time, it appeared the bed was going to carry her!

To her amazement, the iron bed rose up from the marble floor, hovered a few inches from the surface, and then, gathering speed, took flight toward the balcony. Surely the bed would be too wide for the narrow opening? She held her breath and shut her eyes, expecting an impact, but either the bed narrowed or the doorway expanded because soon she was seeing the balcony from the other side, as the bed soared higher and continued its flight over the Academy terrace far below. She sat up on the bed, feeling more steady than she had just now when it was still rooted to the floor. Her energy seemed to be similarly restored and she was able to enjoy the rush of the breeze on her face and the stunning view down over the Academy gardens. There was the jacaranda tree and the lecture theater down by the harbor. And there, running by the dockside, was a pack of students. Grace remembered Captain Platonov talking about the morning run. She searched for Connor in the crowd, but all the students were dressed alike and she was simply too high up now to identify him. She wondered what the students would think if they looked up and saw her. Part of her hoped they wouldn't, but another part made her wish Connor would glance skyward to witness her extraordinary ride.

Within seconds, unnoticed, the bed flew beyond the edge of the land and was speeding over the harbor and out beyond the tall stone arch, out to the open ocean. The speed of travel increased. The landscape raced by as it had on Grace's last journey. Ocean blended into rock into sky in one continuous flowing stream of light.

Then the mist engulfed her, crisp and thick as newly fallen snow. It was cool and she folded her arms across her chest instinctively. But it never became too cold. She luxuriated in the mist, letting its soft arms engulf her. All too soon, it began to part. She found that she was indoors once more, still on a bed, but not lying fully on it — hovering a couple of inches above it. When she glanced up, there were silk hangings above her head. The ornate stitching on the cloth was familiar. She realized that she was no longer on the Academy bed but back on her bed in her cabin on the Vampirate ship. Just as if she had never been away.

Except, the candles were not burning. Not all of them, anyhow. When Grace had occupied the cabin, she had been surrounded by burning candles at all times of day and night. Now, just one tall candle was lit. It burned away in a glass, set on the nightstand. It made her ponder.

The candles had always been a mystery. They had never seemed to burn down and, even when she had thought she'd extinguished them, they had sparked back into light. She had realized that they were not in her control. But what might it mean that now — now that she had left the ship — only one candle was lit?

She stepped down from the bed, keen to renew her acquaintance with the rest of the room. There was the little writing desk. She had taken several of the pens and notebooks from it and those that were left were in disarray. The pens were scattered on and around the desk, and the jar they had been stored in had fallen to the floor. Instinctively, Grace reached out for it. But, as before, she was unable to properly touch anything on the ship. The mess remained.

There was further disarray on the other side of the room, where the hairbrush and other items had fallen from the dressing table. The ship must have passed through rough waters to cause all this chaos. Cushions had been thrown from the bed to the floor. Grace reached out her hands again, in a last attempt to clear up the clutter. But, instead of gripping the cushions, her hands closed on thin air.

Her eyes fell on the gramophone, with the pile of old records stacked beside it. Indeed, a record was turning even now, though somehow she had not registered the sound earlier. A woman's voice — strangely familiar —

was singing above a background of violins and the crackle of the ancient recording:

> *I wish I could forget you, yes I do,*
> *But to forget you would be like forgetting*
> *my own name. . . .*

How, she wondered, had she not heard this when she first arrived in the room? Perhaps the mist not only cut off her sight but her hearing, too, carrying her into a state of suspension while it wove its curious magic about her. But now the song and the singer filled her head. The woman's voice was high and breathy:

> *But to forget you would be like forgetting how to smile*
> *To somehow fail to remember how to speak. . . .*

She stepped closer to the gramophone, watching the black disc turn and trying to read the writing on the label. She couldn't be sure, but she thought she recognized the name there. She sat on the edge of the bed, waiting for the song to finish.

> *Yes, to forget you*
> *Would be worse, much worse,*
> *than never having met you.*

At last, the disc slowed and eventually stopped turning. Grace looked down and saw that she had been right.

*Miss Darcy Flotsam,*
*accompanied by the Royal Palm Revue,*
*sings Songs of Love.*

Grace smiled. So Darcy Flotsam had once made a record. It was strange hearing her friend sing on the ancient disc. The vinyl record was over five hundred years old! It truly was a wonder it had survived. She wondered how much the recording had distorted Darcy's voice, and realized that she had yet to hear her friend sing for real. She'd have to ask her next time she saw her.

Just then, she noticed for the first time that she was not alone in the cabin. This time, her eyes did not deceive her — there were no mirrors here. She was fully alert, perhaps even in a state of heightened sensation. And there, as clear as day, was the chair, and there, sitting in it, was Lorcan. How could she not have seen him before? He appeared to be asleep, bundled up in a blanket which she recognized as one he must have grabbed from the bed. He looked far from comfortable, one arm hanging down over the side of the chair, the other clamped over his eyes and forehead.

Grace stepped closer. Lorcan's breathing was uneven, coming in fits and bursts as if he were in the throes of a dark dream. Should she wake him? He did seem to be deeply asleep, in spite of her arrival and Darcy's singing. She looked at him, hoping he might wake of his own accord. How she longed to see his blue eyes again — they had always been such a comfort to her. But when she had last visited the ship, his face had been turned away from her and in shadow. Now she was similarly frustrated as his arm rested over his eyes. Oh, if only he'd wake up, she thought.

Grace stepped backward, sitting down on the corner of the bed, watching Lorcan as, in times before, she knew *he* had watched her. It was strange watching somebody sleep. It felt intrusive, as if you had caught them at their most defenseless. And as you watched them, motionless, you couldn't help but wonder — if only for a moment — whether they had died, and watch furiously for signs of life.

Cheng Li's voice filled Grace's head, reminding her of the questions she must ask Lorcan. Sitting with Cheng Li in her room at the Academy, it had seemed entirely logical that she must ask Lorcan and the others some very searching questions. But now that she was here, the importance of those questions receded. All she wanted was to see him open his eyes.

Suddenly, Lorcan gave a deep groan and his whole body twisted. Had he woken? No, he had simply reached some new portal of sleep, for he assumed a new position in his chair — but then stopped still just as suddenly as if they'd been playing "musical statues." His hand had fallen from his face and now hung down on the other side of the chair. A dark shadow fell across his face. Grace leaned nearer, realizing with a shock that it wasn't actually a shadow. There was a livid bruise spreading out around Lorcan's eyes, purple at the edges but darker, almost black, toward the center. His eyebrows were singed and — Grace felt sick to see — over the eyelids and brows, Lorcan's pale skin was blistered and burnt. It looked unbelievably painful.

She felt a pull on her heart, remembering that he had tried to prevent her from seeing this devastation last time. That was why, though he had allowed her into his cabin, he had remained in the darkness and kept his face hidden from her. He had been protecting her, as he always did.

Grace could barely look at his terrible disfigurement. She stole another brief glance but it was too much. She turned away with a sob. As she did, a hand reached out toward her shoulder.

"Grace?"

"Oh, Lorcan," she said, turning slowly back toward him.

She had expected his eyes to open but, even though he was awake now, they remained tightly closed.

"Grace, what are you doing back here?"

She was confused. Hadn't *he* called her back, then?

"Never mind me," she said. "What about *you*?"

She couldn't help the tears that were welling in her eyes. But she must fight them. She must be strong for him. She sought for words to distract her, to distract them both.

"What are you doing in *my* cabin?" she asked, trying to smile.

He smiled faintly, his mouth rising at either side but his eyes remaining steadfastly shut. "My, how possessive you are. I come here sometimes . . . to think about . . . things."

"And to play old records?" Grace said, her heart still weak with sorrow.

"Darcy has a fine voice, doesn't she?"

"Yes," Grace said. "Yes, she does."

"You should hear her sing for real."

"Lorcan" — she couldn't defer the moment any longer — "Lorcan, what happened to your eyes?"

He said nothing, simply shrugging.

"Tell me," she said.

"It's not so bad," he said. "I'll be all right in time."

She braved another look at him. "Your face looks so raw," she said. "Can you not open your eyes, even a little?"

"Still a bit too sore," he said. "But they're nothing for you to trouble yourself over."

"How long have they been like that?" she asked, though she was sure she knew the answer. "What happened?" As if she needed to ask.

He did not speak, raising his hand back over the wound. She was unsure if he was doing so to spare her distress at the sight of it or because even the faint light of one candle was too much for him to bear.

"It was three months ago, wasn't it?" She was unable to

hold back any longer. "It happened the morning Connor came onto the ship. Darcy sounded the Dawning Bell but you stayed out on the deck, even though it was getting light. You stayed out . . . to protect me." She was close to tears. "This is my fault."

"No, Grace. It's no one's fault."

"Yes, it is. You can't go out in the light. Only the captain can. But you went out and stayed out — to protect me."

"You needed me."

She shook her head. He was such an honorable man. Only, he wasn't, she reminded herself, a man. He was an immortal. Vampires lived forever, didn't they? And, thanks to her, he might now be blind through eternity. Then another dark thought took hold. What happened if a vampire took on an injury as harsh as this? Could Lorcan die a second time?

Her heart was racing and her head was spinning. She needed to see the captain now. He'd have the answer. But if he did, how could he let Lorcan suffer like this? When she'd visited the last time, Lorcan had said that the captain's powers were being tested. Did this mean that even he could not help Lorcan? This was terrible, just too terrible.

She looked back toward Lorcan but the mist had already started to separate them. Despairingly, she stretched out her hands to him. Though he could not see, he must have sensed her because his hands reached back toward hers.

But their fingers could not touch. An invisible curtain still held them apart. The mist began to descend more thickly.

"No!" she cried. "Not yet. I can't leave now."

But the mist was now so thick she could no longer even see him. Still, she reached for his hands, though she knew in her heart it was useless. Then the motion began and she was thrown backward by it, torn away from him. She felt herself racing away, this time without the bed, as if she were bodysurfing on the most urgent of tides.

But why? she thought. Why am I torn away just when I need to stay?

The thoughts were still turning over and over in her mind as she opened her eyes and found herself once more in her room at the Academy. She lay, sprawled on the bed, on top of the pillows and counterpane.

There was a knocking at the door and she sensed from its loudness and urgency that whoever it was had been knocking for a while.

"Come in," she called, bringing herself up to a seated position.

"Grace!" Connor bounded into the room, walking straight past her and flinging open the curtains to the balcony. "Grace, what are you still doing in bed? It's a glorious morning. I've been for a run and . . ."

Connor finally looked back at his sister.

"Grace, you look awful. What's the matter?"

Grace sighed, pulling herself up into a sitting position.

"I slept really heavily. It must be . . . must have been all that food at dinner last night."

Connor laughed. "Well, go and have a shower — quickly! We've been invited to sit in on Captain Quivers' Knot class after breakfast. It's only the juniors but it should be fun. Come on, Grace. Get a move on! We don't want to miss breakfast!"

Grace looked at her brother. He had absolutely no idea what she was going through. She ached to tell him but she couldn't. Not yet. He wouldn't understand. He didn't want to know about the Vampirates. Far better he focus all his energies on Academy life. One battle at a time, she told herself. Once she'd made sure he wasn't going back to *The Diablo*, then — and only then — would she try to tell him about her own adventures.

22

# KNOTS

Jacoby, Jasmine, and a couple of other students joined them on the terrace for a quick breakfast. It was already a bright, hot day and Grace was thankful she had had the wit to grab her sunglasses as Connor had propelled her at high speed out of her room.

Jacoby chatted away to Grace in a friendly manner and she made all the right noises in return though, of course, her mind was still far from the Academy. It didn't seem to bother Jacoby in the slightest. He was the most easygoing of companions. Grace toyed with a muffin and a small glass of orange juice as the kids around her made light work of pancakes, eggs, bacon, sausage, and fruit.

"We better get a move on," Jacoby announced, as the school bell began to chime. Grace couldn't help but think of the Dawning Bell aboard the Vampirate ship — the bell that sent the vampires back inside. The bell that Lorcan had ignored to save her. She felt guilty to be wearing sunglasses, thinking how safe she was, compared to her friend. Her friend, who she had caused such pain.

"Where did you say your first port of call was, Connor?" Jacoby's bright voice cut across her dark imaginings. It was lonely to feel so bleak in such sunny company.

"Captain Quivers' Knot class," Connor answered his friend.

Jacoby laughed. "I see they're starting you off with the basics. OK, I'll show you guys down there. Come on, Grace. How is your marlinspike hitch, by the way?"

Grace looked at Jacoby quizzically through her dark shades.

He laughed. "Hmm, I'm not sure you've had quite enough coffee for this."

A few minutes later, Jacoby delivered Grace and Connor along one of the tributaries of the Octopus to a small, bright classroom full of low desks and excited little kids, making the kind of high-pitched noise that little kids make on a sunny morning. Grace realized that she probably ought to take off her glasses indoors. As she did, her eyes were assailed by the bright colors that buzzed from every surface of the room — from the kids' paintings and collages which lined the walls to the models of sea creatures proudly displayed on shelves. Looking up, she saw that the students had even made their own mobile of swords, to mimic the glass cases in the Rotunda. Each had painted their own imagined sword and written their name proudly beside it. Captain Samara Pescudo of *The Meltemi*, Grace read with a smile.

At the front of the class, Captain Quivers was handing out small baskets of colored ropes to kids aged, Grace guessed, between six and seven. Beside the teacher, one of the young students carefully presented each of his classmates with something like a thin rolling pin. His fellows rushed back to their desks with a pin and a basket of rope each.

Just then, Captain Quivers looked over and smiled up at them.

"Good morning, Grace and Connor. How are you both this beautiful day?"

"Very good," said Grace, smiling brightly in spite of herself. She liked Captain Quivers. "Thanks for letting us crash your class."

"Crash is the right word," said Captain Quivers, "— fifteen juniors and this amount of rope! I hope you're good at *un*tying knots!" She chuckled. "You go and grab a spare seat, my dears." She turned back to the class. "Once you have your knot pin, please attach it to your desk. Come on, now, you should be able to do this for yourselves by now. Let's try to show our guests how clever and self-sufficient we all are."

The twins watched as the kids clicked the pin into position at the front of their desks. It formed a small bar jutting out at the front. The more organized kids were now laying out strands of different colored ropes on the desk. Grace could sense a competitive spirit rising between some of the would-be pirates. She and Connor grinned at each other as they took their seats. Already, Grace felt herself starting to come back to life, back to the Academy.

"Okay then," said Captain Quivers, "is everyone organized? Good. Well, take a blue rope, and tie me an overhand knot."

Immediately, tiny hands buzzed into action, reaching for the small lengths of rope and knotting them expertly around the bar at the front of their desks.

"Lovely work. Now take a red rope and do me a figure of eight."

Once more the hands whisked up the rope and expertly wound it around the length of wood. Captain Quivers cast her eyes about the room, nodding encouragingly. "Remember, nice and tight, Nile," she said, smiling at one of the younger-looking boys. He nodded earnestly, drawing the rope together more tightly.

"And now," said Captain Quivers, pausing to glance around the room. The kids were silent, holding their breath with excitement, waiting to know which color of rope and knot would be called next. Grace stifled a giggle. It was wonderful to see such youthful exuberance — she suddenly felt very old. I'm just fourteen, she thought. It isn't so long ago that *I* was a kid in a classroom like this. But now . . . now she might as well have been as old as Captain Quivers, there was such a gulf of experience between her and these bright-eyed children.

". . . grab a green rope and make me a . . . carrick bend."

Immediately the air was full of green rope, twisting and turning as tiny fingers and thumbs made light work of Captain Quivers' latest challenge.

"Lovely, lovely, lovely!" said Captain Quivers. "Now, class, we have two special visitors with us today. Everyone say hello to Grace and Connor Tempest. Grace and Connor are visiting us from the very famous pirate ship, *The Diablo*. Yes, that's right, *The Diablo*. Who can tell me who the captain of that ship is?"

Immediately hands shot up, with some of the kids dangerously near to straining their limbs with effort.

"Yes, Mika?"

"Captain Molucco Wrathe," the girl announced with perfect diction.

"That's right, Mika. Well done. Hands down again, everyone."

There was a buzz of excited chatter as the kids took proper notice of Grace and Connor for the first time.

"Now, since we have Grace and Connor with us today, I

thought you might like to take a break from your rope-work to ask them just a few questions about life on a real pirate ship — if that's okay with you?" As she turned to Grace and Connor, the children's hands were already up and straining.

"What's Captain Wrathe like?" asked a small, ginger-haired boy at the front of the class.

"Good question, Luc," said Captain Quivers.

"He's an amazing man," said Connor. "Imagine all the exciting stories you ever heard about him and then some more!"

"Is it true he has a pet snake?" inquired a girl in the center of the class.

"Absolutely." Connor nodded. "He's called Scrimshaw and he lives in Captain Wrathe's hair."

There was a sigh of awe around the room, and a loudly hissed, "I told you!"

Captain Quivers nodded at another girl. "Yes, Samara, a question from you?"

"I want to ask Grace — did you always want to be a pirate?"

Grace shook her head. "No, not really. It all happened by accident."

The girl looked disappointed.

"Have *you* always wanted to be a pirate?" Grace asked her.

"Oh, yes." Samara nodded very rapidly. "My name is Samara Pescudo and one day I am going to be a pirate captain, just like my mummy and daddy." Others around her nodded their agreement. They had been well schooled already, thought Grace.

"Have you done much fighting?" one of the boys asked Connor.

"Yes," Connor answered. "You have to be ready to defend yourself and to attack at all times on the ship."

"Which swords do you use?" another boy asked, too excited to remember to raise his hand. All eyes turned to Connor.

"I use a rapier," he said.

"Just a rapier?" the boy persisted.

Connor nodded. "Just a rapier."

"We generally teach combat with two swords here," Captain Quivers interjected. "You'll see this lot in action a little later."

Grace was taken aback. Weren't these kids a little young to be wielding swords?

"It's Combat Workshop this afternoon," one of the kids told Connor. "Are you going to come along and watch us?"

Connor shrugged. "I'm not sure. Would you like us to?"

"Yes!" the boy shouted, beaming. The others joined in the chorus.

"It is rather a special Combat Workshop, today," Captain

Quivers told Connor and Grace. "It would be well worth coming along. We have a little surprise in store for our young pirates."

"What surprise, Captain Quivers?" It was little Samara again.

"Well now, it wouldn't be a surprise if I told you, would it?"

"We're going to get our swords today!"

"That's a good guess, Luc, but I'm not saying anything. My lips are sealed." Captain Quivers mimed zipping up her lips.

"We're either going to get our swords or maybe Mister Tempest's going to do a demonstration or something."

"Well," said Captain Quivers, "you'll just have to wait and see, won't you. Now, do we have any other questions for Connor and Grace or shall we return to our knots?"

A hand shot up again.

"Yes, Mika?"

"Please, Connor, which knots do *you* use on *The Diablo*?"

"To be honest," Connor said with a smile, "I only know a few of the basics — a figure of eight, a reef knot . . . and a sheet bend. You guys could probably run rings around me."

The children laughed.

"Well," said Captain Quivers, "let's put that to the test, shall we?" Smiling, she passed Connor a spare basket and a pin. "Here's some rope, Connor. And some for you, Grace, dear." She gave Grace another set. "And I'm going to show everyone a new, very useful knot — it's called the marlinspike hitch . . ."

There were worse things on a sunny morning than sitting in a class of lively children, playing around with colored ropes, thought Grace. They were a cheerful and amusing bunch, and Mika, with whom she sat, was just delightful — barely seven years old but already a born teacher, patiently showing Grace how to tie each knot that Captain Quivers announced — the marlinspike hitch, the lariat loop, the bowline.

She wasn't sure if it was being cocooned in the warm classroom, the friendly atmosphere Captain Quivers had created, or just the irrepressible energy of the kids themselves, but Grace realized that she was thoroughly enjoying herself — for the first time in a very long time. The rope-making challenge allowed her to forget for a moment the bigger dilemmas she faced. Perhaps it was the simplicity of just taking colored ropes and twisting them into knots. Sometimes you got it right first time; sometimes, you didn't. But, even then, there was no problem — you just unpicked your work and had another go. If only her life was always as simple as this.

Grace felt a sudden sense of protectiveness over Mika and her young classmates. She glanced around the room at the eager apprentice pirates, their heads full of dreams of sun-drenched oceans and easy adventures. It all seemed so safe here — tying colored knots and making clay models of octopi or mobiles of swords or even messing about with Captain Avery on boats in the harbor. But, out beyond the harbor walls, another world lay in wait for them — a world Grace could not even have imagined at their young age. It would change them, just as it had changed her and Connor.

She glanced over at Connor now, amused to see him flailing about with the colored ropes. He seemed to have gotten into a real mess, and was being helped out by two of Captain Quivers' young students. Possibly, he was just humoring them. It was good to see him laugh and joke with the kids, here in a room where the swords were only made of cardboard and, at worst, would give you a paper cut. Suddenly, Grace realized that she wasn't filled with sadness at what was going to happen to the kids in the room. It was two other kids she was in mourning for — two kids who, through force of circumstance, had had to grow up far too fast.

23

## LITTLE DOVES

As the bell chimed for afternoon classes, Jacoby led Grace and Connor through the sunny grounds to the gymnasium complex. Inside the bright, high-ceilinged gym, they found Cheng Li, who had changed out of her usual clothes and was dressed instead all in white, her feet bare. As usual, she did not look up to greet them as they came into the room. Her face was bent low over a bowl of incense. In her hands was a small, leather-bound book.

"Please take a seat to the side," she said, still without looking up.

Jacoby removed his shoes and encouraged Grace and Connor to do the same. Then the three of them walked over to a row of seats at the side.

Cheng Li paced carefully across the matted floor. She lit a second bowl of incense and waited for the smoke to rise.

The school bell chimed once more. Shortly afterward, the gymnasium door opened and in trooped the fifteen children of the lower class, all dressed in white robes like their tutor. They look so sweet — like little doves, thought Grace, as they took their positions, spread evenly across the mats, though the wings on their backs were just two short lengths of bamboo held in place by straps. As the children settled silently into position, Cheng Li turned toward them and began speaking softly.

"First check your head. This is neither tilted up nor down. It does not lean to the side, nor is it crooked. It floats perfectly, like the sphere of the full moon." She paused. "Your eyes glance neither to the left nor to the right but remain in the center. Your sight extends from the center to each side, *without* your eyes moving. Behind your observing eyes, behind your eyelids, is an eye which sees deeper into all situations you encounter. Engage this all-seeing eye now."

The children stood like statues, as their tutor surveyed them coolly, moving between them as softly as a breeze through blossom.

"Now, let your attention fall to your neck and shoulders . . ." Cheng Li took the young students through similar mantras until their bodies were fully engaged. Every now and then she stopped to gently turn a neck, or correct the posture of a spine. Grace was dazzled by the control the young students exerted. Either they were naturals or they had already been rigorously trained. Whichever, it was undeniably impressive, but at the same time a little spooky. In Captain Quivers' Knot class, they had still seemed like children. Here, it was as if Cheng Li was moulding little warriors out of clay.

"Now, drop both shoulders, keep your back straight — do *not* stick out your rear — and put strength from your knees to the front of your feet. Extend your stomach so that your hips will not be bent."

Once more, the young pirates made the infinitesimal adjustments to their posture to meet Cheng Li's satisfaction. Nodding, she made her way back to the front of the class. "I am impressed. You have all learned your lessons well. You have laid the foundations for becoming not merely pirates, but warriors."

She turned and picked up the leather book she had been holding before. "And now," announced Cheng Li, "Let's get working on a fresh attack strategy. Divide yourself into your combat groups . . ."

At these words, the children deftly rearranged themselves across the mats, and Cheng Li began her briefing. "Today, we'll start to look at another technique for deflecting an enemy's blade," she said. "I'm going to show you how to deliver a diagonal downward cut."

There was a buzz of excitement as Cheng Li continued her instruction.

Grace leaned across to Jacoby. "Aren't these kids a bit young to be learning about diagonal cuts?" she asked.

Jacoby smiled but shook his head. "This is key stuff," he said. "When these kids return to their parents' ships, they have to be able to defend themselves."

"Well, yes," said Grace, "I understand that. But these children are only, what, seven and eight years old? Shouldn't they be allowed to just play, like normal children?"

Jacoby shook his head once more. "They're not *normal* children, Grace. These kids have been chosen to be the future leaders of the oceans. One day each of them will control a fleet! They *have* to start young. Besides, do they *look* like they're having a bad time?"

Far from it! That was perhaps what bothered Grace the most. In front of her eyes, Mika, Samara, Nile, Luc, and all the others had mutated from the joyful young kids of the morning class into tiny killing machines. As they swung their twin bamboo sticks up and down, they looked like lethal clockwork toys.

"What do *you* reckon to all this, Connor?" Jacoby asked.

Connor said nothing. He was watching the kids intently, using his own hands to mirror the maneuvers Cheng Li demonstrated with her katana blades.

Jacoby smiled, but Grace frowned. She leaned back into her seat, continuing to watch the lesson in silence. As she did so, she reflected on her own actions. She had brought Connor here to the Academy, to rescue him from certain death aboard *The Diablo*. She had wanted him to fall under the spell of the Academy and he was showing every sign of doing so. But, Grace thought with a shiver, had she taken him out of the frying pan and into the fire? Was there no escape anywhere from death at the hand of another's sword?

It wasn't, she reminded herself, sword fighting in itself with which she had a problem. She had brought Connor here because the Academy reared its pirates to act in a strategic, coordinated way. If Connor stayed here and embraced the Academy's teachings, he would become a more thoughtful pirate. He would almost certainly return to the oceans as a captain, not as mere rapier fodder. But still, Grace found little comfort in the thought. Whether Connor stayed on board *The Diablo* or took up residence at Pirate Academy, the same fate ultimately awaited him. He would be engaged in swordsmanship on a daily basis and his life would be endangered with the same frequency. Her only chance to save him was to dissuade him from being a pirate altogether. But that seemed a remote possibility now.

"Isn't this amazing?" he said, suddenly turning to her. "The Academy is *such* a cool place. I'm so grateful you persuaded me to come here. It's *really* opened my eyes."

Grace smiled, though she felt sick. But worse was to come.

"This is excellent work," Cheng Li said, facing her

students. "You have learned our teachings well. Do not for a moment grow complacent, however. You are like young birds at the beginning of a long journey. Though today takes you a step closer to your destiny, there is still far to fly."

At these words, the gymnasium doors opened once more and in strode Commodore Kuo, dressed in an elaborate red silk robe, bearing the Academy insignia of the dagger, compass, anchor, and pearl. Behind him came two students of the upper class, pushing a tall lacquered chest on wheels.

The young children on the mats turned around excitedly. There was a buzz of chatter but Cheng Li silenced it with a glance.

"Commodore Kuo," she said. "We have just seen exemplary work from the lower class."

"I'm delighted to hear this," said Commodore Kuo, smiling. He strode forwards to address the young students himself, but not before giving a friendly nod in Grace and Connor's direction.

"Now, my young warriors," he said, addressing the children on the mats, "the time has come for you to step up to the next level of your learning here. The prefects will now pass among you with silk sashes. These must be bound tightly across your eyes."

As he spoke, the two older students who had arrived with him moved across the mats, drawing each small child to his or her feet and blindfolding them. In a moment or two, all the younger students were blindfolded with red silk sashes, of the exact same hue as the headmaster's robe.

"Now, remember what I told you before," Cheng Li said, "there is observation and there is seeing. The lids of your eyes do not need to be open to see. You must sense your enemy's sword even when you cannot observe it."

As she spoke the words, the headmaster took a key and opened up the lacquered chest that had been brought with him. The two prefects helped him to open it and it fell away, revealing rows of gleaming swords.

"Now," Cheng Li said, "using your all-seeing-eye, and making no sound, make yourself ready."

Connor turned to Jacoby. "Wow!" he said. "What's going on?"

Jacoby simply smiled. "Watch and learn, my friend. Watch and learn!" At these words, a shiver shot down Grace's spine. She felt a deep sense of foreboding. In spite of this, she could not remove her eyes from Commodore Kuo.

The headmaster beckoned Connor over. Instinctively, Connor stood up and padded toward him. Grace watched as the headmaster whispered something in Connor's ear. Connor nodded and Commodore Kuo lifted a pair of small swords from the lacquered chest. Connor carried the swords over to one of the children on the mats, extending them toward the child by the hilt.

After a moment, the small hands suddenly shot out,

each seizing a sword by the hilt. Connor let go. Now, the child held a daisho in each hand and a broad smile broke across his face.

Between them, the older kids and adults bestowed the same gift upon each of the children. At last, they all stood in a row, still blindfolded, their small fists gripping the hilts of their sharp, steel blades. Grace could see them struggling to suppress their excited smiles.

The prefects closed the lacquered case. Connor sat back down next to Grace. Commodore Kuo stood before his diminutive warriors as Cheng Li passed swiftly behind them, removing their blindfolds. The children's eyes shone like jewels as they had their first sight of the daisho in their hands.

"Let these blades be your most treasured possessions," said Commodore Kuo. "These swords represent our trust in you and our belief that you are the future of piracy. Use these weapons not in sudden anger nor for quick gain but with precision and with honor in the way that your teachers show you. These blades in your hands now connect each of you back through time to the noble line of pirates who came before you. They connect you forward into the future to the line of pirates to come. But, most importantly, your daisho connects each of you to one another — to your comrades at the Academy and also in the Pirate Federation."

He bowed toward the kids, then walked over to Connor and Grace.

"I'm so glad you could be here to see this," he said, "It's one of the most exciting moments in the Academy year."

Grace nodded, unable to speak for the risk of saying the wrong thing.

In front of her, the prefects were lining the kids back up again.

"What's happening now?" she asked.

"Ah, well," said Commodore Kuo, "now, they're being taken to the sword store. They don't keep their swords with them at this age. We wouldn't want any mishaps!"

Her work done, Cheng Li padded forward across the mats to join them.

"I was just saying how pleased I was that Grace and Connor could be here to witness this," said the head-master.

"Yes, indeed," Cheng Li said.

"Why," said Commodore Kuo, "it seems only yesterday that an especially talented young seven-year-old was standing on that mat, stretching out her arms to receive her daisho." He smiled. "And now look at you, Cheng Li."

She smiled in the way she did when she was just a little embarrassed.

Now, Commodore Kuo turned to the twins. "So, Connor and Grace. You may not have come here in time to receive all the training we can offer, but there is still plenty to share with you, should you want to stay."

Grace glanced at Connor. What was he thinking? She no longer knew which way she wanted him to jump. Perhaps it was time to stop interfering and let him make his own choice. She remembered thinking that he had made a mess of things by signing Captain's Wrathe's articles. And how she had believed that she was better at making decisions for the two of them. And where had it led them? To an Academy which created killing machines out of seven-year-olds. And then there was the small matter of her unfinished business with the 'ship of demons.' *Oh yes,* she thought. *Yes, I really am blessed with great decision-making skills.*

"Grace, you're looking a little peaky," said Cheng Li.

She turned to see Cheng Li smiling at her.

"Would you like to go for a walk?" Cheng Li asked.

Grace considered for a moment. She knew that Cheng Li was offering more than a walk. They'd have a chance to talk about things and for her to tell Cheng Li about her latest journey to the Vampirate ship. It was a tempting offer, but suddenly Grace hungered to be alone.

"Thank you," she said. "Actually, I thought I might go for a swim before supper."

"A swim?" Cheng Li said, amused.

"Yes," replied Grace. "I missed out on Captain Platonov's run this morning and I could really do with some exercise."

"Great idea!" Connor said. "We'll come with you, won't we, Jacoby?"

"Sure," Jacoby said. "We might even ask Jasmine to come along." He whispered to Connor, "I never pass up the chance to see her in a bikini."

Commodore Kuo beamed at the three of them. "Excellent," he said, "excellent. Have fun, guys."

They turned and walked out of the gym. As the door swung shut behind them, Commodore Kuo turned to Cheng Li. "It's good to see Connor and Grace making new friends, isn't it?"

"Oh yes, Headmaster," said Cheng Li, smiling. "Yes, isn't it?"

"I don't suppose I can tempt you to a bout of swordsplay before dinner?" he asked. "For old time's sake."

"I'd make mincemeat of you, John," she said, smiling.

Commodore Kuo laughed. "At least, I'd die a happy man."

"Death is death, John. Whether you die smiling or with tears in your eyes, it amounts to the same thing. A whole heap of nothing."

## 24

## EXILE

Grace went through the motions of swimming and, later, dinner with Connor, Jacoby, and Jasmine. It wasn't as elaborate as the previous night's dinner with the captains, but it was more relaxing and the Academy food was still delicious. However, Grace wasn't there — not really. She felt herself withdrawing from the Academy and letting all her thoughts drift to the Vampirate ship. Perhaps if she made things right there, then she'd be able to settle in properly here. Wasn't that how karma was supposed to work?

After dinner, Jacoby suggested a pool tournament. Connor was keen and Jasmine said she'd join them later, after she'd finished some reading she had to do for the next day's classes.

"Brains as well as beauty, you see," Jacoby said to

Connor as Jasmine departed for her room. "What about you, Grace? You'll join us to shoot some pool, won't you?"

Grace smiled but shook her head. "I'm exhausted," she said. "I think I'll have an early night."

Jacoby looked a little disappointed. "Just us then," he said to Connor. Grace bid them both good night. And as she headed off toward the accommodation block, she heard Jacoby saying to Connor, "Let's make this more interesting with a wager . . ." She smiled. The two of them were incorrigible.

As Grace crossed the terrace, she saw a familiar silhouette standing there, looking out to the harbor.

"Cheng Li."

Cheng Li turned toward her. "Hello, Grace. Off to bed already?"

"Yes," said Grace. "It's been a long day."

Cheng Li shook her head. "You're not talking to the headmaster now, Grace. There's no pulling the wool over my eyes. We share *everything*, remember." She reached out her hand to Grace's shoulder.

"Come on, a quick walk round the Academy gardens won't kill you. You can get it off your chest — whatever's bothering you. And the fresh air will ensure you get a great night's sleep. Come along."

"Cheng Li, I'm just not sure I fit in here. Connor does, but I don't think I do. And I'm worried for Connor — I thought if I got him away from *The Diablo* he'd be safe. But since we've been here, he seems even more set on being a pirate. So we're no safer here than we were with Captain Wrathe!"

"We brought Connor here because we both know this is what's best for him," Cheng Li said. "He'll have a glorious future if he stays at Pirate Academy. In a few years, he'll return to sea as a deputy captain, just like I did."

"But will he be safe?" Grace persisted.

Cheng Li came to a standstill, smiling. "You each have such an admirable desire to protect the other. It's understandable after everything you've been through. But don't you see, Grace, there's no such thing as safety in this world, *our* world?"

"You mean the *pirate* world," Grace said. "But we weren't born into that world. Maybe it isn't for us."

"What then?" Cheng Li said. "Tell me what other plan you have? Would you prefer it if you and Connor headed back to a life of drudgery in Crescent Moon Bay? Really? Is that what you'd like? Because if it is I can borrow one of the Academy tenders and sail you down the coast tomorrow morning. We can have you checked into the orphanage by teatime!"

Grace looked hard at Cheng Li.

"No," she said, after a lengthy pause.

"What was that, Grace? I'm a little hard of hearing."

"I said NO," Grace repeated. "That isn't what I want."

"Of course it isn't!" exclaimed Cheng Li. "You may not have been born into the pirate world but it has claimed you . . . well, it's claimed Connor at least. We still have to work out exactly where *you* fit in. But we will. We *will*."

Grace sighed. Cheng Li's words were invigorating as well as reassuring.

"Get some sleep," Cheng Li said. "It's been a long day and tomorrow won't be any different. Life at the Academy is no free ride. Maybe tomorrow you'd like to do some combat practice with me? I heard a rumor that you're actually pretty talented in that area, and it might help you work out some of your tension."

Grace smiled. "Could be fun," she agreed.

"All right. Well, let's see how you feel in the morning. Off you go, now. And promise me, you'll stop worrying about Connor. Everything is working out just as I planned."

"Just as *we* planned," Grace corrected her.

"Yes, of course, that's what I said."

Up in her room, Grace tried to sleep but, tired as she was, the minute she changed into her nightclothes and got into bed, she felt wide awake. She closed her eyes, willing her mind to come to rest, but it was just no good. Instinctively, she reached for Lorcan's Claddagh ring. It had helped to calm her before. *Before* the visions had begun. But now, as she pressed it between her thumb and forefinger, nothing changed. The temperature remained constant. There was no vision of any kind. It seemed as if Cheng Li was right. The ring had served its purpose. Nevertheless, touching it brought her closer to Lorcan in her own mind and that, she concluded, could only be a good thing.

She remembered someone saying that if you couldn't get to sleep, the worst thing to do was to stay in bed. So she threw back the covers and walked across the room toward the balcony. She opened up the shutters and stepped out into the cool night air, lifting her face into the breeze, then looking out across the grounds, down to the harbor. The Academy looked so beautiful by night. Some of the students had taken musical instruments out onto the terrace and were playing now. They were actually pretty good — their haunting, rhythmic, almost tribal music both calming and utterly suited to the hot night. Grace watched them play, then shut her eyes, letting the music flood her senses and conjure its own pictures.

Suddenly, Grace's head was full of a different, but similar, music — the music that she had heard on board the Vampirate ship as an overture to the Feast. She stood dead still, recognizing the start of another vision. Every time, it seemed, the vision came a little differently.

Now her mind's eye was full of the vampires and

donors making their way to the banqueting hall, several decks below sea level, dressed in all their finery. This didn't seem to be a fresh vision, but rather a memory. She remembered the elaborate sense of ceremony and etiquette. She remembered the fine china, crystal, and linens and the strange lack of symmetry of a table set along only one side. And the hundreds of faces she had never seen before — the pairings of vampires and donors talking softly together across the table and then leaving the banquet to go to their cabins, where "the sharing" would begin. Connor had been appalled at the idea of "sharing." Was it really so repellant? The vampires simply had a need that had to be met and the captain, in his infinite wisdom, had devised a humane way for this to happen.

A peal of laughter brought her attention back down to the kids on the terrace below. They were talking between songs. Then, once more, her head was filled with the strange rhythmic music and her thoughts raced back to the Vampirate ship. Was it possible, she wondered, that a Feast was taking place there this very night?

She felt a sudden jolt. Her body lurched forward, against the balcony. Using the railing to steady herself, she drew upright again. As she did so, she realized that the balcony had torn itself away from the building and that she was now hovering in midair above the terrace, looking down at the musicians. One of them looked up and smiled, but he did not appear to really notice her. She clung on tightly as the balcony began to swoop through the air, out toward the harbor and through the night.

This time, she had more of a sense of the exhilaration of motion. She actually enjoyed the journey. The wind raced through her hair and she felt as if she were hurtling on her own private chariot through space and time. The sky was setting and all around her were the hot oranges and pinks of the dying light, as if the earth and sea were on fire and she was riding through the flames — a part of it, yet disconnected.

At last the flames gave way to velvet darkness and she lost the sense of rapid movement as she became enclosed in a blanket of black. Then, just as suddenly, the sky was filled with starlight and the balcony continued onward, her eyes dazzled by the light of the stars and moon. It was the most incredible adrenaline rush she had ever felt. How blessed she was, she thought, to be able to experience the world in this way. How many others were granted a chance like this?

Then the stars began to fade as the balcony entered the inevitable mist. She was a little sad to leave the night sky behind but she knew that it was only a staging post on her journey. So she submitted to the mist, aware that it was like the anteroom which led onto the Vampirate ship. In a matter of seconds, she would be there again. She sighed, looking forward to seeing Lorcan. This time, she decided, she was going to talk to the captain. This time, she was going to find out more about Lorcan's wound and what she could do to help.

As the mist slipped away, she found herself back on the deck of the ship. Just as before, she could not feel her feet on the boards — as if she were hovering just a little above them. It was nighttime and Darcy had lit all the lamps. Music was playing. Familiar, percussive music. Grace felt a frisson. She had been right. Tonight *was* the night of the Feast.

The deck was crowded with vampires, taking their *passagiata* — an extended stroll around the deck in all their finery — before the Feast got underway. A group of them were striding straight toward her, as if they did not see her. She darted to one side, just in time. A moment later and they would have trampled her underfoot. She turned and watched them pass. They appeared utterly unaware of her — no doubt solely possessed by the hunger that had been growing in them and which would, in a matter of hours, at last be sated.

She watched another pack of them take their turn around the deck. One of them stared at her strangely as he passed, his head almost twisting off its axis. Grace shivered. She remembered seeing him at the last Feast she had witnessed. She didn't know his name but his face had unnerved her then, just as it did now. But, thankfully, in an instant he was gone and another gaggle brushed past her, without even glancing in her direction.

She made herself as comfortable as she could against the deck rail, still feeling as though there was an invisible barrier between the rail and her body. She was pleased to be back, though. And this time, she was going to get some answers.

"Well, look who it isn't!"

Grace was tugged out of her reverie by the familiar cockney voice.

"Darcy!"

There, before her, was Darcy Flotsam, resplendent in a dress of sky blue chiffon with a trim of gold sequins. "Figurehead by day, figure of fun by night!" exclaimed Darcy, reaching out her arms to hug Grace. They passed straight through her.

"Oh!" sighed Darcy. "I hoped you was back for real this time!"

Grace shook her head. "I wish I was, Darcy. But I don't know how to make it happen. Do you?"

Darcy shook her head. "You'd have to ask the captain about that. All I know is that when you're on a visit — like you are now, like I was to that pirate ship of yours — well, the only people who can see you and hear you are those of us who've got a connection with you. The captain explained that much to me."

Grace nodded. Now she understood why some of the ship's inhabitants appeared to stare right through her, while to others — like Darcy and Lorcan — she seemed as real as the very boards of the deck.

"Oh, Darcy," Grace said. "After I saw you last time, I did what you said. I went to see Lorcan."

Darcy nodded sadly. "He's in an awful way."

"I know, Darcy, and it's all my fault."

Darcy shook her head. "No, Grace. He knows you think that. But it *isn't* your fault."

"Yes," Grace insisted, "it is. But I'm going to help him. I'm going to find a way back here *properly* and I'm going to find a cure."

Darcy looked at Grace sadly.

"What is it? Has something else happened?"

"His sight shows no signs of improving," said Darcy, "but it's worse than that. He refuses to take blood. He's growing so weak. He has taken to his bed. Oh, Grace, I don't know how long he can survive. Tonight is the Feast but Lorcan won't even leave his cabin for blood. It's as if he's given up."

Grace was chilled by this latest turn of events. She had to do something to help — but what? She didn't know how long she could stay this time, and not being able to touch anything or anyone was becoming more and more frustrating.

"I must go," Darcy said. "I wish I could stay and talk, but I must go and take my seat at the table."

"Of course," Grace said, "You go. You must. I'll wait here, as long as I can. Come and look for me later."

Darcy nodded. Her face was wet with tears.

"Fabulous dress!" Grace called after her.

When Darcy turned again, she was smiling through her tears and she gave Grace a delicate curtsy.

The strange Feast music grew to a crescendo and Grace watched as the deck completely cleared. She imagined the twin lines of vampires and donors arriving at the banquet hall and taking their places. She was tempted to go and watch but something held her in place up here — some power which she couldn't quite explain.

She felt her eyes drooping with tiredness. No. She tried to fight it, not wanting to be carried away from the ship — not after so brief a visit. But her lids were heavy and there was nothing she could do. Her eyes closed and she fell into a deep state of relaxation, as if she were floating on the dark waters once more. She did not fight the feeling, knowing that it would carry her wherever it wanted.

The next thing she heard was a cry, or rather, a roar. Her eyes opened and she found, to her surprise, that she was still on the deck of the Vampirate ship. She hadn't been taken anywhere else — she had simply drifted off to sleep. She was unsure of how much time had passed, but the music had faded now so she sensed that the Feast was over and that the vampires and donors were in their cabins, where the sharing was taking place.

"Stop!"

She recognized the voice immediately. How could she not? It was strong and firm, yet it did not rise above the volume of a whisper.

She scanned the deck and saw the captain striding out across the boards, calling to someone.

"I said, stop!"

She turned and saw that the captain was not addressing one vampire, but three of them. They turned their faces back to the captain. Grace recoiled. Their eyes were aflame. She had seen Sidorio look like this before, but witnessing a group of them in this frenzied state was all the more terrifying. She recognized two of the vampires. She had seen them talking — conspiring, she now realized — on her previous journey to the ship.

When they spoke, their words were like flames, licking across the deck toward the captain.

"Need more blood. Need more . . ."

"No," said the captain. "You have taken your fill. More than your fill."

"Need more . . ."

Now Grace saw, as they turned in her direction, that the gaggle of vampires held three donors tightly within their grasp. The donors looked terrified.

"Stop," said the captain once more. "Release the donors. Return to your cabins."

In answer, the vampires let out a communal hiss, their words now unintelligible. Grace shivered, glad that she was hidden from view. She did not think that these vampires would be able to see her, but she didn't want to take any chances all the same.

"I will tell you only once more," the captain said now. "Release the donors."

"Or *what*?" crackled a reply.

"There is no alternative," the captain said coolly. "You have only one option. Release them."

"The captain's way is not the *only* way," returned the hiss.

"The captain is not the *only* captain," crackled another.

"The ship is not the *only* ship," added the third.

"Enough! Release them!" said the captain. At his words, the deck was ringed with a sudden flash of light. The vampires leaped out of its path, pulling in their limbs to protect themselves. At the same time, the donors threw themselves toward the light.

"Go inside," the captain said to them, calmly but urgently. Weak as they were, they needed no repeat of the order.

The vampires had thrown themselves together upon the deck and now the captain approached them once more. Darkness restored, the creatures rose again, their eyes bright, though the fire that had burned before was now dull.

"I have been patient," the captain said, "but my patience has run dry."

The vampires looked at him with eyes that were now full of fear and regret. In a matter of moments, thought Grace, they had gone from being monsters to looking like guilty schoolchildren. But it was all too easy to remember the horror she had seen before.

One of them addressed the captain. "Sometimes this need grows out of control, Captain," he wheedled.

"We are not all as disciplined as you," said a second.

"Sometimes our desire seems to feed upon itself," spoke the third.

"I am aware of all these things," the captain said, still in his measured whisper.

"Then help us," hissed the first.

"You have rejected my help, Lumar," the captain said, sadly. "There is no more I can do for you. It is time for you to leave this ship."

"No, Captain. Do not say such things." Lumar cowered before the captain.

"If Lumar goes, then we must follow," said one of his companions. Some of the vampires' former malevolence was returning in their voices — the wings of the threat opening out like a moth.

"Indeed," said the captain, unmoved. "It cannot be any other way."

"But where shall we go?" asked the third — a girl.

"To find Sidorio," hissed her companion, greed spilling from his voice. "Sidorio will help us to meet our needs."

Grace shivered. So they knew — or at least suspected — that Sidorio was out there in the night, waiting for them. Was it wise of the captain to let others out to join the first exile? Wasn't he just swelling the risk of an enemy force building?

"Go, then," the captain said. "Go and find your other way."

His voice was heavy with disappointment, Grace thought. He turned and headed back toward his cabin.

The three exiled vampires still clung to the deck rail, as if to conspire further.

"I *said* — leave!" The captain turned suddenly and ran toward them. As he did so, the cape he was wearing flashed with veins of light. Above them, the sails of the ship glowed and began to flap. Bolts of fire shot across the wooden boards of the deck.

Grace had to close her eyes to protect them from the glare. When she finally opened them again, the vampires had disappeared.

The captain stood at the deck rail, his head in his hands.

Grace left her shelter and went over to him.

He seemed unaware of her until she was at his side, reaching out her hand toward the strange material of his cape. Even this, she found to her frustration, was beyond her touch.

"Grace," he whispered, "Grace. What are you doing here?" He did not sound pleased to see her.

"I came back to help," she said. "I know things are wrong. I just want to help."

"You cannot help." His whispers filled her head. "You must leave at once, and do not think of returning."

"But, Captain . . ."

"This is how it must be, Grace." He did not turn toward her, his mask facing straight out to the ocean.

"But, Captain," she said again, with tears in her eyes, "Lorcan is so badly wounded. And it is all my fault . . ."

"Yes," the captain said, turning at last. "Yes, so now you know the result of your coming to the ship. And that is why you must stay away."

Tears were flowing down Grace's face now, but she would not give up. Not yet.

"Please, Captain. If I came back properly perhaps I could help."

"You think you could cure Lorcan's blindness? How do you propose to do that? Tell me!"

His voice remained a whisper but she could hear the anger within it nevertheless.

"Speak, child!"

"I don't know, Captain. I don't know how I could help. Or even *if* I could."

"It's very simple, Grace," said the captain. "There is only one way you can help. Go back. And stay away."

Grace couldn't believe her ears. Was this how it ended? Here, on this deck? Was Lorcan destined to stay blind? And now that he refused to take blood, what then? She couldn't bear to leave things like this — his fate unknown. But the captain had spoken and he had no more words for her. He turned and walked slowly back across the deck.

Grace stood there, at the edge of the deck, tears falling once more. They were still falling as the mist enclosed her and she was carried away from the Vampirate ship — *never to return.*

## 25

# ZANSHIN

"Grace! Grace, it's Connor!"

"What do you want?"

"Can I come in?"

"All right."

Connor and Jacoby waited outside.

The door opened and Grace poked her head around it.

"Morning, sleepyhead!" Connor said, reaching out his hand to ruffle her hair.

"Stop it!" she said. "You know I *hate* that!"

"You look rough as guts, sis. What's up?"

"I slept badly, okay? What time is it anyway?"

"Ten to seven. Jacoby and I are going to SSM. It's T'ai Chi with Captain Solomos today. Are you up for it?"

Grace shook her head. "I'll catch you later," she said, closing the door.

Connor shrugged and smiled at Jacoby. "I told you, she's *really* not good in the mornings!"

———

Connor knocked at Grace's door again. He waited.

"Yes?" The cry was faint.

"Grace, it's me!"

He heard footsteps. The door opened again.

"I told you, I'm not coming to SSM —"

"Grace, we've *done* SSM. It's almost half past eight. What planet are you on this morning?"

"I'm just really tired, okay?"

"You look upset."

"I'm upset you woke me up at ten to seven! And now again! I just need to rest. Is it really such a big deal?"

"But it's breakfast time. And then Commodore Kuo's giving this cool lecture about swordsmanship. It's for the final year students but he's asked us along."

"I don't think I'm going to make any classes today," said Grace. "Not this morning, anyway."

"But, Grace, this is the headmaster —"

"Enjoy!" she said, closing the door in his face.

Connor frowned. It was a real honor being invited to attend this class by Commodore Kuo. But he knew from experience that once Grace's mind was made up, it was implacable. Well, let her sleep! He wasn't going to let her put a cloud over *his* day. He turned away and set off in search of Jacoby.

On the other side of the door, Grace slumped down onto the floor and put her head in her hands. She couldn't stop thinking about the Vampirate ship — about Lorcan's fading well-being and the captain's cruel words to her. He might as well have run a blade through her heart.

---

Commodore Kuo nodded to Connor and Jacoby as they entered the lecture theater.

"Ah, Mister Tempest and Mister Blunt. Good morning, my friends. Do take a seat."

Connor wondered if he should explain Grace's absence, but the headmaster didn't seem perturbed so perhaps it was best to say nothing.

Commodore Kuo was standing by a podium, on which he had set some papers and a small, leather-bound book. The lecture theater had enough seats to accommodate the Academy's entire student body but, for this morning's lecture, a semicircle of sixteen chairs had been formed at the front, close to the podium. There were two spare seats at the center, which Connor and Jacoby now claimed. Further along the line, Jasmine Peacock gave them a discreet wave. Connor nodded back, smiling.

The headmaster stepped in front of the podium and looked out toward the audience. The faces of sixteen eager teenagers looked back at him. "Today," he began, "we shall consider the notion of *zanshin*. . . . But before we do, for any of you who have not yet met him, let me introduce you to our guest at the Academy, Connor Tempest."

The Year 10 students now turned toward Connor and he felt as embarrassed as if a spotlight had been turned full-blast upon him.

"Connor and his sister Grace," Commodore Kuo continued, apparently oblivious to Connor's unease, "have spent three months aboard *The Diablo*, under the command of Captain Molucco Wrathe."

It was clear from the muffled gasps and nods that Connor had suddenly risen in their estimation. He smiled to himself. Evidently, whatever doubts the staff had about Molucco's brand of piracy had not filtered down to the student body. To Connor's peers, Molucco Wrathe was simply a celebrity pirate, whose fame was now rubbing off on Connor himself. All of the other students were two or more years older than he — but in one significant respect, Connor was ahead of them, having already lived the pirate life for real.

"And I daresay that in those three months, Connor has had cause to perfect his swordsmanship. Would I be right in thinking that, Connor?"

He nodding, hoping with all his will that the headmaster wasn't about to call upon him for a demonstration.

"May I borrow your sword?" Commodore Kuo asked now.

Connor was surprised but he nodded. He stood and drew his rapier from its scabbard. Then, as Cate had taught him, he gripped the sword at the bottom of its hilt with his left hand and extended it toward the headmaster, the point of the blade facing away from him.

Commodore Kuo reached out his right hand and placed it above Connor's hand on the hilt. As Connor released his left hand, the headmaster nodded and placed his own hand on the hilt.

Connor stepped away and sat down.

"Your training has been good," Commodore Kuo said with a smile. Connor nodded. Cate had taught him many of the rituals involving swords. He remembered her explaining that, in some cultures, offering your sword with the right hand was seen as crude or aggressive. Therefore, it was always best — on those rare occasions when you offered your sword to another — to do so with your left hand.

Now, Commodore Kuo took his own left hand from the rapier and reached into his pocket, withdrawing a square of silk. He rested the blade on his left palm, the small silk cloth preventing his own flesh from touching the metal. This went beyond Cate's teachings but Connor imagined that it was another part of the infinite — and endlessly fascinating — ritual of swordsmanship.

"There's a difference between Mister Tempest and the rest of you," Commodore Kuo said, looking up from the blade. "And the difference is this. We've been teaching you sword-fighting techniques ever since you arrived at the Academy, when we placed those little sticks of bamboo in your hands."

Connor noticed the students smiling at the memory.

"And then you progressed from Basic Combat to the day when you held a real sword in your hands for the very first time — a day I expect all of you remember and will do for the rest of your lives."

Again, Connor saw the quick recognition of the students. He remembered the excited faces of the junior class the day before as they had held their daisho for the very first time.

"You are the cream of the crop," the headmaster continued. "You're in your final year here and we have high expectations of you. We set up this Academy to educate the pirate captains of tomorrow — the best of the best — and here you are. In a few short months, you'll leave here to take up apprentice positions on real pirate ships."

"You bet!" Jacoby exclaimed, unable to rein in his excitement at the prospect.

"That's right, Mister Blunt," Commodore Kuo said, turning to face him. "And you'll doubtless excel at being a deputy; then, before very long, you'll be a captain yourself."

Connor thought again of the vision he'd had — of that curiously familiar scene aboard deck, when he was captain and his crew were calling to him because someone was hurt.

"You have learned much since you arrived here at the Academy," Commodore Kuo continued, "but the biggest lessons still lie ahead of you. And one of those lessons will come the day you use your sword — not in practice, not in Combat Workshop, but for real — to defend your life."

Sunlight streamed into the room and bounced up from the blade of Connor's rapier onto Commodore Kuo's face.

As the light met Connor's eyes, Commodore Kuo's voice receded and Connor found himself back on that deck, just as before.

There he was, in the heart of a battle. The swords clashed against each other. He saw rigging being torn and heard cannon firing and the cries of pirates running in and out of the fray. Then came the cries.

"Captain," he heard. "Captain Tempest."

Connor smiled to hear himself addressed once more as "Captain." It sounded great. It sounded right. But then the vision changed.

"Come." He heard a distraught voice. "Captain Tempest . . . Come . . . Captain Tempest. He is wounded . . . He needs . . ."

They were the exact same words he'd heard before, but this time the vision was clearer. The first time, he had thought they meant a wounded crew member. Now, he knew that it was he who was wounded.

He heard the voice once more, cut through with sobs.

"Captain Tempest is cut. Please come . . . please come . . . so much blood . . . I'm not sure how much longer he can last. . . ."

Connor felt a sense of coldness flooding through him. The vision was so clear, so precise. Was it a foretelling of his own death? He couldn't believe it.

"Mister Tempest. Connor . . . Connor!"

Connor came back to reality and saw that the headmaster was addressing him.

"I'm sorry, Headmaster."

"Did we lose you there?" Commodore Kuo smiled at him.

"I'm sorry," he said again. "The light caught my eyes and —"

"I was just asking you," Commodore Kuo's voice cut across his own, "have you, these past three months, had to use your sword to defend your life?"

As he spoke, he offered the sword back to Connor, reversing their previous gestures so that now he held the rapier in his left hand as he extended it by the hilt.

"Yes," Connor said, as his hand gripped the hilt above Commodore Kuo's, "yes, I have." His hand was shaking — a reaction perhaps to the vision. He did his best to steady it. He could see that Commodore Kuo had noticed his trembling arm. He steadied it with his other hand and eased the rapier back into its scabbard. Commodore Kuo placed a hand on Connor's shoulder. The solidity of his touch helped to calm Connor.

"Before you sit down again, can you share with the rest of us what it feels like to use your rapier in that way?"

Connor thought back to his first attack with the pirates of *The Diablo* through to their last, ill-fated venture onto *The Albatross*.

"It's a mixture of feelings," Connor said.

"Go on," encouraged Commodore Kuo.

"It's exciting. After your training, you want to use your sword as best as you can. It's a challenge — like any sport."

"You bet!" Jacoby exclaimed again, his hands miming the swipe of swordplay.

"But," continued Connor, his hand touching the hilt of his rapier, "the very first time you hold a sword in your hand, you're aware that this isn't a sport like any other. This isn't a toy. It's an instrument of death. You hold this awesome power and responsibility in your hand. You have to respect the sword and honor your opponents."

"Okay," said Commodore Kuo. "And you have all these thoughts in the heart of the attack?"

"No." Connor shook his head now. "Before. These are the thoughts that go through my mind beforehand. Cutlass Cate — she's the weapons trainer on *The Diablo* — she teaches us to empty our minds before the attack itself."

"Excellent," Commodore Kuo said. "Okay, Connor, please take a seat again."

Connor did so with no further urging, glad to slip out of the spotlight again. He was still shaken up by his premonition, if that's what it was. But maybe it was nothing of the sort. Maybe it meant nothing at all.

As he sat down, Jacoby leaned across and whispered, "You looked a little freaked up there. What happened? Did Jasmine flash you a smile?"

Connor shook his head. "It was nothing," he said. That's what he had to believe. But his hands were still shaking a little.

When Connor looked up again, he noticed that Commodore Kuo had written a single word on the blue chalkboard at the front of the class. It was the strange word he had spoken a couple of times before.

*zanshin*

Commodore Kuo surveyed the class through his spectacles.

"Connor told us just now that before entering into attack, he has been trained to empty his mind. This is one way of viewing the concept of *zanshin*. Now, as you know, here at the Academy we draw on some very ancient warrior traditions and this notion of *zanshin* goes right back to the ancient flowering of Japanese martial arts, or *bujutsu*." He wrote out *bujutsu* on the board in his immaculate script. "Now, can anyone remember from our previous discussions the Japanese word for engaging in combat?"

His eyes scanned the room, as did Connor's. He noticed that several hands were raised.

The headmaster gave a nod. "Yes, Aamir?"

"*Kamae,*" said the boy confidently.

"Absolutely," said Commodore Kuo, adding *kamae* to the list of words on the board.

"Now, *zanshin* is the state of mind that every successful combatant must employ before entering into *kamae*, or combat. It means an exceptionally high state of alertness in which you will be ready to defend and attack in all directions, a full three-hundred-and-sixty degrees about the body. You will have no area of weakness." He smiled lightly. "*Zanshin* will then combine with your doubtlessly flawless combat technique to result in perfect action and a successful result." He turned to write another few words on the chalkboard.

"Now," he said, stepping to one side and tapping the board, "who can tell us about the concept of the 'one-stroke-victory'?"

Connor wished that he could answer the question, but though the sensations the headmaster described were utterly familiar to him, his language was new. He watched as the well-educated finalists raised their hands in the air.

"Yes, Jasmine," said Commodore Kuo.

"The one-stroke-victory is another concept dating back to the flowering of *bujutsu*," Jasmine said, "and more specifically to the technique of *iai-jutsu* or," she smiled at Connor, "the immediate drawing of the sword." Turning back to Commodore Kuo, she continued. "The true art of *iai-jutsu* rests on bringing down your adversary with one stroke of the sword. Any additional stroke required constitutes a failure of the true art."

At Jasmine's words, Connor immediately thought of the way he'd seen Cheng Li operate in battle. He'd noticed at once how minimal her actions were. While other pirates, Bart included, wove around the deck, thrusting their swords this way and that, you might blink and miss Cheng Li's actual engagement of her twin katanas. And yet, when she did use them, in Cate's view, she was the most effective of swordbearers. Clearly, this was one legacy of Cheng Li's rigorous Academy training. Connor felt like a sponge, eager to learn more of these techniques. But he was only at the Academy for a few more days. How could he ever hope to amass the knowledge that Cheng Li had learned in ten years here? Suddenly, in spite of his practical knowledge of piracy, he felt lacking. If only he could stay longer.

"Very good, Jasmine," said Commodore Kuo. "Yes, the one-stroke-victory was very important to our forebears and, if you look at it in terms of *zanshin*, you can understand why. *Zanshin* places you in an optimum state of alertness. In such a state, with the three-hundred-and-sixty-degree awareness I spoke of before, you should be fully able to execute the one-stroke-victory. Failure to do so means you have wasted that *zanshin*. Now, with every further stroke you take, you further waste your *zanshin*. And, with every further stroke, you expose yourself to risk and reduce your own chance of survival."

Again, Connor recognised the sensations Commodore Kuo was describing. Swordfighting wasn't entirely like sport. However much stamina you developed — and Connor knew that he had just about as much as any human being — fighting drew more deeply on your reserves than any mere sport. And often, after the lengthy psyching-up process, the actual battle was over very quickly. A few seconds might be all it took. It was the way you capitalized on your adrenaline — or *zanshin* — in those seconds that determined your fate.

"Now don't think," said Commodore Kuo, "that the concept of *zanshin* is reserved merely for that moment on the battle deck. The successful pirate needs to maintain *zanshin* away from the obvious arena of combat, twenty-four/seven . . ."

As Commodore Kuo continued his discourse, Connor listened intently; more aware than ever that he had a lot to learn.

Connor couldn't believe how quickly the double period of the Swordsmanship lecture had gone by. As Commodore Kuo wound up the discussion, Connor glanced at the clock and saw that a full hour and twenty minutes had slipped past. He shook his head. Back at CMB High, his brain would have felt totally numb after a double dose of Physics or Geography. But, challenging as Commodore Kuo's lesson was, he could have listened for another hour or more.

"You looked a little shell-shocked when I called you up," Commodore Kuo said, appearing before him. "I hope I didn't embarrass you."

Some of the other kids were starting to file out of the lecture theater, no doubt on their way to their next class. Jacoby waited at Connor's side.

"No," Connor said. "It's a lot to take in, that's all."

"But you knew what I was talking about," said Commodore Kuo. "I could sense it. Come on, let's walk and talk."

Connor nodded and began walking out with Commodore Kuo on one side and Jacoby on the other. "Yes, a lot of what you said struck a chord with me. But all these terms are new to me. Not just *zanshin*, but *kamae* and *bujutsu* and *iai-jutsu* . . ."

"Well, of course," said Commodore Kuo, as they

stepped out into the sunlit gardens. "You haven't had the advantage of Academy training, like these kids have. These guys are — what — two years older than you? Plus, they've had almost ten years of studying here at the Academy. But you know more than you think — look at the way you offered your sword to me for inspection. The way you did that also dates back to the classical Japanese warriors."

Connor was surprised.

"Your trainer — Cutlass Cate? — has instilled a remarkable level of knowledge in you during your time aboard *The Diablo*. You really have much to be proud of, Mister Tempest."

Connor flushed with pleasure.

"How's your sister today?"

The question took Connor off-balance. "She's okay, I think . . . I mean, I guess. She wasn't feeling too well this morning, but . . ."

Commodore Kuo smiled. "Well, it's a beautiful day. I'm sure she'll perk up. Right — I have to go and teach Captaincy Skills to Year 6 now. Enjoy the rest of your day."

He began striding up the hill. Then he turned back and looked at Connor curiously. What was he thinking? Connor wondered. It was disconcerting.

"I was just thinking," said the headmaster, "just *wondering* if we can tempt you to stay a little longer at the Academy? I feel we could teach you much about piracy.

And you could teach us too. You have a lot to give, Connor Tempest."

"Thanks," Connor said, not knowing exactly what else to say.

"Well, look," Commodore Kuo said. "I know it's a bit of a wild thought. And I know Molucco will be keen to have you back and all that. But would you . . . would you at least think about it?"

Connor nodded. At this moment, there was nothing he wanted more than to stay. But could he really do it? After everything that had happened, could he leave Captain Wrathe and *The Diablo* behind?

He thought once more of his vision. It chilled him to the core. But he was going to fight it. If death *was* stalking him, then he'd give it a duel to remember. He was going to prepare himself by becoming the very best pirate that he could be. Not just a pirate, but a warrior. Not just a warrior, but a captain. Yes, he thought, even if one day — a long, long way off — I am struck down on the deck of my ship . . . I will die a pirating legend.

26

# THE SEED

"Grace!"

"Connor! Not again!"

"No. It's not Connor."

"Cheng Li!"

Grace jumped off the bed and opened the door to her room. On the threshold stood Cheng Li, dressed for combat and holding a spare sword. She smiled at Grace and brushed past her into the room.

"I thought we were going to have some combat practice today, Grace," she said, "but we haven't seen you all day. Why, you're not even dressed yet. It's almost dinnertime, Grace! Is something wrong?"

"Yes," said Grace, unable to rein in her emotion. "Yes, something is very wrong."

Immediately, Cheng Li dropped the sword on the bed and enfolded Grace in a hug. It was an uncharacteristic gesture but exactly what Grace needed.

"Whatever's the matter?" asked Cheng Li, as she held Grace in her arms. "Tell me. You know we share *everything*."

Grace told Cheng Li the whole sad tale of her latest — her *last* — trip to the Vampirate ship. Once more, Cheng Li listened intently until Grace's very last words.

"I don't know what to do," Grace said. "Everything has changed."

Cheng Li shook her head. "Nothing has changed."

Grace couldn't believe her ears. "It has! The captain has told me he doesn't want me to return. That I must stay away."

"Agreed," said Cheng Li. "But you have friends aboard that ship. You have, in your own words, 'unfinished business.' It no longer matters what the captain thinks. What matters is how you find peace of mind."

Grace shook her head. "I can't go against the captain's wishes. I can't."

"What about Lorcan?" Cheng Li said. "He needs you. The captain's all but given up on him. You haven't!"

"But if the captain himself can't save him, what can I do?"

"Well, we won't know that, Grace, until we get you back on the ship."

Grace looked into Cheng Li's smoky eyes. Her heart was racing. Could she really do this?

"Look," said Cheng Li. "Darcy Flotsam came to find you, to ask for your help, didn't she?"

Grace nodded.

"And Lorcan gave you the Claddagh ring and sent you visions of himself . . ."

"Yes," Grace nodded. "Yes, he did!"

"Visions which might just as well have been pleas for help," continued Cheng Li. "Grace, you do have unfinished business with that ship. I think the captain is preoccupied with these rebel Vampirates — Sidorio and the others. He isn't thinking straight. He certainly isn't thinking about poor Lorcan. As you say, if he isn't taking blood, who knows how long he has left? By the time the captain turns his attentions to his plight, it could be too late."

As ever, Cheng Li had thrown Grace a lifesaver.

"All right," said Grace, flushed with a new sense of purpose. "All right. Let's do it. But *how* do I get back on the ship?"

---

"Tell me again, Grace, how do you think you found the Vampirate ship in the first place?"

Grace sighed. They'd been over this so many times already. "I was in the water, fighting for my life — and losing the battle. Much like Connor was. You found him. And, in the same way, Lorcan must have found me."

"I found Connor in the daylight," Cheng Li said. "The light was dying but it was still daylight. I could never have seen him in the darkness."

"So Lorcan must have found me in the light too."

"But he can't have, can he? From everything we know now, Lorcan couldn't have come out in the light."

"No, you're right. But there was the mist . . ."

"Yes, the mist you found yourself in when you arrived on the ship . . ."

"The same mist which came down when Connor and I were reunited on the deck."

"It's as if the Vampirates generate that mist themselves," Cheng Li said, thoughtfully. "Could that be possible?"

"Yes," Grace said, excitedly sitting up. "I remember something now. I remember when I first arrived on the ship, the captain said something to Lorcan about moving me inside before the mist rose."

"It's not conclusive evidence," Cheng Li said, "but we're not dealing with hard facts here. It's my belief that the Vampirates — well, the captain at least — can create a mist to act as a protection for those who cannot usually go out in daylight. But they can't control how long it lasts. Wait . . ."

"What is it?" Grace asked, excitedly.

Cheng Li lay there, her eyes closed. "It's close, Grace. There's something we're so close to, but it's just out of reach." She opened her eyes again. "Do you think it's possible that you found the ship, rather than it rescuing you? Maybe *you* are meant to save it?"

"But it did find me. I was drowning in the ocean. There's no getting away from that."

"Yes, there is," Cheng Li said, suddenly sitting up straight. "It all depends how you frame the story, doesn't it? Think outside the box, Grace."

Grace had never seen Cheng Li so intense.

"Take yourself back to Crescent Moon Bay, to before the storm. Take yourself back to the room at the top of the lighthouse."

As Grace heard Cheng Li's words, she closed her eyes and pictured herself once more up in the lamp room, surveying the bay beneath her.

"Now what?" she said.

"Take yourself back," Cheng Li said. "Your father has died. The lighthouse has been repossessed by the bank. You're running out of options in that terrible town. And so . . ."

"And so?"

"And so, you look out to the ocean and you send a signal into the night to come and rescue you."

"What kind of signal?"

"We don't know that. But a signal that you somehow knew how to make and that the Vampirates recognized."

Grace gasped.

"What?" said Cheng Li. "What is it?"

"I think we're on to something," Grace said excitedly. "I just remembered something the captain said to me. It was the first night that I met him."

"What did he say?"

"I asked him what he wanted from me. And he said . . . he said . . ."

She could hear the whisper all over again . . .

"*What do I want from* you? *Grace, it was* you *who sought me out, was it not?*"

Grace opened her eyes again, finding Cheng Li staring intently into them.

"I thought he was just talking about that night, Cheng Li. I thought that he meant I had gone to find him on the ship. But what if he meant *more* than that. What if he meant that I had sought out the ship itself?"

Cheng Li nodded, as excited by the discovery as Grace.

"You've been asking the wrong question, Grace. It's an easy enough mistake to make. The question isn't how you can get *back* to the ship — it's what do you want from that ship. What is it that connects you to the Vampirates in the first place?"

"But I can't find that out until I'm back there. And we

don't seem any closer to working out how I can do that than we were *hours* ago."

"Yes, we are," said Cheng Li, beaming. She slid off the bed, padded across the room and unfastened the shutters. The breeze blew across them, carrying a spray of jasmine blossom inside.

"It's just a thought," Cheng Li said, smiling at Grace, "but why don't you just wait for another storm? Perhaps when the conditions are the same, history *will* repeat itself."

# 27

# THE CREW

Stukeley is getting good at surfing. Really good. Well, he reflects, as he paddles through the water, he has certainly had time to practice. Most nights, he and the captain find themselves on a beach somewhere along the coast. They make shelter there for a day or two, then move on somewhere new. They always keep to the coast. The captain maintains he has a plan, but Stukeley is no longer sure of that. The captain speaks less and less each day — and he didn't exactly start off full of chit-chat. Sidorio only truly comes alive when the hunt is on. Then, he is a different man — a different *creature* — altogether. Afterwards, he is full of dark jokes and strange tales. But before long the energy drains away, like the tide retreating back across the rippled sand.

Sometimes, Stukeley feels lonely and thinks of Bart and Connor and his other old mates. But he can't dwell on such memories — it's too painful. Besides, with every passing day, his memory grows dimmer and dimmer. He is ceasing to be one thing while not yet becoming another. Caught in this limbo, he grabs his board and races out into the water, watching the waves and waiting. When you're out there, surfing, you can forget about everything except the breaking swells and the intricate energy of the water itself. Just as he now feels the tide shifting and raises himself up to a sitting position on the board, steering it around with his hands to optimize his position.

He is changing — in ways subtle as well as profound. Each night, his ability to see through the darkness grows sharper. Now, he can surf with or without the moon, seeing the shape of the distant waves clearly, irrespective of the given light.

The dark waters begin to lift, and again he presses his body flat against the board, waiting for the wave to strike.

As it does, in a perfect motion, he jumps up onto the board and begins his journey back toward the shore. This is a good one. He's caught it just right. He can feel the power of the swell, propelling him toward the beach. It is deserted but for the lone figure in the center, constructing a fire.

The wave takes him all the way into the shallows. He jumps down, exhilarated, and lifts his board out of the water. Hoisting it under his arm, he runs toward the fire, still puzzled at how quickly the air dries his skin and clothes.

"Did you see me out there, Captain? Did you see me ride that perfect wave?"

Sidorio does not look up from the fire he is constructing on the sand. "No."

The captain sets another branch of driftwood in the center of the fire. Stukeley wedges his board into the sand and crouches down, helping to stoke the fire.

"No," says Sidorio again, pushing Stukeley's hand away roughly.

"What's wrong, Captain?"

"Nothing's wrong."

"Won't you have a surf, yourself? The waves are amazing tonight."

Sidorio says nothing and continues adding kindling to the fire.

Stukeley glances back to the water, considering returning for another wave. He watches the tempting rise and fall of the water. As he does so, he suddenly sees a small boat lifted by the waves.

"Look, Captain!"

"What now?" This time Sidorio raises his dark eyes. He looks furious at the fresh interruption, but Stukeley doesn't care. This is important.

"Look at that boat. It's coming into shore."

"Where?"

Suddenly, the campfire bursts into flame. Sidorio stands up and follows Stukeley's gaze out to sea. There is the boat and an indeterminate number of figures clinging on to it as it rolls down over a breaking wave and is propelled toward them.

Stukeley turns to the captain for guidance. A decision will have to be made and it is the captain's prerogative to make it. When the boat and its inhabitants reach the shore, there will be only two ways this could go. Either they'll find a way to get rid of the travelers or else they will make a fresh kill. Which is it going to be?

They have feasted already tonight but that is not, Stukeley knows, always decisive.

"There is no sating of the appetite," Sidorio has told him. "Take what you will."

He glances once more at the captain, expecting a sign. But the captain is glued to the spot, his eyes empty as he watches the figures climb down from the small bark and push it through the shallows and onto the pebbled shore. Then the figures look over and one of them waves. There is no escape now. They have definitely been noticed.

"What shall we do, Captain?"

Still no answer comes.

The boat safely grounded, three figures make their way across the beach toward them. The shapes begin to define themselves — two men and a woman, one of the men tall and almost as broad as the captain himself. He strides with the same sense of purpose and now he waves again and opens his mouth.

"Sidorio! Hey, Sidorio!"

His ears must be tricking him. Stukeley turns. The captain is smiling. Stukeley turns back and sees the tall man striding forward, breaking into a run.

"Sidorio! It *is* you!"

"Lumar."

Now the captain strides forward to meet the stranger. Stukeley follows, at a slight distance. He is intrigued but unnerved. He watches the captain and the first of the strangers embrace. Could this all be part of the captain's plan?

As he watches the captain greet the other two travelers, Stukeley becomes less nervous. Hasn't Sidorio always said there will be others? Besides, now he will not be alone with the captain and his dark, silent moods. All in all, this must be a good thing, mustn't it?

"Stukeley!" The captain is calling to him. The eager lieutenant runs over to his captain's side.

"This is Stukeley," the captain says, in a tone that makes Stukeley swell with pride. "My lieutenant."

He draws closer.

"This is Lumar," Sidorio says. "An old friend."

The first of the strangers draws forward and reaches out his hand. The man is of similar build to Sidorio but his skin is black and his head close-cropped with silver stubble that shines like sharkskin in the moonlight. He is dressed somewhat like Sidorio, too, in clothes that speak of the military and of the sea.

"Well met, Stukeley," Lumar says, with something of a smile. His voice is rich and sinister as an old churchyard bell.

The handshake is firm, though the hands are, like Stukeley's own, icy cold.

"This is Olin." The second man steps forward and looks not so much at Stukeley as through him. Their hands meet briefly. Olin is tall and thin, dressed in a long cape, with a hood covering his head. His face is lean and angular inside it, the bones almost pushing through the pale skin. When his hand touches Stukeley's, it is like having a wet fish run through his fingers. Stukeley is pleased when Olin steps backward and allows the third traveler to present herself.

"And this is Mistral," Sidorio says.

A woman steps forward. Like Olin, she is wearing a cowl, but she draws it back and he sees a length of fine blond hair uncoil itself. Stukeley freezes. Mistral is the most beautiful woman he has ever seen — so beautiful, that the sight of her erases the memories of all the girls from his past. She smiles softly at Stukeley and he feels his heart flip over on itself as she extends a soft pale hand toward him. He reaches out his hand, as if to hold a fragile flower, and bows to kiss her fingers. She is wearing several small rings, and his lips brush the cool metal.

He glances up to find her smiling.

"How charming," she says, before stepping back again, in line with her traveling companions.

Sidorio turns to Stukeley. "I told you they would come," he says. "Didn't I tell you?" His eyes are gleaming wildly.

Lumar addresses the captain. "We had to leave. There was nothing left for us on that ship."

"The rules," hisses Olin, "the rules no longer made sense to us."

"The captain's ways are tired," says Mistral, drawing her hands across her chest, perhaps against the cold. "We must find new ways."

"We knew," intoned Lumar. "We knew that you would lead us to new ways, Sidorio."

Sidorio nods. He seems possessed of a fresh energy, thinks Stukeley. Perhaps it was the waiting that proved so burdensome to him. Now that more of the crew have joined them, perhaps his real work — whatever it might be — can begin.

"I have such plans," Sidorio announces to the group. The others all smile and nod. "But come, travelers. Come, warm yourselves at my fire."

He extends his hand and they begin walking toward the fire, which is now burning as brightly as if Sidorio has harnessed the moon itself and embedded it in the heart of the beach.

Stukeley watches closely as Lumar places his hand on Sidorio's shoulder.

"It's good to see you again," he says.

"Yes," agrees Sidorio. "But how did you find me?"

"Like will find like," Lumar says with a dark smile. "There will be others," he adds. "This is merely the beginning."

28

# A GLORIOUS FUTURE

"So, what's bugging our pirate prodigy?" Jacoby asked, as they tucked into breakfast on the sun-drenched terrace. Connor sighed. "Is it *that* obvious?"

"Afraid so," Jacoby said. "You were happy enough during Krav Maga but you've barely said a word since then. And you keep jiggling your knees under the table, O tense one. What's up?"

"I've been doing a lot of thinking."

"Uh-oh," Jacoby said, spearing a strip of bacon, "Thinking. That's a dangerous business!" He crunched the bacon between his teeth.

Connor pushed his plate away, though it was still half full of food.

"Now, I'm *really* worried," Jacoby said. "Usually you

leave your plate so clean it's like you never used it. You better start talking, Connor Tempest. What's eating you?"

"You know that I'm only here for a week, right?"

"Oh, of course, yes."

"Well, it's day five already. I've only got two more days left."

"Time certainly has flown." Jacoby smiled. "Though sometimes it feels like you've been here forever!"

Connor looked gloomy.

". . . in a *good* way," Jacoby added.

Connor nodded. "The thing is . . . I don't think I'm going to be ready to leave on Sunday."

Jacoby crunched through another strip of bacon. "Then stay."

"It isn't as simple as that," Connor said. "You're forgetting that I'm signed up to Captain Wrathe. It's my duty to return to *The Diablo*."

"Well, sure," Jacoby said, "*eventually*. But I'm certain Captain Wrathe can survive another week without his Boy Wonder. And I'm certain Commodore Kuo would be pleased to extend your stay."

"Yes, I think Commodore Kuo would be happy enough," Connor said, "but I'm not so sure about Captain Wrathe. He's not a huge fan of the Academy."

"No?" Jacoby said, tearing apart a blueberry muffin. "Why's that?"

"Lots of reasons. For one thing, he doesn't think you

can be educated to be a pirate. He reckons that either you have it in your veins or you don't."

Jacoby shrugged. "Maybe there's some truth in that."

"Maybe," Connor said, "but I've learned so much since I got here. And, if I stayed, I could learn so much more." He was surprised at the undertow of yearning in his own voice.

"So go talk to Kuo," Jacoby said, "and let him square it with the Wrathe."

Connor frowned. He just couldn't see the two captains sitting down and discussing this amicably.

Jacoby suddenly grinned. "Here's an idea. How about you stay here and I go back on *The Diablo* as your substitute? I'd kill to get out on the ocean for real."

"It *is* awesome," Connor said, remembering the sense of freedom he always experienced when *The Diablo* was coursing through the open ocean. Suddenly, he was flushed with warm memories of the ship and his crewmates.

"I *do* want to go back," he said, "just not yet."

"Then drink up your pomegranate juice and go talk to Commodore Kuo," Jacoby said.

"Talk to Commodore Kuo about what?"

Jacoby and Connor looked up to find Cheng Li hovering at their table. She had arrived silently. Neither one knew quite how long she had been there.

"I was just saying," Connor said, "that is . . . I was just wondering . . ."

Cheng Li gave him a sidelong glance, one eyebrow raised in amusement.

"He wants to know if he can extend his stay," Jacoby said with a broad smile.

"I see," Cheng Li said.

"He's worried about how Captain Wrathe will react," Jacoby continued, "but I think Commodore Kuo can handle him."

"Oh you do, do you?" Cheng Li said, glancing up at the Academy clock. "Jacoby, isn't it time for your Marine Biology class?"

Jacoby followed her eyes to the clock-face which hung over the terrace, encircled by bougainvillea.

"Oh yeah. Connor, we'd better get a move on or we'll be late for class."

"That's okay," Cheng Li said. "You go on and tell Captain Solomos I have borrowed Mister Tempest for important Academy business."

"It's very cruel of you to cut me out of the conversation, just when things are getting exciting," Jacoby grinned, "but okay, Mistress Li. If it helps Boy Wonder's cause — who am I to complain?"

He jumped up out of his chair and winked at Connor. "Later, buddy." They knocked knuckles while Cheng Li slipped down into the chair Jacoby had vacated.

"Well," Cheng Li said, as Jacoby jogged off down the hill toward the Biology lab, "I must say, Connor, you've established yourself here at the Academy even more quickly than I anticipated."

Connor shrugged. "I just wish I didn't feel so torn. I know my duty is to Captain Wrathe and my crewmates on *The Diablo*. But I really like it here. And I'm learning so much."

Cheng Li beamed from ear to ear. "I knew you would. We're cut from the same cloth, you and I. As talented as we are naturally, still we hunger for more knowledge."

Connor was so used to Cheng Li's arrogance it barely registered now, but perhaps she was in danger of overestimating him. He had never hungered for knowledge before. Certainly not the kind of knowledge they shoveled in your direction at Crescent Moon Bay High. But it was certainly true that, when it came to piracy, he wanted to know everything. His ambitions grew with each passing day.

"What are you thinking?" she asked.

"Oh, it's pointless, really," he said. "I was just hoping that Commodore Kuo might let me stay another week or so. But what difference would that make? You spent ten years here. Jacoby's been here almost that long. I can never catch up."

"Well, no, not in a single week. Of course not. But, at the risk of swelling that head of yours, you are prodigiously talented, Connor. There's no Academy student, besides Jacoby, to rival your skill at swords. And I know that I speak for the rest of the tutors when I say how impressed we are at your ability to hold your own in the classes here — and often with kids older than yourself."

Connor blushed. Getting praise from a teacher was an entirely new experience for him.

"It's strange, isn't it?" he said. "There I was, a few months back. Stuck in that dead-end town for all those years. And then Dad died and I nearly followed him to the grave. But I survived and you rescued me and . . . well, it's as if I was waiting all that time. All those years. Waiting for piracy to claim me. Like it was my destiny, like it was in my blood all along."

Cheng Li was nodding furiously. "Yes. Yes, those are my thoughts exactly. You might be the son of a lighthouse keeper, Connor, but you were born to be a pirate."

"Born to be a captain?" Connor asked, thinking once more of his vision of the future.

"A captain and more besides. Perhaps, one day, a commodore — the captain of captains. There is a glorious future for you," Cheng Li said, smiling. Then her expression changed as if a chill wind had blown across the terrace. "But we have to unpick some of the unfortunate circumstances that have arisen."

Connor looked at her curiously.

"We have to free you from Captain Wrathe's articles," she explained.

"But the articles are binding . . . for life. I signed them with my own blood."

Cheng Li smiled once more. "What nonsense," she said. "There are always ways. Especially with a man like Wrathe.

It's just a question of what he requires in exchange. You know what he's like. Now don't take offense, boy, but you could probably buy back your freedom with a sapphire trinket."

Connor's face fell once more. Would Molucco really swap him so easily? And even if this was the case, how was he supposed to lay his hands on a sapphire? He had nothing to his name, other than the small amount of booty he'd acquired after the raids. Certainly, there was nothing in his possession to tempt a man of Molucco's vast wealth.

"Oh, poor boy," Cheng Li said, leaning back in her chair. "Did you think I meant you'd have to *buy* your way out of servitude? Of course not! You are not alone anymore, Connor. You have supporters of considerable power and influence. John Kuo is not merely Headmaster of the Academy. He's one of the most powerful operatives in the Pirate Federation."

"What exactly *is* the Pirate Federation?" Connor asked.

"I think you should ask Commodore Kuo that question. I shall set up a meeting for you later. Why don't you go and get on with your lessons and I'll talk to the headmaster."

Connor stood up from the table and slung his bag over his shoulder. "Thank you," he said, "for everything."

"Don't thank me yet," she said. "Just remember that you owe me . . . and that one day I'll call in that debt." She was smiling but Connor felt a strange chill. He had no doubt that she was utterly serious.

He began walking away, his head heavy with all the dark

thoughts bubbling away inside. Suddenly he turned back. Cheng Li had stood up and was heading across the terrace. He had to run to catch her. She turned, hearing his tread.

"Yes?"

"I don't want to betray Captain Wrathe. He's done so much for me."

Cheng Li nodded, and extended a hand to rest on his shoulder. "I do understand, Connor." She sighed. "But, it was hasty of you to bind yourself to his crew in perpetuity. There are bigger and better opportunities for you. Don't think he doesn't know that. Don't think for a moment that he didn't know what he was doing when he bound you to those articles."

Slipping through the door, she left Connor outside, weighing up her words. Was it true? Had Molucco taken advantage of Connor's naivety to bind him in service before he discovered what other options existed? It was a harsh accusation. But if Cheng Li was right and Molucco had pulled a fast one, then perhaps it was time to break away. Whatever the cost.

As he zigzagged down the hill, he glanced over his shoulder, back toward Grace's window. The shutters were still closed. It was after ten and there was no sign of life up there. He wished he'd asked Cheng Li how Grace was, but he'd been so preoccupied with his own dilemma. Well, he could check on Grace during break — or, failing that, over lunch. It wasn't, he thought with a frown, as if she were going anywhere.

29

# THE GATHERING STORM

Connor did not, as it happened, get around to checking on Grace during break. Instead, he found himself lounging under one of the pomegranate trees with Jacoby and Jasmine — taking shelter from the sun, snacking on the ripe fruit, and talking enjoyable nonsense until it was time for Captain Larsen's Swords class. This was a double lesson, taken at a brisk pace by the formidable Danish captain.

Next came a single session of Captaincy and Crewbuilding Skills. According to the timetable, Cheng Li was due to teach the class but, in fact, it was Commodore Kuo who entered the seminar room, to the surprise of his waiting students.

"I know you were expecting Mistress Li, but I'm afraid you've drawn the short sword today," he said with a smile.

No one objected. The headmaster was one of the most popular teachers in the Academy and the students treated any extra time with him as a bonus, not a chore. Captaincy and Crew-building had quickly become one of Connor's favorite classes anyhow, and the way Commodore Kuo taught it was far less didactic that Cheng Li. Rather than telling you how to do things, Commodore Kuo was more inclined to set up a scenario and then invite different suggestions.

"Remember," he said, "when each of you attains the rank of Captain, with most affairs there will be no clear sense of right or wrong. There will be a hundred possible resolutions and it will be your responsibility to choose the right one for you and your crew."

The forty-minute lesson breezed by, with Jacoby and Jasmine violently disagreeing on how to deal with a dispute between crew members and Connor and Aamir offering their ideas on how to tackle a lack of supplies when far out at sea. In each case, the headmaster expertly drew out the students to make a case for their chosen solutions and then refused to judge one person's proposal over another — instead turning to the other students to air their views. The class broadly endorsed Jasmine's rather more thought-out approach to resolving conflict and seemed impressed with Connor's pragmatic ideas on imposing rationing *in extremis.*

As the lunch bell rang, the students were still deeply

engrossed in discussion. Finally, it fell to Commodore Kuo to shoo them out into the sunshine.

"Mister Tempest," he called softly as Connor collected his papers. "Might I have a word?"

Connor turned back. His heart was racing. Clearly, Commodore Kuo knew of his request. Now he would learn his verdict. What passed in the next few moments would decide his entire future.

"Let's walk and talk," the headmaster said, gesturing for Connor to go on ahead. They began the climb toward the terrace at a safe distance from prying ears.

"Mistress Li told me about your earlier chat," the headmaster said, "and well, of course, I'm delighted that you're keen to extend your stay here." He paused before continuing. "How long exactly were you thinking you might like to stay?"

Connor cleared his throat as he gathered his nerve. "Perhaps . . . perhaps another week?"

"Just a week?" Commodore Kuo looked amused. "And are you satisfied that in another week, you'll have soaked up every last bit of knowledge we have to offer?"

"No, no. Of course not," Connor said, feeling foolish. "But I have my duties . . ."

"I know, I know. You have your duties to Captain Wrathe and the crew. It's very commendable of you to think that way, Connor. But let's suppose, just for a moment, that I had a magic wand and I could fix it for you to stay here as long as you wanted, irrespective of your current commitments. Then would you want to stay just a week?"

"No, I . . ."

"A month, perhaps?"

"Well, maybe . . ."

"Until the end of the year?"

Connor felt a rush of excitement at the words. The path before them began to climb steeply up the hill. To their right, the waters glistened in the harbor.

Commodore Kuo's dark eyes reflected the sun on the ocean.

"Suppose I could fix it for you to become a full-time student here," he said. "To play with the curriculum so that you had some private tuition as well as group classes — to fast-track you, if you like. How would that be?"

Connor sighed. "That would be cool. Really cool."

"That's what you'd like? Well, in that case, we'd better try to get our heads around the possibilities. Leave it to me, Connor." He tapped his head lightly. "Give these old gray cells a chance to ponder things." He smiled. "I'll get back to you later. In the meantime, enjoy your lunch."

With a pat on the shoulder, he left Connor on the terrace. As the headmaster walked away, Connor saw Jacoby waving him over. He was sitting at a table with Jasmine, Aamir and some of the others from the class. They had saved him a space. Smiling, he stepped forward to join them.

During the post-lunch triple period of Nautical Attack Strategy, the heavens opened. In a classroom at the end of one of the coiling arms of the Rotunda, Captain Solomos and his students paused their studies to turn and watch as the sky grew dark and thick clouds expelled jets of rain over the Academy grounds. Then they resumed their debate, only to be interrupted by a whip-crack of thunder.

"A storm," Captain Solomos said, his eyes lighting up with characteristic drama. "It's a while since we've had a storm as violent as this." He snapped shut his textbook. "Class, let's park our earlier discussion. Instead, let's consider how we might use such weather to stage an inspirational attack."

As Connor was packing up his books at the end of NAS class, Captain Solomos called him over. "Commodore Kuo asks you to go to his study," he told Connor with a smile, "to continue your earlier conversation."

Connor nodded and headed back along the snaking corridor to the headmaster's study. He knocked on the door.

"Enter!" called Commodore Kuo.

Connor stepped inside the wood-paneled room, finding the headmaster at his immaculate desk, reading through some papers.

"Ah, Mister Tempest. Please, take a seat. Some tea for you, perhaps?"

Connor accepted the small bowl of fragrant tea.

"I've been thinking about our earlier discussions," said the headmaster, "and I have a proposition for you."

Connor nodded. He took a draught of the tea.

"How much do you know about the Pirate Federation?" Commodore Kuo asked him.

"Next to nothing," Connor admitted.

"Excellent," said the headmaster, a twinkle in his eye. "We like to keep it that way with those outside the Federation. But it's a very different matter for those on the inside."

Connor leaned forward. Now, the headmaster had his full attention.

"It must be clear to you," continued Commodore Kuo, "that piracy is in a state of significant and rapid change at the moment. This is due to the work of the Federation all over the globe." He stood up from his desk and indicated a glass globe at Connor's side. "Give it a spin," he said.

Connor reached out his hand to the globe and did so. As the glass spun, its surface turned black and hundreds of lights began to twinkle at him, like stars in the night sky.

"You see those lights?" Commodore Kuo said. "Each

one represents a cell of the Pirate Federation — all over the world. More are coming online all the time."

Connor was impressed.

"There's a great and growing gulf between those pirates who operate within the Federation," explained Commodore Kuo, "and those — like Molucco Wrathe — on the outside. Those of us in the know are busy forming alliances, not only across the oceans, but also on land. In a short time, our influence will be unstoppable. And rather than working as disparate crews, often coming into conflict with each other, you'll see the formation of vast fleets of pirate ships united in one cause."

It was heady talk. Commodore Kuo came to the front of his desk and sat upon it, facing Connor.

"Such an organization needs leaders, and one of my jobs within the Federation is to recruit the leaders of the future."

His gaze bore into Connor. Connor thought once more of the vision he'd had of becoming a pirate captain. But would he — *could* he — become a captain within the Federation itself?

"I'm going to tell you something now, Connor, something which must remain within these study walls. Do you understand me?"

"Yes, sir," said Connor.

"Excellent. First — more tea?"

Connor shook his head. He was too intrigued to be

distracted in any way. The headmaster brought his hands together in a steeple.

"It was I who recruited Mistress Li to the Federation. I knew from her time in the Academy what a valuable asset she would be — and so it has proved."

Outside, there was a crack of lightning. The headmaster glanced over his shoulder.

"I love a storm," he said. "Don't you?"

"Not so much, actually," said Connor, the thunder a reminder of the very worst time in his life.

"Oh, of course not. I'm sorry. How insensitive."

"I have a question," Connor said, refusing to let the storm distract him.

"Shoot."

"Was Mistress Li spying on Captain Wrathe? Captain Drakoulis said that was why she was on *The Diablo*. That she'd been sent by the Federation."

Commodore Kuo's face was a mask. He leaned back and calmly poured himself some tea. He took a sip, then cupped the bowl in his hands. "I'm sure you'll understand," he said, "that some Federation matters must be kept confidential. But the main reason for Mistress Li to join *The Diablo* was to complete her apprenticeship as deputy captain. It is our policy to fast-track our recruits to become captains."

The headmaster met Connor's eyes once more and

Connor thought that, for all his diplomacy, Kuo was answering in the affirmative. Cheng Li *had* been sent to spy on Molucco. He wasn't sure what to make of that.

"But if Captain Wrathe operates outside the Federation, why would Mistress Li serve alongside him?"

"A good question, Connor," said Commodore Kuo, "but here's the truth of the matter. No ships truly lie outside of Federation rule. It is just that some captains blind themselves to the fact."

Did Captain Wrathe represent such a risk to the Federation then? Commodore Kuo talked of the *power* that the Federation sought. But what exactly were its aims? And were they so very different from Molucco's?

"There's a big difference," the headmaster said, as if reading Connor's thoughts, "between immediate gain and the more fruitful rewards of delayed gratification. A quick bit of plunder in the here and now is no match for the real treasure of power — *sustained* power in the long run. That's a goal worth waiting for, planning for — don't you think?"

Connor wasn't sure. He had another question — and it was a big one.

"Is Captain Narcisos Drakoulis part of the Federation?" He took a deep breath. "Was his attack against *The Diablo* planned by the Federation?" There was a third question he wanted to — but dared not — ask. Was the Federation responsible for Jez Stukeley's death? As he awaited Kuo's answer, he made a decision. If the answer was yes, then Connor would never work for the Federation in any capacity.

"As I told you before," said Kuo, "some Federation matters must be kept confidential . . ."

Connor's blood froze in his veins. He couldn't believe his ears. The Commodore might just as well have confessed to his direct responsibility.

". . . *but*, I will say that Drakoulis is as wild and wanton in his ways as Wrathe — perhaps even more so. Neither one can be depended upon to execute Federation business."

So now, he was denying it. But it was far from a clear denial. Connor was left wondering which way to turn. He felt he was adrift at sea, not knowing who was his friend and who was his enemy. Images of Captain Wrathe and Narcisos Drakoulis drifted through his mind. Then they both faded and he found himself once more looking directly into Commodore Kuo's eyes. They were kind eyes. Trustworthy eyes. Not the kind of eyes that sent a young pirate like Jez Stukeley to his death.

"You might think," continued Commodore Kuo, with a smile, "that it's unusual to recruit someone at so young an age as you but, understand that I am looking to strengthen the Federation into the farthest reaches of the future. The younger my recruits, the stronger the Federation becomes." He paused. "Indeed, there are other young colleagues of yours here at the Academy who are already working for us."

Connor considered this for a moment. Jacoby! He was

a star pupil. The headmaster must be talking about Jacoby. He'd have to ask his friend if this was the case when he next saw him.

"Do remember," said the headmaster, "what I told you about this conversation remaining within these study walls. Remember, too, that all Federation members are sworn to secrecy . . . on pain of death."

*Okay,* thought Connor. Perhaps he *wouldn't* ask Jacoby the question just yet.

"Enough preamble," said Commodore Kuo. "The fact is that we've been watching you carefully, Connor, the other teachers and I. During this week you've spent with us at the Academy and — I confess — for a time before. And we've come to the conclusion, unanimously, that we'd like you to join the Federation. We think you'd be one of our very brightest recruits. And, without wishing to overstate my case, I think we could offer you a world of opportunity such as you can only imagine."

Connor felt excited and intrigued by the offer. It was flattering to realize that they held him in such high regard, albeit a little disconcerting to know he'd been watched. It was becoming clear to him that the Federation had eyes everywhere.

"You don't need to decide immediately, of course," said Commodore Kuo, "but it would be helpful if we had an answer ahead of Captain Wrathe's return at the weekend. I'll need to prepare the ground, so to speak. And, it goes without saying that in order to join the Federation, you must first commit to study here at the Academy."

Connor nodded. His head was racing with the new information.

"Tell me," said the headmaster, "what are your initial thoughts?"

Connor cleared his throat. "My initial thoughts are that . . ." he took a deep breath, feeling he was about to dive from a very great height, ". . . yes, I want to join the Federation . . ."

"That's wonderful news."

". . . but I don't see how I can do it without upsetting Captain Wrathe. And he's been so good to me."

"I understand your concern," said the headmaster, standing up and walking toward a portrait of himself in younger days, "and it's entirely to your credit." He moved the picture to one side. Behind it was the dial of a safe, which Kuo began turning back and forth. Eventually, the safe door opened and Commodore Kuo dipped in his hand and retrieved a small velvet bag. He returned to his chair and began untying the clasp of the bag.

"All we need to do is talk to Molucco in his favorite language," said the headmaster, smiling. He undid the bag and shook it open. A slew of perfect sapphires poured out across the table.

Connor gasped. The headmaster smiled, reaching out toward the jewels.

"Now, how much do you suppose it will take to sweeten Molucco?" he asked. "One lump or two?"

---

Grace was standing on the balcony, watching the storm. She didn't hear the knock on the door.

She turned to find Cheng Li entering her room, bearing a tray of food.

"I brought your supper," said Cheng Li, setting it down on the table. "I figured you'd prefer to eat alone."

Grace nodded, reluctant to be distracted from the storm. She turned back to her view of the gardens. Cheng Li walked out and joined her on the balcony.

"It's becoming quite a storm," Cheng Li said.

"Yes," said Grace. "It brings back memories."

Cheng Li was about to speak but hesitated.

Grace nodded. "I think it's time."

"Are you sure?" Cheng Li said. "I mean, we could be wrong. We could be crazy!"

Grace shrugged. "A storm like this only comes once in a while. It would be a shame to waste it."

"If that's the case, then come inside and have something to eat," said Cheng Li. "You're going to put yourself through quite an ordeal tonight. You had best get your strength up."

# 30

# NOW WE ARE FIVE

Since "the Others" arrived, Sidorio has lost all interest in surfing. Now, only Stukeley surfs while the captain spends his time deep in conversation with the crew. Each night, they build a fire and the four of them sit around it, like old crones — talking in soft voices, plotting. Stukeley surfs alone. I am too young to spend all my time sitting and plotting, he thinks. In truth, he no longer knows if he is young or old. Age has lost all meaning for him.

Ever since the rest of the crew arrived, Sidorio has barely said two words to Stukeley — to *his lieutenant*! It is disorientating. Curious creature though he is, Sidorio has become the center of Stukeley's world. He is the one who brought him back. That Stukeley will never forget. Sidorio is his captain and his father. It is an unbreakable bond. But now Sidorio ignores him.

For a time, he loses himself in the surf. A storm is brewing and the waves are strong — he enjoys their strength. Rain falls upon him and lightning crashes around him. It only adds to his fun. He is an amazing surfer now. He is happy as a child, while the "grown-ups" talk their talk on the sand. He is glad to be separate from them. The one called Lumar prattles incessantly, as if *he* is the captain. Stukeley can't understand why Sidorio doesn't put him in his place. The one called Olin says little, but the way he watches you is unnerving. His eyes fix on you and do not let go. If you meet them, your own eyes begin to burn from the intensity of his stare.

The only one Stukeley likes is the girl — Mistral. She always smiles at him and makes room for him at the fireside. He wishes that she had turned up without the other two. *She* is a welcome addition to the crew. If only the others would go on their way — but yet, they stick limpet-like to the captain.

At last, Stukeley has had his fill of the surf and rides the last wave in. His feet hit the sand and, as usual, his clothes and skin are dry — even in the driving rain. He runs through the storm toward the fire. At first, he wonders how they keep it alight in the midst of the storm and how they hear themselves talk above the roar of the thunder and the slap of the sea against the cliffs. But, as he reaches the fire, he finds the noise of the storm recedes. The sand is perfectly dry here, too. It is as if they are protected from the storm by an invisible globe.

Mistral turns and smiles at him. The light of her gaze is brighter than the fire itself.

He throws down the surfboard and joins the circle. "So," he says, deciding to try and be friendly, "what ya talking about?"

"Ah, Lieutenant Stukeley," says Lumar, glancing up and smiling with no trace of warmth. "We talk of many things."

"Many things, Lieutenant Stukeley," echoes Sidorio.

Stukeley can feel Olin's hungry eyes upon him. He refuses to return his glance, turning his gaze instead to the flames. As he does so, he feels a soft hand on his shoulder.

"We're making plans for the next stage," Mistral says.

He turns toward her. She reaches out her fingers to his forehead and brushes back a stray lock of his hair. He trembles at her touch. She smiles once more.

"The boat we came in is too small for us all," says Lumar. Sometimes his voice is so soft, Stukeley can barely hear his words. But Lumar always sits beside Sidorio and the captain always hears his words, as if they are pouring melting honey into his ears.

"The ferryboat is also too small," announces Sidorio.

Five pairs of eyes turn to the two small barks, tethered close by. They leap on the rough water — the ocean is like a horse trying to throw its riders but the little boats hold their own. Stukeley looks fondly at the ferryboat. It served their purposes well enough when it was just the captain and Stukeley and their surfboards. How long ago was that? It feels an eternity.

"We need a ship," Lumar says softly.

"We need a ship," Sidorio booms.

"Yes," says Lumar, nodding, as if the idea is new. "Yes, we need a ship."

"A ship." These are the first words Olin has spoken in Stukeley's presence all night.

"That is our plan," says Mistral, smiling at Stukeley. He is prepared to go along with *any* plan she might suggest.

Sidorio stands up, towering above them. Saying nothing, he walks away from the circle, toward the boats.

"Come," says Lumar to the others. "We shall journey along the coast tonight. We shall see which ships are in these waters and think further upon this."

"Is that a good idea?" Stukeley asks, forgetting, for a moment, his hatred of Lumar. "Won't we get into trouble out in the storm?"

Lumar smiles — a full, proper smile this time. It is the most evil smile Stukely has ever seen. "The weather need trouble you no more, Lieutenant. There are no more storms for the likes of us."

Lumar's words are proved true. As rough as the weather grows about them, somehow the small ferryboat moves firmly through the waters, as if they are quite calm. Nor does the rain soak the five passengers. Once more, Stukeley imagines they are protected by a small globe.

Nevertheless, he thinks, the ferryboat, though bigger than the bark the others arrived in, is too small. A ship *would* be better. On a ship he could get away from Lumar and Olin whenever he wanted. A lieutenant would have his own quarters. And on a ship, he could be alone with Mistral. The more he thinks about it, the more he sees the possibilities. He wants a ship. He wants it now. This is how his appetite works, these days.

But as the small ferry hugs the coast, they pass no other ships. The sea is empty — for which ships would wish to contend with such weather?

"Patience!" Lumar says, smiling once more. "We must have patience. All our desires will come to pass. If not tonight, then soon."

Stukeley detests the way Lumar speaks. Grand words. Saying nothing. He seems to feel the need the fill the air. Better to be silent. Silent like the captain. The captain, who brought him back from the other place.

They sail on, around the corner of the coast. Stukeley

watches the rain lash the dark cliffs — the droplets of water illuminated by soft moonlight. Stray bushes appear to stretch from the cliff edge. Some are torn clean off by the wind and tumble down into the black waters. The ferry sails on, untroubled. They turn the corner of the cliff and, as they do, they see lights in the distance. Lights on a hill.

"What's this?" asks Lumar.

They all look up as a broad arch comes into view.

The lights and the arch strike a vague chord of recognition in Stukeley.

"Is that a harbor?" asks Mistral.

"Beyond the arch?" says Lumar. "Yes, I believe it is!"

"Shall we take a closer look?" she asks.

Lumar turns. "What do you say, Captain?"

They all look to Sidorio.

He is standing, looking toward the tall arch, and through it. There is a strange look upon his face.

"You seem perturbed, Captain," says Lumar. "What is troubling you?"

Sidorio gives no immediate answer. His eyes are racing through the arch and over the water, on to the dock, then climbing the hill. "The girl," he says at last.

"The girl?" Lumar echoes.

"What girl?" asks Mistral.

Sidorio shakes his head slowly. "The girl with the book." He is talking to himself as much as to the others.

"I'm afraid I'm not following, Captain," says Lumar. This time, the frustration in his voice is evident.

Their ferry has reached the arch. Now the arch is protected, like the boat, from the falling rain and crashing lightning. Still, Sidorio stands, staring into the distance. Stukeley gets to his feet to join him.

"Careful, idiot!" Lumar says. "You'll unbalance the boat."

"Surely nothing can unbalance *this* boat?" says Stukeley with a smile.

Lumar glowers at him.

"Look," says Mistral, pointing to the carvings. "It's an Academy."

*Academy.* The word triggers an echo somewhere in Stukeley's mind. As does the arch and the lights on the hill. He knows enough to know that he has been here before.

"Shall we go through the arch?" he asks Sidorio.

"The girl and the book," Sidorio repeats. "She knows my story."

Stukeley nods, encouragingly. "Would you like us to go on, through the arch, Captain?"

But there is no reply. Sidorio's eyes are empty now. They all see it. In place of his eyes are pools of fire. The hunger is upon him. And it is catching. Each one begins to feel the same gnawing hunger, rising from within. Until five pairs of eyes are aflame, like beacons in the dark night.

31

## INTO THE FIRE

Grace pushed back the bedroom shutters and stepped out onto the balcony. Although wet, the dark night was warm and sultry and the falling rain did nothing to slake the heat. If flood and fire could come together, then this is what it would feel like.

The storm had long since taken possession of the Academy and was now rampaging through the gardens like a pack of savage beasts. The trees were being tugged back and forth by invisible hands, bending them like giant wishbones, ready to snap. The ordinarily placid glass channels of water were churning like rapids, racing from the terrace down toward the dock. And down, down in the harbor, the Academy boats were shaken violently by the dark, troubled waters, denied, tonight, their peaceful slumber.

Grace watched it all, as the warm rain soaked her skin and hair and clothes. She watched it all and thought of that night some three months before, when she had last witnessed such a storm — not from the relative sanctuary of a balcony but from far out in the dark waters themselves. She watched it all and she thought of the Vampirates. It was the perfect weather for their reunion.

She felt a shoulder brush against her own and turned to see that Cheng Li had joined her on the balcony. Grace smiled, full of purpose.

"Are you absolutely sure about this?" Cheng Li asked her.

Grace nodded. "I'm sure."

Cheng Li rested her hand on Grace's shoulder for an instant. Together, they watched the havoc of the storm.

"You know the risk you're taking?"

Her words were almost lost in a sudden roar of thunder. Grace waited for it to pass before she answered.

"It's worth the risk." She thought of Lorcan and felt the adrenaline sweep through her. "Come on, let's do it now, before I lose my nerve."

She stepped back inside the cabin. Cheng Li followed, drawing the shutters closed behind her. "You should leave Connor a note," she said.

"I thought you could tell him."

Cheng Li considered for a moment. "A note would be better."

"Okay," Grace said, not wanting to waste any more

time. Not wanting to waste this storm. But the harsh weather was here for the night. A few more minutes would not prove decisive.

Grace carefully unlocked the vanity case that Darcy had given her and took out a pen and one of the notebooks. Reluctant to spoil the books, which had taken on a special meaning for her, she carefully removed a double page from the center. She managed to extract the page without a trace. She smoothed out the sheet and considered what to write. Inspiration came quickly. She scribbled the words, then blew on the ink to speed its drying. As she did so, a few droplets of rainwater splashed down from her rain-wet hair to the sheet. The water met the not-quite-dry ink and blurred her handwriting. It was messy, but it was still legible and she was loathe to waste any more time by starting again.

Waiting a moment, she folded up the paper and then — careful to keep her wet hair back — added a "C" to the outside, propping it on the bedside table.

She slipped the pen and the notebook back into the case and locked it shut once more. It bothered her to leave it behind, but she could at least take the key with her, ensuring that no one else could open it. Silly, really, she thought — all this fuss over a few secret notebooks. But then, she had precious little left these days besides those secrets.

"Ready?" Cheng Li asked. She had been standing with her back to Grace, watching the storm.

Grace nodded. "Let's go."

Cheng Li held open the door for her and they stepped out into the darkened corridor, moving swiftly and silently along the row of closed doors, down the stairs and out into the Academy gardens.

"Be careful," Cheng Li said, shouting over the howling wind, as they reached the rain-lashed grass. "You don't want to slip at this point."

Grace nodded. There was no way she was going to slip now. Nothing was going to prevent her from fulfilling her mission. She was more convinced than ever. This was the only way.

The two of them were soaked by the warm rain as they made their way down the hillside. Not another soul had ventured out into the grounds and, glancing back, Grace saw that all the Academy's shutters were tightly fastened. No one bore witness to their movements.

At last, they made it to the dockside. Grace paused to catch her breath. The harbor waters looked like a soup that has boiled too long, the thick liquid jumping and sputtering over the edges of the stone. Thank goodness for the moon — and the intermittent flashes of lightning — bringing light into the hot darkness.

Cheng Li said something, but her words were drowned out by thunder. Grace noticed that the jacaranda tree had been so shaken that its seat and the harbor path were both strewn with blue flowers. In the aftermath of the storm, the once beautiful tree would be almost bare. It was a sad sight, but Grace could not afford to dwell upon it.

Cheng Li leaned in closer. "Let's go out to the very end of the harbor wall."

Grace looked up. Ahead of her, the wall snaked out toward the water. On either side, the water reared up against it, leaving a trail of foam on the sleek stones. Getting from one end to the other would be a challenge. But Cheng Li was right. The farther out she entered the water, the greater the chance that the Vampirate ship would come for her quickly, before the dark waters dragged her down beyond even a vampire's grasp.

Her wet clothes already pulling at her like an undertow, Grace clambered up the steps to the top of the wall. Cheng Li followed. They held on to each other for support as they made their way forward. On either side, the waters were agitated and unpredictable. They were forced to stop for a moment as a rogue wave jumped clean over the sides of the wall. Once the water cleared, they struggled on. Grace was chilled to the bone now, in spite of the warmth of the rain.

Now the end of the wall dropped away and down into the dark, agitated waters. They stood side by side at the water's edge — allies against the storm. Then Grace stepped forward and Cheng Li stepped back. They had come as far as they might together. Now it was up to Grace alone. She looked out across the water to the Academy arch, which marked the divide between the Academy walls and the ocean beyond. Through it, a smoky mist obscured the horizon. Could the ship already be there — hovering on the other side of the arch, cloaked in mist — waiting for her? Her heart almost broke with longing. Let it be there. Let it be so.

Grace turned to find Cheng Li shivering. "Go inside," she told her, "I'll be all right."

"But what if they don't come?" Cheng Li said. They were both shouting above the noise of the storm.

"They will come," Grace cried.

"All the same . . . ," Cheng Li said, rooted to the spot.

Grace shook her head. "This isn't a game, Cheng Li. They need to think I'm in real danger. I need to *be* in real danger. That's why they came to me last time. If they know you are here, they might not come. I have to do this alone." It was all so clear to her now.

Cheng Li gazed at Grace with an intensity that drilled through her. The older girl stepped forward as if to embrace her, but then held back.

"I always knew you were extraordinary," she said. "Good luck, Grace!"

With that, she turned and staggered back across the wall. Grace watched her go, thinking how small and frail Mistress Li suddenly appeared, framed by the might of the storm. Even the twin katanas on her back seemed useless now — little more than knitting needles in the face of the elements. She thought suddenly of the kids' game — *rock, scissors, paper.* Strange how each was rendered useless, depending on what you were up against.

As Cheng Li faded back into the night, Grace turned once more toward the water. Beyond the arch, the dark mist was growing thicker but, above her, the moon slipped out from the cover of clouds and a beam of light shone down upon her face. She had a sudden sense of calm. This was her moment. She stepped right up to the edge, as if this was the diving board at Crescent Moon Bay's municipal pool. As if this was just another Friday afternoon swimming class.

"Out of the frying pan and into the fire," she cried. Then she jumped off the edge of the wall and down into the water.

It was shockingly cold. She shot down below the surface. Suddenly, she was insulated from the noise of the storm raging above. It was pitch-black and calm here. She held her breath, extending her limbs and floating beneath the furor for a moment. As her breath began to run out, she pushed down her arms and swam back toward the surface. Pushing her head up and out of the water, she was shocked by the chill night air and the noise of the storm. It seemed louder now — but whether this was because of the contrast with the calm beneath or because the weather had taken a turn for the worse, she was not clear.

She glanced around, hoping for a sign of the ship. There was none. It was too soon. She looked back toward the harbor. Cheng Li had disappeared, just as she'd told her to. Grace was seized by a momentary panic. What on earth had she been thinking of — throwing herself into the roiling waters in the heart of the rainstorm? This was madness! At that moment, she had a sudden vision of her dad, standing on the wall, staring down at her with a smile.

*"Sometimes madness is wisdom, Gracie."*

She smiled back at him. Then a wave lashed at the wall and he disappeared. The waters rose around her and she knew that she was alone — utterly, definitively alone.

She trod the waters bravely, feeling herself carried farther and farther away from the edge of the wall, out toward the arch. The sea was colder here and her energy was draining away. Surely it was time for the ship to come through the arch? Surely they wouldn't wait for her to struggle any longer?

She lost all sense of time. It could have been an hour or only a few seconds. Pictures flashed through her head like a movie replaying the scenes of her life. She was back in Crescent Moon Bay at her father's funeral; setting off with Connor on their boat; waking up on the Vampirate ship; stealing her way toward the captain's cabin; facing Sidorio; attending the Feast . . . the scenes played slower and slower, as if the spool of movie film had grown tangled and broken. And then the pictures stopped altogether. And there was only inky darkness, soaking into her through her head and hands and feet. She was coming to the end of something. If they didn't come for her now, this was it.

She dipped down beneath the surface again and felt the waves swallow her whole. She was starting to sink, like a stone, through the layers of water. Still, she felt strangely calm. She had risked all. She had been wrong. Now, what lay in wait for her?

There was a moment of nothingness. Perhaps the first of many such moments.

And then, she felt the shock of a pair of hands closing about her shoulders and pulling her. Pulling her back up through the dark water. Lorcan. It had to be Lorcan! He had taken his time. But he had come for her, just like she knew he would. She couldn't help but smile as her body went limp.

## TROUBLED SOUL

"Lorcan. Lorcan, you came. I knew you'd come."

Once more she was gazing into his blue eyes. His wound had cleared completely, as if the act of saving her had somehow saved him, too. Of course. As if she needed any further sign that their destinies were linked.

"Grace!"

She smiled up at him, ecstatically — losing herself once more in the blue.

"Grace!"

Now her vision was blurred. She was losing him. She had a sudden sense of panic.

"Grace!"

It wasn't his voice. It was . . .

"Connor!"

Her eyes opened and she found herself looking up into her brother's eyes. She couldn't piece it together. It was as if someone had simply pulled Lorcan's head away to reveal her brother's beneath. Connor let out a sigh of relief, but there was terrible anger and pain in his green eyes.

"Where's Lorcan?" she asked.

He shook his head.

Her head was propped on a single pillow. She looked beyond Connor. She was in a bed, indoors. In a vast room, dimly lit and filled with other — empty — beds. What was this place? She had never been here before.

"Where am I?"

"You're in the infirmary, Grace."

Connor's lips hadn't moved.

Grace turned her head to one side.

A woman's face gazed down at her. The gaze was more inquisitive than sympathetic.

"I'm Nurse Carmichael," she said. "I run the infirmary here at the Academy, missy. You're in *my* care now."

Grace felt a sudden shiver. Her mission had failed. The Vampirate ship hadn't come for her. Lorcan hadn't rescued her. Then who?

A droplet of water fell onto her brow. She looked up. Connor's hair was wet. So was his face and neck and, as far as she could see, his clothes.

"It's a miracle you got to her in time," she heard Nurse

Carmichael say. Her accent, ironically, was not so very different from Lorcan's.

"I saw her from her own window," Connor explained, his breath short. "The moon came out from the clouds and I saw her standing on the wall. And jumping. I ran to her. . . . I never ran so fast in my life."

Grace looked up at Connor again. He was crying. He struggled to continue speaking.

"Why did you do it, Grace?"

"To find the Vampirates again." Wasn't it obvious?

"By . . . by killing yourself?"

"No." She shook her head. "No, of course not —"

Her words were interrupted by Nurse Carmichael. "Your sister's a very troubled soul, I think."

*Troubled soul?* What was she talking about?

"I found your note," Connor said.

She glanced up. In his hands, unfolded, was the note she had hastily scribbled. Her words were clear, in spite of the smudging.

Connor,
Please don't be angry with me.
I had to do this.
You have your journey and I have mine.
We'll be together again soon.
Until which time, love Grace

"What a terrible note for a brother to find," said Nurse Carmichael. "What a terrible way to say good-bye."

What was she going on about? It wasn't a good-bye note. Well, not *that* kind of good-bye note. They were getting it all wrong. Grace was filled with frustration, not least because, in spite of all the thoughts racing inside her, her ability to speak was severely impaired. As if she was still floating under the surface of the water. She struggled to break through as she heard a burble of speech pass from Connor to Nurse Carmichael and back again.

"Ask Cheng Li." She managed to push out the words.

"What?" Connor said.

"Ask Cheng Li. She'll tell you. She knew the plan." Grace drew in, then out, another breath. "She helped me."

"What nonsense!" Nurse Carmichael said. "What slander! Mistress Li is sleeping. This is some more of her madness, I'm afraid."

*Madness.* The word snaked through Grace's head. Once more she saw her father standing at the edge of the wall.

*"Sometimes madness is wisdom, Gracie."*

"You best go and get some sleep, young man," Nurse Carmichael said.

"Shouldn't I stay with her?" Grace could hear the sorrow in Connor's voice. How could she reassure him that she was okay? Her plan may have failed, but it wasn't the plan he thought it was.

"No point in that," the nurse said. "I'll put her to sleep in a moment. She'll be out in an instant. Best thing for her."

*Put* her to sleep? How? Grace lifted her hand to Connor's, having a sudden premonition.

Too late. The prick of the needle was no deeper than a mosquito bite, but in a second it numbed her and she sank once more into nothingness.

The last thing she heard was the nurse, her accent a wicked distortion of Lorcan's.

"There. Safe now."

# 33

# A SIMPLE PLAN

It is a simple plan — to take a ship. It doesn't matter *which* ship. And, as for *when*, well, sooner is better than later but, if not tonight, then tomorrow or the night after that will suffice. These things are worth considering for a moment or two, given how decisive the events of this night will prove.

To take a ship will mark the beginning of the second phase. There are five of them now, and soon, if Sidorio and Lumar are to be believed, there will be more — many more. They can't simply rove from bay to bay in a mess of rowing boats, like water gypsies. Of course not! They must have one ship *to begin with* — and a plan for more. It not only makes practical sense — it delivers a clear message. They are a force to be reckoned with!

There will be no more aimless wandering, Stukeley realizes with a tinge of sadness — no sailing into a new cove each night and setting up camp there. Things began to change the moment the three strangers arrived. Sidorio has woken up to a new purpose. Lumar, in particular, seems to have the effect of propelling him forward in thought and action. His presence works some kind of alchemy upon Sidorio — transforming the base metal of his primal, confused notions into clear, resolute steel. At first, Stukeley suspected that Lumar would simply take over control, but he seems content enough for Sidorio to remain as captain. For now, at least. There is something about Lumar which Stukeley doesn't like or trust.

The plan, such as it is, has led them to watch for ships these past few nights from a deserted lighthouse where they have set up an impromptu base. Like so much else in the dilapidated building, the lamp itself is broken, but Lumar and Olin set about fixing it. Now, the lighthouse is back in business, sending a glow out upon the dark waters of the rock-strewn bay. The watchers in the lamp room have no need of the light to see any ship that passes into the bay. That isn't the point — the point is to draw a ship to them, to draw it in tight to the rocky shore, a fly caught flailing in their honeyed web.

On the night of the storm, the five of them are gathered in the lamp room. Stukeley hates it up here. There isn't room for five and the enforced intimacy only makes him more aware that he is the outsider among long-time allies. In such close confines, the heat from the lamp is unbearably intense. The bright ball of light scares him. It reminds him of the sun and he is all too aware what damage the sun can do him now — part instinct, part the lessons Sidorio has drummed into him. Lumar sees his fear and laughs at him.

"Don't worry, Stukeley," says Lumar, "we'll make a vampire of you yet! You see if we don't!"

And Stukeley keeps silent, but, "I already am one," he wants to say. "We were doing just fine before you came out of the night. And I'm still lieutenant." But he says nothing and worries to himself on account of the fact that Sidorio has not called him lieutenant for several days now. They all call him Stukeley now, plain old Stukeley. As if they've demoted him without ever bothering to tell him. He needs to do something to remind the captain of his worth. But what?

He doesn't have to wait long for his answer. The storm brings a ship their way. There have been other ships on other nights but, in the clement weather, they had no need to shelter in the crook of the bay. They sailed on and past, without so much as a wave of thanks up to the lamp room.

This ship, this night, is different. The storm is electric. Stukeley enjoys watching it from this perch. It is as if he is sitting above the weather. As if he is sending down darts of thunder and spears of lightning onto the sorry vessel below.

"Captain, we're on!"

Lumar swings the lamp across the water. Sidorio and the others quickly move to the windows, locating the ship. It is bravely battling the elements which attack it from all sides.

"All right then, let's go," says Lumar.

Sidorio coughs. Only *he* may issue orders.

"That is, we should go, should we not, Captain? This is, is it not, the opportunity we have been waiting for?"

"Yes," booms Sidorio. "Come one, come all. The ship will be ours."

He steps outside onto the parapet. Stukeley follows him into the storm, glancing up as a torrent of water comes down over them. Stukeley darts back inside but Sidorio laughs. He stands there, on the low wall, surveying the land and seascape as if he is emperor of it all. Then, with a cry, he leaps off into the darkness, somersaulting through the air.

"The captain is in high spirits," Lumar says to the others, his eyes bright. "Come Mistral, come Olin, let us join him. Stukeley, you stay here and shine the lamp until we give you the sign."

When was this decided? This is some ruse of Lumar's.

The three of them begin their descent while Stukeley stands alone — trapped with the ball of light he has grown to detest. He directs its beam across the ship's sails, making a game of it. He watches as the ship finds its way out of the worst of the tides into the calmer nook of the bay, right up flush to the rock at the foot of the lighthouse.

Stukeley plays the light over the ship's sails and up to the crow's nest. He plays it across the ship's flag — the skull and bones. A pirate ship, he realizes. Wasn't he once a pirate himself? Or has he imagined that? He is getting so confused — unable to separate dreams from memories. It is all such a jumble in his head. Sometimes, it is easiest not to think too hard at all — just to do what you are told and exist in the moment.

He swings the lamp back over the ship. Something registers in his memory — like a stone thrown into water, sending out small ripples. But the ripple is enough to make him stop, to force him to think, even if thinking is difficult. There *is* something familiar about this ship.

Below, the captain and his three accomplices are putting out toward the ship in their small ferryboat. He watches as the boat dips into the water. As they let go of the shore, they are quickly propelled toward the ship. Stukeley plays the light direct upon them until, to his amusement, he sees Lumar signaling frantically up at him, his arms crossing back and forth with increasing speed. Stukeley understands what he is saying — he isn't stupid — but still he waits for a moment before moving the glare of the light away and back onto the ship's deck.

The deck. He looks down. Pirates, the size of ants, are scurrying back and forth across it, slipping and skidding on the wet surface. Again, a dim memory stirs. It is more of a sensation than a thought — the feeling of his worn boots on a slippery deck. The strain to balance. That is when he knows. He has been on that deck before.

The small ferry has reached the side of the ship and now the four comrades begin their ascent. This will be the most challenging part. Sidorio is more agile than the others. He goes first. Then Olin. Next Mistral, carrying a covered basket. Lumar is the fourth. Stukeley watches as they reach the deck. Watches as one of the pirates stops in his tracks and notices the newcomers. And that is when he sees a familiar face. Fascinated, appalled, he looks down. He feels a coldness spreading through him as if a hole has been torn through his skin. He opens his mouth and cries.

"Nooooooooooooooooooooooooooooooooooooooooooooo ooooooooooooooooooo!"

―⁓

"Take us to your captain," Sidorio shouts to the pirate.

"We've come from the lighthouse," Lumar adds, "with information on this stretch of coast, and," he points to Mistral, "supplies."

The pirate looks them up and down and calls over one

of his fellows. But there is no time to deliberate. There is a lull in the storm but it mightn't last for long. The pirate beckons them forward.

"Follow me!" he says.

And so they do — Sidorio at the head, closely followed by Lumar, then Mistral, and last of all Olin. They hurry into the narrow passageway inside the ship.

"The captain is in his cabin, with his deputy," the pirate announces. He hammers on the door.

"Who is it? Enter!" comes the cry from inside.

The door is thrust open.

"Captain Wrathe, here are four visitors from the lighthouse. They come with information and supplies."

There is a pause and then the voice booms back.

"Come on in, then. Come in. This is no time to hang back in the shadows."

"Indeed," says Lumar, stepping forward. "Captain *Wrathe*, is it? Pleased to make your acquaintance. My name is Lumar."

The four of them proceed into the captain's cabin. Olin pushes the door shut behind them.

---

Up high in the lighthouse, Stukeley scans the deck frantically. Where are they? Where have they gone? But his lamp already knows the answer. They have made it inside. Their simple plan is coming together. They cannot be stopped.

But he decides it is worth a try at least. He lets go of the lamp and propels himself down the spiral stairway. He flies — two, three, four steps at a time. It seems like an eternity of stairs. Who knows what mischief will have been done in the time it takes him to descend?

He runs out of the building into the wet night. The waves are making a vicious noise. He sees the ferryboat, empty, bound to the side of the ship. He sees their other small bark tied to the rocks. He could take it out to the ship but, in his heart, he knows it is too late. He can feel it.

Then, as if he needed confirmation, he hears the first scream. It is not long before others follow. Even above the roar of the storm, the screams of men and women are easy to discern and distinguish.

He sees the pirates running back and forth upon the deck. He sees the fallen — those who have failed to escape the touch of the four strangers. He sees the others — who have been luckier, but who now throw themselves from the ship in order to be free. They jump down into the savage waters, which — though not so far from land — are deep and unpredictable. They should save their screams — they cannot afford to waste their breath.

There must have been more than a hundred and fifty crew on the ship. But finally, there are no more screams.

And, as alarming as the sound of their agony was, the absence of it chills him more. The four strangers have brought this ship to silence. Stukeley witnesses it all. He sees the fallen bodies sliding back and forth across the deck, slimy now with blood as well as spume. He sees the other bodies fighting to survive in the surrounding waters. They last out bravely but not for long. Perhaps one or two — a handful at best — will make it to the land. Whether their fear will allow them to survive the night remains to be seen.

At last, he sees a familiar figure step out onto the deck. It is Sidorio. His chest is puffed out. He is smiling.

When the pirates flooded out, they seemed like ants, utterly diminished by the ordeal. In contrast, Sidorio seems like a giant. He strides into the center of the deck, balancing himself expertly — as if he has simply swapped his regular surfboard for this super-sized one.

Without a moment's pause, he looks up and meets Stukeley's eyes through the distance and the darkness.

"Lieutenant Stukeley!" he booms. "Come and join us! There is blood for you here. Plenty of blood." He laughs. "We have our ship! We have our ship!"

His words fly through the air and bring a smile to Stukeley's face. There, he thinks to himself, his concerns for the pirate crew forgotten. He called me lieutenant. I am still his lieutenant!

"I'm on my way, Captain!" he calls back, already running to join him.

"We have our ship!" Sidorio calls once more.

Stukeley unties the small boat. He cannot get there fast enough.

Above them, the lamp of the lighthouse spins madly around, illuminating the chaos. Their simple plan has been accomplished.

## 34

# AFTER THE STORM

Connor slept fitfully and, when Jacoby knocked on his door the next morning, he was still in his nightclothes, his head as heavy as lead.

"Wow! You look awful!" Jacoby said, bounding into Connor's room, full of beans in his Academy tracksuit. "Better get a move on, man. It's already quarter to seven."

"I don't think I can do SSM today," Connor said.

"Why not?" asked Jacoby. "Are you feeling sick?"

Connor shook his head. "It's Grace," he said. "She tried to take her own life last night."

Jacoby's jaw dropped open. "No! Why? How?"

"It's a long story," Connor told him. "But it ended with her throwing herself off the harbor wall."

Jacoby shook his head. He couldn't believe what he was hearing.

"I saw her. I was up in her room. I . . . I saw her jump. And I ran . . ."

He was shaking at the memory. Jacoby put his hand on Connor's shoulder. "You did good, mate. You did real good."

It took a moment for Connor to steady his breathing. He was determined not to cry in front of Jacoby. "She left this," he said, passing Grace's note to his friend.

Jacoby scanned the words. "Wow, that's heavy, man. And look at the way the writing is all blotchy. It looks like she was crying when she wrote it."

Connor nodded. He had noticed that, too, of course.

"I don't understand," Jacoby said. "I know that Grace wasn't having the best of times here. And I know she's been a bit sick. But why would she want to do something like this?"

"Like I say," Connor said, "it's a long story. And it's time you were off on your run."

Jacoby shook his head. "I'm not going anywhere, mister. I'm not leaving you like this. So, now you have plenty of time to tell me *exactly* what's been going on."

Connor looked into his friend's eyes. It would be a relief to tell him about Grace's obsession with the Vampirates. Even if it was a betrayal of her trust, so be it. She had betrayed him in the worst way last night. Now it was every man for himself.

⟶⟞⟝⟵

Jacoby walked with Connor to the infirmary. They pushed open the heavy door and stepped into the long room, lined with rudimentary iron beds. Only one, in the center of the row, was occupied. As they began walking toward it, a figure stepped briskly from the shadows.

"Oh, hello," Connor said.

"Good morning," said Nurse Carmichael, not quite smiling. "How did you sleep?"

"Not well," Connor said.

"I'm not surprised," replied Nurse Carmichael, shaking her head. "What a night!"

"How is she today?" Connor said.

"Still sleeping." The nurse smoothed her starchy uniform. "Best thing for her."

"Let's go and see her," Jacoby said.

"Not much to see," said Nurse Carmichael.

"All the same." Jacoby nudged Connor forward. They walked past the nurse to the bed where Grace was tucked under the tight white bedsheets.

"She looks pale," said Jacoby.

She did. Connor looked at his sister. She was peaceful

now at least, her hair fanned out on the pillow, her hands crossed over her chest like an old statue in a churchyard. Connor couldn't help listening out for her breath. It was faint, and it came like a distant breeze.

"Like I told you, not much to see." Nurse Carmichael appeared at the bedside.

"When will she wake up?" Jacoby asked. "Are you *sure* she's okay?"

The nurse fixed him with angry eyes. "Are you questioning my expertise, Jacoby Blunt?"

He shook his head. "I just —"

"Because it isn't so long now since I was rubbing witch-hazel on your grazed knees and elbows, young man. I think I'm just a bit better qualified to judge the situation, don't you?"

Jacoby raised his hands in defeat and stepped back from the bed.

"Will you let me know when she wakes up?" Connor asked.

"Of course," said the nurse in a gentler tone. "I shall send word immediately. But it could be a while yet. You're best getting on with the business of your day. A busy mind can't dwell."

Connor nodded. He took a last look at his sister's deceptively peaceful face, then turned away. "We'd better get to lessons," he said to Jacoby.

The two of them walked back to the door.

"Well, at least this decides one thing," Jacoby said.

Connor turned to him quizzically.

"You can't leave the Academy until she's better, can you? No matter what Captain Wrathe thinks about it."

Connor hadn't thought of that. "I suppose not," he said.

Jacoby smiled. "I'm not going to say that every cloud has a silver lining. But, at least she's okay. And this will give you some more thinking time."

Connor nodded. As they stepped out into the sunshine, he felt a little lighter of heart.

Behind him, the heavy door of the infirmary swung shut.

As it did so, the heels of two other visitors — who had entered via the opposite door — clicked across the marble floor toward Grace's bedside.

"Headmaster, Mistress Li," said Nurse Carmichael, nodding to them.

"How is our patient today?" Commodore Kuo asked the nurse.

"As well as can be expected," she said. "Her body is still in shock. I've given her something to kill the pain."

"Very good," said the headmaster. He and Cheng Li looked down at Grace. Nurse Carmichael leaned in closer. For a while, the three of them said nothing, observing her breathing.

Then Nurse Carmichael stole a sidelong glance to Cheng Li. "The girl said something strange before she went to sleep," she said.

"Oh?" Cheng Li met Nurse Carmichael's stare straight on. She was one person the nurse would not intimidate.

"She said that you knew all about this — all about her *plan*."

"She said this to you?" Cheng Li asked.

Nurse Carmichael made sure she had both visitors' attention. "Not to me, specifically. She was talking to her brother."

"I see." Cheng Li nodded. Nurse Carmichael thought she saw an uneasy look pass between Mistress Li and the headmaster. She made her face a mask.

"I told them, of course, that it was nonsense. That you were sleeping . . ."

The headmaster and Cheng Li were still locked in a glance.

"I was right, wasn't I? You *were* sleeping, Mistress Li?"

Cheng Li opened her mouth to speak, but it was Commodore Kuo's smooth voice that filled the air.

"I don't think Mistress Li has any need to explain herself to you or anyone else," he said. "This has been a distressing incident, but Grace is safe now." He turned the full beam of his gaze upon Nurse Carmichael. "The best thing would be for all of us to take good care of her and create the minimum of fuss."

"Oh, yes," said the nurse, her eyes darting away. "I quite agree. No fuss."

"Then we all understand each other," Commodore Kuo said. "And now, if you'll excuse us, we have students to teach. We'll leave you to your . . . gentle healing."

He gave her a formal bow and then swiftly ushered Cheng Li toward the door.

Nurse Carmichael watched them go. Thoughts were popping in her head like fireworks. She glanced down at the sleeping girl. What secrets could she tell, she wondered. What secrets lay beneath that smooth unconscious mask?

---

*A busy mind can't dwell.* The nurse's words of wisdom proved true. Once the day's lessons were underway, Connor felt himself start to regain a sense of normality. The weather returned to calm sunshine and for Captain Grammont's Practical Piracy and Ocean-faring class the students took to the boats in the harbor to practice maneuvers. Connor felt a tug at his heart as he caught his first glimpse of the wall in the daylight. Jacoby squeezed his friend's shoulder. And, as Connor looked up, the harbor wall was bone dry and the waters were low on either side, like mirrors reflecting the bright sun. It was as if last night had never happened — as if it had all just been a nightmare.

"Come on," Jacoby said, "Grammont's dividing us into threes . . . Jasmine! Jasmine, wait up!"

—⁓—

The morning raced by and, now that the fine weather had returned, they were able to lunch on the terrace once more.

"Any word on Grace?" Jacoby asked Connor.

Connor shook his head. "But I'm going to check on her before afternoon class."

"Cool," said Jacoby, "I'll come with you."

"Me, too," said Jasmine.

Connor nodded and smiled. It was good knowing he had his friends around him at a time like this.

As he was finishing up dessert, Connor saw Commodore Kuo approaching from the end of the terrace. He glanced up, expecting the headmaster to stop and talk to him. They hadn't seen each other since the previous evening. Kuo must have known about Grace, and Connor felt sure that he would have something to say on the matter.

But the headmaster didn't seem to notice him, walking past their table at a brisk pace and entering his study from the door on the terrace. It slammed behind him.

Connor looked up and saw that Jacoby and Jasmine had both been watching, too.

"What's eating the Kuo?" asked Jacoby.

Connor shrugged.

"Beats me," Jasmine said, finishing the last mouthful of chocolate pudding. "Mmm, that was delicious. I'm going to be on a sugar high all afternoon!"

"Me, too," Jacoby said. "Combat Workshop should be fun today!" He turned to Connor. "Right, shall we go and check on your sister?" he said.

Connor was lost in thought.

"Calling Mister Tempest! Earth to Mister Tempest!"

"Sorry?"

"I said, how's about we take a stroll down to the infirmary and check how Grace is doing? We could even take her some cake. I'm sure that witch Carmichael won't be feeding her anything but liquid nasties."

"That sounds good," Connor said. "But first I think I'm going to go and have a quick word with Commodore Kuo."

"Are you sure that's a good idea?" said Jasmine. "He doesn't seem in a great mood for a chat."

"That's just it," Connor said, "I think his mood might have something to do with me and Grace. If I talk to him, I might be able to smooth it over."

He could see from their expressions that the other two didn't think this was a good idea. But he knew his own mind. Besides, they hadn't been privy to the discussions he and Commodore Kuo had been having. He knew that the headmaster would have thoughts about what had happened with Grace and he wanted to hear them. He stood up and tucked his chair back under the table.

"I'll only be five minutes," he said.

"Okeydokey," Jacoby said, "I guess I'll just have to endure five minutes alone with Peacock." He feigned boredom. As he yawned, Jasmine threw a raspberry at him. It bounced on his nose, leaving a blood-red stain.

Connor grinned and walked across the terrace. He had planned to go to the headmaster's door off the Rotunda but, as he passed the study, he saw that the glass door onto the terrace was ajar. It must have bounced open again after Kuo had slammed it. As Connor headed toward it, he heard the headmaster's voice.

"Things are getting out of hand."

He had never heard such steel in the headmaster's tone. It brought him to an immediate standstill.

"I thought this was what you wanted."

It was Cheng Li. Now, Connor froze to the spot.

"It's a very delicate situation," he heard Kuo say. "We had him just where we wanted him — but it's a fine line."

Were they talking about *him*? They must be. Or was it just arrogance to think that?

"I really don't see what has changed," Cheng Li said. "If anything, we're closer to the result we want."

Connor felt his head begin to pound. If they were talking about him, what did this mean? Had they had something to do with what had happened to Grace? He remembered in a flash Grace saying that Cheng Li had known her plan. Nurse Carmichael had dismissed this as madness but Grace and Cheng Li had certainly spent enough time together. He felt as if he was putting together a jigsaw but didn't yet have all the pieces.

"Connor . . ."

It was Kuo's voice. So they *were* talking about him.

"Connor!"

No, they weren't talking *about* him. They were talking *to* him. The French door to Kuo's study opened and the headmaster leaned out and stared at him with a curious expression.

Connor was trapped and exposed.

"I think you'd better come inside," said Commodore Kuo, beckoning him from the bright terrace into the darkness.

35

# LETTING GO

Connor's heart was beating wildly as Commodore Kuo closed the door behind him. His friends were only a couple of feet away on the terrace — he could see their backs through the window — and yet he sensed extreme danger, as if he was willingly walking into a cage at the zoo.

"Take a seat," said Kuo.

Connor sat down in the chair opposite Commodore Kuo's desk. Kuo sat down in his own chair, but Cheng Li remained standing, her hand resting on the globe.

"It goes without saying," said Commodore Kuo, "that we're extremely shocked and distressed by what happened last night. And I can only imagine how you must be feeling."

Connor heard the words and waited. Wasn't the headmaster going to say anything about catching him outside, listening in on the conversation? Wasn't he going to try to explain away the words he must know Connor had overheard?

"I'm terribly sorry not to have come and seen you earlier," said Kuo, "but I'm afraid I was distracted by urgent Federation business. It's really no excuse but I feel I must offer it."

"Thanks," Connor said.

Cheng Li stepped across the room, moving to the headmaster's side. "We came here from the infirmary, Connor. Grace seems to be stable now."

Connor nodded.

The headmaster smiled at him. "How are *you* doing, Connor?"

Connor shrugged. "I'm okay, I guess. It was a big shock."

Commodore Kuo nodded.

"I mean, first of all, finding the note."

"The note?"

Commodore Kuo clearly hadn't heard this part. Connor reached into his jacket and produced the folded note. Commodore Kuo slipped on his glasses and read Grace's blotchy handwriting. "May I?" he asked Connor, before offering it to Cheng Li. Connor nodded. What did it matter? Let them all read it. Let them all see the fragile state of his sister's mind.

"So you found this note and then . . ." Commodore Kuo raised his eyebrows, inviting Connor to continue.

"I had gone to her room to talk to her. The shutters had been closed all day. I suppose I wanted to try and talk some sense into her. To get her to try to take part in life at the Academy. So I got to her room, but there was no answer. I knew she had to be inside — where else would she have gone? When she didn't answer, I panicked. The door wasn't locked so I went inside and then I saw the note. The storm was so bad that the latch on her shutters had broken. They were flapping in the gale. The moon was bright on the harbor and as the shutters opened I saw a silhouette on the harbor wall. I knew it was her. And I knew what she was going to do . . ."

He was shaking again. Commodore Kuo stood up and moved swiftly to Connor's side of the desk, placing his hands on Connor's shoulders for support. "It's okay," he said, "there's no need to tell us any more."

There was silence in the study as Connor struggled to regain his composure.

"Except," said Cheng Li, "why you think she did it?"

Connor could sense a look passing between the head-master and Cheng Li over his head.

"You're more likely to know that than me," he said, the words tumbling out before he had time to censor them. "You've spent far more time with her than I have since we got here."

Cheng Li nodded. "That's true. And, I confess, I do feel partly to blame for what happened."

Connor was surprised. Such an admission was uncharacteristic. He looked up, eager for Cheng Li to continue.

"As you know, Grace was profoundly affected by what happened to her on the Vampirate ship," said Cheng Li. "She feels a strong bond with its crew."

This was not exactly breaking news. "It's not good for her," Connor said. "Look where it's led her."

Cheng Li nodded. "I agree. It's not good for her, but it's natural enough."

Commodore Kuo left Connor's side and returned to his seat. Once seated, he addressed Connor. "Perhaps you are aware of Stockholm syndrome?"

Connor shook his head. The headmaster slipped his spectacles down his nose and took their stalks in his hands. "In simple terms, Stockholm syndrome refers to the strong emotional attachments we can form with the very people who threaten our lives. It's a survival mechanism — a way to endure terrible violence. It only takes a matter of three or four days to occur. It is precipitated when we are placed, like Grace was, in a life-threatening situation where the threat of death is then removed. The victim is then flooded with feelings of relief and comes to see her captors as the 'good guys' — as people who have not threatened her but in fact saved her." He paused. "We rather think that this is what Grace is suffering from."

"Since her arrival here," Cheng Li said, "I've been letting her talk through her experiences on that ship. I've encouraged her to do so. I know that you felt uncomfortable hearing about such things — and who could blame you? — but I felt it was important that Grace had someone to tell them to."

"Getting them out of her system," said Commodore Kuo, "was the first step in curing her."

"But," Cheng Li continued, "things took a very different turn last night. Grace's state of mind was clearly more fragile than I realized. And, as I say, I feel that by encouraging her to talk about the Vampirates, I may have unwittingly led her to take extreme action."

Connor nodded. "You mean like trying to kill herself?"

The headmaster and Cheng Li were clearly surprised by the starkness of his words. But then they nodded.

He shook his head. "I don't think she *was* trying to kill herself," he said. Commodore Kuo leaned forward, fascinated.

"I did at first," Connor continued, "it was the obvious explanation. But I've been thinking it over. It just isn't something Grace would ever consider. I know how much my sister wanted to return to the Vampirate ship. I've been trying *not* to think about it, but I know it's true. Perhaps you're right and it is that syndrome you mentioned. Whatever, she feels she has unfinished business there. I think that, last night, she was simply trying to get back onto the ship."

Cheng Li and Commodore Kuo looked at him curiously.

"By jumping into the harbor in the middle of a storm?" said the headmaster after a pause.

Connor nodded. "Of course. That's how she ended up on the ship in the first place. We were shipwrecked in the middle of a storm and one of the Vampirates, a guy named Lorcan, fished her out of the water. I think that Grace was hoping that history would repeat itself."

"That seems a little far-fetched to me," Commodore Kuo said.

Connor noticed that Cheng Li was silent. She had spent time with Grace. *She* knew that it wasn't far-fetched, he could sense it.

"When she came to after I rescued her," Connor continued, "she was calling for Lorcan. In fact, for a moment, she thought I *was* Lorcan." He smiled. "Grace wasn't trying to end her life. Like she wrote in this note, she was just trying to continue on her journey."

Commodore Kuo shook his head slowly. "You're made of stronger stuff than I thought, Connor. You're really fine with this?"

Connor nodded, smiling. It was as if, while he had been talking, something had clicked into place inside his brain. He *hadn't* been fine with it — not at all. From the moment he and Grace had been reunited on the deck of the Vampirate ship, he'd been trying to erase all thoughts of what had happened to her there. He'd avoided hearing her talk about it, denied her the chance to get it out. And, all the time she'd been closeted with Cheng Li he had just kept his head down and busied himself with life at the Academy. But now, suddenly, he saw the situation for what it was. Since the shipwreck, they had both embarked on journeys. And, just as he could not turn back the clock and walk away from piracy, now he understood that her journey was equally unstoppable. He hadn't wanted to let Grace go. But now, at last, he could.

"So where does this leave us?" Commodore Kuo asked him. "Do you still want me to work out an agreement with Captain Wrathe — to free you from his articles so you can stay here? And begin both your Academy and Federation training?"

Connor nodded. "Nothing has changed."

"Of course he must stay here," Cheng Li said. "He can't leave Grace now."

"This has nothing to do with Grace," Connor said, surprised at his own steel. "Of course, I'll do what I can to help her recover. But we have to start making our own decisions. We want different things from life. We're set on different paths. She can stay here with me or she can go back to *The Diablo*. She can even go back to the Vampirate ship — if she can find it. It's up to her to decide."

Outside, a bell began to chime. Through the window, Connor could see Jacoby and Jasmine getting ready to return to class.

"Afternoon class," said Cheng Li.

Connor stood up, feeling strangely powerful. "I'd better catch up with the others."

The headmaster nodded, chewing on the arm of his spectacles.

Connor excused himself and exited through the terrace door, closing it securely behind him. After he had gone, the headmaster and Cheng Li looked toward each other.

"I must confess," said Cheng Li, "he surprised me."

Commodore Kuo smiled. "You must learn to trust the tide, Mistress Li," he said. "Sometimes all you have to do is sit back and wait."

The final lesson of Connor's day was Combat Workshop. At four o'clock, he and Jacoby arrived in the gym dressed in their tracksuits, along with the rest of their class. Captain Platonov was waiting for them, but he was not alone. At his side was Cheng Li.

As the students assembled, Platonov clapped his hands. "Attention, everyone. Attention. In a moment, we will resume our usual practice. But today, we must make do without Mister Blunt and Mister Tempest."

Connor and Jacoby turned to each other in puzzlement. Their fellow students were equally surprised.

"Mister Blunt, Mister Tempest, perhaps you would go with Mistress Li?"

Shrugging, Jacoby and Connor stepped to the front of the class. Cheng Li smiled and led them out of the gymnasium door. Behind them, Connor heard Platonov barking out commands to Jasmine and the others.

"What's up?" Jacoby asked Cheng Li. "Where are you taking us, Mistress Li? Are there some secret Academy dungeons we didn't know about until now?"

There was a broad grin on his face. Nothing seemed to faze him, thought Connor.

Cheng Li seemed equally amused. "What a feverish imagination you have, Jacoby. Perhaps one day you will write a book? No, there are no dungeons — not to my knowledge, at least."

Indeed, she was leading them *up*stairs rather than down. They emerged into another corridor, and then Cheng Li pushed open a door and they found themselves in a second, smaller gym.

Connor was puzzled. It was dark in here. Then, as Cheng Li hit the lights, he saw, in the center of the room, two sword stands and, on each one, a glass case.

The three of them walked across the matting on the floor to the stands. As they did so, Jacoby gasped and Connor felt his heart begin to race.

"It's the Toledo Blade," he said. "Commodore Kuo's Toledo Blade."

Cheng Li smiled.

"And Molucco Wrathe's Sapphire Rapier," said Jacoby. "It's even more beautiful up close!"

Connor was confused. "But the headmaster said that these only ever come out of their cases on Swords Day."

Cheng Li nodded, as she took a pair of keys from the chain around her neck and unlocked the two cases. "That is correct, ordinarily. But it has hardly been an ordinary few days, has it? The headmaster wished to make a gift to you."

"The blade?" Connor could barely speak as Cheng Li opened up the case, revealing the sword in all its magnificence.

"No, not the blade itself. But the chance to use it, once."

Both Jacoby and Connor focused on Cheng Li's every move as she took both swords from their cases and laid them on a velvet-covered rest on a nearby table.

"Tomorrow night, there will be another dinner in your honor. It was to have marked the end of your stay, but now it will mark the beginning of your becoming a full-time student here."

This, of course, was news to Jacoby. He let out a cheer and slapped Connor on the back. But Cheng Li did not wait before continuing.

"All of the captains will attend. And, prior to the dinner, the entire student body will gather to watch you and Mister Blunt perform an exhibition of swordplay with these blades. This will take place on the practice deck . . . on the 'lagoon of doom.'"

"Wicked!" cried Jacoby. "I claim the Toledo Blade!"

Both Connor and Cheng Li glared at him.

"I'm joking, I'm joking! I'll take Molucco's rapier."

"That's quite enough of your clowning," Cheng Li said. "We have barely twenty-four hours until you perform in front of the entire Academy. It has fallen to me to choreograph your swordplay. And I have to show you some very complicated moves." She put on her gauntlets. "Connor, you chose to join the Academy as a full-time student? Well, this is where your real Academy training begins!"

---

"I think I'll sleep for a week after that," said Connor, as he emerged from the showers after sparring with Jacoby for two hours solid.

"No rest for the wicked," Jacoby said, vigorously drying his hair. "Didn't you hear Mistress Li? She wants us back in that gym at seven sharp tomorrow morning. You know what that means?"

"No Saturday morning lie-in?"

"Worse than that, mate. No swimming class — *ergo*, no chance to ogle Jasmine in her bikini."

Connor laughed. Jacoby Blunt was incorrigible.

After their extended sword workout, Connor was dog-tired that evening. By the time he'd eaten dinner, he was ready for bed. Incredibly, Jacoby came to life again after eating and suggested a pool tournament. Connor couldn't face it and was thankful when Aamir and a couple of their other classmates took up the challenge. They all wished him good night and headed off to the games room, leaving him on the terrace.

Connor looked down to the harbor. It was so tranquil tonight — amazing what a change twenty-four hours could bring. He yawned and stretched out his legs. They were as heavy as lead. He could fall asleep right here, right now — only, there was one last thing he needed to do before bed. Drawing himself to his feet, he walked across the terrace and down the steps through the gardens.

The light was on over the infirmary door. Connor knocked but there was no answer, so he pushed it open.

It was dark inside. The dormitory was so big that the lamps hanging from the ceiling were inadequate to light it properly, even if the bulbs *had* been of an appropriate wattage. One lone bedside lamp was on, in the center of the room. He walked toward the light, aware of the noise his feet made on the cool marble floor.

In a moment, he stood at Grace's side. She was still sleeping, but she looked much more comfortable than the last time he'd seen her. Before, her hands had been crossed awkwardly, like a statue. Now, one was curled under her head on the pillow and the other rested over the top of the sheet.

Connor sat down on the bed and looked at his sister's face. She appeared content now. He was pleased to have reached the point where he could feel comfortable simply being with her again. For a time, he just sat there, watching the rise and fall of her breathing. It was deep and regular. There seemed little chance that she would wake but there was color in her cheeks and her dip in the ocean some twenty-four hours earlier appeared to have left her with no permanent damage. He was glad. He was more than glad.

"You're right," he said to her. "We each have our own journey to make. I'm sorry that I didn't see it before. I'm sorry I tried to stop you. I'll never do it again."

He reached out for her hand. But, as he tried to touch it, his hand went straight through it and met the bedclothes. Confused, he reached out once more, but again his own fingers pushed through hers, as if she was made only of air. He must be really tired, he thought, steadying himself and, for a third time, reaching for her hand. He drew on all his powers of concentration. But, once again, his hand passed straight through hers.

He felt cold panic spreading through him. He stepped back and looked down at her, again watching her breathing, looking once more at the expression on her face. She was not only content. She seemed to be smiling at him, up from the depths of sleep. Something clicked inside his head. He decided to try one more thing. Her hair had swept down over her eyes. He reached out to brush it clear, but his fingers went straight through her head. The next time, he didn't even try to pretend. He just put his hand straight through her ear and burrowed it down into the pillow. Grace smiled at him, eyes closed, as if he was tickling her. He stepped back, smiling now himself.

"They came back for you," he whispered. "They came back for you, Grace, didn't they? I don't know how they did it, but that's where you've gone."

And in that moment he knew this was how it was supposed to be. This was what she wanted and needed. The headmaster and Cheng Li could pontificate forever about which syndrome Grace might or might not have. Whatever — for now, his sister belonged on the Vampirate ship. It was her home.

"What's all this commotion?"

Nurse Carmichael marched down the center of the ward. Connor grinned. His whispers hardly qualified as commotion. The nurse really was living on the edge.

"Oh it's you," she said. "Come to see your sleeping sister again?"

Connor nodded. "I just came to say good night to her."

"Well, you've said it now, so off you pop," said the nurse. "We don't want her waking in the middle of the night, do we?"

Connor shook his head. "No," he said. "No we don't. But I wouldn't worry, Nurse Carmichael. I don't think Grace is going to wake up any time soon."

The nurse regarded him peevishly. He took a final look at the phantom of his sister, then smiled at Nurse Carmichael and patted her on the shoulder, before brushing past her and walking to the infirmary door. Nurse Carmichael flinched. She brushed her uniform as if a bird had pooped on her shoulders, and headed back toward her cubicle.

## 36

## COMBATANTS

Connor's next day at the Academy was destined to be a long one. At seven o'clock, he and Jacoby were back in the gym, where Cheng Li was waiting for them. Connor still felt tired but his body soon came to life as Cheng Li led them in some preparatory exercises, then talked them through the moves for their exhibition fight in more detail.

They spent the rest of the morning perfecting them. There was a lot to concentrate on. The Toledo Blade was heavier than Connor's usual rapier but it felt good to hold. The handle was bound in an odd, rough leather. At least, he thought it was leather. When he asked Cheng Li, she reminded him that, like Commodore Kuo's boots, it was made from stingray skin — much tougher and more waterproof than regular leather. He looked at the hilt and saw that the tiny bumps were actually fine scales. Even after so much use, the scales still glittered, as if the handle had been embedded with tiny starlike jewels.

There was nothing, however, to match the hefty sapphire embedded into the hilt of Molucco's old rapier, which Jacoby had taken to as if it had been crafted especially for him. As it moved back and forth before him — Jacoby maneuvering it expertly through one strike then another — Connor saw that the sapphire served not only a decorative purpose but a practical one, too. It was so polished on its multiple faces that when it caught the light at a certain angle it dazzled you, as if the sun was shining directly into your eyes. You had to squint, making you lose your focus and the core of your concentration.

The hardest thing about the fight, Connor and Jacoby agreed — during a ten-minute break on the sun-drenched gymnasium steps, was going to be not harming each other. In spite of their retirement from regular combat, the swords were kept sharpened and oiled in readiness for their use — and they were both razor keen. Jacoby was more used to exhibition combat than Connor — who had been thrown more quickly into real-life attacks — but both boys agreed that it was if these swords craved an actual body hit. As if they had a mind of their own, and resented being out of action for so long. It was as if the blades themselves had a mind for battle and a thirst for blood.

By lunchtime, they had the fight nailed. Cheng Li took back the swords and locked them away in their cases. The two combatants would not see them again until they entered the "lagoon of doom" that evening, in front of their audience — the entire student body and faculty of the Pirate Academy.

"Are you nervous?" Connor asked Jacoby as they sat down to lunch.

"Nervous? Are you kidding? I'm petrified. I might hurt you."

"Funny," Connor said. "Very funny."

"It's good to see that being petrified hasn't spoiled your appetite," said Jasmine, smiling as she indicated Jacoby's fully-laden plate.

Jacoby looked up at them. "Hey, Coach Li said to load up on carbs. That's all I'm doing."

"Oh, *that's* what you're doing, is it?" Connor laughed. He continued with his more modest meal. He felt too sick with rising adrenaline to eat much. He'd have to make up for it at the post-fight feast.

The fight was due to commence when the Academy clock struck six, but by five-thirty the atmosphere in the harborside amphitheater was electric. The students began taking their seats, ranged in their year groups, the tutors joining them at the end of the rows. Flaming torches lit the walkways up the steep stone stairways, along the front of the lagoon and the small pier leading out across the turquoise waters to the practice ship.

In the lagoon itself, the ship had been lowered and brought forward so that the deck became a stage, visible to the entire audience.

Right now, the deck was filled by some of the older kids who had formed a rock band. They had been given the opportunity to warm up the crowd.

"This music is making me feel very old indeed," Commodore Kuo said to Cheng Li, in the seats in their very front row.

"You *are* very old, John," she said with a smile. "You just choose to ignore that fact most of the time."

He gave her a wounded look, then broke into a smile. "How are our boys doing?"

"Very good," she said. "At last the Toledo Blade is in the hands of a rightful warrior."

"Touché," said Commodore Kuo. "You know how to inflict a body blow."

---

Connor and Jacoby waited in their own seats close to the pier. Connor glanced back at the crowd, feeling as if he was about to be thrown to the lions.

"Hey," Jacoby said, "don't sweat it, Connor. This is just a little showcase to get the Academy rocking on a Saturday night. This is one of the reasons they made a stage here. Happens all the time."

Connor nodded. He knew that. He'd competed in sports events too many times to let his nerves get the better of him. This was a bit different, though. It was more of a performance than a competition. He had to balance executing the perfect moves, without harming Jacoby. The last thing he wanted was to hurt his new best mate.

At last the rock song faded away and was followed by a roar of cheering from the crowd. The kids cleared their instruments from the stage and began walking over the pier toward Commodore Kuo, who had stepped up to greet them. Now he welcomed them back onto dry land and turned to the crowd.

"Thank you to . . . The Vagabonds of, erm, Death," he said. "I'm usually more of a trad jazz man, but really that was most . . . impressive. Most refreshing." He glanced at Cheng Li who mouthed "old" at him.

As the clapping started to subside, Commodore Kuo turned to address the audience.

"Tonight, we have a special treat for all of you . . . for all of us. As you know, it is our custom here at Pirate Academy to have an annual Swords Day. On that day — the very last day of the school year — all the swords which hang in the Rotunda are brought down and the most accomplished of our students here get to use them in exhibition fights, which honor their illustrious forebears — the captains who once used these swords for real."

He cast his eyes from the row of tutors to the kids. "Sometimes, I think of these swords as the treasure of the Academy. Not because they are made of the finest metals — often enriched with jewels — by the best craftsmen the world over. *No* — I think of these swords as treasure because each of them has so many stories to tell. Each of these blades has fought in a hundred or more battles. If only they could talk, if only they could share their experiences with us. But, you know what? In a way, they do. When an ancient sword comes into the hands of a young pirate, I'm convinced that there's an electric charge between the energy of the young combatant and the energy within the blade."

He paused, giving the audience a moment to reflect on his words. "But the *real* treasure of the Academy isn't the ancient blades which hang over us. The real treasure is *you*. Each of you. The swords represent our past, but you . . . you are our future. Each and every one of you is destined for greatness. You will each continue the fine and noble traditions of piracy. Some of you are distinguishing yourselves already as expert navigators. Others are showing themselves to be fine leaders and strategists. And then there are those of you who are dazzling combatants."

There were some whoops from the crowd. They knew the fight was about to commence.

"Tonight, I have lifted the rule that our ancient swords are taken out of their cases only on Swords Day. Tonight, I have decided to celebrate the fighting talent here at the Academy. Tonight, two of our finest combatants will take to our stage and show you some dazzling moves, taught to them by the tutors here and, in particular, by Mistress Li."

This was greeted by applause and, nodding, Commodore Kuo extended his hand toward Cheng Li. Blushing, she finally stood up and acknowledged the cheers.

"Yes," the headmaster said. "Mistress Li has only been teaching here three months, but she's already made a huge impact on Academy life. And, on that subject, we come to someone who has been here just one week but who, I am pleased to say, will now be joining the Academy as a full-time student. I'm delighted that he'll be fighting tonight with my very own Toledo Blade. . . . Put your hands together and give a rousing Academy welcome to Connor Tempest!"

Connor and Jacoby exchanged a handshake they'd evolved over the past few days. Then Connor walked over to join Commodore Kuo. As he reached the headmaster's side, the headmaster extended his hand and shook it in a more conventional fashion.

"Connor has proved himself to have exceptional skill in combat situations," said Commodore Kuo, "and so we had to look to the very best of Academy students to take him on. You know, of course, who I am talking about." The crowd cheered and some of them shouted out his name. "Yes," continued the headmaster, "you all know who I mean. What you *won't* all know is how this boy performed in his very first Combat class. But I was there, as was Captain Avery and Captain Singh. We remember the skill that this boy — then just six years old — demonstrated with those little bamboo sticks. Well, a few years have passed since then, and tonight he'll be using Molucco Wrathe's Sapphire Rapier. His name may be blunt, but he's as sharp as they come. . . . Let's welcome Jacoby Blunt!"

Now Jacoby took a deep breath in and out, then jogged out to join Connor and the headmaster. He, too, shook the headmaster's hand.

"I've said enough," said Commodore Kuo. "All that remains is for me to say that, whether you are a gifted fighter or not, I want you to watch this battle and appreciate the pure skill these two display. And remember — whatever your talent is, strive to be the best that you can be. That's all we ask of you here at Pirate Academy. And now, gentlemen, let me present you with your swords."

The swords in question were resting on stands erected at the front of the pier. Connor and Jacoby each knelt on one knee before the stand bearing their sword. The headmaster lifted first the Sapphire Rapier. He took it in his left hand, extending it toward Jacoby.

"Use this sword with wisdom and precision," he said to Jacoby. "Honor your forebears and make your mark upon history."

"I will," said Jacoby, receiving the sword in his own left hand and remaining kneeling while the headmaster moved to the second stand.

Kuo ceremonially wiped his hands with a silk cloth that had been set there for this purpose. It was a symbolic cleaning so that the same hands had not touched both swords. Setting down the cloth, he took the Toledo Blade in his left hand, pausing for a moment as he gripped his long-time ally.

There was a spontaneous burst of applause in celebration of Commodore John Kuo's long and illustrious career. He waited for it to subside, smiling softly.

"Use this sword with wisdom and precision," he said to Connor. "Honor your forebears and make your mark upon history."

"I will," said Connor. He took the sword in his left hand, his fist enclosing the stingray bindings of the handle. He thought of the blade's long history.

At a signal from the headmaster, four students came forward and removed the sword-stands from the arena.

"Gentlemen, take your starting positions," said Commodore Kuo, before walking back to his seat.

Connor and Jacoby walked together along the pier onto the practice deck. They had been well-rehearsed.

They took their position in the center of the deck, back to back.

The Academy clock began to strike six o'clock. The sixth strike was their cue. Connor waited, letting breath come in and out with the striking of the clock. One . . . two . . . three . . . four . . . five . . .

37

# THE LAGOON OF DOOM

*Six!*

Connor spun around and launched at Jacoby with the Toledo Blade. Jacoby extended the Sapphire Rapier. The swords made first contact and each combatant felt the electric connection of the blades. Now, the friends were no longer smiling at one another. There was too much to concentrate upon, as they began moving through the first of Cheng Li's challenging sequences.

Connor quickly shed all his nerves. Though this was an exhibition fight, he still felt that heightened sense of awareness the headmaster had called *zanshin* in his lecture. When his sword struck Jacoby's, the noise in his head was louder than the school bell. When Jacoby swung the rapier toward him, Connor saw the sapphire, bluer than the waters of the lagoon. Every noise and color, every sense, was intensified. He drew on a deeper focus and energy. It enabled him to jump higher in the air, to swing the sword back and forth in a fraction of the time it would usually take. He was utterly and completely in the zone. Even as he drew on the calm well of energy in his core, he had the extra awareness that this was going well. He was aware of the roars of the crowd as the first sequence came to a close with him apparently having the upper hand over Jacoby. But it was all choreography — each would have his moments of glory as the exhibition fight continued.

"Stunning work," Commodore Kuo whispered in Cheng Li's ear. "Connor has such a natural ability."

She nodded. "I just hope Jacoby remembers all his instructions."

Kuo nodded, then drew back, focusing again on the two young fighters as they moved into their second sequence. This was more complex than the first — Cheng Li knew how to work an audience. The sequence began with some fast parrying back and forth across the deck. Then Jacoby took the upper hand, forcing Connor low and apparently defenseless. It was at this point that Connor had to summon all his strength and athleticism and not only push Jacoby back but assume dominance in the fight.

Once more, he felt that sense of *zanshin* — that three-hundred-and-sixty-degree awareness all around his body.

He could see Jacoby and the extended rapier. He could see the narrow band of room he had for his maneuver. He could see the audience, watching with bated breath and, in front of them — like the two eyes of a giant beast — Cheng Li and Kuo, their faces boring into him. He saw all this without ever losing his core focus on Jacoby's eyes. It took him back to his very earliest days of training, not here at the Academy, but on *The Diablo*. When Bart had told him, "Always watch your opponent's eyes. The sword can lie, but the eyes don't." Connor looked into Jacoby's eyes. And he saw something wrong there — a lie, behind the familiar eyes of his new friend. He registered it but fought hard to give nothing away. Peturbed as he was, he held his focus and executed the complex turnaround, pushing Jacoby back and taking control.

Again the crowd roared its approval. Cheng Li and Commodore Kuo joined in the clapping.

"Breathtaking," said Kuo.

Cheng Li inclined her head toward him. "You ain't seen nothing yet."

As they began the third sequence of strikes, Connor never let his attention drift from Jacoby's eyes. He was sure he wasn't mistaken. Jacoby was lying to him. Connor continued making his moves, using the Toledo Blade with more skill and dexterity than he had ever used with his rapier. He decided to stick to every nuance of the moves they'd choreographed, increasingly certain that Jacoby would start deviating from them. There was no time to be shocked by the betrayal or to think through the layers of those others who must have betrayed him. That would not save his life. *Zanshin* would.

It happened in the middle of the sequence. Connor kept to his marks perfectly, but as Jacoby launched the next attack, the blade of his rapier came much closer than they had rehearsed. He could feel the hot steel against his ear. Then he realized it wasn't the blade that was hot. The steel had pierced the skin of his ear. It was bleeding.

Jacoby looked panic-stricken. He glanced over Connor's shoulder to the audience. Perhaps he had meant to wound Connor, but not so soon. Connor was not distracted for an instant. He maintained his alertness, showing no panic or fear. If the fight was halted now, he would know that he had been wrong — that nothing was amiss and it was a simple error. But if no one intervened then he had a very different answer.

No one intervened.

Unshaken, Connor continued to focus on Jacoby, eye to eye. Neither spoke. There was no need for conventional speech. It was all in the eyes. Connor let Jacoby know that he knew. Jacoby acknowledged the fact. But Jacoby seemed far more shaken than Connor. There was another secret buried deep in Jacoby's eyes that Connor could not yet unearth.

Now, Connor had to make a lightning-fast decision.

Should he stick to the scripted moves and defend himself only when Jacoby attacked or should he let go of the routine and simply treat this as any other fight? He decided to opt for the former approach. Jacoby had clearly been schooled in another routine altogether but he was either having trouble remembering it or was simply unable to implement it. Whatever he was up to, he seemed disadvantaged in his role as aggressor. Connor decided to let him make his attacks and make his mistakes. He had more experience of real combat than Jacoby. A little blood wasn't going to weaken him.

They moved into the fourth sequence they had rehearsed. This one was supposed to be dominated at the outset by Jacoby. As his opponent initiated the fresh attack, Connor could tell that something was wrong. All of Jacoby's assurance was fading away. Though his physical moves showed all his usual strength, it was clear to Connor that his opponent's fighting spirit had drained away.

Once more, Connor had to make a lightning-fast assessment of the situation and to decide his tactics. This was complex, though. If this was any other adversary, he could take the victory in a decisive fashion. But, in spite of Jacoby's betrayal, he was not ready to inflict serious harm upon him. It had been easier defending himself when he had only to contend with Jacoby's attack. Now, he faced the infinitely more complex situation of an enemy who appeared to have lost heart. Of course, it could all be an elaborate bluff. But, looking into Jacoby's eyes, Connor knew that it wasn't.

He had to maintain his alertness and so, for the next few moves, he concentrated fully on that, taking himself back to that full state of *zanshin*. He kept focused on Jacoby's eyes and the blade of the rapier. He took in the rapt attention of the crowd, separated from him by the narrow band of water. He saw the masklike expressions on Cheng Li and Commodore Kuo's faces. They, too, must know that he had sensed their betrayal. But they were masters. They gave nothing away.

Connor held all these sights and thoughts in his head, and then he heard a stray sound coming from the direction of the harbor. He was drawn back into combat with Jacoby — an athletic and challenging sequence which took them from one side of the deck to the other. Connor could hear more noise from the dockside, but he couldn't afford to miss a beat. Was this some new part of whatever plan was unfolding? He had to do something, and fast. He made a quick decision.

As they parried to the point furthermost at the right of the stage, Connor slipped in an extra strike, which knocked the rapier out of alignment. Jacoby stumbled to hold tight to it and, as he did so, Connor drew the Toledo Blade forward toward Jacoby's neck. In his panic, Jacoby dropped the rapier. The audience gasped. Connor held the blade across Jacoby's neck, only an inch from his skin.

"Start talking," Connor said. "And talk fast!"

Jacoby wasted no time. "I didn't want to do it, Connor. They made me. They wanted to shake you up, to see how good a fighter you really were."

"They were going to have you kill me."

"No," Jacoby said. "Believe me, that was never the case. Just to shake you up. I didn't want to. Look, you saw how I screwed up out there."

Connor hesitated. One incorrect impulse now could prove decisive. He searched Jacoby's eyes. In them, he saw a true picture of confusion and regret. He did not see anything there to suggest a killer.

He drew the tip of the Toledo Blade away, remaining alert to a surprise attack. As he stepped back, he scooped up the Sapphire Rapier in his left hand then held up both weapons to the crowd — weary, bloodied, but victorious.

The crowd began to cheer, louder than ever before.

Commodore Kuo jumped up and called to them to join him at the front of the pier.

But neither combatant moved — each too stunned by events.

"Come on, pirates!" Commodore Kuo called, with more force.

Connor looked at him with disdain. They could just defy the headmaster and remain out on the practice deck. But actually he needed to confront him. Connor strode off along the pier, leaving his opponent behind.

"Well fought," said Kuo to Connor as they met.

Connor glared at him in disbelief. "Don't patronize me," he said.

"I'm sorry?" Commodore Kuo looked puzzled.

"You set me up. You and Cheng Li. You set me up against my best friend."

Kuo shook his head, beaming at the roaring crowd. "I wanted to see what you were really made of, Connor. Exhibition fights are all well and good, but I needed to see what you could pull out of the bag in a real conflict scenario. And you passed. You passed with flying colors. Your place in the Pirate Federation is now assured."

"You know what you can do with your Federation?" Connor said, angrily extending both swords in the direction of the headmaster. A new roar from the crowd drowned out his words. The headmaster jumped onto the pier. Connor kept the twin blades trained on him. The headmaster looked at Connor down the length of the blades.

"Connor, I think you had better look behind you."

Connor paused. Was that the best Kuo could come up with? It was little better than a pantomime trick.

"Connor, behind you."

Connor shook his head. His days of doing Commodore Kuo's bidding were over.

"Connor, look behind you!"

This time, it wasn't the headmaster who spoke. It was an altogether more welcome voice.

"Molucco!"

Connor turned, never happier to see his old ally, who stood before him in all his finery.

"That's *Captain* Wrathe, to you!"

"Captain Wrathe!" Connor stepped forward. He was so pleased to see Molucco, he could have thrown his arms around him — were it not for the two blades he held in his hands.

"Is that . . . it can't be! Is that my old rapier?" Molucco said.

"Yes." Connor extended the hilt toward him. The captain took it and weighed it in his hand. He looked sad for a moment.

"What are you doing here?" Connor asked. "You aren't due until tomorrow." He smiled, adding hastily, "Not that I'm not glad to see you."

"Something terrible has happened," said Molucco. He removed his hat and Scrimshaw slipped into view, extending himself toward Connor in greeting.

"What is it?" Connor said. "What's wrong?"

"It's my brother," Molucco said. "My dear brother . . . Captain Porfirio Wrathe." He broke off as a large diamond of a tear rolled down his cheek.

"What of Porfirio?" Commodore Kuo spoke, drawing close to Connor's side.

"Murdered most savagely," said Molucco. "And with him, his crew . . . all but a handful."

Connor shuddered. "What happened?"

Captain Wrathe shook his head. "There's a time for telling tales and there's a time for action, my boy. Now go and fetch your things. I need you back on *The Diablo*. It's every pirate to his mettle. I will not wait for this deed to cool before I take my revenge."

Connor nodded. "I'll be quick," he said.

"I think you're forgetting something," Commodore Kuo said. "I think we should all go into my study and talk things through in private."

Connor shook his head. "That won't be necessary. There's nothing for us to discuss."

"But Connor . . . ," Commodore Kuo began.

Shaking his head, Connor brushed past the man who had once inspired such respect in him.

Cheng Li stood up and moved out into the walkway. "Connor, compose yourself."

"Don't *you* talk to me," he said. Her betrayal hurt even more deeply.

"Listen to me," she said. "You may not like me very much at the moment but there are things you don't understand."

"You always tell me there are things I don't understand," he said. "But the fact is, there are plenty of things that are perfectly clear to me."

He moved past her, up to the flame-lit walkway. He was determined to get to his room and collect his stuff. The

Academy students — blind to the truth of the fight — patted Connor on the back, praising his swordplay.

"You can't go," Cheng Li said. Her words brought him to a standstill. He turned.

"Why not?"

"Because you can't leave Grace here," Cheng Li said, smiling at him, sure in the knowledge she was one step ahead of him.

But not this time. "Grace isn't here," Connor said. "She left already."

Seeing the dumbstruck expression on Cheng Li's face was intensely satisfying. He wasted no more time and began running up to the top of the amphitheater and onto the hill beyond.

—～—

Connor quickly packed up his things and headed down the Academy hill for the last time. His head was hot and aching from everything he had been through and the wound on his ear could do with some attention — but certainly not from the likes of Nurse Carmichael. He wanted no more of this place or the people within it.

A barbecue had been set up on the terrace and the students were busy piling up their plates and tucking in. It wasn't easy to slip past them unnoticed, but thankfully most were too preoccupied with the food to bother him.

He sincerely hoped that Commodore Kuo and Cheng Li would stay out of his way. The last thing he needed was another confrontation with them. They had hurt him badly and nothing good would come from hearing their excuses and rationalizations. His eyes scanned the terrace. A table had been set for the teachers at one end. Of course! He was supposed to join them for dinner. Well, forget it — there would be one empty place tonight.

He headed down the path toward the dock. A figure stepped forward from the trees at the side of the path. Connor stepped back. It was Captain Lisabeth Quivers. What did she want?

"Connor, I just wanted to say that I'm sorry."

He paused, looking at her carefully. There was genuine regret in her voice.

"I'm sorry that your visit to the Academy has ended like this. Sometimes the headmaster takes things a step too far."

This was the understatement of the year. "He almost had me killed," Connor said.

"I can't excuse his actions and that isn't my intention," said Captain Quivers. "I don't want to delay you — I know you have urgent business with Molucco. All I wanted to say is that we're not all the same — at the Academy, or at the Federation. If you ever change your mind about things, I'd be honored if you felt you could contact me."

It was an honest request from a decent woman. He appreciated the gesture.

"Thank you," he said, shaking her hand. "I have to go now."

She nodded and smiled. Then they set off in their different directions.

*The Diablo* was waiting in the harbor and it was a sight for sore eyes. Connor couldn't wait to get on board and sail away from the Academy. But before he made it, another person crossed his path. Jacoby.

"I'm sorry. I don't think we're talking," Connor said, carrying on walking.

"I deserve that," Jacoby said, following him. "And you don't have to say anything. But I'm really sorry, Connor, I really am. I'm your friend . . ."

Connor stopped and turned. "Your definition of 'friend' is a little warped."

"They made me do it," Jacoby said, "but I should have said no."

"Yes," Connor said. "Yes, you should have."

He continued walking. He was right at the harborside now.

"I'm not going to beg for forgiveness," Jacoby said. "That would be crass and you'd only say no, the way you feel right now. But I *am* your friend, Connor — at least, I want to be. I did wrong but I'll find a way to make this up to you. It may take a while, but I'll do it."

"Good-bye," Connor said, reaching for the ladder which hung over the side of the ship.

Without turning back, he glanced up the rope ladder. At the top was Bart, waving and smiling down at him. "Hey buddy," he called, "welcome back!"

Connor smiled and began climbing up the ladder toward his real friend.

38

## THE RETURN

Grace stood under the sails of the Vampirate ship. Her
heart was pounding. Was she really back? She could feel
the deckboards under the soles of her feet. There was no
invisible barrier keeping her at one remove. She reached
forward and her hand touched the mast itself. As she did
so, a vein of lightning rose from the base of the sails, illuminating them so that for a moment they seemed like vast
bronze wings.

She heard a door creak open. Glancing along the deck,
she saw that it was the door to the captain's cabin. She
stood, frozen to the spot. She thought how fearless she
had been that first time she had sought out the Vampirate
captain. Now, she was filled with fear as well as other

emotions. Now, she knew so much more than she had then, *felt* so much more.

"Come, Grace." His whisper filled her head. As usual, it was devoid of emotion.

Was he still angry with her? She frowned. Whatever he might feel, *she* was still angry with *him*. She strode off across the deck, toward his cabin.

As she crossed the threshold, her eyes searched for the familiar cloaked and masked figure. There was no sign of him. She stepped further inside. The cabin door swung shut behind her. She kept on walking through the darkness, glimpsing light in the distance. At last, she saw his silhouette through the balcony shutters. He was standing at the ship's wheel.

"Am I really back this time? *Properly* back?"

The captain turned toward her. She found herself infuriated by his mask. Why was he so scared to reveal any emotion? He just stood there, like a statue, saying nothing for a time. She was filled with anger now.

"Yes, you're back." At last, his whisper filled her head. "And I'm glad."

His mask crinkled slightly. She recognised that he was smiling at her. She was pleased but she still had unfinished business with *him*.

"You're glad?" she said. "But you told me to stay away."

The captain turned away from the wheel. Once more. Grace watched as the ship's wheel turned back and forth, free from its master's touch. The captain walked toward her and extended his gloved hands.

"I know that I hurt you. Grace. And I am sorry. There were many things on my mind — many *challenges* I had to address . . ."

Grace felt tears pricking her eyes. "Nevertheless," she said, "you don't just push your friends away. You don't tell them to leave. You let them stay and help!"

Again, he said nothing and she wondered if she had overstepped the mark with her outburst. But his hands rested on her shoulders and he bowed his head.

"I apologize, child. You are right. I lost myself for a time. There were new threats, new dangers that I had to address. But it is no excuse for my . . . cruelty to you."

Grace was taken aback. She couldn't believe the Vampirate captain was apologizing to her. But, as gratifying as this was on one level, she was disturbed to hear his words. Suddenly, she felt as if he was coming to *her* for support. She wanted to help, she'd been willing them to let her help for so long, but now she felt a sudden burden of responsibility.

The captain led Grace into his inner sanctum and indicated for her to sit down with him at his table. As usual, it was strewn with maps but also, this time, with numerous old books. It reminded Grace of when she had been in the middle of homework, desperately searching for answers, wherever they might lie.

"Things have — as you know — been difficult here since you left," continued the captain. I did not want to involve you in such dangerous situations. This ship was not a safe place for you."

"Pirate Academy wasn't so safe, either."

"I saw that. That's why I came to fetch you in the end."

"Not before I nearly drowned myself!"

He shook his head. "That was unnecessary, Grace. And foolish."

"I realize that now," she said, embarrassed. "But I didn't know what else to do. I was so desperate to come back here. I thought that if I put myself in the same place . . ."

"I know *why* you did it," he whispered. "And I admire your bravery. But you must learn to wait sometimes. Your father had a saying — *Trust the Tide*." He paused. Grace wanted to ask how he knew about her father and his sayings, but before she could, the captain went on.

"The night you threw yourself into the harbor, I was sinking in dark waters of my own. I couldn't come to you then. But I knew that Connor would. He is brave, your brother. Brave and true."

"Yes." Grace nodded. Suddenly, she felt very stupid and ignorant.

"*I'm* sorry, too," she said, her head hanging low. "Really, I am."

"Don't look so gloomy," the captain said. "You are

courageous and wise, Grace. You have great powers, but you do not yet, I think, quite understand the extent of them. Or how best to use them."

"What kind of powers?"

Her spirits were renewed and she was hungry to hear more. But the captain was not one to be rushed.

"Look at the way you were able to communicate with your friends aboard this ship. And then you were able to journey here several times . . ."

Grace was confused. "I thought *they* were calling *me*," she said. "First, Darcy came to see me. Then I had those visions of Lorcan. And then I began making spirit journeys here. I thought *you* were calling me back."

"Darcy made her own spirit journey to you," the captain said. "I was angry with her at the time — I didn't want you to be dragged back into danger — but I could not remain angry. You touched Darcy — that's why you can communicate so strongly with her. You touched Lorcan — and others, too." He bowed his head once more. "But when you came here, Grace, it was not through our doing. No. It was you who chose to embark upon those journeys."

*Her?* Could it be true?

That time under the jacaranda tree . . .

And then on her academy bed . . .

And, last, on the balcony . . .

Had she brought these journeys upon herself? It was hard to fathom. And it certainly hadn't been a conscious decision, as much as she had wanted to help.

"Yes, Grace. *You* chose to come to us, just like the first time."

*Just like the first time?* What did he mean?

"The first time — the very first time — I was just caught in a storm," Grace said. "I was drowning. Lorcan rescued me then."

The captain said nothing for a moment. She knew that his silence was merely a veil over thoughts he was not yet ready to voice.

"How *is* Lorcan?" she asked, anxious to know the latest news.

"One thing at a time," said the captain. "You must learn, my child, to be patient."

Grace sighed. As much as she liked the captain, he could be tremendously infuriating. She had forgotten this trait during her absence.

Suddenly, he drew himself up once more and walked toward the fireplace. His long robe trailed behind him. Light sparked along its network of veins.

"There's someone I would like you to meet," he said.

"Who? Why?" She hoped he would not scold her again for these new questions.

"His name is Mosh Zu Kamal. He's an old friend of mine. My guru, you might say."

*Guru?* Grace knew that the word meant leader or teacher. She was surprised to discover that there was someone senior in rank to the captain. But then she remembered how vulnerable the captain had seemed before. It was reassuring to know that he *did* have someone to turn to in crisis.

"He's the one who came up with the idea of the ship," the captain continued. "He's the one who, at the beginning — when I was so very lost — showed me the way."

Grace was greatly intrigued at the thought of such a person — not that the term "person" seemed quite adequate to describe the guru of the Vampirates. "Where is he? Does he travel on the ship? How come I haven't already met him?"

The captain smiled. This time, he seemed amused by her torrent of questions. "He does not travel on this ship, though from time to time he does visit us. On this occasion, however, *we* will visit *him*. We are journeying there now, as a matter of fact."

"Where?" Grace asked.

"He lives in a place called Sanctuary," said the captain. "It is at the top of a great mountain."

Grace glanced down at the map spread out across the captain's table.

The captain shook his head once more. "I'm afraid you won't find Sanctuary on any map, my child."

Grace was puzzled, but excited. If it wasn't on a map,

how could the captain navigate toward it? How would they ever find it? Now, she *really* knew she had returned to the Vampirate ship! Now, she knew why she had had to come back. This place had so many mysteries — and she was only skimming the surface of all its magic.

"We're heading there now?" she said, deciding to focus on more tangible things. Was it far, she wondered? And were they journeying there purely on *her* account?

The captain smiled once more. "Actually, there are several things about which I must consult Mosh Zu. Firstly, I believe that he will be able to help Lorcan . . ."

"You mean to heal his blindness?"

"I mean only what I say, Grace. Mosh Zu will help Lorcan."

Grace frowned. Was the captain saying that Lorcan would remain blind? That this guru of his would only help him to adjust to his new condition? It wasn't good enough! Lorcan *had* to regain his sight! She still felt so responsible for what had happened.

"It isn't your fault," the captain said, once more guessing her thoughts. "I was wrong, before, to say that it was . . ."

"But it is my fault," she said, ruefully. "Of course it is. He wouldn't have gone out into the light if he hadn't been trying to save me."

"That part may be true. But Lorcan is not helping himself to heal."

Grace nodded. She remembered all too vividly her last spirit journey to the ship. The night of the Feast. She remembered Darcy telling her that Lorcan would take no more blood from his donor.

"Isn't there anything *I* can do to help Lorcan?" she asked, despairingly.

"Yes," said the captain to her surprise. "Yes, of course. And you know what it is."

"I do?" she asked.

"Search for the answer," the captain said. "It lies within you."

He looked suddenly troubled once more. He had that look she had seen before — the look that signaled it was time for him to be alone.

"You want me to go now, don't you?" she said.

"It's not a question of want," he answered. "There are things I must do — further questions I must ponder."

"About Lorcan?"

He shook his head. "There are other urgent matters to which I must now turn my attention."

"Can I help? You know I'd do anything in my power."

The captain rested a gloved hand on her shoulder.

"You already *are* helping, Grace." he whispered. "More than you know."

# 39

# A NEW KIND OF ENEMY

It was a very different Ma Kettle's that Connor and his crewmates on *The Diablo* stepped into that night. The tavern was no less crowded than usual, but the mood was somber. Usually, you had to struggle to hear yourself think above the din of chatter and music, tomfoolery and petty scraps. But tonight, the voices were low and hushed. Everyone had heard about what had happened to Porfirio Wrathe and his crew. No one could quite believe it.

"Here you are, Lucky!" Ma Kettle said, squeezing Molucco's hand. She was, Connor noticed, dressed more plainly and conservatively than usual. Sugar Pie was at her side, holding a tray of drinks. She too was dressed and made-up more simply. Without makeup, she looked more beautiful than ever, he thought. She smiled softly at him. He glanced away, embarrassed.

"Everyone's waiting for you," Ma Kettle told Molucco. "They all came. I knew they would. Will you address them now, or would you like a little strengthener first?"

Molucco gazed at her sadly and shrugged. The simplest of decisions seemed to torture him in his grief.

"Here," said Ma Kettle, passing out glasses from Sugar Pie's tray. Each glass contained a slug of translucent red liquid. "Coral brandy," said Ma. "Iffy taste but it packs a punch! They say it makes you as strong as the coral reefs. One for you too, Mister Tempest. And you, Bartholomew."

Ma and Sugar Pie took the final two glasses.

"To Porfirio," said Ma, raising her glass high. They all brought their glasses together, then drank the brandy. Connor winced. It was, without doubt, the most disgusting drink he had ever tasted in his life. But once the putrid taste receded, he felt a strange warmth spreading through his entire body.

"Let's go then," said Ma, taking Molucco's hand once more.

She led Captain Wrathe to the stage in the center of the tavern. Connor and Bart stood to one side, looking out at the massed ranks of pirate crews who filled the bar.

"They've come from far and wide," said Bart, "to show their support for Captain Wrathe."

Connor looked back at Molucco as the captain made his

way to the front of the stage. "He's really shaken up, isn't he?" he said.

"Buddy, you should see him in private," answered Bart. "He's just barely holding himself together."

"I can't say I blame him," Cate said, arriving at their side. "What happened to Porfirio was horrific."

Connor nodded. He was still trying to take it all in.

"Friends," said Molucco, his eyes roving across the serried ranks, "I thank you all for coming here tonight. Your support means so very much to me at this time." He paused. "To lose a dear brother leaves the very deepest of wounds. But to lose him in such a monstrous way, well, it cuts to the very heart of a man." He paused. "This news has left my hoary old heart broken." A fresh tear edged down Molucco's face. Ma Kettle stepped forward and pressed a handkerchief into his palm. He gripped it but allowed the tear to flow freely. The crowd waited patiently for him to continue.

"Forgive me," he said. "I am not here to crave sympathy."

"You have it already!" cried one of the pirates from the pit.

"Thank you. You're very kind, sir, but really, I'm not here to ask for condolences." He took a deep breath. "I'm here to request action."

"Just name it!" cried one of the pirates in front of Connor.

"Yeah," added another. "We're right behind you."

"Aye!" several hundred pirates boomed together. The hairs on the back of Connor's neck stood on end. He'd never seen so many people united in one cause.

But there was one rogue voice. It came from the shadows. "Leave this to the Federation. The Pirate Federation should handle these matters." The voice sounded familiar, thought Connor, but he was unable to see the speaker.

Molucco shook his head. "What need have I for the Federation, when I have friends? We shall band together and defeat the enemy."

The crowd cheered Molucco's sentiments.

"I think," Molucco said, "that most of you now know the horror that passed two nights ago. My brother's ship was sailing through a terrible storm and sought shelter in a bay not far from here, close to a lighthouse. Porfirio and his brave crew were battling the elements and looked to the people in the lighthouse to bring them aid." His voice grew stronger as he continued. "But the crew of that lighthouse did *not* bring aid. They brought *death*."

As Molucco paused once more, you could have heard a pin drop on Ma Kettle's grimy floorboards.

"We do not know exactly what occurred," Molucco said. "Out of a crew one hundred and fifty strong, only seventeen men and women survived that night. I've talked to those that did and only a few of 'em still have their minds. They have told me that the savagery committed by that lighthouse crew was beyond anything they have ever witnessed in all their time at sea." Molucco stepped to the front of the stage and extended his hand. "Friends, be very clear. This is a new kind of enemy. A veiled enemy. They do not seek gold. They do not seek advantage upon the ocean. All they seek is blood."

Molucco's words chilled Connor. Just as they chilled every pirate — man and woman, young and old — who gathered in Ma Kettle's pit that night. But they chilled Connor more deeply, as he thought of Grace returning to the Vampirate ship. A return which Connor had *allowed*. Not that he'd have had much chance of stopping his sister, Connor thought, ruefully. Grace was adamant that in the main the Vampirates were peace-loving. He hoped with all his heart that she was right. That it was only a few renegades who fit Molucco's terrifying description.

"Porfirio's ship is not far from here," Molucco continued. "These monsters have taken it for their own and are cruising along the coast. But they shall not have it." He raised his voice and boomed out at the audience. "They shall not sail away on my brother's ship."

"We'll take 'em!" cried a pirate captain.

"Yes," Molucco said. "Yes, reaching the ship will not be difficult. But once we board it, then what?"

"Molucco!" a voice called from the side of the stage.

"Yes, Captain Gresham."

"Molucco, there are, so we understand, only five of these . . . demons."

"Yes," Molucco said, "aboard this ship, yes. It seems incredible, but yes, the survivors tell me all this death and devastation was caused by five alone."

"We cannot be complacent then," said the other captain.

"No," Molucco agreed, shaking his head. "Five may seem as nothing to a multitude such as ours, but these are no ordinary five. They do not employ swordplay — nor are they deterred by it."

"We need a different weapon," said the captain.

Molucco nodded. "A new kind of weapon for a new kind of enemy. But what?"

The tavern was quiet, then a noise began to rise like a breaking wave as the assembled pirates debated their choice of weapon. Connor watched the crowd. In its center, he saw a tall stranger, dressed in a dark leathery cloak and a mask. In spite of the mask, Connor could see that the stranger was looking directly at him — and at him alone. And, as he did so, inside Connor's head a voice whispered:

"Fire."

Connor thought his eyes and ears must be deceiving him — an aftereffect of the coral brandy, perhaps. But the masked stranger continued to stare at him and Connor's head was filled once more with the curious whisper.

"Tell them, Connor. Fire."

Instinctively, Connor opened his mouth and shouted, "Fire!"

The crowd drew suddenly silent. A thousand heads turned toward him.

"Not here," Connor said. "Our weapon. We'll take fire to them."

"Yes!" Molucco cried. "That's it! Simple, effective —
brilliant. Yes, Mister Tempest. Our weapon shall be fire."
Suddenly, he was all business again. "Now, can I ask all
the captains and deputies here gathered to join me in the
booth and we will devise our tactics. . . ."

Connor looked back at the crowd, which was starting to
disperse. The masked stranger returned his gaze and nodded.

"Connor, let's go and grab a seat, buddy," said Bart.

"Sure," Connor said, turning to his friend. "Sure, I'll be
with you in a minute. There's someone I have to talk to."

"Who?"

"That man over there — the one in the mask."

"Mask? I don't see anyone in a mask."

"Right there in the middle of the bar."

"I think someone's had a bit too much brandy . . ."

But Connor had left his side and was striding through
the bar toward the masked stranger. He beckoned Connor
to the side of the room and up the stairs. Connor followed,
heading up toward the gallery of private booths.

The stranger stepped inside the first booth and Connor
followed, drawing the velvet curtain behind him. His
heart was racing.

"Connor." The words seeped into Connor's head like
melting ice. The stranger held out a gloved hand. Connor
reached for it.

"You're the captain, aren't you?" Connor said. "The
captain of the Vampirate ship."

The captain nodded.

"It's good to meet you at last, Connor Tempest." Again, Connor's head was filled with the whisper.

"You too, sir."

"I thought you might be angry with me."

"Angry, sir? Why?"

The captain sat down. "Because Grace came back to my ship. Because she cannot stay away."

"I was angry, well, frustrated, at first," said Connor, sitting down himself. "I thought that after everything that's happened, we should stay together. But I know now that she needs to be there. I was selfish — I thought I could get on with being a pirate and just expect her to come along for the ride. But, in the end, I realized that we had to go our separate ways — for now at least."

The captain nodded. "Then you are wise, Connor Tempest. Wise, as well as strong."

"She is safe there, isn't she?" Connor asked. "It is a safe place?"

The captain paused. "Is anywhere truly safe?"

It wasn't the answer Connor had hoped for.

"Don't look so worried, Connor. I will do my utmost to protect Grace, and she has other friends on board who feel the same. Besides, Grace is very strong."

"I know," Connor said. "She's the stronger of the two of us. She always has been."

The captain seemed surprised at the statement. And Connor had surprised himself by admitting the fact.

"I should be getting back now," the captain said.

"So soon?" Connor replied. Suddenly, he had a hundred questions for the captain.

"You can always come and visit us, you know. You are very welcome."

"But how do I find you? Even Grace had difficulty finding her way back to the ship."

The captain shook his head. "Not really," he said. "It's not really so hard to find."

He rose from the seat and began to make his way out of the booth.

"Wait!" Connor said.

The captain turned.

"You told me to tell them to take fire."

"Yes," said the captain.

"But the . . . the people who murdered Porfirio are . . . they're Vampirates too, aren't they?"

Connor was surprised how much emotion the captain could convey through the strange mask. He looked sad and weary.

"They are exiles. I gave them shelter for a time. But no more."

"So you want them to die as much as the pirates do? Can they die a second death?"

The captain considered the matter.

"I do not wish hurt or death upon any living creature," he said, "but, in this case, I fear the alternative." He paused. "There is one more thing, Connor. Something important."

"Yes? What is it?"

"Among the exiles, you may see someone you think you know. But do not be fooled. He is not as he appears — only an *echo*. You must be very strong, Connor. You must lead the way. Do not let him prevent you and your comrades from doing what you *must* do."

What did he mean? Connor frowned. Why did the captain talk in riddles?

As if he had read Connor's thoughts, the captain smiled. "Because you will know, Connor. When the time comes, you will understand and you will act. You don't need as much help as you think you do. Your destiny is not to follow, but to lead." He reached out his hand once more. "Until we meet again, Connor Tempest."

Connor shook the captain's gloved hand. As he did so, he felt a wave of strength and determination pour into him. It was the strangest sensation — as if it was coming directly through the captain's veins into his own. And there was one more mystery. As Connor held tight onto the captain's hand, he had the strangest feeling. There was no logical explanation — but he was certain that it was a hand he had held before.

## 40

# DONOR

Grace was too troubled to sleep. She pushed back the curtain over her porthole. It was light outside. On the Vampirate ship these daylight hours were the hours of rest, but she had not yet adjusted her circadian rhythms.

She stepped down from her bed and, slipping on Darcy's coat once more, made her way out of the cabin and along the corridor. She pushed open the door to the deck and, feeling the sudden blast of cold air, stepped outside.

It was a brisk day, but she found the breeze somehow soothing. It ruffled her hair and massaged away her headache. The sound of the wind and the unsettled waters below helped to drown out the constant noise inside her head. She rolled the sleeves of the coat right down over her hands to keep them warm and walked up to the railing that ran around the edge of the deck.

All around her the sea was gray and choppy. As far as she could see, there was no sign of any other ships. And no sign of land — of Sanctuary, whatever it might look like. She wondered how far into their journey they were. Was this still the regular ocean or had they already passed into uncharted waters?

Her musings were interrupted by a light touch on her neck. At first, she took it to be the breeze, blowing up the collar of her sweater. But then it came again and she realized it was the hand of a fellow traveler. No one should be up here during the light hours. No one save the captain — and his hands were always gloved. She could tell that this was a bare hand. Feeling suddenly fearful, Grace slowly turned around.

"Hello," said a small, delicate young woman. She looked familiar.

"Hello," said Grace, trying to place her companion. She was tiny and very pretty, though also very pale.

"I'm Shanti," said the woman, "Lorcan's donor."

Of course! Now, she recognized her. She had seen her with Lorcan the night of the first Feast. Grace had envied Shanti that night — envied her not only her beauty but the easy intimacy she shared with Lorcan. Now, Shanti looked older and more frail. Her brow was stitched with worry lines.

"You're Grace," said Shanti, stepping forward and joining Grace at the deck rail. "Lorcan often talks about you."

Grace was pleased with that information. She felt awkward, though. She had never talked to a donor before and, although the captain had explained something of the relationship between vampire and donor, she still had many unanswered questions.

"When did you get back?" Shanti asked her, turning her eyes out to the gray sky.

"Yesterday," Grace said.

"And you're going to stay, this time?" There was an edge to Shanti's voice. Was she somehow jealous of Grace? She sounded as if she might be — though she surely had nothing to be jealous of. Still, Grace decided, she should probably tread carefully.

"I'm not sure how long I can stay," Grace said, truthfully. "It's not really up to me."

"I don't understand," said Shanti, the wind toying with her long, dark hair.

"Nor do I," Grace said, smiling as she turned toward her companion. "It's all a mystery to me."

Shanti continued to gaze into the distance. "What's a mystery?"

"This ship," Grace said. "The Vampirates. The donors. I really know very little. I didn't even know that donors could come up to this deck."

"We're allowed up here during the daylight hours,"

Shanti said. "But not after the Nightfall Bell." She shrugged. "It's for our own protection. Besides, we need to get a good night's sleep. Sleep keeps us strong. Sleep makes our blood pure."

Grace nodded. Things were starting to make sense.

"Not that it matters much any more."

"Why not?" Grace asked.

Shanti shrugged, still refusing to meet Grace's eyes. "What good's a donor's blood when a vampire refuses to feed?"

She sounded very hurt now. Of course — Lorcan had stopped taking blood since he had been wounded. It might have been a relief to his donor, thought Grace. But, looking at the girl, she saw that nothing could be further from the truth.

"I'm sorry," Grace said.

"What good is sorry?" said Shanti. There were tears in her eyes.

Grace reached a hand out to her shoulder but Shanti quickly shrugged away her touch.

"Leave me be!" she said. "I don't need sympathy from *you*."

"It's just I feel responsible," Grace said. "Lorcan wouldn't be in this state if it wasn't for me."

At last, Shanti turned to face her head on, tears working their way across her cheeks. "I am very well aware of that fact," she said.

"You care for Lorcan," Grace said. Of course she did. How could you not care for him?

But Shanti shook her head. "I'm not crying for *him*. It's me. I had a good thing going on this ship. If he chooses not to take my blood, then there's nothing left for me here. I'll have to leave."

Grace was puzzled. "Where would you go?"

"That's the question, isn't it? I can't go back to the places I came from. They don't exist any more. Not since the floods. I've got no home, no family, no . . . no nothing. This ship was my last chance."

"Lorcan's appetite will return," Grace said. "I know it will. And even if it doesn't, well, surely the captain would let you stay."

Shanti shook her head. "You don't understand. You said it yourself. It's all a mystery to you. Well, it's plain as day and night to me. I made a deal, you see. Every donor makes the same deal. As long as you're supplying blood, you're fine. But if something happens to stop that — well, they have no need for you. It's good-bye and good luck."

Grace was shocked at Shanti's words. She couldn't believe the captain would run things in this way. He had always been so kind, so caring, toward her.

"You couldn't understand," Shanti said, each word dripping with pain and bitterness. "What would you know of having nothing in this world? Of having nowhere to go?"

Grace was about to answer the question but then she realized that no answer was sought.

"No, you couldn't possibly imagine. When the floods came, I lost everything I had in this world, everything except my bones and blood. And I made a deal with the devil for them. It was the last chance. The very last chance. But it had its upside." She paused, her words had come in such a torrent, she needed to catch her breath. "*They're* all immortal, of course. That comes easy to them when they cross. But us lot — well, it isn't the same for us. We're only immortal so long as we're with them, feeding them. When they stop feeding, age catches up with the likes of us."

So that was why she looked so much older than when Grace had seen her at the feast. How old was she? Grace wondered. How much catching up was there left for Shanti to do? No wonder she was so angry at Lorcan — and at Grace.

"Shanti, I'm sorry about what's happened. I really am. But I'm here to help Lorcan get better. I know he will."

Shanti snorted, tearing her hands from the deck rail. "Maybe he will. And maybe he won't. It doesn't matter to me any more. Because even if he does decide to take blood again, it isn't my blood he wants any more, is it?"

The woman glared at Grace, then began striding off across the deck. Grace turned and followed her.

"What do you mean? If he doesn't want your blood, then whose?"

"Oh come on," said Shanti, "I thought you were supposed to be clever!"

With that, she turned and threw her small, frail body at the door. In a moment, she had disappeared back indoors.

Her words resounded in Grace's head. What was she saying? That Lorcan wanted *her* blood? Was the only way to cure Lorcan to become his donor?

Grace thought of what the captain had said when she'd asked how she could help.

*"Search for the answer. It lies within you."*

Grace began to tremble, suddenly aware of the blood pumping through each and every vein within her body. Was this what Lorcan needed? If she truly wanted to save him, was this the price she'd have to pay?

# FIRE

It was a simple plan that Molucco and the eleven other pirate captains had devised. To surround the ship and bring fire to it from all sides. So much fire that it would take an ocean to quench its heat. To leave its murderous squatters no possible chance to escape. Molucco knew that it meant his brother's ship — along with his brother's body and those of the crew — would burn away to ashes. But, with Porfirio gone, this, he had decided, was the right, true end. "Like the pirates of old," he announced solemnly, "his ship shall be his funeral pyre."

And so, that night, twelve ships set sail along the coast. *The Diablo* was, of course, at the front of the fleet. On the deck of each ship, a controlled bonfire had been prepared — ready for the cue when each pirate force would light their torches and make ready for simultaneous attack. Watching the preparations, Connor kept thinking about what the Vampirate captain had told him.

*"Among the exiles, you may see someone you think you know. But do not be fooled. He is not as he appears — only an echo."*

What did he mean — an echo? And who was the captain talking about?

*"You must be very strong, Connor. You must lead the way. Do not let him prevent you and your comrades from doing what you must."*

The captain seemed so confident that Connor could control the others, but he was still new to the crew. True, he had Molucco's ear, but he was far from sure that he could command the rest of his comrades in the heat of battle.

*"When the time comes, you will understand and you will act. . . . Your destiny is not to follow, but to lead."*

Was this true? Connor thought again of his vision of becoming a pirate captain. Perhaps today would be his first test toward that goal.

The ship's cannon roared. It was the sign. The rogue ship had been sighted. *The Diablo* adjusted its course. Connor looked back and saw the amazing sight of eleven ships moving in formation, each carrying perfect circles of fire — like small planets — through the night.

The ships turned toward their target, gathering around it like bees in a hive. The ship idled in the water, its sails furled. The pirates could see no sign of life aboard — but the empty deck bore the terrible, bloody evidence of the slaughter. A fresh siren sounded. On each ship, the pirates armed themselves with flaming torches. A second siren. And now, the pirates began throwing torches from all sides at the deck of the ship. Before long, the deck was ringed with flame.

"This is for Porfirio," cried Molucco, sending a flaming torch straight toward the mast.

The pirates on *The Diablo* cheered as the sails began to carry the flames. The cheers were taken up by the other ships until there was a wall of sound around the circle of fire.

Suddenly, figures appeared on the deck of the ship. Connor looked closer. There were four of them — three men and a woman — and they were cowering amid the fire. Connor's eyes roved across them — these monsters! There was a tall black man, his silver hair reflecting the flames. Then a taller, thinner, younger man. And a girl — a beautiful girl, but a monster nevertheless. And then . . . And then there was the fourth vampire. Connor recoiled. It was Jez!

Connor looked at Jez, remembering the last time he had seen him, lying in Molucco's cabin after they had brought his corpse back over the wish. He remembered the moment, on the deck of *The Albatross*, when Jez's life had finally left him. As long as Connor lived, he would *never* forget that moment. Suddenly he understood the Vampirate captain's words. *Amongst the exiles, you may see someone you think you know. He is not as he appears — only an echo.* Here was the echo. It *wasn't* Jez.

At Connor's side, Bart paled in horror. Connor turned to his friend, who pointed, dumbstruck at Jez — or whatever Jez had become.

"It isn't him," Connor told him. "It looks like him but it *isn't* Jez."

Bart's face was pure agonized confusion. "I don't understand. Look at him . . ."

"It's complicated," Connor said, suddenly understanding the Vampirate captain's words. "After Jez died, after we buried him, he was brought back to life. Well, brought back to *something* . . ."

Bart shook his head. "You're telling me my old buddy is a *vampire*?"

"He's a Vampirate," Connor said.

"The crew that rescued Grace?"

Bart was — understandably– struggling to take it in. But now Connor saw that other members of the crew had noticed "Jez" and were holding their fire. He had to do something. If they ceased the attack, who knew what danger might spring from this?

"It isn't him!" Connor cried. "It *isn't* Jez." He climbed higher on the deck. "Trust me, it isn't Jez!"

The pirates looked back at Connor, all wide-eyed confusion. They too had seen Jez die. They had seen his coffin thrown into the sea.

Across on the other ship, Stukeley looked uncertainly toward them through the leaping flames — his eyes betraying a mixture of fear, surprise, and confusion. And then he saw Bart. And something broke through the confusion.

"Bart!" he called. "Connor! *The Three Buccaneers!*" It was recognizably Jez's voice.

"It certainly *sounds* like him," Bart said, his face wracked with pain.

"You saw him die," Connor said, urgently. "Remember that. You saw him die. Together, we threw his coffin overboard." Connor turned to address the rest of the crew. "It's a trick! We all saw Jez die. We were all there when we buried him at sea. This is a trick, I promise you, the cruelest kind of trick. But this is the crew that murdered Porfirio Wrathe and his crewmates. We *must* continue the attack!"

There was a moment when Connor thought he'd failed to reach them but then, suddenly, the crew began raising their torches once more. They hesitated, looking toward

Bart. The implication was clear. He had been Jez's best friend. Let him make the final call.

"Yes," Bart cried, "Connor's right. It's a trick. I held my buddy when he died. That isn't him! Unleash the torches!"

Connor knew what a terrible moment it was for Bart. This was the very end of the Three Buccaneers. As the pirates around them renewed their attack with extra vigor, Connor and Bart closed their eyes. When they opened them again, moments later, they could no longer see or hear Jez through the flames.

Gradually, the shrieks of Jez's three companions also ceased.

Then it was like watching a ship entirely made of fire — from the prow to the stern, from the mast through the sails and rigging. The entire structure was starting to break apart, unmaking itself and tumbling into the dark waters below.

A siren sounded. The pirates' work was done. The ship was destroyed and with it its murderous crew. Revenge, thought Connor, was a painful thing. It left no real satisfaction, but instead, a sense of revulsion and guilt and dirt. He wished *The Diablo* could sail away right now, job done.

But suddenly, Connor heard a roar and saw a vast figure emerge from the center of the flames. Connor's eyes popped. It was Caesar — the stranger who had met the crew of *The Diablo* at Ma Kettle's and led them to the

Vampirate ship to rescue Grace. Caesar, who had mysteriously disappeared from the ship. Now, Connor thought he understood why. But he needed confirmation. He climbed up the rigging so that he was on a level with the monster's eyes.

"Caesar!" he cried. "Caesar!"

The other pirates looked up at Connor and then over to the burning ship. Those who had met "Caesar" began to nod. But now, understanding was starting to spread. Something was seriously warped on that other ship — its crew was not what it seemed. They were, after all, demons.

Now, the lone surviving vampire turned to Connor. It was like looking at the face of the devil — his eyes burning with the same fire as the flames that hungrily ate his ship. Connor tried to look away but the sight, though gruesome, was too compelling.

"My name is not Caesar, idiot! My name is . . . Sidorio!"

Of course! It all made sense now. This was the vampire who had preyed upon Grace. This was the one the Vampirate captain had exiled. He had led the pirates to the Vampirate ship not to rescue Grace but to destroy the Vampirates. . . .

"Give me a torch!" Connor cried to one of the pirates below. "Quick, give me a torch!" One was passed up to him. Suddenly, he felt like a senior officer.

"This is for Grace!" Connor cried, launching the torch straight at Sidorio. It hit the deck right in front of him.

"And another!" Connor called to the pirates below. Quickly, another torch was passed up to him.

"This is for Jez!" Connor cried, sending the torch up through the air. It struck Sidorio's side. A terrible flame rose up from his flesh — or whatever he was made of. Dark smoke began to rise above him.

"Fire," roared Sidorio's voice. "Fire only makes me stronger."

"Another!" Connor cried. "Pass me another and gather all the remaining torches. We'll throw them together."

The pirates passed Connor another torch, then took up their own. Connor looked down upon the pirates of *The Diablo*. For a moment, they were *his* crew. Bart, Cate . . . even Molucco was looking up at him.

"And this," Connor cried, staring across the water and the fire at the burning giant, "this is for Porfirio!" He launched his torch through the night sky. It flew up in a high arc, meeting the hundred other torches thrown from the crew. They rained fire on the deck of Porfirio's old ship. Nothing, no one, was visible within the flames. The only noise was their hungry cackle. The only smell was the noxious smoke as the ship burned away to nothingness.

Then, above the crackle of the fire, came a louder roar. *"Fire only makes me stronger!"* But the voice was changed, somehow. Sidorio was a vain creature, thought Connor.

He would protest his power to the very end, but he could not possibly survive this latest attack.

But, to Connor's amazement, the flames began to form into the shape of the monster, until he was five, ten, twenty, forty feet tall. The giant loomed angrily at them from high above.

*"Death cannot take me,"* it roared. *"Death cannot take back the dead."*

As his words finished, the fire suddenly subsided. The terrible image of Sidorio vanished. And, suddenly, though his heart was pounding wildly, all Connor was looking at was a burning ship. A funeral pyre for Porfirio Wrathe and his crew. And, in some way, thought Connor, for Jez, too.

For a long time, Connor hung there on the rigging, watching the ship smolder away, becoming one with the waters which had borne it. Were the oceans safe again now? Had Sidorio's tide of terror come to an end?

At last, he looked down and saw that Cate, Bart, and Molucco had gathered beneath him on the deck below.

"Come down!" Molucco called to him. "It's over now!"

Connor clambered down the rigging, suddenly stunned from everything that had happened, chilled and shaking with deferred emotion.

As he reached the deck, Cate and Bart stepped forward and hugged him. It was exactly what he needed.

"You were awesome!" Bart said.

"A real hero!" added Cate.

Captain Wrathe nodded, holding out his arms to Connor.

"You saved the day. Mister Tempest. If it hadn't been for you . . . if it hadn't been for you . . ."

Connor shook his head. "I just did what any pirate would have done — for his captain — and his friends."

As Connor fell into Captain Wrathe's hug, he thought of the question the Vampirate captain had asked him.

*"Is anywhere truly safe?"*

A shiver broke through his entire body. One battle was over but another would not be too far away. They were pirates. This was what it *meant* to be a pirate.

Over Molucco's shoulder, Connor watched the fleet of ships sailing off through the night. I'm part of all this, he thought. I chose this and I'd choose it again and again and again, whatever the dangers.

42

# A MILLION MYSTERIES

Grace was waiting on deck as daylight faded away into dusk. They had sailed through the gray ocean and sky into clearer waters but she still had no clue as to whether Sanctuary might be near or far. She hadn't seen the captain to ask him. He was busy with his plans — and now, she had plans of her own.

As the sun fell into the obsidian waters, Grace looked down at the ship's figurehead, waiting for Darcy Flotsam to wake. It happened just a few moments after the sun was finally swallowed by the waves. Grace heard a cracking sound and then saw the first sign of movement from below. Darcy's neck lifted slightly, causing another small crack. Then her neat bob swished from side to side.

*Crack-swish. Crack-swish.* Next her arms jerked into motion — *creee-ak* — and soon her legs, too. She must have been aware she was being watched because she twisted her face up toward Grace and winked before turning back and diving into the water.

She disappeared under the water with a delicate splash and surfaced again a few feet away, smoothing back her sleek black hair and gazing around in wonder, as if she were looking upon the world for the very first time. She paddled about a little bit, then swam around the ship to climb up the ladder and join Grace on the ship's deck.

"Good evening, Grace," she said, dripping water all over the red deck boards. "Are you back for good?"

"Yes, Darcy," said Grace. "At least, I hope so."

"Then what's wrong?" Darcy asked. "I can read you like a book, Grace Tempest. In fact, a good deal better. And I can see you're in one of your agitated moods."

Grace smiled. Somehow, whatever was happening aboard the ship, Darcy — with her strange ways and words — always made her feel better.

"Darcy, I need to ask you a favor."

"A favor, eh? Well, ask away, and I shall certainly consider your request most carefully and come back to you with an answer *toute de suite*." As she spoke, she made her way toward the ship's bell.

"Wait!" Grace cried.

Darcy stopped in her tracks and turned. "Please, do be

patient, Grace. You know it's my duty to sound the bell. It is my responsibility to wake the crew."

"Yes, I know," Grace said. "That's the favor I need to ask you."

Darcy wrinkled her nose and furrowed her brow. "I'm a little confused now."

"Darcy, please will you wait to sound the Nightfall Bell tonight? I want to bring Lorcan up here and I thought it would be easier if we had the deck to ourselves."

"Oh, Grace." Darcy's face fell. "But I thought you knew. Lorcan won't come up on deck any more. He's too scared after what happened. He lives in fear of light."

Grace nodded. "I know that, but I'm not going to give in. With your help, tonight, he *is* going to come up onto deck. I'm just not taking 'no' for an answer."

Darcy smiled. There were tears in her eyes. She understood what Grace was about to do. "You're a wonderful person, Grace Tempest. A wonderful friend."

A wonderful friend, thought Grace. What she was going to offer to Lorcan tonight exceeded even the offering of a friend. She looked back up to find Darcy smiling.

"Of course I shall do as you ask. I shall just light the lamps, so they're all ready for later. Then, I'll go and change into a pretty, dry dress and redo my hair and makeup. Would half an hour give you enough time?"

Grace nodded. "Plenty. Thank you, Darcy. Thank you very much."

"You're most welcome," said Darcy. "Now, off you go and fetch Lieutenant Furey from the gloom of his cabin."

Grace nodded, smiling, and dashed back inside the ship. She marched purposefully but quietly along the corridor and then down one set of stairs to Lorcan's cabin. She knocked on the door and, without waiting for an answer, pushed it open.

He was lying in the shadows, one candle glowing feebly at the side of his bed.

"Who is it?" he asked, his voice tired and frail and broken.

"It's me — Grace."

"Oh," he said, his voice empty of emotion. "Are you back on another visit?"

"No," she said, approaching the bed. "Not on a visit. This time, I'm back for good."

The words caught his attention and his head twisted toward her. His wound had been freshly bandaged and the dressing of white cloth was neatly tied around the back of his head. His skin was almost as pale.

"Back for good, you say?"

"Yes." She reached out her hand and touched his arm. He trembled at her touch, but she knew she had made her point.

"Come on," she said. "It's time you got up."

He shook his head. "I'm tired."

"Of course you're tired, Lorcan," she said. "You're not taking care of yourself. You won't leave your cabin. You've stopped taking blood. No wonder you have no energy. Come on — get out of bed! I'm taking you up onto the deck."

He froze. "No, Grace."

"You'll be all right," she said. "I know you're scared, but I'll be there with you — every step of the way. Besides, it's pitch black up there. The moon isn't even out yet."

"How can it be dark?" Lorcan said. "Darcy hasn't sounded the Nightfall Bell. Unless I slept through it."

"No," Grace said. "She hasn't struck the bell yet because I asked her not to. I thought it would be easier for you if the deck was empty."

He pulled himself upright with some effort. "Grace, you're very kind but I'm not going up onto the deck."

"Yes, you are," she said, sounding a lot more resolute than she felt. She pulled back the bedclothes. "Come on!" she said, in her firmest voice. She could see he was thinking about it now.

"It'll be cold up there," he said.

"That's why you're going to wear your cape. Now, come on, sit up and I'll help you on with your shoes."

Not feeling overly optimistic, she turned her back on him for a moment and went to fetch his boots from the other side of the cabin. When she had located both of them, she turned back and found him sitting up, waiting for her. Her heart raced with happiness. She wanted to cry out but she had to keep strong and stay focused. There was a lot to do in a short period of time.

"Here you are," she said, setting the boots down on the floor and kneeling in front of him. She lifted his right foot into the boot and began tightening the laces. That foot done, she repeated the operation with the left one. Then she drew herself up in front of him.

"There," she said. "Now you must stand up."

He paused, taking a breath. She realized he was weaker than she thought.

"Shall I help you?" she asked.

He nodded, slowly. She was happy to do it but distressed to find that he was so much weaker than she had realized. Whether from lack of blood or exercise, Lorcan had lost all his former vitality. She wondered if he would ever get it back.

"On the count of three," she said, reaching her hands out to him. He clasped them, his touch as chill as ever.

"One . . . two . . . three!"

He rocked up and onto his feet. They wobbled together unsteadily for a moment or two and then he was standing. Standing properly.

"Well done," she said, straightening his shirt. "And now, let's put your cloak around you."

She took his heavy cloak from the chair and placed it over his shoulders. She began bringing the two cords together to tie them, but he shook his head. "Let me do it."

"Yes, yes of course." She placed the cords in each of his hands and stepped back.

His fingers fumbled with the ties and, on his first attempt at a knot, he failed completely. The cape slipped from his shoulders, down onto the floor. Grace knelt down and picked it up again, placing it back over his shoulders.

"Thanks," he said, clearly embarrassed and frustrated.

Grace stepped back again, wanting nothing so much as to make the knot for him, but knowing how important it was that he do this small thing for himself.

It was torture watching him fail to tie the cords for a fourth, fifth, and sixth time but Grace refused to give in. Each time, she whispered words of encouragement to him, pulled up the cloak, and handed him back the ties. On the seventh attempt, he managed to entwine the cords. He wouldn't have won any honors in Captain Quivers' Knot class, thought Grace, but the knot held the cloak tight around his neck and that was all that mattered.

"I think you're ready," Grace said, opening the door.

"Let's take it slowly," Lorcan said. "I'm a little unsteady on my feet these days."

"Of course," said Grace, looping her arm through his. "Just lean on me."

And so they made their way, very slowly at first, along the corridor and up the stairway. Their speed increased as they moved down the second corridor, but Lorcan leaned against her the whole way, his body frail and in need of support.

"We're at the door to the deck now," she said,

immediately feeling him tense up. "It's okay, Lorcan. Really, it is. You're going to be just fine."

"It *is* dark out there, isn't it?" he said.

"Yes."

"Just check again for me."

"All right." She pushed the door open the tiniest fraction. It was fully black outside, save for the stars and the thin crescent moon.

"It's dark," she said. "Oh, Lorcan, it's a beautiful dark night. *Please* come outside." She held open the door and waited. "If you won't do this for yourself, at least do it for me."

He nodded and, reaching for her support once more, stepped out into the night air.

"There, now," she said. "You're outside. How does it feel?"

"It feels good," he said, breathing it in. "It feels good."

She walked him up to the deck-rail. Instinctively, he reached out his hands to the metal. He held onto it and leaned forward, just as he had so many times before, raising his face to feel the ocean breeze.

"I've missed this," he said.

"I've come back," Grace said. "And now you must make your way back, too."

"What do you mean?" he asked.

She sighed. It was now or never.

"You have to start taking blood again," she said. Her

heart was pounding now. But her fate was sealed. It had been sealed long ago. There was no turning back. "I saw Shanti earlier today," she said.

"Shanti," he repeated, as if the name stirred only a far-away memory.

"Your donor," Grace said. "I saw her and she told me that you had stopped sharing with her."

He said nothing, his tightly bound face rising in the air. He was harder to read than the masked captain these days.

"You must take blood again," Grace said. "If not Shanti's then . . . then, you must take mine."

He turned to face her. Though much of his expression was blocked by his bandage, she could tell he was shocked.

"Grace, I would never take your blood. Shanti is my donor . . ."

Grace nodded. Tears were running down her face — whether of pain or joy or relief she was unsure. "It's just that Shanti thought you didn't want her blood any more. But that you might take mine. That I might become your new donor."

"And you'd have done that for me?" he said. His hand slipped a little along the deck-rail. It met hers, the sides of their little fingers pressing against each other.

"You saved me, Lorcan," Grace said. "You saved me and cared for me and protected me. And, of course, I'll do whatever it takes to save you."

He dropped his head.

"I've been so stupid," he said.

"Why? What do you mean?"

"I didn't think you were coming back," he said. "And I missed you. I missed you so."

His words thrilled her. Of course they did. But at the same time, she felt a strong sense of responsibility. Had he really stopped taking blood, not out of despair for his blindness, but because he missed her? She had never mattered so much to anyone, other than Connor, before. Her feelings were an unfamiliar blend of delight and fear.

"Look out at the ocean," he said. "What do you see?"

She looked into the distance.

"I see very little, except . . . except these dark waters going on and on and on for ever."

He nodded. "That's what it's like for me. But it isn't just the ocean that stretches out for ever. It's time. Imagine if all that ocean was a patchwork of days and nights and hours and minutes. Stretching on and on for all time, without any end. Imagine if you had to face all of that on your own."

"But you're not on your own," Grace said.

"Not now," he answered, the side of his finger pressing against hers.

They stood there for a time, saying nothing. Tears streamed down Grace's face but she left the wind to dry them.

"I'm cold," she said, shivering.

"Here," he lifted up his arm. "Come inside my cloak."

She came closer, tucking her body against his as he brought the warm cloak back around them.

"Lean on *me* now," he said, drawing her closer to him. She smiled.

"We're going to find a cure for you," she said. "That's where we're traveling to now, you know. To a place called Sanctuary. To meet a friend of the captain's — a man called Mosh Zu Kamal."

Lorcan took a breath. "Is that a fact?" he said. "Is that a fact?"

"The captain told me himself," said Grace. "He's not going to give up on you, and neither am I."

Lorcan smiled. "Welcome back to *The Nocturne*, Grace," he said.

She twisted her head, puzzled. "*The Nocturne*? What's that?"

"Why, 'tis the name of this ship, of course."

"Really? I didn't even know it *had* a name."

"Ah well, Grace. There's a million mysteries aboard this ship and you've only just begun to scratch the surface of them. I reckon you'd better stay a while longer if you want to find out some more."

She smiled and drew deeper into the warmth of his cloak.

"Yes," she said. "Yes, I might just do that."

PLENTY AND SATIETY,
PLEASURE AND EASE,
LIBERTY AND POWER.